DEATH IN ST JAMES'S P...

KU-611-241

Also by Susanna Gregory

The Matthew Bartholomew Series

The Thomas Chaloner Series

Death in
St James's Park

Susanna Gregory

SPHERE

First published in Great Britain in 2013 by Sphere

Copyright © 2013 Susanna Gregory

The moral right of the author has been asserted.

*All characters and events in this publication, other
than those clearly in the public domain, are fictitious
and any resemblance to real persons,
living or dead, is purely coincidental.*

All rights reserved.
No part of this publication may be reproduced, stored in a retrieval
system, or transmitted, in any form or by any means, without the prior
permission in writing of the publisher, nor be otherwise circulated in any
form of binding or cover other than that in which it is published and
without a similar condition including this condition being imposed on the
subsequent purchaser.

A CIP catalogue record for this book
is available from the British Library.

ISBN 978-1-84744-434-9

Typeset in Baskerville MT by Palimpsest Book Production Limited,
Falkirk, Stirlingshire

Printed and bound in Great Britain by Clays Ltd, St Ives plc

Papers used by Sphere are from well-managed forests
and other responsible sources.

MIX
Paper from
responsible sources
FSC
www.fsc.org   FSC® C104740

Sphere
An imprint of
Little, Brown Book Group
100 Victoria Embankment
London EC4Y 0DY

An Hachette UK Company
www.hachette.co.uk

www.littlebrown.co.uk

In loving memory of Angelyn Riffenburgh

Coventry City Council	
WHO*	
3 8002 02063 820 3	
Askews & Holts	Jan-2013
CRI	£19.99

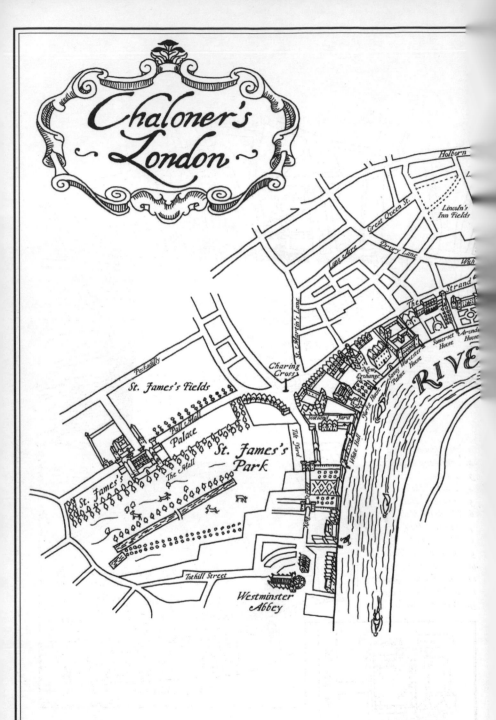

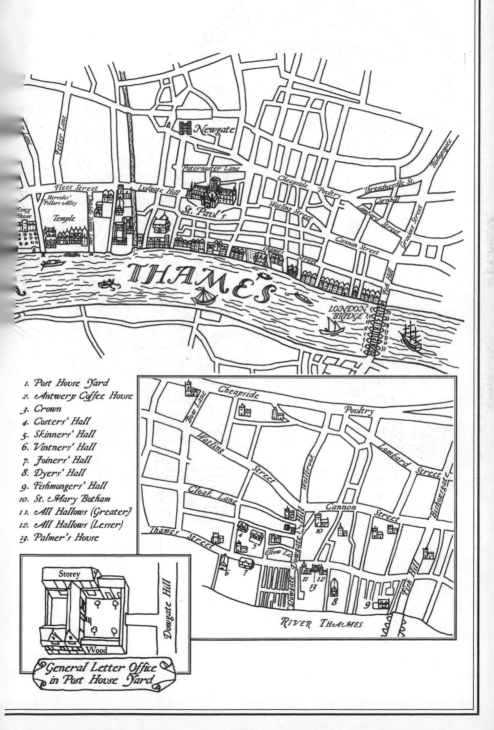

General Letter Office in Post House Yard

Prologue

Dorset, Summer 1657

John Fry was a man with controversial opinions. He had shocked the House of Commons with his unorthodox theology, he had written pamphlets that had been burned for their profanity, and he sincerely believed that beheading King Charles had been a very good idea. Naturally, his schismatic views had earned him enemies, and he suspected half of England would be delighted to learn he was laid low with the flux.

Through the sickroom window he could see the gently rolling hills and corn-rich fields that surrounded his house. He could see the river, too, glints of silver between a line of noble oaks, which made him recall the many hours he had spent there as a youth, reading, filling his mind with philosophy and political theory. He sighed, bitter in the knowledge that all his learning and dedication had been for nothing. He had fought bravely in the civil wars, but his dream of a republic had turned to ashes – Cromwell had transpired to be a worse tyrant than the King, and his regime every bit as oppressive. Fry had been told, quite categorically, that if he penned another contentious tract, he would be sent to prison without the courtesy of a trial.

His thoughts stirred him from his sickly languor, giving him the strength to sit up against the pillows. No! He would not be silenced by Cromwell or his bullying Puritan henchmen. It was his moral duty to point out the flaws in the current government, so that was what he was going to do. Filled with sudden vigour, he called for his wife to bring him pen and paper. She regarded him uneasily, but did as he asked. As soon as they arrived, he began to write, and he did not stop until a veritable mountain of letters lay on the bed beside him.

'Find a fleet-footed servant to run to the post office, Anna,' he instructed, as he signed the last one. 'The London mail leaves within the hour, and I want these missives to be in the hands of their recipients by the end of the week.'

Gingerly, Anna picked up a few and read the names. Major Smith of Hounslow, Henry Wood of London, Major Wildman in Amsterdam. She looked into her husband's bloodshot eyes. 'But these are all notorious malcontents who want Cromwell deposed.' She spread the letters in one hand like a fan.

'Yes.' Fry gripped Anna's wrist. 'And they are right – it *is* time to be rid of him. I had such high hopes when we won the war, but Cromwell's rule has degenerated into a military dictatorship, and we cannot accept it any longer. It is time for another rebellion.'

Anna regarded him in alarm. 'But if he is ousted, who will take his place? Do you want the monarchy restored?'

'No!' Fry was shocked by that notion. 'These last fifteen years have convinced me more than ever that the only sensible form of government is a republic. We cannot have yet another petty despot dispensing unfair laws – I want democratically elected representatives.'

Anna pulled away from him and gathered all the letters. Her husband was a passionate and determined man. If anyone could set the country alight, it was him, and perhaps this wave of determination meant that he was not as ill as she had feared. She felt tears prick as she stared at the missives in her hands; what they contained could bring misery and hardship to countless thousands again – yet more harsh years of violence, hatred and anguish. She was tired of uncertainty and conflict, and while Cromwell was far from ideal, he did bring a measure of stability to a war-weary nation.

'Hurry, good wife,' said Fry softly. There was compassion and understanding in his eyes: he knew why she hesitated. 'Or you will miss the post. And then help me dress. There is much to be done if we are to succeed.'

But within two weeks John Fry was dead. Speculation was rife. Had he left his sickbed too soon? Had he been assassinated, because the letters he had written had caused such a stir? Or was he not dead at all, but had gone into hiding, so that he could mastermind his plan without interference? Tongues wagged, and there were more theories than could be counted, but only a select handful of people knew the truth. And they were not telling.

St James's Park, London, December 1664

When Andrew Leak had first been handed the bottle of poison, he had regarded it in disbelief. There was barely a dribble, and he was sure there would not be enough for what he had been charged to do. However, the fellow who had hired him – Leak believed he was an apothecary – soon put him right: it was one of the most deadly substances ever created, and a single drop was more than enough to kill.

Leak had been extremely careful with it after that. Worryingly, the apothecary had worn gloves when he had handed it over, although whether to protect himself from spillages, or to ensure that no part of him was visible when he dealt with his minions was impossible to say.

'Who is he?' Leak asked, as he followed his friend Smartfoot over the wall and into St James's Park. It was a dark night, with thick clouds blocking out the moonlight, and they stumbled constantly, unfamiliar with the place and its terrain. 'He even takes care to whisper when he meets us, to make sure we cannot identify his voice. Yet I am sure I should know him if I saw his face.'

'Do not think about it,' advised Smartfoot. 'It might transpire to be dangerous.'

'The whole business worries me,' Leak went on unhappily. 'Oh, the money is good, but this is peculiar work. I do not understand why he wants us to kill the royal waterfowl.'

'No questions,' said Smartfoot warningly. 'That was the agreement.'

Both men stopped walking when a gale of laughter and music wafted from the nearby Palace of White Hall. The King was holding another of his soirées, where he and his debauched friends would carouse until dawn. Leak frowned disapprovingly as the revellers launched into a bawdy tavern song. It was one thing to hear such ditties in a Seven Dials alehouse, but another altogether for His Majesty to bawl them. Leak expected better of

4

him and was disturbed by his coarseness. He said nothing, though, and after a moment, he and Smartfoot resumed their journey.

'Here is the Canal,' whispered Leak eventually, lighting a lamp so they could see what they were doing. 'You grab a swan, while I pour the toxin down its throat.'

However, they soon discovered that 'grabbing a swan' was easier said than done, because the royal birds were kept in peak condition and were powerful creatures. Neither man had any idea of how to lay hold of one, and after several furious encounters that the birds won handily, Leak and Smartfoot decided to opt for something smaller and less feisty.

Unfortunately, the ducks had been disturbed by the fracas, and had scattered into the darkness. Only one remained, its filmy eyes and dull feathers suggesting it was ill. Thoroughly rattled by the whole business, Leak grabbed it with one hand and groped in his pocket for the phial with the other. He forced open the bird's beak, and without thinking pulled out the stopper with his teeth.

As soon as he tasted the searing bitterness on his tongue, he knew he had done something very stupid. His stomach clenched in horror, and he spat frantically, so it was left to Smartfoot to drip the poison down the bird's throat. Once released, the hapless fowl flapped a short distance and then was still.

'Not exactly a swan,' said Smartfoot dispassionately. 'But it will have to do. And we had better be on our way, because we cannot afford to be caught. It is probably treason to damage the King's property.'

Leak could not reply, because his tongue was on fire, and the pain grew worse as he followed Smartfoot towards the wall. Then his throat began to hurt as well; he could feel it swelling, cutting off his breath. He staggered, hands to his neck, then pitched forward and began to convulse, eyes wide in his terrified face. Smartfoot hurried back to help, but then thought better of it, afraid to touch him lest he should be poisoned, too.

Leak's desperate struggle for life went on for a very long time, while Smartfoot paced in agitation, longing to run away, but kept rooted to the spot by fear of the apothecary. It was over eventually, and Smartfoot struggled to pull himself together. Now what? He could not leave Leak where he was lest he was identified – and the apothecary would not approve of that. Yet he could not carry him away on his own. He looked around quickly. Nearby was a part of the park that had been left to grow wild. It was not an ideal place to hide a body, but it would have to do.

He donned gloves, grabbed Leak's feet and began to haul. He found a slight dip in the ground, rolled the body into it, and covered it with handfuls of dead leaves and twigs. It did not take long, and he was soon racing towards the wall again.

He was shocked: the apothecary had not been exaggerating when he had bragged about the potency of his poison. Smartfoot's stomach churned, and he had a bad feeling that he knew what would happen the next time he was summoned: the victim would not be a bird, it would be a person.

London, Tuesday 10 January 1665

Post House Yard was a pretty square, located just off the busy thoroughfare named Dowgate Hill. It was dominated by the General Letter Office, the place where the country's mail was received and dispatched. This was a handsome building taxed on thirty-three hearths, although there was a wing at the back that was disused and was said to be falling into disrepair. It boasted an imposing stone façade, and five marble steps led up to its grand front door.

The other buildings in Post House Yard were equally attractive – a row of neat, brightly painted cottages on the right, and the elegant mansion owned by the eccentric Sir Henry Wood on the left. The square was cobbled with pale pink stones, and someone had planted two long borders with a variety of shrubs and trees.

The two conspirators stood in one of these gardens. It was a clear night, and they could not afford to be seen, so they were grateful for the shadows cast by a spreading yew.

'I am not sure about this,' the first muttered unhappily. 'Gunpowder is so indiscriminate. We might harm a lot of innocent bystanders.'

There was a crackle as the second man fingered a letter. 'It says here that we should not allow that possibility to discourage us – that there will be casualties in any struggle for justice.'

'I suppose that is true. When do they want this explosion to take place?'

'At noon on Thursday.'

The first man gaped his disbelief. 'But that is when the domestic mails are collected! The square will be teeming with people – we might kill dozens of them.'

The second shook his head quickly. 'Not if it is done properly, and the noise and commotion will work to our advantage. It means that our powder-laden cart is less likely to be noticed, which will increase our chances of success.'

'I do not like it.'

'Neither do I, but the situation cannot be allowed to continue. You know this – we have talked of little else for the past four years. Look!' The second man pointed at the sky. 'It is the comet. It appeared on the very evening that we received our instructions, and it has grown steadily brighter ever since. It is a sign of God's approval – what we are doing is *right*.'

The first man nodded, but he remained uneasy. In two days, the dead would litter Post House Yard, and London would never be the same again.

8

Chapter 1

Because Dowgate Hill ran from north to south, it served as a funnel for the wind, which was unusually bitter as it scythed towards Thames Street. Dawn was approaching, but London was reluctant to wake, and Thomas Chaloner, spy to the Earl of Clarendon, did not blame anyone for not wanting to leave their beds that day. He wished he was in his. Roofs shimmered white with frost, parts of the river had frozen over and snow was in the air.

Not for the first time, he wondered whether there was an easier way to earn a living. His Earl neither liked nor trusted him, even after two years of faithful service, and employed him only because he needed help to stay ahead of his many enemies. The Earl deplored the necessity, and had awarded him the title of 'Gentleman Usher' to disguise his true function. His master's disdain for him and his skills meant Chaloner was regularly given duties that were dangerous, foolhardy or demeaning – such as lurking in filthy alleys on nights when not even a dog should be out.

Of course, it was the civil wars that lay at the heart of the trouble. Chaloner's family had sided with Parliament, after which he had been eagerly accepted into Oliver Cromwell's intelligence service. But Cromwell had died, the Commonwealth had collapsed and Charles II had been restored to his throne, which meant opportunities for men like Chaloner were now few and far between. Thus he was not in a position to tell the Earl what to do with his dreary assignments, and was forced to be grateful that someone was willing to overlook his past and hire him.

Unfortunately, he was unsure how much longer even this dismal state of affairs would last – he had returned from a mission in Sweden the previous week to learn that his master had appointed a 'marshal', a man whose duties were disconcertingly similar to his own. George Gery was an intensely devoted Royalist, and Chaloner could only suppose that the Earl no longer wanted a former Roundhead in his retinue, and was manoeuvring to replace him.

Chaloner stamped his feet and blew on his fingers, fast reaching the point where, even if the two men he had been ordered to arrest did appear, he would be too cold to do much about them. Shoving his frozen hands inside his coat, he tried to forget his concerns for the future, and reflect on what little the Earl had told him about his quarry instead.

Joseph Knight and Lewis Gardner worked in the nearby General Letter Office. A postal service had been established the previous century, although it was notoriously unreliable – letters were opened by government spies, mailbags were 'lost', and charges were made for missives that were never delivered. Chaloner had been bemused when he had been ordered to apprehend a pair of dishonest clerks: the Earl, who was also Lord Chancellor of England, did not usually trouble himself with such petty affairs.

Chaloner was on the verge of assuming that the culprits had somehow learned of the trouble they were in and were not going to come home, when two men appeared. One was small and nervous, while the other was stocky with bushy flaxen hair and a round, homely face. He looked like a country bumpkin, although he moved with a catlike grace that said he would be a formidable opponent in a brawl. They matched the descriptions the Earl had provided.

The small one, Knight, opened the door with a key, while Gardner stood with his back to the wall scanning the lane. Chaloner waited until they had gone inside, then slipped from his hiding place. The door had been secured again, but that was no obstacle to him; he was good at picking locks. Then he crept along a corridor to where he could hear voices. Twelve years in espionage meant eavesdropping was second nature, and he began to listen without conscious thought.

'We are wrong to run,' Knight was saying. 'We should take our tale to Controller O'Neill.'

'O'Neill will not listen,' predicted Gardner. 'Now gather what you need quickly. If we are caught, we will be hauled off to Newgate Gaol, never to be seen again.'

'But taking flight will make everyone assume we are guilty.' Knight's voice was unsteady. 'We should stay in London, and prove our innocence.'

'No one is interested in our innocence. Now for God's sake hurry!'

Personally, Chaloner thought Gardner was wise to be

11

wary of the legal system. Miscarriages of justice were frequent and brazen, and London's prisons were vile places. He owned a deep and abiding horror of them, and would certainly have gone on the run to avoid a sojourn in one.

'What about the other business?' Knight swallowed hard. 'The murder. Are you sure you had nothing to do with it?'

'Of course,' replied Gardner, although it was not the most convincing denial Chaloner had ever heard. 'Why?'

'Because it preys on my mind,' explained Knight miserably. 'The taking of a human life is rather different to the pilfering of a few pounds.'

Gardner gestured impatiently that Knight was to pick up his bag, while Chaloner frowned. Were they innocent of dishonesty but guilty of murder then? He sighed softly. Why did the Earl insist on sending him on missions armed with only half a story? Apprehending killers was hardly the same as snagging petty thieves, and he would have asked for assistance had he known. But the pair were preparing to leave, and it was rather too late to be questioning his orders now. He drew his sword and stepped through the door.

'You are under arrest,' he announced. 'By the Lord Chancellor's warrant.'

Knight issued a shrill shriek of terror, but Gardner was made of sterner stuff. He hauled a gun from his belt and took aim.

Chaloner had never liked firearms. They were unpredictable, took an age to prime and were noisy, something that was anathema to spies, who lived in the shadows. Moreover, he had been wary of gunpowder ever since he had been injured by an exploding cannon at the Battle of Naseby, damaging a leg that had never fully recovered.

His mistrust was borne out when Gardner's weapon flashed in the pan, producing nothing more deadly than a puff of smoke.

Furious, Gardner hurled it at him with one hand, while hauling a second dag from his belt with the other. Knowing that both were unlikely to misfire, Chaloner grabbed Knight to use as a shield, confident that Gardner would not shoot when his friend might be injured. He was mistaken.

Gardner fired at Chaloner's head, the crack of it deafening in the small room. Knight screamed again, and Chaloner was sure he felt the hot singe of the ball as it streaked past his ear. Swearing under his breath, Gardner drew his sword, forcing Chaloner to do likewise.

Firearms were not often discharged on Dowgate Hill, and the sound had attracted attention. Footsteps and muffled shouts indicated that residents in the neighbouring houses were astir, while a group of passing apprentices had paused in the street outside. Chaloner could see them through the window, edging forward in an uncertain semicircle, curiosity vying with the knowledge that it was dangerous to loiter in a place where shots had been discharged.

'You cannot escape,' he told Gardner firmly, still gripping Knight around the neck. 'And fighting will only make your situation worse. No one will believe your innocence if you—'

With a roar of rage, Gardner leapt at him, and Chaloner only just managed to parry the murderous swipe. It was wild, but delivered with considerable strength, making him stagger, and giving Knight the opportunity to wriggle out of his grasp. Gardner struck a second time, at which point Chaloner decided he had better launch an offensive of his own before he was skewered. He surged forward, blade flashing, although his frozen limbs rendered his movements disgracefully clumsy. Even so, he soon had his quarry retreating.

But he had reckoned without Knight, who seized a pot from a table and lobbed it. It caught him on the side of the head, dazing him just long enough to allow Gardner to dart past. He managed to grab the hem of the clerk's coat, but his fingers were too cold to grip it properly, and the material snapped free. And then Gardner was gone, bellowing for Knight to follow.

Chaloner blocked the smaller clerk's way. Terrified, Knight lashed out with his fists, but he was no warrior, whereas Chaloner had been trained to fight by Cromwell's New Model Army. It was an unequal contest, and did not last long.

'Enough,' said Chaloner irritably, pushing his captive against the wall. 'You will hurt yourself if you continue to wrestle with me.'

Knight stared at him, eyes wide with a combination of fear and resignation. 'Please,' he whispered. 'Let me go. I have done nothing wrong.'

It was not for Chaloner to judge. He took Knight's arm, and pulled him along the hallway towards the door. Outside, the apprentices had swelled in number, and they watched in silence as he steered his prisoner through them. Their mood was sullen, their sympathies firmly with the man who was being taken into custody, and Chaloner sensed it would take very little for them to stage a rescue attempt. So did Knight, who began to shout.

'Help! I am innocent of any wrongdoing. Please do not let him have me.'

Several lads stepped forward, but Chaloner still held

his sword, and they fell back when they saw he was prepared to use it. Knight in one hand and weapon in the other, he marched past them, aiming for Thames Street, where hackney carriages were available for hire.

'No!' wept Knight, still trying to pull away. 'You do not understand! You sign my death warrant if you drag me off to gaol.'

'Shall we go to White Hall instead, then?' asked Chaloner acidly. Knight's terror was making him feel guilty, which he resented. It was hardly his fault the man had involved himself in something unsavoury. 'So you can tell the Lord Chancellor that there has been a mistake?'

'Oh, thank God!' breathed Knight in relief. 'Yes, take me to Clarendon. I have a tale that will make his hair curl. I shall tell him everything.'

Although the suggestion had not been made seriously, on reflection Chaloner saw no reason why he should not oblige. He knew for a fact that the Earl would be at work, despite the early hour, as he was currently suffering from gout, which made sleeping difficult. He might even appreciate a diversion from his discomfort. Moreover, Chaloner would do a great deal to avoid setting foot in a gaol, even if it was only to deliver a prisoner to one.

Dawn had finally broken, although heavy clouds meant the morning might never be fully light, and the wind carried the occasional flurry of snow. The tiny white pellets danced across the frozen mud that formed the streets, and Chaloner wondered whether they would settle.

'I am innocent,' Knight said miserably, as he was bundled into a coach. 'I swear it on my soul. But there is a deadly conspiracy unfolding at the Post Office, and its perpetrators are eager to silence me. That is why they have contrived to have me arrested.'

'They have committed murder already?' Chaloner climbed into the hackney after him. There was ice on the seat, a result of the window shutters being removed so that the inside of the coach was exposed to the elements. He could only suppose that the driver did not see why his passengers should be protected when he was obliged to huddle on a box at the front. He considered decanting to another carriage, but did not have the energy for the argument it would inevitably provoke.

Knight nodded. 'I do not know who the victim was, but someone told me the culprit had a lot of fluffy yellow hair and a farmer's face, and . . . well, you saw what Gardner looks like. That horrid Clement Oxenbridge is at the heart of it, of course. He is evil, sly and dangerous, and if you are ordered to arrest him, I advise you not to go alone. He would kill you for certain.'

'Would he now?' murmured Chaloner, although he knew he had not comported himself particularly impressively that day, so Knight might be forgiven for thinking his martial skills were lacking. 'Who is Clement Oxenbridge?'

'A wealthy man, although no one is sure of the exact nature of his business. Or where he lives, for that matter. And he would not appreciate anyone trying to find out either.'

'I see. And what manner of "deadly conspiracy" has he devised?'

'If I tell you, you will have no reason to take me to White Hall, so I shall wait until we meet Clarendon, if you do not mind.'

16

A sudden crack had Chaloner reaching for his sword, but it was only a ball of frozen mud lobbed by the group of tanners who had gathered outside St Paul's Cathedral to pelt passing traffic. He might have dismissed their antics as youthful high spirits, but the lads were surly and scowling, and it was clear there was nothing light-hearted about their mood.

'Have you noticed how unsettled London is at the moment?' asked Knight, peering out of the window at them. 'It feels like it did during the wars – turbulent and volatile.'

'London is always unsettled,' said Chaloner, thinking that in all his travels, he had never encountered a city that was more prone to violent undercurrents. If there was not one plot in the making, there was another.

'This is different,' insisted Knight. 'Look.'

He pointed, and Chaloner saw the tanners approached by a large group of butchers. As rivalry between the two trades had always been fierce, Chaloner expected a scuffle at the very least, but the leaders only exchanged a few words, before steering their followers off in different directions.

'You see?' said Knight. 'If they are not quarrelling with each other, it means they aim to fight someone else. Rebellion is in the air, you mark my words. Mr Bankes is worried, because he keeps pressing me for information about it.'

'Who is Mr Bankes?'

'A man interested in London and her troubles. He frightens me, if you want the truth. I have never met him, but the letters he writes demanding information are terribly aggressive. However, he is right to be concerned – I smell another civil war in the offing.'

Before Chaloner could ask whether that was the nature of the intelligence Knight planned to pass to the Earl, the hackney rolled to a standstill. He leaned out of the window, and saw that a coach had broken an axle on the Fleet Bridge and was blocking traffic. There was nothing he could do to expedite matters, so he sat back to wait for the snarl to clear. Moments later, the door to his hackney was wrenched open. He drew his sword without conscious thought.

'There is no need for that.' The speaker was a Yeoman Warden from the Tower of London, identifiable by his distinctive uniform. 'However, I am afraid we must commandeer your vehicle. We have an important prisoner to convey to White Hall, and our own carriage is broken.'

Chaloner was about to tell him to find another, when a second yeoman arrived with the prisoner in tow. The captive had the pale, wan look of a man kept locked up, although a certain chubbiness suggested he was not deprived of victuals. He had a thin black moustache, protuberant eyes and a mane of grey-brown hair. Chaloner recognised him immediately.

John Wildman, always known simply as 'the Major', had been an officer in Cromwell's army, although his talent had been for making fiery speeches rather than fighting. Chaloner had heard one of his homilies before the Battle of Naseby, and recalled how it had set the soldiers alight with revolutionary zeal. After the wars, the Major had decided that Cromwell was worse than the King, and had plotted to assassinate him. The scheme had failed, but Royalists had loved him for it anyway, so Chaloner was astonished to learn that he was still incarcerated. Intrigued, he decided to find out why.

'I am bound for White Hall with a prisoner, too,' he

18

said, sheathing his sword. 'And London feels uneasy today. It will be safer for us to travel there together.'

'Fair enough,' said the first yeoman, climbing in and indicating that his charge should follow. 'The city's current agitation makes me reluctant to leave the safety of the Tower, to be frank. But the Major has been summoned, and we can hardly let him out on his own.'

'I would not escape,' said the Major tiredly. His voice was weak and slightly hoarse, a far cry from the strident bray he had effected at Naseby. Chaloner studied him. The Major had been a lively and colourful figure during the wars; now he was grey, drab and defeated, a mere shadow of the man he had been. Chaloner could only surmise that the Tower had broken him, as it had so many others.

He gave no indication that he recognised Chaloner, but that was not surprising – Chaloner had been fifteen years old at Naseby, and although he had claimed the Major's indignant attention by challenging some of the points in his tirade, he had changed considerably from the fresh-faced, slender boy of twenty years before.

'I have been arrested, too,' Knight told the Major unhappily, as the carriage began to trundle forward slowly. 'I have done nothing wrong, of course.'

'Neither have I,' averred the Major. 'I was taken eighteen months ago, accused of conspiring against the King, although I have never been formally charged. I have begged for a trial, to prove my innocence, but I have always been refused. My imprisonment is illegal – it is against the writ of habeas corpus to keep a man locked up indefinitely.'

'I hope that does not happen to me,' gulped Knight. 'But I have seen you before. Were you friends with the

19

Postmaster – not O'Neill, but his predecessor, Henry Bishop?'

'Bishop is my friend still,' said the Major with a sad smile. Then it faded. 'But do not mention that snake O'Neill! Being Postmaster is lucrative, and he wanted the job for himself, so he told a lot of lies to get poor Bishop ousted. And because I am Bishop's friend, he included me in his fabrications. It was largely his testimony that saw me locked in the Tower.'

'Bishop was excellent at running the postal services,' said Knight. 'But Controller O'Neill – did you know he prefers that title because he thinks it sounds grander than Postmaster? – is nowhere near as efficient.'

He lapsed into silence at that point, and stared out of the window, leaving Chaloner to wonder whether Knight had been arrested just for preferring his previous master to the current incumbent.

'The Major has led a very interesting life,' said the first yeoman conversationally, after a short pause during which the carriage crawled forward at a snail's pace. His indulgent grin suggested he was rather fond of this particular inmate. 'There are tales that say *he* was the hooded axe-man who beheaded the first King Charles—'

'Those are untrue!' cried the Major, distressed. Chaloner believed him: by all accounts, the kill had been a clean one, the work of a professional executioner. 'I cannot imagine why I should be accused of so vile a deed.'

'Then he decided that Cromwell was no better, so he plotted to blow him up,' the yeoman went on approvingly. 'Along with half that vile usurper's Council of State.'

'Now that is true,' the Major conceded. 'Cromwell was a dictator, and I wish I had succeeded. However,

20

those dark times are behind us, and these days, I am a man of peace. All I want is to go home to Norfolk, and live in quiet seclusion.'

Chaloner longed for peace, too, and if he never drew his sword again, it would be too soon. He fully understood why the Major should feel likewise.

'Why are you going to White Hall?' he asked politely. 'To beg for a trial?'

Unhappiness filled the Major's face. 'If only it were that easy! No, I am summoned because important people believe I have valuable information to impart. They are not interested in my plight, only in the fact that certain faithful friends are in the habit of corresponding with me.'

'But you improve your chances of freedom with every visit you make,' said the yeoman encouragingly. 'And as long as you take us with you, these government officials have even given you leave to enjoy a tavern or a coffee house on the way home.'

'Only so I can gather intelligence for them,' said the Major bitterly. 'Do you know my family motto? It is *nil admirari* – surprised at nothing. However, I *shall* be surprised if they keep their word and let me go. But this is a gloomy subject, and we should discuss something more uplifting. Does anyone like music? I have a particular affection for the viol.'

So did Chaloner, and the rest of the journey passed very agreeably.

White Hall was where the King, his family, his ministers and his favourite courtiers lived and worked. It dated back several centuries, and had been extended and rebuilt as and when funds had been available, so it boasted an eclectic mixture of styles. It was vast, with approaching

21

two thousand rooms, although parts of it had grown shabby under successive rulers who had either no money or no inclination to invest in repairs and refurbishment.

When they arrived, the palace guards invited the Major to warm himself by their fire before his appointment, indicating that he had visited often enough to make friends. Chaloner left them exchanging tales of London's growing restlessness, and escorted Knight across the Great Court to the offices that had been allocated to the Lord Chancellor. They overlooked the Privy Gardens, which were pretty that day, dusted as they were with a light coat of rime. He ascended the marble staircase to the upper floor, Knight shuffling dejectedly at his side.

It was too early for most of the Earl's staff to be at work, and the only retainer in evidence was Will Freer, a stocky, soldierly fellow with a ready grin. Marshal Gery had hired him, which meant Chaloner felt compelled to regard him with a degree of caution, although Freer was likeable and friendly enough.

'Where you are going?' he hissed in alarm, as Chaloner and his prisoner passed. 'You cannot take vagrants to see the Earl, man! He will have a seizure and you will lose your job.'

'I am not a vagrant,' objected Knight, offended. 'I am a postal clerk. I wore this rough cloak today because . . . because the weather is cold.'

He had worn it to conceal his identity as a person of means when he had escaped from London, but Chaloner let the lie pass. 'He has something to tell Clarendon.'

Freer regarded him worriedly. 'I would not go in there if I were you. The Earl is in a bad mood, and Gery is with him.'

The Earl was always in a bad mood as far as Chaloner

was concerned, and he did not care whether Gery was there or not. He nodded his thanks for the warning, and tapped on the door anyway. When he heard the call to enter, he opened it and strode inside, indicating with a gesture that Knight should hang back until told to come forward.

The Earl of Clarendon was short, fat and fussy, and his portliness was accentuated rather than flattered by his close-fitting silk suit and the frothing lace under his several chins. He sported a fashionable T-beard – a sliver of hair over the upper lip with a small tuft on the chin – and an enormous and very costly wig. His gouty feet were propped on a stool in front of him, warmed by a fire that was high enough to risk setting the entire palace alight.

Gery was standing in front of him, tall, strong and dour; Chaloner had never seen him smile. He was so devoted to the Royalist cause that he was unable to forgive anyone who had sided with Parliament during the wars, and he hated Chaloner with a passion that verged on the fanatical. He firmly believed that former Roundheads were responsible for everything that was wrong with the world, and was in favour of rounding them all up and hanging them. He was not a particularly clever individual, and always gave the impression of barely controlled rage. Chaloner could not begin to imagine what had possessed his master to hire such a person.

'Well, Chaloner?' asked the Earl, steepling his chubby fingers. 'Have you carried out my instructions? Are Knight and Gardner safely installed in Newgate Gaol?'

Gery gave a start of surprise. 'You ordered the arrest of Knight and Gardner, sir? But why?'

'Because Spymaster Williamson applied to me for warrants,' explained the Earl. 'But all his people were

23

busy quelling trouble with the apprentices, so I sent Chaloner instead. I know you have been investigating irregularities at the Post Office, Gery, but you had gone home. Why do you ask? Is there a problem?'

'No, sir,' said Gery, although the reply between gritted teeth suggested otherwise.

'Good,' said the Earl, a little coolly, then turned to Chaloner. 'Well?'

Chaloner gestured behind him. 'Knight has something to tell you, sir. He—'

'You brought him here?' interrupted Gery sharply. 'A common felon?'

'Please, My Lord!' Knight scuttled forward and dropped to his knees. 'I have never done anything dishonest in my life. These tales against me are wicked lies.'

'Yes, yes.' The Earl moved away in distaste, and looked at Chaloner. 'Where is Gardner? Or am I to assume that he is already under lock and key?'

Chaloner braced himself for fireworks. 'He escaped.'

'Escaped?' echoed Gery, while the Earl scowled his irritation. 'I thought you were a soldier. Surely apprehending a pair of clerks should not have been beyond your capabilities?'

'Please listen to me, My Lord,' begged Knight, sparing Chaloner the need to reply. 'These charges are a fiction, invented by men who hate me for my integrity.'

The Earl glowered at him. 'The Spymaster had proof that you "lost" several letters.'

Knight clasped his hands together. 'We all lose letters, My Lord, but that is hardly surprising when thousands of them pass through our hands each week. It happened less when Mr Bishop was in charge, but Controller O'Neill has introduced "improvements" that are less efficient than—'

24

'You blame O'Neill?' interrupted the Earl indignantly. 'A royally appointed official?'

'No, sir,' said Knight miserably. 'But I have never defrauded the Post Office, not even during the Commonwealth, when I might have done it as an act of rebellion against a regime I never liked.'

'Oh, yes, everyone is a Royalist now,' muttered the Earl acidly.

'I asked to be brought here because I have information to share with you.' Knight swallowed hard, clearly frightened. 'It is about a man named Clement Oxenbridge.'

'Clement Oxenbridge?' repeated Gery disdainfully. 'Never heard of him.'

'Then you should remedy the matter,' said Knight with a small flash of defiance. 'Because he is the most deadly villain in London.'

'A Parliamentarian, then,' surmised Gery. 'Stand up, Knight. We have heard enough of your bleating, and it is time you were in Newgate. The Major will be here soon, and it is unfair to keep him waiting for the likes of you.'

'The Major's appointment is with you?' asked Chaloner, surprised. He had not imagined that Gery would speak to a man who had earned his fame in the New Model Army, even if the Major had later changed sides and done his damnedest to murder Cromwell.

'It is with me, actually,' said the Earl. 'He has proved himself extremely useful these last few weeks, and I may order his release from the Tower if it continues.'

'Wait!' cried Knight, as Gery stepped towards him. 'There is a great and terrible plot unfolding in the Post Office, one that might result in another civil war.'

'There is no plot,' said Gery contemptuously. 'Only a

25

lot of greedy and unscrupulous clerks who cheat their customers. Fetch the palace guards, Chaloner. They can escort him to Newgate.'

'I will take him,' said Chaloner, thinking that Knight might confide in him now that he had been given short shrift at White Hall, and there was something about the tale that had the ring of truth in it. No one wanted another war, and he was inclined to take such warnings seriously, even if Clarendon and Gery were not.

'Do not defy me,' barked Gery. 'Fetch the guards.'

'Do as he says, Chaloner,' sighed the Earl tiredly. 'As my marshal, he outranks you.'

With no choice, Chaloner went to do as he was told, although the Earl's pointed reminder of his reduced status made him wonder yet again why Gery had been hired. The moment the door had closed, he heard the murmur of voices. He could not make out the words, but he could tell that Knight was doing the talking and Gery was asking questions.

He frowned, perturbed. Gery had deliberately excluded him from the discussion now taking place, so what did the marshal not want him to hear? Freer was watching, which meant he could not press his ear against the wood, as he might have done had he been alone, so he was obliged to walk away. As he went, he was assailed by a strong sense of foreboding, and the distinct sense that all was not well in his master's household.

Knight wept so disconsolately when the palace guards led him away that Chaloner half wished he had let him escape. When they had gone, Chaloner began to walk down the stairs again, but Gery ran after him and grabbed his arm. The spy freed himself with more vigour than was strictly necessary, objecting to the liberty. Gery regarded him frostily.

'What did Knight tell you when you were alone together? Did he mention the Post Office?'

'Not really. Why?'

'If I find out you have lied to me, Knight will not be the only one locked in Newgate. You will join him there, in the deepest, dankest dungeon the keeper can provide.'

Chaloner tried not to shudder at the notion, sure Gery would implement the threat if he knew the extent of his aversion to such places. He masked his disquiet with a question. 'Why should it matter what Knight said if you believe his claims to be a fiction?'

Gery scowled. 'Because the enquiry into corrupt practices at the Post Office is *mine*, and I do not want you interfering. You might spoil the traps I have laid. Stay away from it and its clerks. Is that clear? Now go back to the office. Clarendon wants to see you.'

He had turned and stalked away before Chaloner could offer any response. Stifling a sigh – he was tired, cold and wanted to go home – Chaloner returned to his master.

'Gery has offered to track down Gardner,' said the Earl, once the intelligencer was standing in front of him again. 'Thus you may leave the matter to him. And there is no truth in Knight's allegations, so you had better forget them.'

'What allegations?' asked Chaloner, aiming to learn what had been discussed after he had been sent out.

The Earl waved a weary hand. 'About Clement Oxenbridge and the so-called Post Office plot that will bring about another civil war. It is a canard, so ignore whatever he told you.'

'Are you sure that is wise, sir?' asked Chaloner,

immediately suspicious. 'It is a serious claim, and if Knight is right—'

'Do not argue with me,' snapped the Earl. 'I am not in the mood for your insolence today.'

'It is not insolence, sir,' objected Chaloner. 'It is concern. The government is still too new to be completely stable, and we will be at war with the Dutch soon. It would be sensible to explore any rumour of plots that—'

'My marshal specifically asked me to tell you not to interfere. He dislikes you for your former loyalties. You see, not everyone is as liberal as me when it comes to that sort of thing.'

'No, sir,' said Chaloner flatly, thinking the Earl mentioned his past so frequently that it somewhat belied his claims to open-mindedness.

The Earl softened slightly. 'I have not yet thanked you for looking after my son in Sweden. He has said little about his experiences, but I have heard from other sources that you rescued him from several unpleasant situations. You served me well.'

With a pang of alarm, Chaloner knew that the discussion was a prelude to him being sent on another overseas mission. He had spent more time away than in London since entering the Earl's service, having been dispatched first to Ireland, then to Spain and Portugal, followed by Oxford, Wimbledon, Holland, Tangiers and finally Sweden. He was heartily sick of it, and had hoped that he had earned a few weeks' respite, not the mere six days that he had had at home since his most recent jaunt.

'It is good to be back, sir,' he said quickly. 'Hannah . . .'

He had been going to say that his wife was pleased to have him home, but he was not entirely sure that was true. They had been married less than six months, yet although they had spent all but a few days of it apart, their relationship was already in trouble.

'Well, I am afraid she will have to manage without you again,' said the Earl briskly. 'Because I have business that needs attending in Russia.'

'*Russia?*' cried Chaloner. That particular country had a reputation for being populated by brutal, superstitious peasants with a deep-rooted hatred of foreigners. No traveller who survived its perilous highways, warring brigands and deadly diseases had anything good to say about it. Was the assignment Gery's idea, to rid himself of a man he hated? Permanently?

'I imagine you speak the language,' the Earl continued blithely. 'I know for a fact that you understand French, Spanish, Portuguese, Latin and Dutch.'

'But not Russian, sir,' said Chaloner, aghast. 'And I cannot go in January anyway. It has no ice-free ports, and will be impossible to reach until May at the earliest.'

'I have it on good authority that there will be no ice this year. Something to do with tides, sea temperatures and the position of the moon. But it will not be for a few days yet, and I have an important task for you first. Three birds have died in St James's Park.'

'In suspicious circumstances?' asked Chaloner, still wrestling with the appalling prospect of a trek to such a remote and inhospitable place. And he was mistrustful of the 'good authority', too, doubting the Earl knew anyone who was qualified to make such a judgement.

Clarendon eyed him balefully. 'I hope you are not being facetious. But yes, the ducks did die before their time, and I want you to discover why. Most of the creatures in that park are gifts from foreign ambassadors – including Russia's – and they will be vexed if they learn we have not taken proper care of them. It is a mission of vital diplomatic importance.'

Chaloner nodded, but his sense of presentiment intensified. He had proved himself to be loyal in the past, so why was the Earl relegating him to a petty enquiry while Gery explored whatever was unfolding at the Post Office? Was it because the marshal had poisoned the Earl against him? Or was there another, more sinister reason?

'It would be helpful if you made a start today,' said the Earl, when there was no reply. 'Or did apprehending that little clerk sap your energy?'

'No,' said Chaloner, rather more curtly than was wise. 'Is there anyone particular I should talk to about these birds?'

'Well, I do not think interviewing their companions will help.' The Earl chortled, the first time Chaloner had heard him laugh since he had been back. 'Unless you speak Duck.'

Chaloner left the Earl's offices in an agitated frame of mind, and was so engrossed in his concerns that he did not see Hannah until she stepped in front of him. Silently, he berated himself for his inattention. In his line of business, that sort of carelessness saw men killed.

She was frowning, and he wondered what he had done to annoy her now. Nothing came to mind: Gery had kept him busy with petty enquiries since his return from Sweden, so he had barely seen her. They had quarrelled once, though, the night he had arrived home, when he learned that she had hired two more servants, taking the number to five. It meant they were living well beyond their means, and visions of debtors' prison loomed like a spectre.

'You look like a tradesman, Thomas,' she declared irritably. 'We have our reputations to consider, you know, and sometimes you embarrass me with your eccentric habits.'

Chaloner had dressed for apprehending felons, and his clothes were mostly grey and brown, two colours she decried as vulgar. He was still chilled to the bone, but imagined he would have been considerably colder had he worn a courtly suit of silk in place of his practical wool long-coat.

'I am sorry,' he said, lacking the will for an argument. 'I did not expect to come here today.'

She nodded, and some of her annoyance receded. She was a small, vivacious, fair-haired woman with an engaging smile, although few would have called her pretty. She was lady-in-waiting to the Queen, and she loved her post, White Hall and her mistress in equal measure.

'Have you heard the latest news?' she asked, bursting with the need to gossip. 'Roger Palmer is home, after serving two years in the Venetian navy.'

Chaloner wondered what he was expected to say. He was not interested in Court chatter – least of all about Lord Castlemaine – although he knew he should be, as only a foolish intelligencer did not learn about the people among whom he was obliged to move.

'There will be trouble,' predicted Hannah gleefully, when there was no response. 'His vile wife will have to curtail her sluttish behaviour now.'

'Why?' asked Chaloner. 'Their marriage is dead. He has no control over her or she over him.'

'True,' acknowledged Hannah. 'Indeed, she began her affair with the King within weeks of their wedding. None of her four children are Palmer's – the King has claimed them all as his own. Unfortunately for everyone concerned, Palmer is a papist – divorce is out of the question.'

31

'I see.' Chaloner supposed it was a covert reference to their own situation. Hannah had converted to Catholicism when she had been appointed to serve the Queen, which meant she would not countenance an annulment either, no matter how disastrous their union.

'We had a nasty shock today.' Hannah flitted to another subject. 'Mary Wood is dead of the small-pox. Do you remember her? She and her husband own a mansion near Dowgate. It is not somewhere I should like to live, as I imagine it is very noisy.'

Their own house on Tothill Street was not exactly a haven of peace, given that it was near a number of taverns, not all of them reputable. But London was like that – respectable homes often rubbed shoulders with insalubrious alehouses, and Dowgate was not much different from Tothill Street in that respect.

'Did you know Mary well?' he asked, not sure whether to offer sympathy or congratulations.

'Yes, she was the Queen's dresser. There are rumours that she was murdered, but I doubt they are true. She became unwell last month, and I hope she did not pass the disease to the rest of us before she collapsed and was carried home. Of course, I did not like her very much.'

'No?'

'When things went missing from the Queen's jewel box, it was nearly always Mary who had last been seen with them. Of course, her faults are forgotten now she is dead – everyone is extolling her virtues. Do you know her husband? Sir Henry is sixty-six years old, and Mary was thirty-eight, but they still managed to produce a baby.'

Hannah's voice was bitter. She wanted children herself, but her first marriage had been barren and her second

32

was proving to be the same. As Chaloner had fathered a child – dead of plague in Holland – she had accepted that the fault lay with her. Chaloner had been mildly ashamed of his relief, suspecting there would have been no end of trouble had she believed otherwise.

'Do you mean the fellow who is Clerk of the Green Cloth?' he asked.

Hannah nodded. 'Which, as you will know, means he has very little to do, yet is still paid a handsome salary. His duties are mostly arranging royal journeys, but the King likes being in London, so Wood is rarely obliged to tax himself.'

Chaloner considered what he knew of the man. 'A few days ago, he told my Earl that eating live wasps would cure his gout.'

'I hope he followed the advice.' Hannah loathed Clarendon, partly for the shabby way he treated her husband, but mostly because he was vocal in his disapproval of the Court rakes, many of whom were her friends. 'But Wood does say and do some very peculiar things. For example, he tried to make Controller O'Neill drink a toast to his health out of a jug that contained a dead toad.'

'Why?' asked Chaloner, repelled. 'Did the Post Office lose one of his letters?'

Hannah laughed. 'Probably! That place has not been the same since Henry Bishop was dismissed and O'Neill appointed in his place. You were not in London at the time, but it caused a tremendous stir. Bishop and O'Neill hate each other now, and are always spoiling for a spat.'

'Then perhaps that is why Wood offered O'Neill a dead toad – he sympathises with Bishop.'

'Perhaps, although Wood is extremely strange, and

33

there is no knowing with him. But he will miss Mary. He always said that she made him feel young again.'

'Who started the rumours that she was murdered?' Chaloner supposed he should keep abreast of the matter lest he was asked to investigate. 'And why?'

'I have no idea, but it will be malicious nonsense. Mary died of the small-pox, and that is that. And if you do not believe me, ask Surgeon Wiseman. He tended her, and I doubt any sly murderer could deceive him.'

'No,' acknowledged Chaloner. Wiseman knew his trade.

Chaloner was deeply unsettled by the prospect of travelling to Russia, and he had not liked the way he had been ordered to stay away from whatever was brewing at the Post Office. He knew his concerns would keep him awake if he went home to bed, so he decided to follow the Earl's orders and make a start on the ducks instead. He was partial to birds anyway, and disliked the notion of someone picking them off.

St James's Park was enclosed by high walls, and was accessible through a number of gates, all of which were guarded to exclude undesirables. However, Chaloner entered unchallenged that morning, the sentries evidently having decided that no one was likely to venture into their domain on a day when the wind was bitter and snow was in the air. Unfortunately, the men who tended the plants and birds had apparently thought the same – the place was deserted, and there was no one to question about what had happened to the ducks.

The grass was white with frost, and the Canal – the wide, straight body of water that formed the park's centrepiece – had frozen over. A number of disgruntled fowl stood along its fringes or in irritable confusion on

34

its iron surface, fluffed up against the chill. Chaloner walked around it in its entirety, bending to inspect the banks every so often, but he discovered nothing useful. He shivered. Perhaps the birds had just died of cold. Many were from warmer climes, after all, and would not appreciate such frigid weather.

He stood for a while watching them, impressed by their variety and colours. There were several kinds of swan and goose, countless ducks, two cranes, including one with a wooden leg, a flock of penguins and a glorious pinkish creature that he believed to be a flamingo, a species he had read about but had never seen.

Other birds were kept in cages, and he had been told in the past that the two white ravens were a gift from the King of Denmark, the parrots were from wealthy members of the East India Company, the hawks had come from the Queen Consort of Poland, and the pelicans were from the Tsar of Russia. He was not surprised that His Majesty felt obliged to protect his collection.

He lingered until the cold bit harder still, and when one of the drakes released a sound that was uncannily like a mocking laugh, he decided to go home. He had almost reached the King Street gate when he saw a conscientious gardener struggling to cover a plant with a piece of material. The wind kept catching it, and the fellow was red-faced and irritable, but his expression brightened when he saw Chaloner.

'Excellent! Would you be so kind as to help me? The cover has blown off my bananas, and unless I replace them quickly the frost will have them and the King will be vexed.'

'I thought bananas only grew in hot countries,' said Chaloner, wondering if the man was making sport of him.

35

The gardener beamed. 'I was given some seeds. Three plants are now in the Inner Temple, which is where I usually work, and two are here – His Majesty heard about my success and asked for a pair, you see. However, they do not like the cold, and they will die unless I protect them.'

Chaloner was somewhat startled to note that the bananas were going to be swathed in a generous length of best quality worsted. It meant they would be far better clad than most Londoners, who would give their eye-teeth for such luxury.

It was easy to wrap the plants with two pairs of hands, and the gardener soon had his charges bundled up the way he wanted. He was older than Chaloner, with a brown, lined face that indicated a life spent outdoors. He said his name was Seth Eliot, and that he had been a gardener at the Inner Temple for twenty years.

'Do you know what happened to the birds that died?' asked Chaloner.

'Only that they were found by the Canal,' replied Eliot. 'Why? Have you been charged to look into the matter? Edward Storey will be pleased. He is Curator of Birds, and was beginning to think that no one cared.'

'The Earl of Clarendon does. God only knows why.'

'Because he wants to curry the King's favour,' replied Eliot promptly. 'All London knows his star is fading, and that he will leap at any opportunity to ingratiate himself. If he finds whoever killed the birds, His Majesty might be more kindly disposed towards him.'

Although Chaloner knew the King no longer treated Clarendon like a favoured confidant, it was disconcerting to hear it from a gardener. 'Where might I find Edward Storey?' he asked, eager to change the subject.

36

'He lives in Post House Yard, off Dowgate Hill. You cannot miss his cottage – it has a pelican carved on the door.'

'Is it near the General Letter Office?'

Eliot nodded. 'His house adjoins it: they are neighbours.'

Chaloner thanked him, and resumed his walk towards the gate. Was it coincidence that his enquiries should take him to the one place in London where Gery had forbidden him to go? Regardless, if he wanted answers about the birds, he would have to visit Storey. And if he happened to learn a little about the Post Office at the same time, then so be it.

It was not a pleasant trek to Dowgate, because the wind cut through his clothes and more snow was in the air. He tried to walk quickly, in the hope that exercise would warm him, but the streets were too crowded and ice underfoot made speed impractical. He was obliged to slow down even further when his second skid caused him to collide with a cleric, who responded with a stream of startlingly unholy curses.

He arrived at Post House Yard and stared at the General Letter Office, wondering what was happening inside it that Knight had said was so dangerous to the country's stability. The square was busy, because noon on Thursdays was the deadline for domestic mail – letters received after twelve o'clock would have to wait until the next post, which was not until Saturday. Wise people handed in their missives as late as possible, in the hope that the government's spies would not have enough time to open them before they were sorted and sent. Hence, there was an air of quiet industry as people hurried up and down the marble steps.

Those who had finished their business loitered to exchange greetings with friends and acquaintances, getting in the way of those who still had to take their letters inside. A musician was plying his trade near the mansion on the left, and had attracted a small crowd. He was not very good, but flamboyance made up for his lack of talent, along with the fact that he had chosen to play popular tunes that his audience knew. Some were singing along, and Chaloner saw a black-garbed servant emerge from the house and whisper in the performer's ear. He was ignored.

'It is disrespectful,' Chaloner heard one woman say to another. 'Mary Wood lived there, and she died this morning. People should do their caterwauling somewhere else.'

Hannah had mentioned that Wood and his wife owned a mansion near Dowgate, and Chaloner studied it with interest. It was spacious and elegant, indicating that her report of Wood's handsome salary had not been exaggerated. As was the custom for a house in mourning, there was a black wreath on the door and all the window shutters were closed.

Chaloner turned his attention to the brightly painted cottages opposite, and quickly identified Storey's with its carved bird. He was about to knock when his eye was caught by a cart. Vehicles tended to avoid Post House Yard, because the alley into it was narrow and they ran the risk of getting jammed – at which point there would be trouble, because there was no other way in or out. The cart was not very wide, but it was tall, and piled high with firewood. There was no horse in its traces, and it had every appearance of being abandoned.

Chaloner frowned. Fuel was expensive, especially in

winter, so why was no one guarding it? Moreover, it was oddly stacked, with logs laid at peculiar angles. Then he saw a wisp of smoke curl from inside the heap and caught the distinctive reek of gunpowder. In a flash, he knew exactly what was about to happen.

'Run!' he yelled, so suddenly and loudly that it stilled the clatter of conversation in the entire square. 'The cart is going to explode!'

There was a momentary silence, followed by pandemonium. Terrified screams tore through the air as people raced for the safety of Dowgate Hill, shoving aside those who moved more slowly. Several fell and were trampled underfoot. Two beggarly boys trotted towards the cart, and Chaloner could only assume they meant to snag some of the wood before the lot was lost.

'No!' he cried desperately. 'Stop!'

One glanced at him, but the attention of the other was on the log he had grabbed. The smoke from the fuse was thicker now, and Chaloner knew there was not much time. He shouted again, his voice cracking as he tried to make himself heard over the shrieks of the escaping crowd. Those who had been knocked over in the stampede were struggling to stand, while two exceptionally large postal clerks were waddling away far too slowly. Meanwhile, the servant from the Woods' mansion was gaping stupidly, apparently too shocked to join the exodus.

And then the cart blew into pieces with a roar that shook the ground.

Chapter 2

Chaloner opened his eyes to a confusion of noise and smoke. For a moment, he did not understand why he was lying on his back in the open air or why his ears rang, but then his mind snapped clear. Someone was looming over him, a bulky silhouette against the grey sky. The shape was familiar, and he recognised Temperance North, a young woman he had known for two years, although their friendship had cooled when she had made a somewhat unexpected transition from Puritan maid to brothel-keeper. He was still fond of her, though, despite the fact that the affection was rarely reciprocated and they often quarrelled.

'Thank God!' she whispered as he sat up. 'I thought you were dead.'

Tendrils of smoke wafted over a sizeable crater, and all that remained of the cart were jagged fragments blown into the far corners of the square. A crowd had gathered, talking in excited voices, and several bodies had been covered with coats. Other people were sitting on the ground, being tended by friends or passers-by. Among the ministering angels was Temperance's beau, Richard Wiseman, Surgeon to the King.

Chaloner turned his gaze towards the Post Office. Its walls were pock-marked and several window panes had been smashed, but it was otherwise unscathed. Its front doors were open, and people were still moving in and out with letters, indicating that the explosion had done nothing to impede business. Wood's mansion and the cottages had also escaped major damage, although Storey's carved pelican had been obliterated by flying debris.

Still befuddled, Chaloner struggled to understand what purpose such an attack might serve. As an assault on a government institution, it was a failure, because neither the Post Office nor the services it offered appeared to have been affected.

He stared at the hole where the cart had been. Its size told him that a generous amount of gunpowder had been used, yet the vehicle had been left more or less in the middle of the square, where its impact on buildings would be minimal. Had the perpetrators been afraid to go closer, lest they aroused suspicion? Had they been novices, who did not know how blasts worked? Or had their intention been rather to kill and maim? He thought of Knight's conviction that something terrible was underway at the Post Office. Was this the sort of thing he had envisioned? Chaloner supposed someone would have to visit Newgate and ask him.

'Richard and I were on our way to dine in the Crown,' Temperance was saying in the same shocked whisper. 'But he wanted to bring a letter here first. We were just coming out of the Post Office when you started to shout and . . .'

'And what?' asked Chaloner, when she trailed off. 'What did you see?'

41

'A cart flying up into the air on a fountain of flames,' replied Temperance shakily. 'And you tossed backwards like an old pillow.'

'Did you notice anyone loitering before the explosion? Or running away after it happened?'

'Yes! A great many people took to their heels once you began yelling. And thank God they did, or we would have been knee-deep in corpses.'

'But did you see anyone acting suspiciously?' Chaloner pressed. 'Looking as though they were waiting for the blast to happen? Or positioned so that they could watch without being harmed themselves?'

'I could not tell.' Temperance swallowed hard. 'There was chaos afterwards, and the alley to Dowgate Hill was crammed with folk trying to escape, all battling against those who were still coming to post letters. I did not notice much else. I was too worried about you.'

Chaloner was surprised and touched by the expression of concern. He had not known she still cared for him, although he was sorry it had taken gunpowder for her to show it.

'Who could have done such a wicked thing?' she went on, more to herself than to him. 'Someone who does not like the way the postal service is run? Well, who does? We all know about its dishonest practices – charging for letters that never arrive, Members of Parliament sending mail free for their friends, drunken postmen . . .'

'Are there any other buildings of note in the square?' Chaloner did not know why he had asked, because he could see for himself that there were not. He supposed he was still dazed.

'Not really. Sir Henry Wood owns the mansion to your left. The cottages on the right belong to him, too, but

42

he refuses to rent them, lest one of the tenants decides to grow carrots – he is rather odd, and a passionate dislike of vegetables is just one of his peculiarities. The only other resident is Edward Storey, who has the house nearest the Post Office.'

'Do you know him?'

Temperance nodded. 'He is a patient of Richard's and a decent man. I sincerely doubt this atrocity was aimed at him. Besides, all he does is look after the birds in St James's Park, which is hardly a controversial occupation.'

'No,' said Chaloner, although it occurred to him that there might be a link between the dead birds and an explosion near their guardian's home. Or had he been in espionage too long, and was seeing connections where there were none?

When Chaloner stood, his legs were like rubber. Temperance gripped his arm tightly, and continued to hold it long after he had regained his balance and her help was no longer needed. He glanced at her. She was wearing a wig of golden curls, which was far inferior to her own chestnut locks – or would have been had she not shaved them off in the interests of fashion – and her clothes were the best money could buy. Unfortunately, they failed to disguise the fact that she was a very large young woman, almost as tall as he, but considerably wider.

However, she was positively petite compared to Surgeon Wiseman, who was vast and added to his impressive bulk with a peculiar regime of lifting heavy weights each morning. He said it was to improve his general well-being, but it had given him the physique of a prize wrestler. Chaloner pitied his patients, not only because they would

43

be powerless to fend him off once he had decided on a course of treatment, but because he liked to experiment and his massive form alone would intimidate his ailing charges into acquiescing to his unorthodox remedies.

It was not just Wiseman's size that made him an imposing figure, but the fact that he never wore any colour except red; even his hair was auburn, a thick mane that was the envy of wigmakers all over London. His detractors said it was to conceal the excessive amounts of blood he spilled during surgery, although Chaloner suspected it was just because he liked to be noticed.

Chaloner's feelings towards him were ambivalent. Like most sane men, he was wary of the medical profession, which was notorious for doing more harm than good. Moreover, Wiseman was arrogant, insensitive, overbearing and brash. On the other hand, he was principled, honest and loyal to those he considered worthy of his respect. At first, Chaloner had resisted his overtures of friendship, but he was beginning to yield, worn down by the surgeon's dogged persistence.

Wiseman grasped his shoulder and peered into his eyes. 'Headache?'

Chaloner nodded warily.

'It will ease. You are fortunate – I thought you were dead when I saw you fly through the air.'

Chaloner wondered whether Wiseman was as brusque with the King when he was unwell, and if so, why he continued to be employed at White Hall. Wiseman vigorously maintained that he was the best *medicus* in the country, but it was not an opinion shared by most of his colleagues.

'How many dead?' asked Temperance in a small voice.

'Five,' replied the surgeon. 'And a dozen injured. It

would have been much worse if Chaloner had not yelled his warning.' He shot the spy a suspicious glance. 'I assume it was by chance that you happened to be here – that you had nothing to do with the blast?'

Chaloner was offended that Wiseman should think he might play a role in perpetrating such an atrocity. 'No, of course not. I came to visit Edward Storey.'

'About the three dead ducks in St James's Park?' asked Temperance. She saw Chaloner's surprise and hastened to explain. 'It was mentioned at the club last night.'

She was referring to the brothel – although she preferred the term 'gentleman's club' – that she owned in Hercules' Pillars Alley, an exclusive establishment that catered to the needs of the very wealthy. It was patronised by members of Court, and gossip overheard there had helped Chaloner with a number of investigations in the past.

'Surely Clarendon has not ordered you to explore those?' said Wiseman in disbelief. 'How can he squander your talents on so trivial a matter?'

'How indeed?' murmured Chaloner.

Temperance's expression hardened. 'I suppose that horrible Gery is given all the interesting cases now. Such as looking into what is going on at the Post Office.'

'The Post Office?' asked Chaloner, surprised a second time. 'Is it common knowledge that trouble might be unfolding there?'

'I suppose it is,' replied Temperance. 'At least, several people have told me that something untoward is going on. Unfortunately, no one seems to know exactly what.'

'The Earl should have asked you to look into it, Chaloner,' said Wiseman. 'And I told him so when I was tending his gout the other day. Gery does not have your wits.'

45

Chaloner was taken aback by how much this vote of confidence meant to him. 'What did he say?'

'That I should cure his sore foot and leave decisions pertaining to state security to him. He was rather rude, actually, which is unlike him.'

It was not unlike him at all, as far as Chaloner was concerned, and he was amazed that Wiseman had gone as long as he had without a reprimand. Perhaps it was the surgeon's growing friendship with Chaloner that tarnished him in the Earl's eyes.

'I cannot abide Gery,' said Temperance. 'He visits the club sometimes, but he would rather die than smile. Still, he always pays promptly, which is a major consideration, of course.'

'And he is wholly devoted to the King,' added Wiseman. 'Unfortunately, he is also unspeakably stupid. I do not like the fellows he has hired to help him either. Chaloner has always managed alone, so why should Gery have an army of staff?'

'Hardly an army,' said Chaloner. 'Just Will Freer.'

'Freer *and* six soldiers,' corrected Wiseman. 'Louts, who will do anything for money.'

'I have seen no soldiers,' said Chaloner, although it occurred to him that he had been kept so busy since his return from Sweden that Gery could have hired half of London without him knowing.

'They are there, I assure you. However, they are better than the villain he has hired as his secretary – a fellow by the name of Samuel Morland. You seem startled. Did you not know?'

Chaloner did not, and was appalled. 'But Morland worked for Cromwell's government and . . .'

He faltered. Temperance and Wiseman were staunch

46

Royalists, and he did not think finishing his remark with 'betrayed the Commonwealth by selling its secrets' would be very well received. But the truth was that he and Morland had once been colleagues: both had been employed by Cromwell's spymaster, John Thurloe. Chaloner had not trusted Morland then, and the passing of time had done nothing to make him change his mind.

'Who saw the error of his ways and switched sides,' finished Wiseman, making Chaloner glad he had guarded his tongue. 'He is said to be very sharp witted and speaks several languages, but there is something about him that I distrust intensely.'

From that, Chaloner assumed that Morland was still the same slippery, devious, unlikable character he had been in Cromwell's day. He had defected only after the Lord Protector had died, when the Commonwealth was failing, so it had been an act of self-preservation, not loyalty to the Crown, that had driven him to shift his allegiance. Morland claimed he had been sending intelligence to the exiled Royalists for years, but strangely, none of the messages had ever arrived. Somewhat inexplicably, the King believed him, and he had been rewarded with a knighthood.

'Are you sure Gery has engaged him?' asked Chaloner, although he hated to reveal that he, a man who made his living by gathering information, did not know what was happening in his own master's household.

Temperance nodded. 'I heard it from Gery himself, at the club. Well, I had to talk to him about something, and his duties for Clarendon were the only thing I could think of.'

'Did he say anything else about them?'

Temperance's expression was troubled. 'Only that he

47

hates working with men who supported Cromwell, and thinks they should all be hanged and their corpses tossed in the river. Be careful in his company, Tom. He seems a little deranged to me.'

It was good advice, and Chaloner fully intended to follow it.

It was not long before word of the explosion spread, and people flocked to gawp at the place where others had died. They included some folk who had fled but who now returned to inspect the crater, along with a number of postal clerks – it was past noon, so the General Letter Office was closed, and they had abandoned their duties of sorting and stamping to stand in gossipy huddles. While Wiseman returned to the wounded, Temperance took her mind off the shock she had suffered by pointing out specific onlookers to Chaloner.

'That is Roger Palmer,' she whispered, indicating a tall man with a lean, athletic build. He was roughly Chaloner's age, with an open, pleasant face. 'Lady Castlemaine's husband.'

'He visits the club?' Palmer's clothes, like Chaloner's own, were dusty and torn, indicating he had been uncomfortably close to the blast, too.

Temperance shook her head. 'He is too respectable, which is astonishing, given his wife's character. He is also said to be intelligent, although I do not believe it: he would not have married her if he had any wits.' Then she gestured in a different direction. 'Do you see that short, dark fellow with the impish face? That is Controller O'Neill.'

Chaloner looked with interest at the man who ran the

Post Office. The dead had been laid in a line, and O'Neill was hovering over them, his face a mask of distress. His clerks hurried to cluster around him, and while some seemed dismayed by the carnage, others were impassive. Then Temperance tugged on Chaloner's arm, directing his attention elsewhere again.

'Henry Bishop is here, too. He and O'Neill hate each other, because O'Neill conspired to have him removed as Postmaster so he could get the job himself. Anything that hurts O'Neill will please Bishop, and an explosion outside the Post Office *will* reflect badly on its Controller.'

Bishop was middle-aged with mournful eyes, and wore a large brown wig and a fine blue coat. He held a lapdog that had one of the most malevolent faces Chaloner had ever seen on an animal.

'He does not look pleased to me,' remarked Chaloner. Bishop was pale and he absently kissed the top of his dog's head as one of the dead was carried past him.

'No,' conceded Temperance. 'On reflection, he is not the kind of man to condone this sort of thing. He is by far the nicer of the two, and he was much better at running the Post Office. O'Neill told some terrible lies to get him ousted eighteen months ago. He even attacked Bishop's friend the Major, who is still in prison because of the accusations.'

Hannah had said much the same, as had the Major himself, and Chaloner was puzzled. 'Everyone seems to accept that O'Neill's accusations were motivated by self-interest, so why were they taken seriously?'

'Oh, I imagine money changed hands,' shrugged Temperance. 'The Major is a fiery orator, so I suspect the government was delighted to have an excuse to lock him

49

up. It is a pity about Bishop, though: the mail was usually delivered on time when he was in charge, whereas now . . .'

'Do most Londoners think the same?'

Temperance considered the question carefully. 'Yes, I should think so. Anyone who writes letters will deplore O'Neill's shoddy service, while anyone who has met the two will prefer Bishop's bumbling amiability over O'Neill's bombastic insincerity. Bishop plays the viol, too, whereas O'Neill says he has no time for what he calls mindless frivolity.'

The last remark put Chaloner firmly in Bishop's camp. Music was important to him. It helped him think clearly when he was confused, soothed him when he was unhappy, and revived him when he was tired. Unfortunately, Hannah hated him playing his viol, something he considered to be a serious impediment to their future happiness together.

Temperance continued to point out the rich and famous, and Chaloner listened with half an ear, more interested in studying the postal clerks who surrounded O'Neill. After a while, he became aware that he was not the only one watching them. So was a tall, thin man with very dark hair and an unusually white face. However, it was the fellow's eyes that were his most arresting feature. They were jet black and oddly shiny.

A memory from Chaloner's childhood surfaced with such sudden clarity that it made him start. One of his sisters had owned a doll that had looked just like the man, right down to its chalky face and glinting eyes. It had given them both nightmares, so their father had put it on the fire, where it had released the most diabolical of shrieks as the flames had consumed it. The entire family had been disconcerted, while the servants had muttered darkly about witchcraft.

'Clement Oxenbridge,' whispered Temperance, following the direction of his gaze.

'A client from the club?'

'No, thank God,' replied Temperance with a shudder. 'He is said to be a very dangerous person, and I should not like to think of him around my girls.'

Chaloner was thoughtful: Knight had said that a man named Clement Oxenbridge was involved in something sinister at the Post Office. 'Do you think he set the explosion?'

'It is possible. No one knows anything about him – he just appears out of nowhere when there is mischief afoot. I am not surprised to see him here. He probably smelled the blood.'

The blast must have deprived Chaloner of his wits, because her words sent a cold shiver down his spine. He was not usually unsettled by remarks that were patently ridiculous, but there was something about Oxenbridge that was decidedly disconcerting.

'Actually, he is here because he was posting a letter,' countered Wiseman, rejoining them and overhearing the remark. 'He was in front of me in the queue, sending greetings to his mother.'

'His mother?' echoed Temperance incredulously. 'He will not have one of those.'

Wiseman shot her an amused glance. 'Of course he will. How else would he have been born?'

'Through the devil,' replied Temperance promptly. 'Oxenbridge is evil, Richard, and if he tries to approach you, I want you to run away.'

'Run away?' laughed Wiseman. 'I most certainly shall not!'

'But you must,' insisted Temperance earnestly. 'Not

51

only is he the most deadly villain ever to set foot in London, but he is said to have been friends with John Fry. Do you remember him?'

Wiseman nodded, and explained when he saw Chaloner's blank look. 'Fry was a man made famous by his controversial opinions during the Commonwealth. He penned all manner of inflammatory tracts and letters, including some that urged a rebellion against Cromwell.'

'A Royalist, then,' surmised Chaloner.

'No, but not a Parliamentarian either,' replied Wiseman. 'He thought the country should be a republic, and his defiant words won him a lot of supporters. He died eight years ago, and there were rumours that he was murdered.'

'A very dangerous man,' elaborated Temperance, 'only ever happy when Britain was in flames. However, he was not murdered because he never died – he arranged his own funeral, so he could continue his poisonous work unimpeded.'

'You heard that in the club?' asked Wiseman, a little sceptically.

Temperance nodded. 'I also heard that he is in London at this very moment. Doubtless Oxenbridge intends to help him with whatever nasty plan he is fomenting.'

Wiseman opened his mouth to argue, but then thought better of it: Temperance was not easily dissuaded once she had made up her mind, and it was neither the time nor the place for a debate. 'You are shivering, my dear,' he said instead, kindly solicitous. 'And Chaloner is very pale. I suggest we repair to the Crown tavern for some hot ale.'

'Why not the Antwerp?' asked Chaloner tiredly. 'It is closer.'

'Really, Thomas,' said Temperance disdainfully. 'The Antwerp is well known for being the haunt of Parliamentarians. We could not possibly go there. Besides, it is a coffee house now, so women are refused admittance. The Crown, on the other hand, has always been a Cavalier stronghold and it welcomes ladies.'

Wondering when the turbulent politics wrought by the civil wars would ever relinquish their hold, Chaloner followed his friends out of Post House Yard.

Although he knew he should visit Storey, Chaloner was glad to sit next to a roaring fire and feel the warmth seep back into his frozen limbs. Wiseman ordered a jug of sack-posset – mulled wine mixed with milk, which was more palatable than it sounded – and it was not long before Chaloner began to feel better.

He had never been in the Crown before, and looked curiously around the place where Royalists still gathered to ruminate. It was large, comfortable and clean. A number of people sat at a table by the window, where they spoke in loud, bragging voices about what they would do if they ever laid hold of a Parliamentarian. Chaloner sincerely hoped his plain brown long-coat and lack of lace would not lead them to assume that *he* was one.

The ambitious navy clerk Samuel Pepys was there, too, with a group of men from the newly formed Royal Society. He glanced in Chaloner's direction, but did not acknowledge him. Chaloner understood why Pepys was reluctant to admit an association in front of his influential friends: Chaloner's clothes had not been smart before the blast, but now they made him look positively disreputable.

'We shall have something to eat, too,' determined Wiseman. 'Roasted duck.'

'No,' said Chaloner hastily, his encounter with the feathered residents of St James's Park too fresh in his mind. 'Not a bird. Not today.'

Wiseman regarded him in concern. 'How hard did you hit your head when you landed on the ground? Is there any ringing in your ears?'

'Perhaps there is quacking,' quipped Temperance. Then she shuddered and took a substantial gulp of posset. 'I do not think I will ever forget what happened in Post House Yard today.'

'Five dead,' sighed the surgeon. 'Including two boys. Apparently, they had come to collect feathers from Edward Storey. He was out, but their youthful curiosity must have been snagged by the sight of an unattended cart. I suspect they were in the process of filching logs when it blew up.'

'I saw them,' said Temperance. 'They looked like beggars. But why did they want feathers?'

'For hats,' explained Wiseman. 'Storey supplies the Court milliners, and these lads delivered them for him, apparently. The other victims were Wood's servant Joyce, and the Alibond brothers.'

'Not Job and Sam!' cried Temperance in dismay. 'But I know them, Richard!'

Wiseman reached out to hold her hand. 'I am sorry, dearest. They heard Chaloner raise the alarm, but were too fat to heed it – they could not waddle away fast enough.'

'They were portly,' acknowledged Temperance. 'When they came to the club, they ate far more than anyone else. But I liked them, and I shall miss their visits. They were postal clerks.'

'It could have been much worse,' said Wiseman soberly. 'The yard was packed with folk, partly because it was nearing the noon deadline for letters, and partly because someone was playing the flageolet and people had stopped to listen to him.'

'Was the musician among the injured?' Chaloner had only the vaguest recollection of the man – a tall, thin fellow of mediocre talent, whose hat had shielded his face.

'No,' replied the surgeon. 'He must have run away when he heard you yell.'

Chaloner regarded him uneasily. 'Do you think he was there to encourage people to linger, so that the carnage would be greater?'

'I would not think so,' said Wiseman, startled. 'What reason could he have? He probably fled to avoid prosecution – there is a bylaw banning itinerant performers from this part of the city.'

Chaloner was not sure what to think. 'What did he look like?'

'I did not take much notice. Ask Jeremiah Copping, one of the postal clerks who was injured. When I tended his wound, he said he had been listening to the music before the blast. He will probably answer your questions, although he is an arrogant sort.'

Coming from Wiseman, this was a damning indictment.

'Copping was friends with the Alibond brothers,' added Temperance unhappily. 'They often came to the club together. Poor Copping. He will miss them, too.'

'How badly hurt is he?' asked Chaloner. 'And where does he live?'

'He had a large splinter in his neck.' Wiseman's eyes

gleamed at the recollection. 'I removed it with deft efficiency, although he cried like a baby. He should make a full recovery. He lives with his sister, who owns the Catherine Wheel tavern on Cheapside.'

Temperance began to reminisce about the Alibond brothers at that point, while Chaloner struggled to remember exactly what he had seen and heard just before the explosion. He had been trained to be observant, and knew he should have been able to describe any number of people in the crowd, but the images in his mind were blurred and disjointed, like looking through thick fog.

He stopped trying to force the issue, and instead thought about Gery and the new staff he had hired. Why had he picked Morland? The man was brazenly treacherous, and only a fool would trust him. Moreover, the Earl was always claiming that he did not have enough money to pay his staff, so why was he suddenly able to afford Gery, Freer, Morland and six soldiers? Yet again, Chaloner had the sense that something untoward was brewing in the Earl's household. It might even explain why he himself was being packed off to Russia, a distant and very dangerous place from which he might never return.

When he finally dragged his attention back to his friends they were discussing Mary Wood.

'There are rumours that she was murdered,' Temperance was saying. 'Are they true?'

'I was summoned to tend her,' replied the surgeon pompously. 'But she was dead by the time I arrived. It was certainly the small-pox, though: the marks are unmistakeable.'

'There was no evidence of foul play?' pressed Temperance.

'None that I saw.' Wiseman rubbed his hands in gluttonous anticipation when the pot-boy arrived with an assortment of roasted meat. 'Goose! What a treat.'

'Will you examine her again?' asked Temperance. 'Just to be sure?'

Wiseman shrugged. 'Why not? Someone should quell these nasty tales. Perhaps you will join me, Chaloner? The woman was a courtier, so you must be interested. And if I do discover anything amiss, Clarendon will ask you to investigate.'

'He is more likely to ask Gery,' said Chaloner, not without rancour.

'Even more reason for you to come, then,' said Wiseman, clapping a friendly hand on his shoulder. 'You can claim prior knowledge of the case, and solve it to impress him. Come to the Westminster charnel house on Tuesday afternoon, and we shall assess her together.'

'Why so long?' asked Temperance. 'She may be buried by then.'

'Her funeral is next Wednesday – Wood told me himself at Court today.' Wiseman's tone was haughty. 'And I cannot possibly spare the time before that – I shall be too busy with the injuries arising from this blast. Including tending you, Chaloner. You do not look at all well. Allow me to—'

Chaloner stood hastily. 'There is nothing wrong that an early night will not cure.'

Unfortunately an early night was not on the agenda for Chaloner. He arrived at Tothill Street to find Hannah entertaining. He tried to sneak upstairs without being seen, but she had heard the front door open, and came to intercept him. She was unsympathetic when he told

57

her about the explosion, and he was left with the sense that she thought he had been caught in it for no reason other than reckless bloody-mindedness.

Once he had changed into respectable clothes, he went to the drawing room and did his best to play the gracious host, but he was exhausted and his head ached. Moreover, he was not naturally loquacious, and hated the vacuous frivolity of Hannah's courtly friends. The only person there of remote interest was Daniel O'Neill, although only because of his connection to the Post Office. O'Neill was with a woman who looked uncannily like him – elfin, dark and with brightly interested eyes. When Chaloner approached, O'Neill introduced her as his wife Kate.

Kate held a very elevated opinion of herself, and immediately set about informing her listeners – at that point comprising Chaloner, her husband and an infamously debauched courtier named Will Chiffinch – that her embroidery was the best in London. Chiffinch quickly grew bored, and asked O'Neill about the Post Office blast instead. An agonised expression crossed O'Neill's face, and Chaloner studied him closely, thinking that here was the man accused of having the Major imprisoned and Bishop dismissed. Were the tales true? And was his distress at Chiffinch's question genuine, or was he just an extremely able actor?

'It was dreadful,' O'Neill replied. 'Five dead, including the Alibond brothers, who were two of my best clerks. Fortunately, there was very little damage to the General Letter Office itself.'

'The news is all over White Hall that two of your men are accused of corruption,' said Chiffinch. 'And that one is now in Newgate Gaol. Do you think the other left the gunpowder in revenge for being exposed?'

58

There was a flash of something hard and unpleasant in O'Neill's eyes. 'It is possible, because I inherited that pair from Bishop. I should have followed my instincts and dismissed them, as I did the rest of his staff, but they begged me to be compassionate, and like a fool I capitulated.'

'I would not have given in,' declared Kate. 'When Bishop became Postmaster at the Restoration, he re-hired a lot of old Parliamentarians, on the grounds that they knew how to run the place. But it is better to have inept Royalists than efficient Roundheads.'

Chaloner did not agree. He and others like him had been sent home from Holland because the new Spymaster had decided to replace them with untried Cavaliers, and intelligence on England's most serious enemy had suffered a blow from which it had never recovered. And now it seemed the same narrow-minded principles were being applied to the Post Office. He supposed it explained why the service had gone downhill once the more enlightened Bishop had been ousted.

'I have nothing against a little ineptitude,' Chiffinch was saying. 'Indeed, I am prone to it myself on occasion. However, the service you provide is a disgrace, and I cannot tell you how many of my letters have gone astray since you became Postmaster.'

'Controller,' corrected O'Neill tightly. 'I decline to use the same title as that rogue Bishop. And there is nothing wrong with my service. If your missives failed to arrive, then it is because you addressed them incorrectly.'

Chiffinch bristled indignantly. 'I assure you I did not. And you were wrong to expel Bishop's people, because their experience would have helped to—'

'One does not need experience to be a postal clerk,'

interrupted O'Neill contemptuously. 'All they do is accept letters and shove them in bags to be delivered.'

Even Chaloner knew the work was more complex than that, and O'Neill had just displayed a woeful ignorance about the foundation he was supposed to be running.

'Put me in charge,' suggested Kate. 'I will turn it into a decent venture. And there will be no Gardners and Knights to steal our profits either, because I shall hire *honest* men.'

'And how will you do that, madam?' asked Chiffinch archly.

'I can tell a good man from a rogue,' declared Kate, glaring first at Chiffinch and then Chaloner in a way that said she thought they might well belong to the latter category. 'I can distinguish between Papists and Anglicans at a glance, too. I would certainly not have any of *them* working in the Post Office.'

'Any of whom?' asked Chaloner, bemused. 'Catholics or Protestants?'

'Pope lovers,' hissed Kate, eyes glittering. 'They are an evil force in our country, and I applaud the laws that suppress them. I only wish we could burn them at the stake, too, because that would make them think twice about plotting against us.'

Chaloner had no particular religious affiliation, but Hannah did, and he objected to her being insulted in her own home. 'There is no Catholic plot to—'

'There are dozens of them.' O'Neill cut across him sharply. 'And anyone who does not believe it is a fool. Bishop is Catholic, of course, which is why he tried to ruin the Post Office – as a covert act of treason.' He turned crossly to his wife. 'And the Post Office *is* profitable. I make princely sums every week, and the King was very kind to have appointed me to such a lucrative position. I deserved it, of course. There was no one more loyal than me when he was in exile.'

Kate was about to reply when the door opened, and another guest arrived. Chaloner did not know him, although an immediate chorus of impressed coos suggested that everyone else did. The newcomer minced into the room waving a lace handkerchief and wearing a silk suit so tight that it had to be uncomfortable. His face was smeared in white paste, and his red-dyed lips and cheeks were stark against it. Much was explained when the language of the gathering immediately switched to French for his benefit – London fashions were outrageous, but Paris had contrived to take them to new levels of absurdity.

'Monsieur le Notre,' gushed Hannah, hurrying to greet him. 'I am so pleased you could come.'

'He is a landscape architect,' explained Kate in an undertone, seeing Chaloner's mystification. 'Hired to design stunning new gardens at the palace that is currently being built at Versailles. However, *our* King has invited him to London first, to see what can be done about St James's Park. It is a coup for Hannah to claim le Notre as a guest.'

'What is wrong with St James's Park?' asked Chaloner, a little indignantly.

Katherine regarded him pityingly. 'Well, nothing, if you like boring swathes of grass.'

'Perhaps we can dispense with those dreadful birds, too,' added O'Neill. 'They make a terrible mess by the Canal, and I dislike their raucous honking. They should all be shot.'

'Three of them were killed recently,' said Chaloner,

wondering whether the Controller and his wife were responsible. They certainly seemed unpleasant enough.

'We heard,' said Kate. 'The King is vexed, and Clarendon has promised him a culprit. Foolish man! The villain will never be caught – he will be long gone by now. Ah, Monsieur le Notre. How lovely to meet you.'

Finding himself alone, Chaloner stepped into the hallway for a respite. Wafts of conversation drifted towards him. Mary Wood's death was one of the main topics, along with speculation as to whether it would lead her husband to lose what scant wits he still possessed. There was also a lot of discussion about the Post Office explosion, and it was generally agreed that supporters of Parliament were responsible.

'There is a rumour that John Fry is in the city,' O'Neill was informing a group of horrified listeners. 'Fomenting a rebellion that will destroy the monarchy for ever. It will begin with the assassination of a famous person, apparently. I sincerely hope *I* am not the intended victim.'

'But John Fry is dead,' said Hannah, puzzled. 'Eight years ago. It was in the newsbooks.'

'The newsbooks!' spat Kate. 'You cannot believe anything you read in those. Personally, I am of the belief that it is Fry who has been agitating the apprentices. The King should let me lead a party of militia to root him out. Then we could hang, draw and quarter him in Smithfield, as a warning to other would-be traitors.'

Chaloner shuddered, feeling there had already been too much blood shed for politics. Reluctantly, he re-entered the affray, where he was immediately accosted by a drunken courtier with foolish opinions about the Dutch. Time passed so slowly that he went to the clock

Hannah had recently purchased at great expense, and shook it, to see whether it had stopped working. Something dropped out on to the floor, and there was a metallic twang as pieces sprang loose inside.

'I should set it down and disavow all knowledge, if I were you.'

The speaker was le Notre, his eyes bright with amusement. Chaloner did not want to do as he was told, but unless he intended to hold the clock all night, he had no choice but to put it back on the table. He did so carefully, wincing when its face tilted at a peculiar angle inside the case.

'When Hannah notices, tell her O'Neill did it,' le Notre continued. His French had a lazy, aristocratic drawl that suggested he was rather more than a designer of gardens. 'She should not pursue a friendship with him anyway. Or his wife.'

'Why not?' asked Chaloner, taken aback by the presumptuous advice.

'Because they hate nonconformists, and will make bad enemies if they discover her religion.'

Chaloner was uncomfortable. It was not illegal to follow the Old Faith, but it was strongly discouraged, and Hannah would find herself barred from all manner of places and occasions should her conversion become common knowledge. 'She is not—'

'The Queen invited me to her private chapel this morning, and I saw Hannah accept the Host from the priest,' interrupted le Notre. 'But do not worry, I am not a man to betray a fellow Catholic. However, you should warn her against the O'Neills.'

'Very well,' said Chaloner, wondering whether she would listen. 'Thank you.'

'Your King promised religious tolerance when he reclaimed his throne, but it has not come to pass. Indeed, I read in your government's newsbook – *The Intelligencer* – this morning that he has ordered his country to dispense with Lent this year. Dispense with Lent! Whatever next?'

'On what grounds?' asked Chaloner, who had not had time for reading that day.

'The article did not say. It merely reported that the King "doth for good reasons think that in this present year, no proclamation do issue forth for the strict observance of Lent". I imagine these "good reasons" are so that it does not curtail his merry lifestyle.'

Chaloner made no reply, loath to engage in treasonous discussions with foreigners.

'Lord Castlemaine will put him right, though,' le Notre went on. 'He has written a book, an apology for Catholics, which will be published next week. Will Hannah purchase a copy?'

'Will you?' Chaloner was not about to answer a question that might see his wife in trouble.

Le Notre smiled. 'Yes. Palmer is an intelligent man, and will have sensible things to say. But I must not monopolise you, Monsieur Chaloner. Good evening. I hope our paths cross again.'

Chaloner did not. The Frenchman was far too outspoken for him.

Hannah's soirée finished very late, and for once Chaloner was grateful that they had a large body of servants, because there was a lot to clean up. Unfortunately, they did so noisily, and although Hannah seemed oblivious to the racket, it kept him awake well into the small hours. He supposed he could have ordered them to be quiet, but it seemed unreasonable to demand silence so that he could sleep when he imagined they would like to be abed themselves.

He had his revenge the following morning, though, waking long before dawn and clattering in the kitchen until Joan the housekeeper appeared. She was a grim-faced woman whose loose black clothes and beady eyes always put him in mind of a crow. She had given up treating him respectfully months before, when she had realised that the high regard in which Hannah held her meant she was immune from dismissal, and that any disagreements were put down to Chaloner's irascible temper and not her own. She regarded him coldly.

'May I help you with something? If so, please wait in the drawing room.'

It was a none too subtle reminder that Chaloner was trespassing in the domain she considered to be her own. Chaloner did not agree. The kitchen was by far the most comfortable room in the house, and the warmest, too, with a fire burning all day. He also liked the pleasing aromas of baking – unless Hannah happened to be plying her culinary skills, in which case wild horses would not have dragged him there. His wife's inability to cook was legendary, and it was fortunate that the servants prepared most of their meals, or they would have starved.

'I can manage, thank you,' he replied shortly.

'Manage with what?' Joan demanded. 'If it is food you want, I shall see what is available. Some fish-head soup, perhaps. Or boiled vegetable parings, which are very wholesome.'

'Some milk will suffice,' said Chaloner, sure Hannah was not offered such unappealing fare when she visited the kitchen.

He saw the instant glee on Joan's face: she believed cold milk was poisonous. She went to pour him some, handing him a far larger cup than he would have taken for himself. He sipped it gingerly, supposing it was sour and she intended to make him sick, so he was astonished to discover that it was sweet and creamy. He nodded his thanks, and left the house as the first light began to steal across the city's grey streets.

It was too early to visit Storey and expect to be civilly received, so Chaloner wandered rather aimlessly, thinking about Hannah's penchant for people with whom he had nothing in common. Why in God's name had he married her? Was it because they had both been lonely, and it had been an act of desperation? Head bowed, deep in gloomy thoughts, he walked east.

It was another frigid day, and although it was not snowing, the wind was sharp. He skidded frequently on ice, especially at the sides of the roads where water had frozen in the gutters. Like the previous morning, the city was slower to wake than normal, with people reluctant to leave their fires and warm beds. It was quieter, too, with street vendors saving their voices for the crowds they hoped would come later, and there were fewer carts and carriages on the roads.

He passed St Paul's Cathedral, the majestic but crumbling Gothic edifice that was loved by everyone except architects, who itched to replace it with something of their own devising. It dwarfed the surrounding buildings, even without the lofty spire that had been damaged by lightning a century before. What caught Chaloner's attention that day, however, was not its grandeur, but the fact that a large group of youths had gathered outside it, talking in low voices.

He stared at them as he passed. Their clothes suggested they were apprentices from several different guilds, including ones that were traditional enemies. He was uneasy – apprentices were an unruly, volatile crowd, and unrest among them often presaged greater trouble elsewhere. He wondered what they were doing together. Was it anything to do with the rumours that the political agitator John Fry was in the city – that they expected him to lead them in some sort of rebellion? Chaloner hoped not. London had seen far too much trouble over the past two decades, and it was time for a little peace.

He continued walking, threading through the tangle of lanes between Watling Street and Dowgate Hill, and to kill time, he entered the fuggy warmth of the Antwerp Coffee House, hoping a dose of the brew would sharpen his wits. The shop was busy, and the odour of burning beans mingled with the reek of a dozen tobacco pipes and the sharper tang of a badly vented chimney.

He sat at an empty table, and opened the latest newsbook – twice-weekly publications in which the government gave people its versions of domestic and foreign affairs. He learned with some bemusement that le Notre had been right about the King's decision to ignore the strictures of Lent, and His Majesty had indeed issued a proclamation saying that everyone could ignore it that year. He also learned that two Quaker meetings had been raided in Ross for no reason other than bigoted intolerance, and that the French Court was eagerly awaiting the Grand Ballet.

As he flicked through the rest of the paper, he became aware that the conversation at the next table was about Lady Castlemaine, who had amassed massive gambling debts and expected the King, via the taxpayer, to settle them. It occurred to him then that Temperance had decried the Antwerp for being the haunt of disgruntled Parliamentarians, and he was on the verge of leaving when someone mentioned the comet that was currently blazing across the heavens, and the conversation moved to less contentious issues.

He relaxed a little, and sipped his coffee. It had a pleasantly nutty flavour, quite unlike the bitter concoction that was served in the place he usually frequented. He still did not like it, but at least it allowed him to understand why others did. It was probably a good deal more palatable with sugar, but he never took that, as a silent and probably meaningless protest against the way it was produced on plantations.

He had just started to browse a list of all the goods that had been imported through Plymouth the previous year – the government's idea of entertaining reading – when two men approached. He glanced up warily, hoping they had not come to berate him for sitting alone. Coffee houses were not places for solitude, and he had broken an unwritten rule by taking a seat at an empty table.

'Tom Chaloner,' said one softly. 'I thought you would have been dead by now.'

It took a moment for Chaloner to recognise the man who had spoken, because Isaac Dorislaus had aged in the year or so since they had last met. What little hair Dorislaus still possessed was grey, and there were lines of strain and worry around his eyes and mouth.

He and Chaloner had much in common. First, they shared the misfortune of having kinsmen who had been involved in the execution of the first King Charles: Dorislaus's father had helped prepare the charges of treason, while Chaloner's uncle had signed the death warrant. Second, they had both worked for Cromwell's intelligence service, Chaloner as a spy and Dorislaus in the Post Office. And third, they both spoke flawless Dutch – Dorislaus's father had been a Hollander, while Chaloner had lived in The Hague and Amsterdam. However, Chaloner had never been quite sure of Dorislaus's loyalty to the Commonwealth, and when several of his reports to Spymaster Thurloe had mysteriously gone missing, he had suspected that it was Dorislaus who had 'lost' them.

Dorislaus's companion, whose smile of greeting was rather more genuine, was Cornelis Vanderhuyden, another Anglo-Dutchman who had made his home in London. He was a talented linguist, whose speciality was translating scientific tracts. Chaloner had once saved him from a cudgel-wielding mob, and they had been friends ever since.

Vanderhuyden and Dorislaus looked odd together. Vanderhuyden was tall and angular, and wore an expensive suit; Dorislaus was short and portly, and his old-fashioned clothes indicated he had not prospered since the Restoration – his coat was frayed, his hat was full of holes, and the lace on his cuffs and collar, although carefully laundered, was unfashionably plain. He launched into an explanation of his shabby state without being asked.

'O'Neill dismissed me eighteen months ago. He accused me of being a Parliamentarian spy.'

'Well, he was right,' said Chaloner, failing to understand his rancour. 'You were.'

Dorislaus grimaced. 'Yes, but I gave all that up when the Royalists came to power. Bishop trusted me to do my job honestly and diligently, so why could O'Neill not have done the same? I am obliged to make ends meet by hiring out my services as a scribe these days.'

'I imagine the Cavaliers remember your father,' said Vanderhuyden quietly.

An expression of pain crossed Dorislaus's face. 'He paid for his role in the old King's execution – he was murdered in cold blood by vengeful Royalists. But why persecute me? I had nothing to do with it.'

Vanderhuyden patted his shoulder sympathetically, and when the coffee-boy came with the bill, he slapped down a handful of coins before Dorislaus could reach for his purse.

'But you have fared better?' Chaloner asked him.

Vanderhuyden smiled pleasantly. 'O'Neill offered me a princely wage to abandon my scientists and translate for the Post Office instead, so I am now one of his clerks.' He shrugged when Dorislaus shot him a recriminatory glare. 'I was never a spy, so of course he prefers me to you.'

'I wish Cromwell had not died,' said Dorislaus miserably. 'The King is a debauched lecher, more interested in bedding women than in governing the country he was so desperate to have back.'

'Easy!' exclaimed Chaloner, glancing around in alarm.

Dorislaus shrugged. 'We need not worry about speaking our minds here. Everyone in the Antwerp is a Parliamentarian.'

Chaloner stood abruptly. It was no place for one of the Lord Chancellor's gentlemen ushers, and he had been a fool to stay once he had recalled what Temperance had said about it.

'Do not leave, Tom,' begged Vanderhuyden. 'We shall talk about something else instead. What about the explosion at the Post Office? Did you hear about it? I was inside at the time, and it rattled the windows in the most horrible manner.'

70

'Did it?' Chaloner sat reluctantly.

'Two of the dead were fellow clerks,' Vanderhuyden went on. 'Sam and Job Alibond.'

'Famous for their gargantuan appetites,' added Dorislaus sneeringly. He addressed Chaloner. 'We are going to inspect the crater in a minute. It is said to be quite a sight.'

'Are there rumours about who might have been responsible?' fished Chaloner.

His question was aimed at Vanderhuyden, given that he worked in the Post Office, but it was Dorislaus who answered. 'I heard one yesterday. Apparently, arrest warrants were issued for two dishonest clerks and—'

'Knight and Gardner had nothing to do with the blast,' interrupted Vanderhuyden indignantly.

'So you say,' flashed Dorislaus. 'However, we are all aware that something nasty is happening in Post House Yard, although we do not know what because our *friends* will not talk about it.'

Vanderhuyden looked pained. 'I cannot talk about my work, Isaac. It is confidential, as you know perfectly well. But even if I could chatter, there would be nothing to tell.'

'Then why is Marshal Gery interested in the place?' demanded Dorislaus.

'I have no idea,' Vanderhuyden snapped back. 'But he is wasting his time. There are minor infractions, of course – mislaid packages, drunken letter-carriers – but nothing serious.'

He was distracted at that moment by an acquaintance who came to ask whether he had seen the comet. While he was replying, Dorislaus gripped Chaloner's arm and spoke urgently in his ear.

71

'If you have any affection for your Earl, you will monitor what Gery does in his name. Clarendon's position in government is tenuous, and he is fast losing the King's favour. You see, something wicked *is* unfolding in the Post Office, no matter what Vanderhuyden says, and it may be used to harm your master.'

'Why should you care?' asked Chaloner, wondering why Dorislaus should encourage him to defy a ruthless, violent man like the marshal. Did Dorislaus want him in danger because he knew Chaloner had suspected him of treachery during the Commonwealth? But *how* could he know? Chaloner had never discussed his concerns with anyone. Of course, Dorislaus had always been astute, which was why he had been such a good spy.

'Because he is the only member of the Privy Council with principles,' replied Dorislaus. 'And because I am certain that whatever is happening in the Post Office needs to be stopped. I wish I could tell you more, but information about the place has stopped flowing completely. And that in itself is suspicious. Do you not agree?'

Chaloner stirred his coffee. 'I recommend you take your concerns to Spymaster Williamson.'

'Williamson!' spat Dorislaus in disdain. 'He tries his best, but his operatives are fools.'

Chaloner continued to stir, watching the sludge at the bottom of his dish turn the liquid thick and muddy. All his instincts told him to distrust Dorislaus, yet what the man said made sense: the Earl *was* in a precarious position, and the stupid, blinkered Gery might well make it worse. Moreover, Dorislaus was not the only person to have expressed concerns about the Post Office.

He made up his mind. The Earl was not much of an

72

employer, but he was all Chaloner had, and loyalty had always been in his nature. If there was trouble afoot, then he had a duty to expose it and protect him. And if the rumours transpired to be groundless, then he would just have to ensure he was not caught disobeying the orders he had been given. It would not be easy, but he had faced greater challenges in the past. His mind made up, he swallowed the coffee and stood.

Chapter 3

Deciding to begin his enquiries immediately, Chaloner accompanied Dorislaus and Vanderhuyden to Post House Yard. It was a Friday, when mail left for the United Provinces, the German states and the Baltic, so people were arriving with letters to be carried overseas. However, it was much quieter than on Tuesdays, Thursdays and Saturdays, when inland collections were made.

Chaloner walked to the crater, joining the score or so spectators who ringed it. An image of the cart was etched vividly in his mind, but everything else remained frustratingly hazy. He tried again to recall the musician, but nothing came other than a vague sense of height and mediocre talent.

'Did anyone here actually witness the blast?' Vanderhuyden was enquiring. 'I heard it from the Post Office, but there was nothing to see except debris and smoke by the time I came out.'

'I did,' replied one man softly. It was Roger Palmer, the Earl of Castlemaine, holding a bundle of letters. Small cuts on his hands and face told of his close brush with the incident.

'What happened?' asked Dorislaus with brazenly ghoulish curiosity. 'I have only been privy to second-hand accounts so far.'

'I was blown over.' Palmer spoke reluctantly, as if the horror of the incident was still with him. 'But it might have been much worse. Someone shouted a warning, which allowed me take the few steps away that saved my life.'

'Does anyone know who set the explosion?' asked Dorislaus, looking around keenly.

The onlooker who replied was Major Stokes, an elderly officer from Cromwell's army who lived in Long Acre. Chaloner kept rooms in the same house, which not only provided a bolthole for when he was working on dangerous cases, but was somewhere to escape from Hannah. Stokes rented the apartment below, and had earned Chaloner's immediate affection by complimenting his viol playing. He had a lined, kindly face with an old-fashioned moustache and faded blue eyes.

'The city is alive with unrest at the moment,' he said soberly. 'So any number of sects might have been responsible – papists, Levellers, Fifth Monarchists, Diggers. It might even have been a courtier, just to make mischief.'

'No,' said Palmer firmly. 'No one from Court is so wicked. Nor is any Catholic.'

'Perhaps it was the apprentices then,' suggested Stokes. 'They have been restless of late.'

'I think they would be more inclined to settle matters with their fists than with barrels of powder,' said Palmer, and Chaloner was inclined to agree. 'However, it may have been John Fry. There are rumours that he has been writing letters, encouraging people to sedition and treason . . .'

'Yes, he has promised to lead a great rebellion,' acknowledged Stokes. 'But it—'

'Then he is a fool,' said Palmer sharply. He turned back to Dorislaus. 'I wish I could remember more about the moments preceding the blast, but a musician was playing a flageolet. My attention was on him, so I saw nothing to help identify the perpetrators of this nasty affair.'

'What happened to him?' asked Chaloner.

'He did not run far when the alarm sounded.' Palmer's expression was distant as he searched his memory. He pointed. 'Just to the trees in that garden. But he made himself scarce afterwards. I do not blame him. This city has a nasty habit of turning innocent bystanders into scapegoats.'

An innocent bystander who waited to see what happened before making good his escape, mused Chaloner. It did not sound very 'innocent' to him. 'What did he look like?'

Palmer frowned. 'Tall, I think, with a hat that shaded his face. But all street entertainers look alike to me, and I would not recognise him again.'

'I knew the Alibond brothers from when I worked here as a clerk,' said Dorislaus. 'I would like to see their killer brought to justice, so I hope there are witnesses who *did* see something that will allow the culprits to be identified.'

'Are they the ones who were too fat to run?' asked Stokes. He shuddered. 'Poor souls!'

'They were hefty,' agreed Dorislaus. 'The other victims were a fellow named Joyce, who was one of Sir Henry Wood's servants, and a pair of beggars.'

Chaloner vaguely recalled a man emerging from Wood's mansion to ask the flageolet player to stop, as it

76

was unseemly to have music and laughter outside a house of mourning. Had he been the victim? It seemed likely.

Because it was open and he was eager to see what he could learn about it, Chaloner went into the General Letter Office, entering with a group of chattering Swedish merchants. It was a large L-plan building, three storeys high, with the lower part of the L being longer and wider than the upright bit. This meant that the bulk of the rooms were at the front, and it was from these that the postal service conducted all its business. The smaller, older, more decrepit wing was rumoured to have been disused since the reign of King James. There was a high wall at the back, and the fourth side of the square was formed by the rear part of Storey's cottage. A modest courtyard occupied the space in the middle.

Customers walked through the imposing front door into a spacious, elegantly pillared chamber known as the Letter Hall. 'Window-men' sat at counters at the far end, ready to receive post – and receive money, too, if a client was rash enough to prepay for a delivery. A door to the left, always kept locked, opened into a short hallway that led to the Sorting Room and the offices in which the postal clerks and their assistants worked.

Chaloner took up station behind one of the columns, watching customers queue at the windows. Palmer was among them, and Chaloner was impressed when the nobleman waited his turn rather than use his status to jump to the front. To pass the time, people discussed the explosion, and there was a minor panic when someone spotted an unattended sack. Palmer was the only one brave enough to look inside, and there were sheepish grins when he announced that it contained wastepaper.

77

But there was only so much Chaloner could learn by lurking in the Letter Hall: he needed to visit the chambers beyond. He waited until the Swedish merchants shielded him from the other clients – they were too engrossed in a debate about import taxes to pay any attention to him – then bent to pick the lock with an efficiency born of long experience.

He stepped quickly through the door, and crept along the corridor to the Sorting Room. He was surprised to find it empty; he had imagined it would be busy at that time of day. Leading off it were the offices belonging to the 'Clerks of the Road', the men with responsibility for the six great highways out of London: Holyhead, Bristol, Plymouth, Edinburgh, Yarmouth and Dover. Each was overflowing with documents, but Chaloner did not attempt to rifle through them. There were simply too many, and it would be better to return at a time when he was less likely to be caught.

A flight of stairs led to the two upper storeys, and a brief inspection told him that these rooms were occupied by minor officials. Meanwhile, the disused south wing was separated from the main building by sturdy doors at each level. The locks on each were substantial, and the ground floor had the added protection of a guard. Chaloner understood why: no Postmaster would want burglars entering through the abandoned part and making off with the post.

Feeling he had pushed his luck far enough – it was broad daylight, after all, and not a sensible time to have invaded – Chaloner turned to leave. He had just reached the door that would take him back to the Letter Hall when it opened.

He was confronted by two men who wore the staid

garb of postal clerks, but whose physique and demeanour suggested they were something else entirely. Both were large, compact fellows who carried themselves like soldiers, and neither had the inky fingers that Chaloner usually associated with people who earned their living among documents.

'You should not be here,' said the first, slightly shorter than his companion and lighter on his feet. Chaloner sensed he would be the most dangerous. 'It is off limits to the public.'

'I came to post a letter,' replied Chaloner in Dutch, grinning inanely in the hope that they would dismiss him as a witless foreigner who had taken a wrong turn. It was, after all, a day when mail was collected for the United Provinces.

'He is French, Smartfoot,' hissed the second with immediate suspicion. 'A papist spy.'

'No, I am not,' said Chaloner, still using Dutch in the hope of averting trouble. 'Surely you can hear the difference between French and Dutch? They sound nothing alike.'

'Let him out, Lamb,' sighed Smartfoot. 'Do not worry – he cannot even speak English.'

'He might, though,' said Lamb, still regarding Chaloner with rank distrust. 'Perhaps we should take him somewhere to find out.'

'No.' Smartfoot stopped his companion from grabbing Chaloner by stepping between them. 'He sounds more like one of those Swedes than a Frenchman, and the Post Office makes a lot of money from them. We cannot afford to offend any.'

'No one will find out,' said Lamb dangerously. 'And I want to interrogate him.'

'I am sure you do,' muttered Smartfoot, opening the door and waving Chaloner through it. 'But we have more important matters to attend than stray Swedes. Now forget about him and follow me.'

Chaloner was just leaving the Post Office when he met Gery. The marshal scowled, and Freer laid a warning hand on his shoulder, one that was angrily shrugged off.

'What are you doing here?' Gery demanded.

'Sending a letter,' lied Chaloner, although all his attention was on the third man in their party.

Samuel Morland was a small, fair, slim man of about forty. He had been Spymaster Thurloe's secretary during the Commonwealth, and his betrayal would have been understandable if he had been treated badly, but Thurloe had been patient, kind and generous. Chaloner had forgotten quite how much he loathed the fellow until he saw the spiteful little face with its slyly calculating eyes. It surprised him not at all that the slippery clerk had managed to inveigle himself a post with the Earl of Clarendon, although he felt his master's security had just suffered a serious setback.

'To a friend you made on your recent visit to Sweden?' Morland asked pleasantly. He was dressed in the latest Court fashion, and looked wealthier than either of his companions. 'I envy you your travels. It must be fascinating to spy on so many different countries.'

'I was not spying,' said Chaloner shortly. Morland's voice had been deliberately loud, and the Swedish merchants had turned to stare at him. Chaloner hoped Smartfoot and Lamb would not appear, because there would be trouble for certain if they heard him speaking

English. 'I accompanied Clarendon's eldest son on a diplomatic mission.'

'You know him, Morland?' asked Gery, suspicion taking the place of anger as he looked from one to the other. 'How?'

'From the Commonwealth.' Malice flashed in Morland's eyes. 'When I was looking after the interests of Royalists, and he was not.'

Chaloner might have said that Morland had been as fervent a Parliamentarian as any until it had served his purpose to change sides, but there was no point. Gery would not believe him, and Morland was far too slippery to be bested in a verbal battle.

'It was a long time ago,' said Freer soothingly. 'It does not matter now.'

'It matters very much,' countered Gery in a hiss. 'And it always will. You are a fool if you dismiss a man's past allegiances.'

'I hear you have been asked to investigate dead ducks in St James's Park, Tom,' said Morland before Freer could respond. He grinned nastily. 'I hope you do not find it too taxing.'

'Well, this is not St James's Park,' snapped Gery, as Morland had doubtless intended. 'And the Earl specifically ordered you to stay away from the Post Office.'

Chaloner regarded him coolly. 'He did not forbid me to send letters to my family. Besides, Edward Storey is the royal Curator of Birds, and his house is near here.'

'I do not believe you,' said Gery immediately.

'Actually, he is telling the truth,' said Morland with a regretful sigh. 'Storey lives next door.'

'And why are you here, Gery?' Chaloner went on an offensive of his own. 'To apologise to Controller O'Neill?'

'Apologise?' Confusion flashed in Gery's eyes. 'Why would I do that?'

'Because the Earl charged you to explore unsavoury dealings here, but you failed to protect it from an explosion. Neither can be very pleased with you.'

'My work is none of your affair,' shouted Gery, outraged. 'Now get out of my way and go and investigate your ducks. And stay away from the Post Office in future, because if I catch you here again, I will . . . I will . . .' He trailed off, too incensed to form coherent words.

'You would be wise to do as he says, Tom.' Morland smiled sweetly. 'You do not want Clarendon to think even more badly of you than he does already. He was telling me only today that you are insolent, disreputable and rebellious. Hardly attractive qualities in a retainer.'

He turned to walk up the steps. Gery followed, still seething. Freer was last. The soldier winked as he passed, an unexpected gesture of support that Chaloner found heartening.

Although he should have gone to visit Storey straight away, it would have been tantamount to following Gery's orders, and the stubborn streak in Chaloner baulked at that notion. Instead, he went to stand next to Stokes, who was still gazing at the crater. There was no sign of the two Anglo-Dutchmen, and he assumed they had been driven away by the cold.

'Do not have anything to do with that villain,' Stokes said. 'He was a spy during the Commonwealth, and was infamous for using bribery and corruption to get what he wanted.'

'Morland?' asked Chaloner. 'Yes, I know.'

'No, I am talking about Dorislaus, who was here earlier.

Do not be fooled by his friendly nature, because it is an act – in reality, he is a liar and a rogue. Perhaps he was a spy too long.'

'I see,' said Chaloner, hoping no one thought the same about him.

'Have you heard of this mysterious fellow called Bankes?' Stokes went on. 'He is interested in the General Letter Office, and has put it about that he is in the market for accurate information. Reports can be left for him at the Crown tavern or the Antwerp Coffee House, and if the intelligence is good, he has promised to pay very handsomely.'

Knight had also mentioned Bankes, and Chaloner wondered how many investigations of the postal service were currently in progress – it seemed Bankes had one; there was Gery's; Spymaster Williamson would certainly be exploring the rumours; and there was Chaloner's own. Would they all fall over each other in their quest for the truth?

'It is damned sinister,' Stokes went on when there was no reply. 'Why should anyone pay for that sort of thing? And what does he plan to do with what he learns anyway?'

They were good questions, and Chaloner supposed he had better track Bankes down and put them to him. Idly, he wondered whether it was Bankes who had left the gunpowder-loaded cart in Post House Yard the previous day.

He loitered with Stokes until Gery, Morland and Freer emerged from the General Letter Office, although none of them noticed him. Part of him was disappointed, as he would have liked Gery to know that he had been defied, but his wiser self was relieved – antagonising a man with the power to make life difficult for him was both foolish and pointless.

He was about to visit Storey when a shiny black carriage drew up beside him. When it stopped, Controller O'Neill alighted, and turned to offer his hand to Kate. She leaned on him rather heavily, causing him to stagger. She issued a shrill shriek of alarm, and might have taken a tumble, had Chaloner not darted forward to steady her.

'Those damned horses cannot stand still for a minute,' grumbled O'Neill, although Chaloner had not seen the beasts move. 'I should shoot them all.'

'Not before I shoot your clerks,' muttered Kate venomously. 'Corrupt, every one of them.'

'Watch your step, Wood,' called O'Neill over his shoulder to the remaining occupant of the coach. 'The nags are restless and may bolt.'

The last passenger was Sir Henry Wood, an elderly fellow with an ugly face, thin hair and a grey beard. He gulped his alarm at O'Neill's pronouncement, and Chaloner was sorry he should have been needlessly frightened. He offered his hand, which was seized gratefully.

'Fanatics,' he whispered as he scrambled out, fixing Chaloner with eyes that were a peculiar amber colour, rather like a wolf's. 'I cannot abide them. Can you?'

'Er . . . no,' replied Chaloner, when he saw that Wood was not going to release his hand until he had received an answer.

'Look what they did to my house,' Wood went on, whipping around suddenly to point at a very small dent on the door. 'Fanatics!'

'They did much worse to my poor clerks,' said O'Neill ruefully. 'The Alibond brothers.'

'He is the Controller, you know,' said Wood, speaking as though O'Neill were not there. 'It cost him thousands of pounds to buy the job, but it is a burdensome responsibility. He should have asked the King for something better. Such as Master of the Revels. That would be far more fun than reading other people's letters.'

'I do not read other people's letters!' exclaimed O'Neill indignantly. 'It would be—'

'Of course you do,' interrupted Wood. 'You and Spymaster Williamson. And then you chew up the ones that are dull or treasonous, spit them out and use them for compost. Personally, I would never set foot in the General Letter Office. It is far too dangerous. Who are you?'

The last question was directed at Chaloner.

'He is Mr Chaloner,' supplied Kate helpfully. 'Married to Hannah, who invited my husband and me to her lovely house the other night. Monsieur le Notre was there and it was—'

'Chaloner the regicide?' demanded Wood. 'I thought he was older. Or has he used magic to shed the years? If so, I would not mind sharing his secret, because I should like to look younger myself. So would my wife, although she is dead now, poor soul.'

'I am sorry to hear it,' said Chaloner, and was flailing around for an expression of condolence that sounded a little more sincere when Wood was off again.

'I cannot bear potatoes. Have you ever seen one? Nasty, malevolent things. But they are nothing compared to radishes, which are agents of the devil.'

'Radishes?' Chaloner had known that Wood was reputed to be eccentric, but no one had mentioned him being insane.

'Terrible creations. But I had best be on my way. Thank you for the ride, O'Neill. It was kind of you, although you should invest in a proper carriage. I do not hold with sledges.'

'It is not a sledge,' objected Kate, startled. 'It—'

'Of course it is a sledge,' snapped Wood. 'There is snow on the ground, is there not?'

'Well, yes, a light smattering,' acknowledged Kate. 'But—'

'Then it is a sledge,' declared Wood with finality. 'Only sledges can glide across snow. It is a scientific fact.' He turned abruptly and scuttled into his house; his next words were yelled through the door that he had slammed behind him. 'Radishes will strike again with their barrels of gunpowder, you mark my words. And they killed my servant Joyce.'

'Ignore him, Chaloner,' instructed O'Neill with a long-suffering sigh. 'He cannot help being odd, and the death of his wife has unhinged him even further.'

'So has the shock of yesterday's explosion, I imagine,' added Kate. 'I suppose he deserves our compassion, but it is hard to be patient sometimes.'

'He will get himself skewered if he goes around making unfounded accusations, though,' said O'Neill resentfully. 'I have never read – or chewed – a letter addressed to someone else in my life, and I certainly do not allow spymasters inside my domain.'

'And I am not a regicide,' said Chaloner with a smile, thinking there was no harm in cultivating their friendship, objectionable though that might be, if he was to investigate the Post Office.

O'Neill smiled back. 'Well then, all is right with the world.'

* * *

86

As Chaloner crossed Post House Yard to Storey's house, he was distracted yet again, this time by Spymaster Williamson, who had arrived with a team of minions to sift through the rubble in the hope of finding clues as to what had happened.

Joseph Williamson had been an Oxford academic before deciding that the government needed his array of dubious talents. At first, his intelligence service had been embarrassingly inept because he had insisted on employing only Royalists, who were mostly novices in espionage. They had improved since and so had he, although his operation still fell far short of Thurloe's. He and Chaloner had worked together in the past, although wariness and dislike persisted on both sides.

'I hear you are investigating the dead ducks in the park,' said Williamson, fixing Chaloner with an expression of haughty amusement. 'Is it true?'

'The King's dead ducks,' Chaloner pointed out.

'Then I hope you find your culprit. We do not want "fowl" killers stalking our streets.' Williamson chortled at his own joke, a curious sound that Chaloner had never heard before: the Spymaster rarely attempted wit. 'However, I hope it will not interfere with your enquiries into yesterday's explosion, a matter that is rather more pressing, as I am sure you will agree.'

'Gery is exploring what happened at the Post Office, not me.'

'Really?' Williamson stared at him, humour evaporating. 'I doubt he is equal to the task.'

'The Earl disagrees.' Chaloner wanted to end the conversation, uncomfortable discussing his master's decisions with the nation's Head of Intelligence. Moreover, being obliged to admit that he had been supplanted by the likes of Gery was galling.

'So can I assume that you have decided to conduct your own inquiry, then?' asked Williamson.

'No, you cannot,' replied Chaloner shortly. Was he really so transparent?

'Of course you are. Why else would you be loitering in the Post House Yard? I do not blame you. Something untoward has been unfolding here for weeks, and your Earl might be accused of complicity if it comes to fruition. The Post Office is not usually a lord chancellor's responsibility, but Clarendon's enemies on the Privy Council have foisted it on him, and will use any trouble to do him harm. And if he falls, so will you.'

'I am *not* investigating,' said Chaloner firmly, afraid Williamson might mention it to the Earl, at which point he would be dismissed for certain. 'Clarendon has forbidden it.'

Williamson frowned his mystification. 'I wonder if his wits are astray following the death of his son. Did he tell you about it? It happened when you were in Sweden. Young Edward died of the small-pox, like Mary Wood.'

Chaloner had been told of the Earl's loss, but it had not occurred to him that grief might be responsible for his master's recent peculiar decisions. If so, the situation was worrisome, because the Earl was responsible for far more important matters than the deployment of his household staff.

'Have you heard anything about what happened here?' asked Williamson, nodding towards the crater. 'I have spies in the Post Office, of course, but they have discovered nothing of value so far.'

Despite his aversion to the Spymaster, Chaloner would

far rather he solved the case than Gery, so he decided to share what he had seen and reasoned.

'The gunpowder was on a cart, concealed beneath firewood,' he began. 'It was a sizeable vehicle, and a horse would have been needed to bring it here. However, the shafts were empty, so the driver had obviously led it away to safety. It was what made me suspicious.'

'It was you who yelled the warning?' Williamson nodded before Chaloner could answer. 'Yes, of course it was. Your vigilance commends you.'

'Whoever is behind the explosion did not bring the gunpowder here himself,' Chaloner went on. 'He hired someone else to do it – someone who is poor, and who baulked at sacrificing a horse.'

'Not necessarily. He might have been fond of the beast.'

'Then he would not have used it to transport explosives. Moreover, gunpowder is expensive, which means a considerable sum of money was invested in the attack. Would the culprit really risk failure just to save an animal?'

'I suppose not.' Williamson was trying to sound un-interested, but there was a keen spark in his eyes.

'Also, if he had delivered the stuff himself, he would have positioned the cart in a place where it would do the most damage to buildings and people—'

'But it was in the middle of the square,' mused Williamson. 'Not only well away from the General Letter Office and its adjoining houses, but where there were the fewest bystanders.'

'Quite. I suspect his hireling either did not care enough about the mission to risk being caught by driving closer, or had not bothered to familiarise himself with the way gunpowder works.'

'Which the real culprit would have done, given the expense. Very well. What else?'

'There was a musician who attracted a crowd of listeners, and who disappeared after the blast. You might want to find out whether his presence was innocent, or whether he enticed people to linger in the hope that they would be killed or injured.'

Williamson nodded slowly. 'Although that would be an unpleasant solution. It means someone left the powder not to destroy a building or disrupt the post, but to beget a massacre.'

Chaloner said nothing. He had met plenty of people in London who would not hesitate to use such means to achieve their twisted purposes, and so had Williamson.

'Anything else?'

Chaloner nodded. 'A man named Bankes has been buying information – about the explosion, and about the Post Office and London in general. Perhaps you should ask why he should be interested, and what he intends to do with the intelligence once he has it.'

'Do you know where I might find him?'

'No, but he can be contacted via the Antwerp or the Crown. It should not be too difficult to lay hold of him when he goes to collect his reports.'

Williamson nodded his thanks, and returned to his men without another word. Seeing he was dismissed, Chaloner walked away.

He knocked on Storey's door, noting that someone had already started to repair the damage to the carved pelican – chalk marks showed where replacement legs would be sited. A plain maid in an unattractive bonnet answered, and conducted him to a parlour at the back of the house.

As he followed, Chaloner realised that although the cottage looked modest from the square, it was unusually deep, and all the windows on the south side looked out on to the courtyard that was shared with the General Letter Office.

Unfortunately, it was not an inspiring view. The flagstones were cracked and sprouted weeds, the sundial was broken, and the shrubs that had once been elegantly petite were now overgrown giants that blotted out the light. Directly opposite was the Post Office's disused wing, a mournful display of sagging gutters, lichen-encrusted walls and windows with dirty shutters.

Storey's parlour was pleasant though, with a blazing fire and cushion-filled chairs. The walls were crowded with paintings, every one depicting a bird, while fowl also appeared in a design woven into the carpet, on the carved handles of the fire tongs, and etched into the coal shuttle.

The Curator of Birds was chubby, clean shaven and white haired. He was entertaining a visitor already, and Chaloner stepped aside so that the maid could go in first and announce him – it was hardly good manners to join them otherwise – but she had disappeared, leaving him to surmise that he was not the only one cursed with unsatisfactory servants. The guest was le Notre.

'Good Lord!' the landscape architect exclaimed in French, as Chaloner stood in the doorway and attracted their attention by clearing his throat. It was impolite, but so was wandering through someone's house on his own to hunt down shoddy domestics and inform them of their duties. 'What are you doing here? Come to steal a clock, to replace the one you broke? There is a nice one on the table.'

'I think Hannah would notice the difference,' replied Chaloner in the same language.

Le Notre laughed. 'Blame O'Neill, as I told you last night. It will serve him right for holding such deeply offensive theories about Catholics. Do you think Palmer's book will cause him to change his mind? Or is he beyond reason?'

'I do not know him well enough to say.'

Le Notre's expression was difficult to read. 'Yet you invited him into your home.'

Chaloner shrugged, reluctant to reveal that it had been Hannah's doing. It would be disloyal, and there was something about le Notre that set warning bells jangling in his mind, despite the man's apparent affability. When he did not reply, le Notre stood suddenly and switched to English, his accent so thick as to be almost impenetrable.

'Farewell, Storey. I will visit you again soon, and we shall resume our discussion about aviaries. Birds are a great ornament to any garden, although only from a distance. Close up, they are smelly, noisy and full of fleas.'

With a bow so elaborate that Chaloner wondered whether it was intended to be a joke, le Notre departed, leaving behind a waft of strong perfume. Storey watched him go with an awe that verged on reverence, and barely listened when Chaloner stated his name and purpose.

'He is a truly great man,' the curator said in a whisper. 'The King of France has appointed him as grand overseer of all the royal parks, and he is going to design a garden of unusual splendour and opulence for the new palace at Versailles.'

Chaloner was unimpressed, preferring the simple beauty of the open countryside to the contrived precision of landscaped estates. 'I see.'

'And he deigned to visit *me*,' Storey went on in the

same hushed tones. 'What a gentleman! What did he tell you when he spoke his native tongue? I have never learned French.'

Chaloner was reluctant to say that le Notre had recommended stealing a clock; it seemed shabby to shatter the curator's illusions. 'He just remarked that it is cold outside today.'

'It is, and you must be chilled to the bone,' said Storey, smiling genially. 'So sit by the fire, and allow me to pour you a cup of hot water. It is most refreshing, and my storks love it.'

'Water?' asked Chaloner, wondering whether to point out that he was not a stork. He watched Storey ladle something into two goblets with swans painted on them.

'What is good enough for our feathered friends is good enough for us,' declared Storey, handing one to Chaloner and taking a hefty gulp from the other.

Chaloner followed suit, but more cautiously, and was startled to discover it really was water, and not a euphemism for something stronger and probably illegal. However, while he was happy to drink milk in the face of common prejudice, he drew the line at water. He had seen men die from it during the wars, filled as it was with dangerous diseases. He held the cup in his hands, enjoying the warmth that seeped from it, but declined to swallow any more.

'Of course, not even le Notre can design something that will keep out foxes,' said Storey, speaking as if this was a theme they had discussed before. 'The cold weather has encouraged these vermin to hunt for prey in St James's Park this year. They are an abomination, and have no place in God's universe. I assume the devil created them. What do you think?'

'I have no idea.' Chaloner was unwilling to be drawn into a debate that might be considered heretical. One never knew who might be listening, and the maid had the look of a Puritan about her.

'They are worthless carnivores that serve no purpose other than to spread misery, pain and terror,' said Storey firmly. 'And I should like to kill every last one of them.'

'You do not know Sir Henry Wood, do you?' asked Chaloner, recollecting the courtier's peculiar diatribe against vegetables. Perhaps all residents of Post House Yard were lunatics.

'He is my neighbour. Just lost his wife, poor man. He does not like foxes either. He saw one near Chelsey last week, and killed it with a musket. It made a terrible mess.'

'I came to ask about your birds,' said Chaloner, to bring the discussion back on track before it ranged too far into the surreal. 'The dead ones.'

'Harriet, Eliza and Sharon,' sighed Storey, and Chaloner was embarrassed to see tears glitter. 'Two Indian runners and a Swedish. Beautiful creatures.'

'Ducks?' asked Chaloner, confused.

Storey regarded him askance. 'Of course they were ducks, man! Poor Harriet was the first, and it was particularly distressing because she had been ill. At first, I thought a fox . . . but then I realised there was something even more sinister. I am glad someone is taking my concerns seriously at last, by the way. The King is fond of his birds, and so am I.'

'How did they die? And when?'

'Take some more hot water, Mr Chaloner,' said Storey, all grim seriousness. 'And make yourself comfortable. My explanation will take some time.'

*　　*　　*

The explanation did not take long at all, because Chaloner kept it on course with questions and prompts, and did not allow Storey to vent as he had evidently intended. Unfortunately, he managed to distil only three facts: that the birds had been killed at night, that footprints indicated more than one culprit, and that scattered feathers suggested the swans had been involved.

Chaloner regarded him in alarm. 'Another bird is the guilty party? Christ! The Earl will dismiss me for certain if I tell him that!'

'A swan did not kill my ducks,' said Storey irritably. 'People did. What I am telling you is that the villains tried for a swan first. But swans are fierce creatures. They do not put up with nonsense.'

'I see. And when did these attacks happen?'

'The first was on a Monday, eighteen days ago. The second was four days later, and the third was the day before yesterday – a Wednesday.'

There was no pattern that Chaloner could see. 'Do you know what killed them?'

Storey beckoned him out of the parlour and into a small cupboard-like room, where the three victims were covered with neatly sewn pieces of black satin, heads visible at the top. They looked as though they were lying in state, an image Chaloner found strangely unsettling.

'I could not bury them,' Storey whispered. 'To smother their beautiful feathers in cold earth. So I thought I would stuff them. Unfortunately, I cannot bring myself to make the necessary incisions. I do not suppose you . . .'

'No,' said Chaloner firmly.

Storey sighed. 'Well, the weather is very cold, so I have a little longer before the matter becomes pressing.' Personally, Chaloner thought it was pressing already.

'Inspect the poor beasts, Mr Chaloner, and see what you think. It is my contention that they were murdered.'

Chaloner had seen enough people dead before their time to recognise poisoning, and he saw it in the birds: blood in their beaks told him that they had been given something caustic. He was angry. The ducks were doing no harm, so why should anyone hurt them?

'You are right: they have been murd— fed a toxin,' he said. 'Do you have any suspects?'

Storey pursed his lips. 'I have no evidence to accuse anyone, if that is what you are asking, but I have my opinions. The villain will be someone wealthy and influential.'

'Why do you say that?'

'Because no one else has access to the park.' Chaloner, who had climbed over its walls on innumerable occasions, sometimes for no other reason than because it represented the quickest way home, regarded him sceptically, and Storey hastened on. 'And toxins are expensive. The poor have more urgent things to spend their money on, like food, clothing and fuel.'

Chaloner was unconvinced. People – rich or otherwise – did all manner of peculiar things for reasons that defied logic and common sense. 'Then which wealthy and influential people do you think might be responsible?'

Storey covered his ducks carefully, then led the way back to the parlour, where he sat for several minutes in unhappy silence. 'My birds are more important to me than the fools at Court, so I shall share my suspicions with you. But please do not say you had these names from me.'

Chaloner nodded acquiescence, and Storey took a deep breath.

'Samuel Morland is at the top of my list, because I saw him strolling around the park on the very day that poor Harriet died. And he is a vile individual.'

Although Chaloner was gratified to hear the name of a man he so despised singled out for such a disagreeable crime, he was reluctant to believe the accusation. What reason could Morland have for dispatching birds? Moreover, the secretary was more used to causing harm with his tongue than with weapons, and Chaloner had never known him target animals before.

'Who else?'

'George Gery, Clarendon's new marshal. I once saw him try to kick a goose, and he unnerves me with his cold, unsmiling face. Then there is Controller O'Neill, who told me that he hates birds because of the mess they make. But birds cannot help the way they—'

'Le Notre does not like birds either.' Chaloner interrupted before they could become sidetracked. 'He just said so.'

'Yes, but he is a landscape architect,' countered Storey, clearly of the belief that this was enough to exonerate anyone. He continued with his list. 'Clement Oxenbridge is an evil villain. Do you know him? He looks like a spectre with his white face and peculiar eyes.'

'Why is he a suspect?'

'Because he is so deeply sinister.' Storey sounded surprised that Chaloner should need to ask. 'He has no home and no obvious employment, yet he is clearly wealthy and appears whenever there is trouble. Rather like the devil.'

'Right.' Chaloner was beginning to realise that he was wasting his time.

'He comes to the park sometimes, and I have seen him *looking* at my birds.' Storey made it sound very disturbing. 'How dare he! His Majesty's fowl are not for the likes of him to gawp at.'

'Is there anyone else?'

'Well, there is a vicious-tempered postal clerk named Harper. And my neighbour Sir Henry Wood often gets odd ideas into his head. He may have mistaken a duck for a radish.'

Chaloner stood, loath to waste more time listening to unfounded speculation. 'Thank you. You have been very helpful.'

Storey trailed him to the front door. When he opened it, he ran his fingers over the disfigured carving. 'It was a terrible thing that happened yesterday,' he said softly. 'Two pigeons were killed, and God only knows how many sparrows.'

'I understand you were out when it happened.'

Storey nodded. 'I should have been in the park, but it was so cold that I spent the day in a coffee house instead, talking about the comet and the effect it is having on starlings.'

'Two of the victims – humans, I mean – were coming to visit you.'

Storey nodded again, sadly. 'Yes, Harold and Henry Yean. I promised them a few flamingo feathers. Have you ever seen a flamingo, Mr Chaloner? Beautiful creatures. Not afraid of foxes either.'

'What do you know about the boys?'

'Cousins from the Fleet Rookery,' replied Storey, referring to an area of tenements and dirty alleys that was the domain of London's poor. The forces of law and order did not venture there, and it was a city within a city, with its own rules and leaders. 'I hired them to run errands for me.'

'They seem an odd choice. Do you not have apprentices or assistants for that sort of thing?'

'I do, but the Yean lads were excellent at trapping foxes.' Storey's face became oddly vindictive. 'And I take any opportunity to teach those murdering, thieving vagabonds not to set their filthy vulpine eyes on birds.'

The following day was colder than ever, and Chaloner woke before dawn to find that Hannah had taken all the bedcovers. He tried to retrieve some, but she tightened her grip in a way that told him she would wake if he persisted, and the sour temper that always assailed her first thing in the morning meant he was unwilling to risk it. He climbed off the bed and dressed in the dark, using the clothes that had been laid in a pile for him by the footman the night before, not because he liked the man making such decisions for him – he did not, and resented someone else rummaging in his wardrobe – but because lighting a candle would disturb Hannah.

He tiptoed downstairs, hoping it would be too early for the servants to be up, and that he could warm some ale over the embers of the kitchen fire. Unfortunately, it was washing day, when water had to be fetched from the well, lye and soap had to be measured out, and a veritable arsenal of boards, bats and dollies had to be assembled for beating the laundry clean. Thus he opened the kitchen door to find his household in the grip of frenzied activity, all conducted in almost total silence – he was not the only one who tried to avoid igniting Hannah's maleficent morning wrath.

Joan sat at the table, issuing low-voiced orders that were obeyed with such a sullen lack of enthusiasm that Chaloner wondered how his wife had contrived to select so many disagreeable retainers. Nan the cook-maid was spiteful; Ruth the lady's maid was lazy and probably dishonest; Robert the footman was arrogant; and Ann the scullion was downright unsavoury.

'Yes?' Joan asked frostily when she saw Chaloner. 'What do you want?'

'Nothing I cannot fetch myself,' he replied, longing suddenly for his family home in Buckinghamshire, where the kitchen was a haven of laughter and good humour. There, he would have been offered cakes fresh from the oven, and regaled with news from the village and amusing tales about the neighbours.

'Yes, drink cold milk,' he thought he heard her mutter. 'It is time the mistress was rid of you.'

'Speaking of poisons, have you heard about Mary Wood?' gossiped Nan, as she mixed ashes with lye in a basin. 'The Queen's dresser? Well, she was fed a toxic substance and—'

'The mistress said she died of the small-pox,' interrupted Joan. 'Who told you otherwise?'

'Dick Joyce, who was Mary's favourite servant,' replied Nan, her superior smile telling Joan whose source was likely to be more reliable.

'Joyce?' asked Chaloner. 'He was killed in the explosion outside the Post Office.'

'How do you know?' asked Joan disapprovingly. 'Were you there? The clothes you wore on Thursday were certainly in a sorry state, and I am not sure we shall get them clean today.'

The eyes of the others brightened at the prospect of a new tale about the capricious eccentricity of their employer, but the gleams faded to disappointment when he declined to reply.

'What did Joyce say, exactly?' he asked of Nan.

Nan was delighted to be the centre of attention. 'I met him an hour after his mistress died. He was terrified that he would be blamed for her death, as he was looking after her at the time – everyone else was out, apparently. Unfortunately, we were interrupted before he could say more, but I am not surprised that something untoward happened. Her husband is very odd.'

'Did Joyce imply that Wood had harmed her, then?'

Nan pursed her lips. 'No, but Wood is insane, so it stands to reason. Last week he told everyone that he was made of glass, and said that no one was to touch him lest they left finger-marks.'

Chaloner laughed.

As the cold milk had chilled him, Chaloner went to the Rainbow Coffee House on Fleet Street for a warming brew, walking there in the pitch dark because dawn was still some way off. He did not particularly like the Rainbow's clientele and its coffee was unpalatable, so he was not sure why he patronised the place. He could only suppose it was because it was predictable and unchanging, and constancy was something that was markedly absent from the rest of his life.

As usual, the owner, James Farr, had burned his beans, so the shop was full of reeking, oily smoke. It was busy, though, even at that hour, as customers stopped off for a dose of the beverage before work. As Farr's infusions tended to be more potent than those available anywhere else, he had a regular and devoted following, and there were many who claimed they could not begin their duties without a shot of Farr's best inside them.

'What news?' called Farr, the traditional coffee-house

greeting. Such establishments prided themselves on being up to date with domestic and foreign affairs, and their patrons were invariably informed of important events long before they could be printed in the government's newsbooks.

'Three ducks died in St James's Park,' supplied Chaloner, supposing the Rainbow was as good a place as any to learn if there were rumours about them.

'That is not news,' said a young printer named Fabian Stedman, who spent so much time in the Rainbow that Chaloner sometimes wondered if he ever went home. 'Who cares about ducks?'

'I do,' said Farr. He and his clients rarely agreed. 'They always sound as though they are laughing, and the noise they make gladdens my heart.'

'Not the ones in St James's Park,' countered Stedman. 'I went to see them once, and all they did was stand around and look miserable.'

'So would you if you had been torn away from Russia and carted here,' retorted Farr.

'If they hail from Russia, then they will be delighted to be in London,' averred Stedman. 'Because we all know about that particular country.' He shuddered theatrically.

'Do we?' Chaloner thought disconsolately about the Earl's plan to send him there.

'Of course,' replied Stedman loftily. 'It snows all the time, its Tsar is a tyrant, its people do not believe in God, and there are no alehouses.'

'No alehouses?' cried Farr, shocked. 'But where do people drink?'

'In filthy, squalid kitchens,' replied Stedman. 'Tell him, Speed.'

Samuel Speed was a relative newcomer to the Rainbow,

having moved into the area when Chaloner had been in Sweden. He was a hook-nosed bookseller of indeterminate age, famous for purveying tomes that no one else carried. Because his wares were frequently deemed scandalous, seditious or heretical, he also sold medicines to help his readers recover afterwards.

'He is right,' obliged Speed. 'I have a report about Russia, if you are interested – *Voyages and Travels of the Ambassadors* by Adam Olearius. It tells what the envoys of Holstein made of the Tsar and his people. Would you like to buy it?'

'I suppose so,' said Chaloner unenthusiastically.

'I shall bring a copy, then,' said Speed, pleased. 'But you will not like what you learn, so I recommend you purchase some of Mr Grey's lozenges to go with it. They have relieved many thousands in case of extremity, and are also an antidote against pestilent diseases.'

'Is he likely to catch some from perusing this text, then?' asked Farr uneasily.

'No, of course not,' replied Speed impatiently. 'I am just saying that Mr Grey's lozenges are good for more than easing a severe shock.'

'Russia must be a terrible place,' mused Farr soberly, 'if even reading about it is perilous.'

'Oh, it is,' Speed assured him. 'It is full of barbarous peasants, whose idea of fun is a game of chess that ends with a brawl. There are no surgeons or physicians, and the cure for everything is a spell in a sweating house. If they are too poor to afford one, they climb in an oven instead.'

'Lord!' muttered Farr, wide-eyed. 'I do not like the sound of that.'

'And no one in that entire benighted nation knows

Latin,' added Speed in a hushed voice, as if he considered this a far more serious deficiency. 'Except perhaps their Secretary of State.'

'I shall not go,' determined Stedman, although the chances of him receiving an invitation were slim. 'And these ducks should be grateful to be in London – the finest city in the world. Do you not agree, Chaloner?'

'The ones who were killed probably would not,' replied Chaloner.

'Such a vile, cowardly deed will be the work of fanatics,' stated Farr. 'And speaking of fanatics, there is talk of a rebellion bubbling in Hull.'

'No, it is in Sussex,' countered Stedman. 'One of my customers told me about it.'

'It *was* Hull,' said Farr firmly. 'I read it in a government newsbook, so it must be true.'

No one remarked on the rank fallacy of this statement.

'Actually, it may be both,' said Speed. 'Because the whole country is on the verge of revolution at the moment. Word is that John Fry has risen from the dead – if he was ever dead in the first place – and is writing letters telling people to prepare for the better society that he will usher in.'

'There are also rumours that someone important will soon be assassinated,' said Stedman. 'I have heard it from several different sources, so I am inclined to believe it.'

'Who will die, then?' asked Farr with ghoulish interest.

'Probably Monsieur le Notre, the French landscape architect,' replied Stedman. 'Or if not him, then the Duke of Buckingham or the Earl of Clarendon.'

'Well, I heard it would be the Major,' said Speed, while Chaloner regarded Stedman in alarm, not liking his master's name on such a list. 'The poor fellow who has been locked in the Tower for the past eighteen months without an opportunity to prove his innocence in a trial.'

'The Major!' spat Stedman in distaste. 'He was an officer in Cromwell's army, and anyone who supported that villain deserves to die. Moreover, it is said that he was the executioner who chopped off the old King's head.'

'If that were true, he would not have tried to blow up Cromwell a few years later,' argued Speed. 'And he spent ages in prison for that particular crime. Surely that proves his loyalty to the current regime?'

'I have also heard that His Majesty might be the victim of this pending assassination,' said Stedman, ignoring the bookseller's point. 'Just because he likes the occasional party.'

'His "occasional parties" are wild debauches that occur with shocking regularity,' said Speed sternly. 'He should learn to control himself, because his people do not approve.'

'It is none of their business,' declared Stedman, the blindly loyal Royalist. 'And I am not listening to any more of this talk. It is sedition, and we want no more of that.'

'No, we do not,' agreed Farr soberly. 'However, the King should not have dispensed with Lent this year. There is nothing wrong with a period of self-denial. It is good for the soul.'

'Good for the Catholic soul perhaps,' countered Stedman sullenly. 'But we Anglicans do not need it.'

'Lord Castlemaine will publish a book about Catholics next week,' said Speed brightly. 'I shall sell it in my shop. And speaking of him, he was blown off his feet by that explosion at the Post Office. I saw him myself, all dusty and dishevelled, when I arrived there shortly afterwards.'

'I do not suppose you saw a musician, too, did you?' asked Chaloner. He shrugged when everyone regarded him curiously. 'I heard one was entertaining when the blast occurred.'

'I did, as it happens,' replied Speed. 'He was running like the devil, clutching a flageolet. He was wearing a faded blue hat, yellow breeches and a reddish cloak.'

'Was the Post Office attacked because it is so corrupt?' asked Farr. 'We all know that everyone who works there is a thief. And that includes Controller O'Neill.'

'True,' nodded Speed. 'The only honest man was Mr Knight – and he is arrested.'

Chaloner winced, and supposed he would have to visit Newgate as soon as possible, not just to find out what Knight knew, but also to see whether there was anything the clerk needed. Clean clothes, decent food and a visitor who believed in him might make his imprisonment easier to bear.

Chapter 4

Chaloner stepped outside the Rainbow Coffee House to find that dawn had brought snow, tiny nodules so hard and dense that they danced across the frozen streets and showed no inclination to melt. Ice formed slick patches on which pedestrians, horses and even carts skidded precariously.

He turned west along Fleet Street, supposing he should report to the Earl before he did anything else. Afterwards, he would go again to St James's Park, although he suspected he was wasting his time given that he had already looked for clues without success. Then he would turn his attention to the Post Office, questioning its employees and suppressing his hatred of prisons to speak to Knight in Newgate. And finally, when the short winter day was over and the General Letter Office was empty, he would break in and see what a systematic search would reveal.

White Hall was deserted when he arrived, and the Great Court looked as though it had hosted a riot. Windows were smashed, the heads of statues had been knocked off, and the ground was strewn with discarded clothing. It was the aftermath of one of the Court's infamous debauches, which explained why the palace was so quiet – the revellers had only just gone to bed, and the other residents were catching up on the sleep they had missed while the party was in progress.

The Earl was at his desk, though. He had not been invited to join the carousing, and would not have gone if he had, being strongly disapproving of such behaviour. Even so, his face was pale, and he had the look of a man who had slept badly. Chaloner wondered why, when his fine new mansion in Piccadilly should have been too far away to have been disturbed by White Hall's excesses. The Earl scowled as his intelligencer approached.

'You went to the Post Office yesterday, after I expressly forbade it,' he snapped. 'Why?'

Chaloner wondered whether it had been Gery, Morland or Freer who had told tales. 'Actually, sir, I went to visit Edward Storey. He lives next door.'

'Who?'

'The Curator of Birds at St James's Park.'

'Oh.' The glower lifted. 'Have you come to report what happened to the poor beasts? The King will be pleased when I expose the culprit.'

'They were poisoned. I plan to interview the park's gardeners and assistant keepers today.'

'Then why are you here?' demanded the Earl, cross again. 'Go and speak to them at once. This is important, Chaloner. I promised His Majesty a solution, and he is expecting one.'

'I shall do my best.' Chaloner hesitated, not sure how to phrase what he wanted to say. 'I am concerned about the General Letter Office, sir. Knight said something

108

untoward is unfolding there, and then that explosion claimed five lives . . .'

The Earl eyed him coldly. 'Yes, and Gery is looking into it. You have other duties.'

'There are also rumours that someone will be assassinated, and London is full of tales about famous agitators waiting to lead the country in a violent rebellion. I cannot shake the conviction that the Post Office plot is related to all this, and—'

'No,' declared the Earl firmly. 'You have allowed yourself to be swayed by Knight's silly ramblings. But the man is a liar, and you should not believe anything he said.'

'What did he say, sir? He refused to tell me until he had spoken to you, but then Gery sent me to fetch the palace guards, and I did not hear what—'

'He spouted a lot of nonsense,' interrupted the Earl briskly. 'Suspicions without evidence. But Gery will investigate regardless, so there is no need for you to worry about it.'

Chaloner nodded, but decided to visit Newgate the moment he left the palace, even more certain that something was seriously amiss. He longed to ask why the Earl had appointed Gery, and why he himself was being deliberately excluded from whatever was going on, but he could tell by the determined set of his master's mouth that he would be given short shrift if he did.

'Go and find this bird-killer,' the Earl went on sternly. 'And leave the Post Office alone. I do not want you impeding Gery's enquiry with one of your own. Do you hear?'

Chaloner tried one last time. 'But I might be able to

help. Whatever is happening there involves murder as well as insurrection and corruption, and Gery—'

'You will stay away! I mean it, Chaloner. Do as you are told.'

Chaloner regarded his master worriedly. 'Is anything wrong, sir?'

'Wrong?' demanded the Earl shrilly. He would not meet Chaloner's eyes. 'Nothing is wrong.'

'Tell me how I can help,' said Chaloner softly. 'No one else need know.'

'There is nothing wrong!' Twin spots of anger glowed on the Earl's plump cheeks. 'Now go and catch the villain who is killing ducks. And if I hear you have disobeyed me, you can look for another appointment, because there is no place in my household for unruly retainers.'

Although the Earl had threatened him with unemployment before, Chaloner was under the distinct impression that this time he meant it. There was no more to be said, and Clarendon had already turned back to the papers on his desk. It was a dismissal, and he did not even glance up as Chaloner bowed and took his leave.

Chaloner closed the door and stood for a moment, thinking. It seemed Dorislaus had been right to urge him to defy his master on the grounds that Gery was a sinister influence – and the Earl was definitely upset about something. Was it the recent death of a son, as Williamson thought? Yet Clarendon seemed more frightened and worried than grief-stricken.

'Did he holler at you again?' came a soft voice from the shadows.

It was Freer. Chaloner glanced around for Gery and

110

Morland, but the soldier appeared to be alone. He nodded.

'Do not take it amiss.' Freer patted his shoulder kindly. 'He mourns his dead child.'

'So I have been told.'

'You must know how he feels,' Freer went on quietly. 'Hannah told me that you lost one to sickness in Holland some years ago.'

Chaloner nodded again, but was appalled that Hannah should have revealed such an intimate detail to a relative stranger. What else had she said? That he was incapable of expressing his feelings, which was one of the things she had come to deplore in him? Unfortunately, it was true, although he was sure he had had no trouble doing it when he was younger.

'You are at work early,' he said, abruptly changing the subject.

'Actually, I am here late – I have been guarding Clarendon. There is a rumour that someone will be assassinated soon, so Gery has ordered him watched at all times. Last night was my turn.'

'You think he will be the victim?'

'Not really. According to popular rumour, the murder will have repercussions, but our Earl's death will not cause many ripples, given his waning popularity. Personally, I suspect the target will be someone like the Duke of Buckingham, who has followers. Or O'Neill from the Post Office. Or Monsieur le Notre, because that will cause friction with France. Or even the Major.'

'Others have said the Major might be the target, too,' mused Chaloner. 'But I cannot see why. He was a fiery speaker once, but he seems broken now.'

'Well, that is hardly surprising after eighteen months

111

in the Tower. However, his death will have serious consequences for Clarendon – if he is murdered, our Earl will be blamed.'

'Why?' asked Chaloner. 'Because he is in the habit of summoning him to White Hall, a journey that renders him vulnerable?'

'Precisely. The poor fellow is dragged here two or three times a week. I think the Earl should visit him in the Tower instead, but he declines to go, on the grounds that he does not like it.'

Chaloner did not like the Tower either, yet even he thought it unwise to put a man's life in danger for the sake of personal convenience. 'Who would want the Major dead? I doubt anyone remembers him now.'

'On the contrary, he is popular because he advocates that any political change must be brought about slowly, gently and peacefully. The death of a committed pacifist will certainly ignite bad feeling.'

Chaloner supposed it might. 'Why does the Earl confer with him so often?'

'Because he is the one who first heard that all is not well at the Post Office. He managed to tell Sir Henry Wood, who happened to be in the Tower pretending to be a lion. And Wood reported it to Clarendon. Obviously, the Earl cannot use Wood as an intermediary – the man is barely sane – and he is reluctant to trust anyone else. So the Major is brought to White Hall.'

'A *prisoner* learned about trouble at the Post Office?' asked Chaloner sceptically. 'How?'

'Because the Major was a frequent visitor to Post House Yard when his friend Bishop was in charge, and several of its clerks still write to him. Thank God he is loyal to the Crown, because O'Neill has erected a wall of silence

112

around the place, and the Major's contacts represent a vital conduit of information. We would know nothing were it not for him. He is extremely valuable.'

Chaloner frowned. 'But O'Neill dismissed all the clerks that Bishop hired, and replaced them with men of his own. The Major cannot still have friends in the General Letter Office.'

'O'Neill made a clean sweep of the *Inland* Office, but he left the *Foreign* Office alone because it is much smaller and – in his view – far less important. The two departments are separate, as I am sure you know, but its clerks chat to each other, and it is the Foreign Office men who pass the Major his intelligence.'

'Intelligence about what, exactly?'

'I cannot tell you more,' said Freer apologetically. 'Gery would dismiss me if he knew I had revealed this much, and I like working here. However, I can say that in return for his help, the Earl has promised to arrange the Major's release. I hope he does not renege. The disappointment will kill the Major if he does.'

As Chaloner walked towards the palace gate, courtiers spilled out of the sumptuous apartment that belonged to Lady Castlemaine, where they had evidently gone to round off their night of fun. She was resplendent in a scarlet gown that hugged the sensuous curves of her body, a body that had cost the King a good slice of his popularity with his people. Her face showed the ravages of good living, though – her skin was puffy, her eyes bloodshot, and there was an unhealthy pallor in her cheeks.

Chaloner was reluctant to thread his way through a lot of people who hated his Earl, lest one of them was

113

drunk enough to start a fight, and he did not want to skewer anyone if it could be avoided. He stepped into a doorway to wait until they had gone, where he discovered that he was not the only one loath to risk an encounter. Two others were already there: Thomas Kipps was the Earl's cheerful, friendly Seal Bearer, while Mrs Chiffinch was unhappily married to the Court rake who had chatted to Chaloner and the O'Neills at Hannah's soirée the other night.

'It is a pity the villains who tried to blow up the Post Office did not target White Hall instead,' said Kipps, uncharacteristically acerbic. Chaloner could only suppose he was resentful because he had not been invited to the Lady's party – he was a great admirer of her thighs, and was even willing to endure Court debauches for a glimpse of them. 'None of these villains would be missed.'

'No, but it almost deprived us of him.' Mrs Chiffinch pointed to Roger Palmer, fresh and fit, who was emerging from the Queen's private chapel where Mass had just ended. 'He was caught in that blast, and his death would have been a waste of an intelligent, decent man.'

'True,' agreed Kipps. 'He is worth ten of any other courtier, present company excluded.'

'His family warned him against marrying her,' Mrs Chiffinch went on. 'They said she would make him the unhappiest man alive, and so she has. She will service any man who asks.'

'Not *any* man,' said Kipps regretfully. 'But she is a beauty! Just look at her lovely—'

'A whore's figure,' interrupted Mrs Chiffinch. 'And not worth our attention. Have you heard the rumours that say a courtier will be assassinated, by the way? Who will it be, do you think?'

114

'Buckingham?' suggested Kipps. 'The King? Clarendon? Unfortunately, all refuse to change their plans, saying they would never get anything done if they panicked every time there is a threat to their lives. It means that everyone else is obliged to do the same, or risk being accused of cowardice.'

'You two *must* look after Clarendon,' ordered Mrs Chiffinch. 'He is the only member of the Privy Council with morals, and we cannot afford to lose him.'

Just then, Sir Henry Wood arrived, sitting astride a small donkey. It was a peculiar sight, and Lady Castlemaine and her cronies burst into hoots of mocking laughter. Wood tried to dismount, but found he could not do it, so Palmer went to assist. Wood promptly flung his arms around Palmer's neck, causing him to stumble, which caused another outburst of hilarity.

The cobbles were icy, and unwilling to see Palmer suffer the indignity of a tumble in front of such an audience, Chaloner hurried to help. It was not long before they had Wood standing on his own two feet, and there was a collective sigh of disappointment from the onlookers.

'I know you,' said Wood, fixing Chaloner with his bright amber eyes. 'You are Chaloner the regicide, and you agreed with me that radishes were responsible for the attack on that dangerous abomination that calls itself the Post Office. Or did you argue for cabbages? I cannot recall now.'

'Neither,' objected Chaloner, unwilling to be associated with Wood's peculiar theories. Or to be confused with his uncle in a place like White Hall, for that matter. 'And I am not a—'

'I cannot talk,' Wood interrupted sharply. 'I must paint

115

myself green as a defence against the comet. Did you know that its presence in our sky is harmful? However, it is very fond of trees, so colouring myself like one should allow me to evade its malevolent attentions.'

'Christ!' muttered Chaloner as Wood scuttled away, leaving a startled Palmer holding the reins of the donkey. 'Should he be in Bedlam?'

'There are plenty who would like to put him there,' replied Palmer. 'But the King remembers his loyalty during the Commonwealth, and turns a blind eye to his eccentricity. Wood is harmless, though, unlike many who haunt this palace.'

'I am not a regicide,' said Chaloner, not sure whether the remark was directed at him.

Palmer laughed. It was a pleasant sound, a far cry from the jeering brays of his wife and her friends. 'You are one of Clarendon's ushers. I saw you in his retinue earlier this week – and again yesterday in Post House Yard.'

'You did?' Chaloner was uneasy, wondering why he should have been noticed.

'Your wife pointed you out the first time,' explained Palmer. 'I had spent the afternoon with the Queen, you see, and they mentioned that you know Portuguese. So do I.'

He had begun speaking that language halfway through his explanation. He was not very fluent, but Chaloner imagined the Queen would be pleased, regardless. She appreciated any opportunity to converse in her native tongue.

'I understand you will publish a book next week, sir,' said Chaloner politely.

Palmer nodded keenly. 'An apology for Catholicism. I

cannot abide bigotry, and London is rather full of it at the moment. My treatise describes our beliefs, and explains why we do not itch to see any country in flames. I hope it will help to eliminate mistrust and suspicion.'

Unfortunately, Chaloner suspected he was harking after a lost cause. England had been happily persecuting Catholics for decades, and it would take a lot more than a book to make it stop.

When the clot of courtiers around the gate cleared, Chaloner started to walk towards it. It was still too early to visit Newgate, so he decided to go to St James's Park first, to question the gardeners. Palmer abandoned the donkey to a passing groom, and fell in at his side.

'Your wife tells me that you are hunting the villain who killed the King's birds,' he said. 'I hope you succeed. I cannot abide people who mistreat animals. Do you have any suspects?'

'Not yet.' Chaloner wished Hannah would not gossip about him.

'No act of depravity surprises me in this vile city,' said Palmer bitterly. 'I already long to leave. For the last two years, I have served in the Venetian navy, which is full of rational, intelligent men. But duty called, and I felt obliged to come home. However, I cannot tell you how much I miss sensible conversation and civilised behaviour.'

'What duty?' asked Chaloner, and then wished he had not spoken when it occurred to him that Palmer might refer to reining in his shameless wife.

'The Dutch conflict,' replied Palmer, to Chaloner's relief. 'I am an experienced sea-officer and cannot sit back while my country goes to war. But my troubles are a rather less immediate worry than these poor ducks. How will you go about solving such a discreditable crime?'

Chaloner glanced sharply at him, but there was no hint of mockery in Palmer's face, only interested concern. 'I was going to walk around the Canal again,' he hedged, unwilling to share his real plans with a man he barely knew, even if it was one who seemed at pains to be congenial.

'Then we shall do it together,' determined Palmer. He smiled. 'And practise our Portuguese at the same time. Do you mind?'

Chaloner did mind, but it was hardly his place to reject the company of an earl. However, Palmer quickly proved himself to be a witty and agreeable companion, even when struggling in a foreign language. He also transpired to be interested in music, and confided that William Lawes was one of his favourite composers. Chaloner also loved Lawes' work, and he felt himself warm to Palmer even more when they discovered a shared appreciation for the bass viol.

'We had better look to your birds,' said Palmer, after a lengthy debate about the best places to buy strings. 'Or the King is still going to be wondering who killed them next week.'

Reluctantly, as he had been enjoying the discussion, Chaloner led the way to the Canal, but had not taken many steps along its bank before they discovered a sad bundle of black and white feathers. Chaloner turned it over with his foot and saw the familiar bloody beak.

'Pity,' said Palmer. 'It was a handsome thing – a kind of northern *penguin*, I believe, otherwise known as a great auk. It is probably one of the flock that came from Iceland. They are quite rare.'

With Palmer at his side, Chaloner walked around the

Canal in its entirety, but there was nothing in the way of clues – no footprints because the mud was frozen, and no indication as to how or where the bird had been caught. Moreover, the day was so cold that there was not a gardener in sight, so there was no one to question either.

'Clearly, the penguin was killed during the night,' surmised Palmer, 'or it would have been found yesterday. *Ergo*, the scoundrels must have climbed over a wall, because the gates are locked at dusk. Shall we explore the perimeter, to see if we can find their point of entry? Perhaps we shall discover something useful there.'

It was a good idea, and Chaloner knew from his own incursions that there were only two or three places where the walls could be easily scaled, so he led the way to the nearest and most likely.

'Hah!' Palmer stabbed his finger. 'Look – someone was sick here.'

Chaloner bent to inspect the mess, then began to search the surrounding area. Nearby were two dead pigeons. He knew for a fact that pigeons were not averse to eating vomit, because he had seen them doing it at White Hall. He prodded them with a twig, revealing a pair of bloody faces.

'But if the toxin was in the sick, it means a person ingested it first,' said Palmer, grimacing in disgust. 'Indeed, it was probably what made him lose his dinner in the first place.'

Chaloner nodded, and pointed to where marks in the grass showed where something heavy had been dragged. They followed the trail to an area of wilderness, then to a mound of leaf litter and twigs. Carefully, Chaloner brushed them away to expose a body.

'Poisoned?' asked Palmer softly, crossing himself.

'Yes. You can see blood in his mouth, the same as the birds.'

'He is wearing a hooded cloak – the kind of attire a villain might don for committing despicable acts under cover of darkness. I would say he is certainly one of your culprits.'

Chaloner agreed. 'And he somehow fell victim to his own poison, which was careless. He died before he could leave the park, and an accomplice must have hidden him here.'

'It looks to me as if he has been dead for some time, possibly since the first duck, which you say was dispatched nearly three weeks ago. He is beginning to rot, despite the icy weather.'

Chaloner nodded. 'In which case his accomplice is extraordinarily ruthless – the terrible fate of his companion has done nothing to stop him from killing more birds.'

'Lord!' breathed Palmer. 'What will you do now?'

'Make a sketch of this man's face, and set about identifying him.'

'I can save you the trouble,' said Palmer. 'I know him. He works at the General Letter Office.'

Chaloner stared at him. 'Are you sure?'

'Yes, and I can even tell you his name. It is . . . it *was* Andrew Leak. We used to exchange polite greetings when he served me in the Letter Hall.'

Chaloner's thoughts were a tumble of confusion. Why should a Post Office employee kill the King's birds? Donning gloves, he examined the body quickly, and although he was no *medicus*, he had seen enough dead men to know what to look for. There was no evidence of a struggle, which would have indicated that Leak had been forced to swallow whatever had killed him, but there was a phial in one of his pockets. It was empty, but marks on the stopper suggested that he had removed it with his teeth.

'I imagine it would have taken more than that to make an end of him,' he said, looking around to see if another, larger bottle had been tossed into the undergrowth.

'Not necessarily,' said Palmer. 'I have spent the last two years in Venice, a city with more than a nodding acquaintance with poisons, and I can tell you for a fact that there are substances so potent that the merest drop can kill. Leak pulling off the top of that little pot with his mouth might well have been enough to claim his life.'

Chaloner set it down quickly. 'I see.'

The next hour or so was taken up with arranging for Leak's body to be removed to a charnel house, and burying the birds and vomit to ensure they harmed no other wildlife. Then Chaloner caught a hackney to Newgate, where he learned that the gaol was closed to visitors that day because it was being cleaned; the prisoners were doing the work, but the turnkeys were so afraid of a mass break-out that they were refusing to open the gates.

Not sure whether to be relieved or frustrated, Chaloner walked to Post House Yard, where he marched purposefully into the Letter Hall. It was busy, because it was nearing the deadline for inland mail, but he demanded an audience with the Controller anyway, safe in the knowledge that Leak's death gave him a perfectly valid excuse for doing so, should Gery happen to appear.

'Chaloner!' exclaimed O'Neill, when he came to see who wanted him. 'If you are here to ask whether you can send parcels for free now we are acquainted, then I am afraid the answer is no. It would be dishonest, and I run a law-abiding operation here.'

'Perhaps we can talk inside,' suggested Chaloner, keen for an opportunity to enter the back rooms legitimately.

O'Neill's eyebrows went up, but he nodded agreement, and conducted him to the Sorting Room, where a dozen clerks were tossing letters into untidy piles. These were then whisked away to the Clerks of the Road, where they were arranged in geographical order.

Meanwhile, another official prowled watchfully. Every so often, he would swoop on a missive and read the name of the intended recipient. Most were dropped again, but some were slipped into the bag he carried at his side. Chaloner could only suppose he was the Spymaster's agent, selecting items to open. Chaloner glanced at O'Neill, who had denied that such practices took place, but the Controller was waxing lyrical about the quality of some new mailbags he had bought, and Chaloner was unable to decide whether he was shockingly ignorant or a masterful bluffer.

He recognised a number of clerks he had seen before, either after the explosion or the following day around the crater, although Smartfoot and Lamb were not among them. He watched their labours with a critical eye, seeing immediately that it was not an efficient operation – piles of letters were moved for no apparent reason, and some clerks repeated tasks already completed by others. Perhaps the Post Office's detractors were right to disparage O'Neill's directorship, he thought.

One clerk did not seem to have any particular function. He sat at a paper-strewn table, but his hands were folded in front of him and his attention was on his colleagues. He had the hungry look of a predator, and he made his workmates uncomfortable – they turned clumsy and fumble-fingered when they sensed his gaze upon them.

'Well, now,' said O'Neill eventually, once he had exhausted the topic of how his sacks were superior to the rubbish purchased by Bishop. 'What can I do for you?'

'I have just found Andrew Leak in St James's Park,' said Chaloner. 'Dead.'

He had not spoken loudly, but the Sorting Room suddenly went silent and work stopped.

'Dead?' echoed O'Neill in disbelief. 'You must have the wrong man. He has been ill, because he has not been to work for the last three weeks or so, but he will not be dead.'

Chaloner watched him carefully. He was clearly shocked, but why? Because Leak had been doing his bidding when he had died, and he had hoped the corpse would never be found? Or because he was a compassionate employer who cared for his people?

'Is that when you last saw him?' Chaloner asked. 'Three weeks ago?'

O'Neill nodded numbly, then turned and beckoned to a burly fellow with eyes that were a curious and not altogether attractive shade of taupe. 'Rea, come here. You and Leak were particular friends. Did you hear what Chaloner said? Leak is dead.'

'I have not seen him since late December,' said Rea, stepping forward with obvious reluctance. 'I suppose I should have gone to his home, to ask after his welfare, but we have been so busy here . . .'

123

'Did he have other work, besides being a postal clerk?' asked Chaloner.

'He told me he ran errands for someone in the evenings,' replied a different clerk. 'He said it was well paid, which is why he mentioned it – to gloat. I tried to press him for details, but he claimed it was a secret.'

'Was he married?' asked Chaloner. 'Perhaps he told his wife.'

'He was not,' said Rea. He glared at the other clerk. 'And he never told *me* that he had another job, and I was his closest friend. He was probably spinning you a yarn.'

'Where did he live?' asked Chaloner.

'Elbow Lane,' replied Rea sullenly. 'Why?'

'Take Mr Chaloner there,' instructed O'Neill briskly. 'Perhaps a search will reveal the truth.'

Chaloner was conducted to a small but neat cottage a stone's throw from Post House Yard. He assessed every inch of it for evidence that Leak had consorted with poisoners, but discovered nothing. Indeed, it was so clean and tidy that he suspected someone had been there before him.

He returned to the General Letter Office and questioned every one of Leak's colleagues, but although all seemed shocked – and some were even distressed – none could tell him what the clerk might have been doing in the park. Chaloner did not mention poison or the King's fowl, and neither did anyone else. Was he to assume that Leak had been approached with an offer of work by someone unconnected with the Post Office, and it was coincidence that one of its officials had been a killer of birds? Somehow, Chaloner did not think so.

* * *

124

Although he rarely discussed his investigations with anyone else, Chaloner felt like doing so that day, so he aimed for Lincoln's Inn, one of the great foundations in London with the authority to license lawyers. It was home to John Thurloe, Cromwell's erstwhile Spymaster and Secretary of State. Thurloe had abandoned politics at the Restoration, and now lived in quiet retirement.

Chaloner cheered at the prospect of meeting his friend, and his step lightened as he walked down Ludgate Hill. As he went, he saw a dozen apprentices standing on the bridge that crossed the Fleet River. They were from the Guild of Skinners, and formed a glowering impediment to traffic. Carters and riders yelled at them to move, but they remained where they were, obstinately defiant.

More from habit than any real concern that he was being followed – Thurloe still had enemies, and Chaloner was always careful when visiting him – he ducked into the porch of the Rolls House on Chancery Lane. As he peered out to survey the street, he saw Morland.

There was a moment when he thought the secretary's appearance was coincidental, but that notion vanished when Morland looked around wildly and stamped his foot in petulant frustration. After standing for a moment with his hands disgustedly on his hips, Morland began to walk back the way he had come. Chaloner set off after him, noting as he did so that the secretary wore an exquisitely tailored suit. As the Earl tended to be mean with salaries, he wondered how Morland could afford to dress himself with such princely elegance.

'Were you looking for me?' he asked, speaking softly and watching Morland jump.

The secretary scowled. 'You startled me. When you disappeared—' He stopped abruptly and glanced at

125

Chaloner to see if he had noticed the inadvertent admission.

Chaloner had, of course. 'Why were you tailing me?'

'Because Gery told me to,' confessed Morland reluctantly. 'He thinks you consort with the wrong kind of people. Thurloe, for example. I assume you are on your way to see him now?'

'I am going to buy a hat for my wife,' lied Chaloner. 'Not that it is any of your affair.'

'I should like a new hat, too. Shall we visit the milliner together?'

'And have you reporting Hannah's tastes to Gery?' asked Chaloner archly. 'I do not think so! He might read something sinister into her preference for wool over silk.'

Morland laughed uneasily. 'Very possibly. Wool is a wicked Parliamentarian fibre, far inferior to Cavalier silk. But we are both old hands at this, Tom – too old for games. Tell me what you plan to do today, and we can both be about our business unfettered.'

'Very well.' Chaloner was willing to agree to anything if it saw him rid of Morland. 'After I have bought the hat, I shall interview the St James's Park gardeners about the ducks.'

'I see.' Morland grinned slyly. '*Is* there a milliner near here? I do not know of any.'

Chaloner pointed to a shop behind them, not such an amateur as to be caught telling a tale he could not substantiate. Morland gestured that he should lead the way towards it, and Chaloner obliged so as not to give the secretary the satisfaction of exposing a lie. He opened the door to reveal a display of such wildly extravagant creations that he wondered who would have the courage to wear them.

'So many feathers,' he remarked, looking around in dismay.

'Feathers are fashionable,' explained the owner as he bustled forward. 'Unfortunately, I have to import most of mine, because Storey, who has care of the King's birds, refuses to sacrifice any. He sends two grubby boys with ones that have been shed naturally, but I need more than that.'

Chaloner frowned. Was that the answer – the ducks had been killed for their exotic plumage? But none had been plucked. Or did someone aim to raid the corpses after Storey had had them cleaned and stuffed?

'Feathers fetch a good price, then, do they?' asked Morland keenly. 'It is worth finding you a few?'

The milliner beamed. 'Yes. So if you hear of a flamingo that wants a good home, let me know. I have ideas for a magnificent hat, which—'

'Touch a flamingo and I will break your fingers,' said Chaloner quietly, but with a look that made the milliner gulp a promise that flamingos would never feature in his creations again.

'Jesus wept, Chaloner!' exclaimed Morland, once they were outside. 'Did you have to terrify that poor man? He is only making a living. Gery is right: you *are* sinister.'

'The warning was intended for you just as much as him,' said Chaloner coldly.

Morland sneered. 'Threaten me again, and I will tell Gery to dismiss you.'

Chaloner rounded on him. 'Where were you last night?'

Morland took a step away, alarmed despite his bluster. 'At home. Why? Are you going to accuse me of killing the King's fowl now? You cannot find the real culprit, so you will invent one?'

'Well, you did express an interest in providing the rogue in that shop with feathers,' Chaloner pointed out, wondering whether Storey might have been right to place Morland first on his list of suspects.

'Not from the King's birds. I am not stupid. I have friends in the East India Company, and they will bring me what I need.'

'You would see birds slaughtered to feed a fashion?' Chaloner was disgusted.

'Why not, if it makes me money? We are all entitled to take what opportunities come our way. But I have better things to do than discuss financial philosophy with you. I shall go back to White Hall and tell Gery that you gave me the slip. He will be angry, but with you, not with me.'

Once he was sure Morland had gone, Chaloner resumed his journey to Lincoln's Inn. He did not enter by the main gate, though, lest Morland should question the porter, and aimed instead for a bramble thicket at the back. Hidden deep inside was a door, all but forgotten and heavily overgrown. He fought his way through the foliage, prised open the gate, and spent several minutes on the other side brushing dead leaves and cobwebs from his clothes.

Term was in full swing and the inn was busy, black-gowned students and their masters swarming everywhere. No one paid him any attention as he made for Dial Court and climbed the stairs to Chamber XIII. Unfortunately, when he arrived he heard the rumble of voices – Thurloe had company. The door was ajar, so Chaloner listened, to determine whether it was a meeting he could interrupt or whether he would have to wait.

'*I* have answered these questions already,' came an aggrieved voice. It was William Prynne, a member of

Lincoln's Inn and a pamphleteer who wrote vicious diatribes on subjects ranging from Quakers and dancing, to lace and playhouses, all of which he despised with equal passion. He had had his ears chopped off for penning libellous nonsense about the King's mother, but the punishment had done nothing to curb his vitriol. Chaloner frowned, wondering why he should be in Thurloe's rooms: the ex-Spymaster usually declined to have anything to do with him.

'I know.' Chaloner was alarmed to recognise the voice as Gery's. What was the marshal doing there? 'But I want to hear it from Thurloe.'

'Prynne is quite right,' came Thurloe's mildly modulated tones. 'He has not been here for some time now. Why do you want to know?'

'That is my business,' retorted Gery. 'Will you tell me if he contacts you?'

'Of course,' replied Thurloe politely. 'I shall send word with Tom Chaloner, a man who can be trusted absolutely. Indeed, I wonder that Clarendon did not ask him to bring me this request.'

'Because he told me to do it,' snapped Gery, nettled by the remark as Thurloe had no doubt intended. 'He also said that you are a valuable source of information, because your old spies still send you regular reports. Is it true?'

'I am not a spymaster now, Mr Gery,' said Thurloe with quiet dignity. 'I know no more than the average Londoner.'

It was untrue, because Clarendon was right: a large number of Thurloe's old informants did continue to supply him with gossip and titbits. But Chaloner was glad he had chosen to be cautious.

129

'*I* am the one with information,' declared Prynne peevishly. 'I am Keeper of Records at the Tower, and I learn a great deal as I trawl through old documents. Moreover, I listen in markets for chatter, and there is nothing you can tell me about current affairs. What do you want to know?'

'John Fry,' said Gery shortly, although Chaloner could tell he was more interested in intelligence from Thurloe. 'What have you heard about him?'

'A very wicked gentleman,' replied Prynne promptly. 'He has been in London of late, writing letters that encourage people to rise up against the government.'

'I sincerely doubt it,' said Thurloe shortly. 'He has been in his grave nigh on a decade.'

'You seem very sure,' said Gery unpleasantly. 'But of course, Fry was a rancorous malcontent whose radical views caused trouble for Cromwell. *Ergo*, he was a thorn in your side, and there were rumours that he was murdered. Do you have any special reason to believe him dead?'

Chaloner held his breath. It was a nasty insinuation.

'Only insecure governments need to silence their detractors,' replied Thurloe coolly. 'So there was no need for assassinations under Cromwell. All I meant was that if Fry did not die eight years ago, then why did he wait until now before reappearing? It makes no sense.'

The door opened suddenly, and Chaloner only just managed to dart into the shadows before Gery stalked out. Prynne was at his heels, wearing the woollen hat that hid his mutilated ears. The pamphleteer was gabbling, and Chaloner was sure he heard the name Oxenbridge. He waited until they had gone, then entered Thurloe's quarters himself.

Chamber XIII was full of heavy, dark oak furniture

130

that Chaloner had once considered oppressive, but that he now found comfortingly familiar. It smelled of beeswax, polish and woodsmoke, and the shelves around the walls were bowed under the weight of an impressive library. Thurloe liked to read, and although most were books on law, there were also smatterings of history, philosophy, science and mathematics.

Thurloe was standing by the window. He was slightly built with brown hair and large blue eyes that often appeared soulful. He was one of the most intelligent, thoughtful men that Chaloner knew, and there was no one he trusted more. The ex-Spymaster glanced up when Chaloner entered, and indicated that he was to shut the door behind him.

'I expected you sooner, Tom,' he said without preamble. 'Thursday, for example.'

'Why?' asked Chaloner, bemused.

Thurloe pursed his lips. 'The Post Office atrocity. I understand you were there.'

'How? Did Temperance tell you?'

'Isaac Dorislaus did,' replied Thurloe. 'He saw it happen, too.'

'Did he?' Chaloner wondered why the portly Anglo-Dutchman had not said so when they had discussed it the previous day. Vanderhuyden had been open about hearing the blast and running outside, so why had Dorislaus seen fit to be secretive?

'Isaac was the most gifted clerk the Post Office had,' Thurloe went on. The ex-Spymaster had always been fond of Dorislaus, which was why Chaloner had never mentioned his suspicions during the Commonwealth – Thurloe was protective of his friends, and would not have listened to accusations of disloyalty against one. 'I

131

urged O'Neill to keep him, but the fool thought he knew better, and not a letter has been delivered on time since.'

Chaloner changed the subject, sure the failings of the General Letter Office went deeper than the dismissal of one official. 'Actually, I came to ask your advice about the dead birds in—'

'I hope you came to tell me about the explosion,' interrupted Thurloe sternly. 'What have you discovered so far?'

'Nothing. Clarendon has ordered me to stay away.'

Thurloe blinked his astonishment. 'What? Surely he will want his best operative on this case, and Marshal Gery is hardly the thing.'

'The Earl does not agree. Moreover, he has let Gery hire some assistants – six soldiers, a man named Freer and Samuel Morland.' Chaloner saw Thurloe's shock. 'You did not know?'

'God and all his saints!' breathed Thurloe. As the ex-Spymaster rarely blasphemed, Chaloner saw the news had unsettled him deeply. 'Morland? *Morland?*'

'He tried to follow me here, which worries me. I think he still means you harm.'

'Almost certainly – to prove himself to his new masters. It is a pity he is so treacherous, because he has many talents. He is skilled with languages and an extremely able inventor.'

'What has he invented?' asked Chaloner sceptically.

'A trumpet that allows deaf people to hear, an engine that pumps water at fires, fountains for Versailles.' Thurloe smiled bleakly. 'We discussed mathematics for hours when he was in my service. I am interested in the subject, as you know. I considered him a friend.'

Chaloner could hear the pain in Thurloe's voice:

132

Morland had wormed his way very deeply into his affections, and the betrayal still hurt.

'I rarely misread people,' Thurloe went on softly. 'But I worked closely with Morland for six years, and never once did it occur to me that he might pass my secrets to the enemy. He played me for a fool. Me, a spymaster who should be used to deceit and treachery.'

Chaloner was not sure what to say, and they sat in silence for several minutes.

'What did Gery want?' he asked eventually. 'And why was Prynne involved?'

Thurloe took a deep breath, pushing Morland's perfidy to the back of his mind. 'Prynne is in everyone's business now the King has appointed him Keeper of Records – a clever ploy on His Majesty's part, because it has won Prynne heart and soul. He was something of a liability before, with his incendiary opinions, but now he is the King's most faithful servant.'

'Gery was asking whether someone had contacted you,' said Chaloner, more interested in the marshal's business than the feisty pamphleteer's allegiances. 'Who?'

'Isaac Dorislaus.'

Chaloner regarded him uneasily. 'You informed Gery that you had not seen Dorislaus for some time, but you must have done if he told you about the explosion. Gery may not be clever, but he is ruthlessly dogged, and if he learns that you lied—'

'I did not lie. I said Isaac had not been here, which is true. We met at my coffee house.'

'Sophistry,' said Chaloner, unimpressed. 'Why is Gery interested in Dorislaus?'

'Apparently, he believes he is a Dutch spy.'

'And is he?'

Thurloe glared at him. 'No, of course not! Isaac is one of few men I know whose loyalty is absolute. He would never betray his country.'

Chaloner nodded, but thought about his own lost reports. It had certainly been to the advantage of the Dutch that they had been mislaid, and Dorislaus had always been bitter that his regicide father had been murdered while on a diplomatic mission to Holland by Royalist agents from England – agents who had almost certainly been encouraged by men who were now members of the government. Moreover, Gery must have had some reason to be suspicious. Of course, Gery was suspicious of Chaloner, too, wholly without cause, so perhaps his mistrust of Dorislaus was similarly baseless.

'I met Dorislaus yesterday,' he said. 'He was with Vanderhuyden.'

'They have always been friends. But never mind this. The Earl is making a terrible mistake by ordering you away from the Post Office. It is your moral responsibility to ignore the instruction.'

'He will dismiss me if he finds out.'

'Better that than the alternative – which may be his execution for treason.'

Thurloe's words sent a chill down Chaloner's spine, but the ex-Spymaster decided that his rooms were no place for such a discussion – even Lincoln's Inn had spies – and suggested a walk in the garden, where he could be certain they would not be overheard.

'In the last few weeks, there have been reports of trouble in places as far distant as Yorkshire, Bristol and Sussex,' he began, once they were strolling along a neatly gravelled path bordered by tiny hedges. 'And there is unrest here in London. It is not easy to coordinate events in such far-flung locations. A lot of correspondence would be needed . . .'

'And you think the Post Office is being used to facilitate it?'

'Sending letters is a lot cheaper than hiring private messengers on horses. However, if you use the post, you run the risk of your missives being intercepted. Unless the clerks are on your side.'

Chaloner shrugged. 'Perhaps you are right, but is it any surprise that the country is dissatisfied? We thought we were getting a king who would heal two decades of civil unrest, but instead we have an indolent rake who is more interested in women than in running his country.'

Thurloe stared dolefully at him. 'I am glad we came out here for this discussion, Thomas, because I should not have liked *that* remark to be heard emanating from my rooms.'

Chaloner grinned. Thurloe was the only person to whom he would have said such a thing.

Thurloe did not smile back. 'His Majesty has his faults, but he is our leader now, so we must do all we can to protect him. And these tales about John Fry worry me extremely.'

'Why? You just told Gery that he is dead. Or was that untrue, too?'

Thurloe eyed him balefully. 'Fry caused untold trouble when Cromwell was in power. He held controversial religious opinions and a very specific notion of what a republic should entail.'

'Him and half the country,' said Chaloner drily.

'Yes, but he was more passionate and determined than most. When our government did not conform to his

135

narrow ideals, he wrote letters urging other malcontents to revolt. He might have succeeded, but he passed away before his plans could be realised. When I heard the news, I travelled to Dorset to attend his funeral – to assure myself that he was really gone.'

'So he is dead? These stories about him wandering around London are a canard?'

'I did not look inside the coffin; perhaps I should have done. However, it is because Fry's letters wrought such havoc *then* that I am so concerned about what the Post Office might be doing *now*. Moreover, I dislike the fact that Clarendon has asked Gery to look into the matter.'

'Why?'

'Because the man is incompetent and will fail. Perhaps Clarendon's judgement is impaired following the recent death of his son. I know I was prostrate with grief when I lost children . . .'

'Williamson said the same. Yet the Earl seems more apprehensive than upset.' Chaloner described his earlier encounters, and his conviction that all was not well. He also mentioned the Major's visits to White Hall. Not surprisingly, Thurloe knew about them.

'I imprisoned the Major for trying to murder Cromwell,' he said. 'But on good evidence. However, he is currently being held on what amounts to a whim, and my informants tell me that eighteen months in the Tower have all but destroyed him.'

'He is a shadow of the man I remember from the wars,' agreed Chaloner. 'But I still do not understand why *he* smelled trouble at the Post Office when Williamson's spies did not. I know Williamson has agents there, because I saw one choosing letters to open.'

'I imagine either they have been corrupted or they are

incapable of interpreting what they see. However, the Major was deeply involved in the Post Office when Bishop was in charge, so I am not surprised that the Foreign Office clerks – you know they managed to survive O'Neill's purge, do you? – still trust him more than anyone else.'

'Even more than Bishop?'

'Bishop was never as good at making friends. However, he was an excellent Postmaster, and the accusations made by O'Neill were patently false, as everyone should have seen when O'Neill promptly asked to be made Postmaster himself. You should encourage the Major to confide in you, Tom. It is in his interests to do so – his freedom depends on a successful outcome, which he is more likely to have with you than with Gery.'

'I cannot visit him in the Tower,' said Chaloner tiredly. 'Gery would find out.'

Thurloe was thoughtful. 'Gery has kept you very busy since your return from Sweden. Other than the birds, what else has he ordered you to do?'

'Find a missing coal shuttle, hunt down some stolen laundry, look into a few mislaid documents, investigate three servants he considered untrustworthy . . .'

'So why does he waste your time with trivialities?' mused Thurloe, more to himself than Chaloner. 'Is it because he knows you are a better investigator than he, and does not want the competition? Or does he have a more sinister reason for his actions – such as that he is keen for whatever is unfolding at the Post Office to succeed?'

Chaloner regarded him doubtfully. 'He is a fervent Royalist. I doubt he supports insurrection.'

'He is a fanatic. Such men are rarely logical or sensible.'

'Well, if he hoped the dead birds would keep me away

137

from the General Letter Office, his plan has misfired. One of the poisoners was a postal clerk.'

Briefly, Chaloner described his discoveries in the park.

Thurloe frowned. 'It will not be a coincidence, you can be sure of that. Leak was a very minor official, and quite expendable – the perfect choice for a dangerous mission.'

'Killing birds is hardly dangerous.'

'I imagine Leak would disagree,' said Thurloe drily. 'However, it will be difficult to learn who else was with him. And someone was, because Storey saw several sets of footprints by the Canal, and you say Leak's body had been hidden in undergrowth.'

'Shall I waylay some clerks and hold them at knifepoint until one confesses?'

'That has already been tried – by Williamson *and* by me. Our agents ended up with blades in their innards. And therein lies the root of the problem: the wall of silence erected around the Post Office by Controller O'Neill. He has even hired henchmen to ensure it is not breached.'

Chaloner had seen some of them himself – the pair called Smartfoot and Lamb, and the feral-faced fellow who had sat at a table and intimidated everyone by watching them. The Foreign Office clerks were brave to defy them and communicate with the Major regardless, he thought.

'The fact that O'Neill has ordered his people not to talk to anyone suggests that he is party to whatever is unfolding,' he said. 'Or do you think he is the innocent dupe of a cleverer mind?'

'You must ask the Major.' Thurloe grimaced. 'He is an extremely valuable asset, and Clarendon is a fool to put him at risk by dragging him to White Hall. He should be interviewed in the Tower, where he will be safe from assassins.'

138

Chaloner did not say that the Earl rarely made good decisions where such matters were concerned, because Thurloe already knew it. After a while, during which their feet crunched on the frozen gravel as they walked, he described what had happened when the cart had exploded.

'Poor Joyce,' said Thurloe softly. 'Sir Henry Wood was a "person of interest" during the Commonwealth, and I paid Joyce to monitor him. I was suspicious of Wood's eccentricity, you see, along with the fact that he insisted on buying the mansion and all the houses near the Post Office.'

'That *is* suspicious. Did you ever ask him for an explanation?'

'I did. He told me it was the only square in London that is unpopular with lettuces. I never did decide whether he was a harmless lunatic or a dangerous dissident.'

'He is the one who took the Major's initial report to Clarendon.'

Thurloe winced. 'Then I imagine the Major was horrified by his choice. I would not want Clarendon in charge of any investigation that my freedom depended on.'

'You suggested earlier that the trouble at the Post Office might result in the Earl's execution,' said Chaloner worriedly. 'And Williamson told me that his enemies on the Privy Council have made him responsible for the place. How? It should have nothing to do with the Lord Chancellor.'

'No,' agreed Thurloe. 'But they outmanoeuvred him, and he agreed to oversee an enquiry before grasping its ramifications – which are that if it fails, he will be accused of incompetence or complicity. Either will see him ruined – or worse – which is why you must ignore his orders and do all you can to save him.'

'Lord!' muttered Chaloner. 'I will try, but—'

139

'You will succeed or look for a new employer,' said Thurloe harshly. 'But to return to Wood, were you aware that Joyce was the second member of that household to die on Thursday?'

'Yes. Mary Wood had the small-pox. Although there is gossip that she was murdered.'

'Ask Surgeon Wiseman to look at her body,' instructed Thurloe.

'He has already offered, but not until Tuesday – three days' time.'

'Then Tuesday it must be. So let us summarise what we know. Something deadly is unfolding at the Post Office, and we suspect it is connected to the unrest that is currently afflicting much of the country. Wood lives next door: his servant was killed in the blast, and his wife is said to have been murdered.'

'The Post Office's other neighbour is Storey, whose ducks have been poisoned.' Chaloner took up the tale. 'And a postal clerk named Leak was one of the culprits. There is another connection, too: the Yean boys, who ran errands for Storey, were also killed in the explosion.'

'And the last victims of the blast are the Alibond brothers, also postal clerks. We must see what we can learn about them. Perhaps they threatened to expose what is happening, and paid the price.'

'They tried to run when I shouted, but they could not move fast enough. I am disturbed by a French landscape architect named le Notre, too. He was in Storey's house when I went to ask about the dead birds. He has been hired to design fabulous new gardens at Versailles – gardens for which you say Morland has invented fountains.'

'Morland,' said Thurloe grimly. 'Yes, we must not forget him. Nor Clement Oxenbridge, a man with no home and no employment that I can discover. He is a mystery, and not a particularly nice one either. There is something deeply unpleasant about him.'

'Temperance said he was friends with John Fry. But he must live somewhere. I will find—'

'I already have a man looking into it, and I do not want you falling over each other,' said Thurloe crisply. 'Leave him to me, please.'

'What shall I do, then?'

'Speak to the Major – in the Tower, if necessary. Then go to Newgate and talk to Knight.'

'Christ!' muttered Chaloner, not liking the notion of braving two prisons in quick succession.

'But first, you must find that musician, and ascertain whether he drew a crowd to increase the number of victims. Start on Cheapside. Street entertainers are rife there.'

Chaloner went to Cheapside immediately, and eventually managed to establish that a flageolet player who wore a red cloak, blue hat and yellow breeches lived in the dangerous, unsavoury area around St Giles-in-the-Fields. He took his life in his hands by entering seedy alehouses that did not welcome strangers, but the trail petered out as the clocks were striking ten. He was too tired to start again by following the lead Wiseman had given him – the surgeon had mentioned that one of those injured in the blast, a postal clerk named Copping, might be able to tell him more about the musician – so he traipsed home on foot, having spent all his money on bribes.

As he passed Long Acre, he was tempted to go to the rooms he rented there, sure Hannah would not miss him. But he had no coal for a fire, and there was nothing to eat. At least Tothill Street would be warm, and Nan the cook-maid baked fruit pies on Saturdays.

He opened the door to his house, and was greeted by the rank stench of burning, which told him both that Hannah was home and that he would not be enjoying anything edible that night. As the kitchen was a perilous place when her culinary experiments did not go according to plan, which was most of the time, he went to the drawing room instead, grateful to find the fire lit. He had done no more than stretch his frozen hands towards it when the door opened and Hannah strode in.

'You are uncommonly filthy,' she remarked, looking him up and down in distaste. 'What have you been doing? No, do not tell me! It is probably better for me to remain in blissful ignorance. I wish you had come home sooner, though. I made pheasant stew, and it was delicious. Shall I fetch you some? It has cooled off, but I imagine it will still taste all right.'

'No, thank you,' said Chaloner hastily. Her stews were barely edible when hot, and cold did not bear thinking about. Her eyes narrowed, so he added, 'I had something in a cook-shop.'

'Very well. Incidentally, I am not inviting O'Neill to my next soirée. He broke our clock.'

'How do you know it was him?' asked Chaloner guiltily.

'Monsieur le Notre told me.' Hannah smiled rather dreamily. 'He really is the most charming fellow. Do you think he will design us an orangery?'

'An orangery?' Chaloner was alarmed. The house they rented was far larger than was necessary for the two of them, but it was still not big enough for such a grand feature. And how would they pay for such a ridiculous extravagance?

'All the best homes have them,' Hannah went on. 'I think I shall see what he says. Do not look so disapproving, Tom. It is cheaper than having a baby, and will go some way to compensating me for not being a mother.'

Chaloner could not see how, but knew better than to say so. However, the remark reminded him of something he wanted to ask.

'Why did you tell Freer about . . .' He faltered, unwilling to speak the name of his dead child, even after so many years. 'About my last family.'

Hannah came to take his hand. 'I am sorry, Tom. It just slipped out. He was chatting to me about the Earl's desolation over his loss, and I said that you would understand grief better than that hard-faced lout Gery. Everyone at Court was sorry when the news came about young Edward – he was a nice fellow and only nineteen. Did you ever meet him?'

Chaloner nodded, although he had found the youth rather wild and extremely arrogant.

'Since he died, people have turned him into a saint, of course,' she went on. 'They have done the same for Mary. No one liked her when she was alive, but now they praise her to the heavens. What hypocrites we all are.'

She went on in this vein for some time, and seeing he was not expected to answer, Chaloner let his mind wander. It snapped back to the present with one remark, however.

'What did you say?'

'That the country will be spared the expense of a trial now that the fellow who cheated the Post Office is no longer with us. Knight was found dead in his cell in Newgate Prison this afternoon. He had hanged himself.'

Chapter 5

Chaloner slept badly that night, racked by guilt. Knight had said that Newgate would be a death sentence, but Chaloner had arrested him anyway, even though he had been far from certain that the clerk had done anything wrong. Lying next to Hannah, he stared into the darkness. Should he attempt to clear Knight's name, to make amends for his part in the tragedy? He decided he would try. Perhaps it would relieve the remorse that weighed so heavily on his mind.

'If you cannot sleep, go downstairs,' came Hannah's irritable voice. 'You are shifting and turning like a man in a fever, and every time I doze off, you jostle me awake.'

Chaloner mumbled an apology, and to stop himself from dwelling on Knight he began to make plans for the day ahead. It was a Sunday, and the Post Office would be closed, so it was a good time to search it for clues. Then he would go to Newgate and ask after Knight, followed by a visit to the Tower to see what the Major was prepared to tell him. Then there was the injured clerk Jeremiah Copping, who might have information about the musician.

144

Another line of enquiry was Oxenbridge, whom Knight had said lay at the heart of the Post Office trouble. Temperance had called him dangerous, and thought he might be helping John Fry with his rebellion; Storey had included him on his list of potential bird-killers; and Thurloe was sufficiently concerned that he had sent someone to investigate him. Thurloe had asked Chaloner to leave Oxenbridge alone, but the man represented an important lead, so Chaloner decided he would ask questions if the opportunity arose. And then there was the mysterious Bankes, who was paying for information about—

'Thomas, please!' snapped Hannah. 'I had a difficult day yesterday, because the Queen was upset over Mary Wood, and I must attend Mass just after dawn. I need to sleep.'

'It is almost dawn now,' said Chaloner, relieved that the night was over at last. He climbed out of bed and set about lighting a candle. 'Shall I walk with you to White Hall?'

Hannah hauled the bedcovers over her head with a groan. 'Go away! But please do not play that wretched viol. It disturbs the neighbours.'

Chaloner knew the neighbours could not hear him through the thick walls, and resented her lie. He said nothing, though, and had almost finished dressing when she sat up.

'I cannot go back to sleep now that I am awake. I told you not to drink that cold milk before we went to bed – that is why you were restless all night. Or is it an investigation devised by your horrible Earl that has you so disturbed? What has he ordered you to do this time?'

'Explore the death of some ducks in St James's Park.'

145

'Ducks?' she asked incredulously. 'Have you fallen out of favour with him, then?'

'I have never been in favour.'

Hannah sounded worried. 'I know I often tell you to look for another master, but do not annoy this one until you have something else lined up. We cannot manage without your salary.'

They would have been able to manage perfectly well on what he could have saved if she had not moved to a larger house and hired staff they did not need, but he kept the thought to himself.

'You would have to sell your viols,' she continued. 'To tide us over until—'

'No,' he said firmly. He had very few personal belongings – a spy's life was necessarily nomadic, and he had lost count of the times he had been forced to abandon all he owned at a moment's notice – but his viols were sacrosanct, along with a book given to him by his first wife.

Hannah was silent for a moment. 'Is anything wrong, Tom? You have been remarkably taciturn since Sweden, even by your standards.'

Nothing, he thought bitterly, except a master who despised him, enquiries that were likely to prove dangerous, the fact that he had been instrumental in sending a man to his death, and a wife who itched to hawk his viols. But Hannah's voice had been gentle, and he knew she was trying to bridge the rift that had opened between them. He went to sit on the bed, and although he thought she would be safer knowing nothing about the Post Office, he did tell her about the birds.

'The poor things,' she said when he had finished. 'Perhaps you should hide in the park, and see whether

146

you can catch these villains in the act. They will certainly strike again, given that they did not stop even when one of them fell victim to his own poison.'

'That might take days.'

'Not necessarily. You say the ducks died last Wednesday, three Fridays ago, and the Monday before that, while the penguin was killed the night before yesterday. The King was entertaining in the Banqueting House on all four of those occasions. And he is due to do it again on Tuesday. Try waiting for these rogues then.'

Chaloner stared at her. 'Why would they strike during a revel?' He answered his own question. 'Because any noise made by agitated birds would be drowned out by the sounds of merrymaking.'

'It makes sensc to me, and it is worth a try.'

Chaloner smiled, heartened. 'Thank you.'

'I have some bad news, Tom. I was going to tell you last night, but you seemed oddly out of sorts after I told you about the suicide of that clerk, so I decided to wait. The Queen is going to Epsom next week, for the waters. I am to ride there before her to make everything ready.'

'So what is the bad news?' asked Chaloner, wondering if she expected him to accompany her. If so, there would be trouble, because the Earl was unlikely to let him go.

Hannah's expression hardened. 'That I am going to Epsom and you will be without me.'

'Oh.' Chaloner saw he had hurt her feelings, and hastened to make amends. 'I shall miss you.'

She regarded him coolly. 'I should hope so. I miss you when you are away, although I confess you are gone so often that I am growing rather used to it. The sooner you abandon that Earl and find someone who will keep you in London, the better.'

'Can we send the servants to visit their families?' asked Chaloner, trying not to look too eager at the prospect of having the house to himself. 'I doubt I will be here much if you are away.'

'That is a kind thought, Tom, but how will you manage without them?'

'With the greatest of difficulty, I imagine,' said Chaloner solemnly.

Once he was outside, Chaloner realised he had been mistaken about the hour; it was not nearing dawn at all, but still the middle of the night. However, it was an excellent time to see what answers could be found in the General Letter Office, so he went there immediately, walking as no hackneys were available. He did not blame their drivers for declining to be out – it was bitterly cold again, and he was half-tempted to return to his warm bed himself.

When he reached Post House Yard, he slipped into the shadows cast by Wood's mansion, and settled down to watch, unwilling to break in until he was sure the place was not under surveillance by another investigation. It was not long before his caution bore fruit – a flicker of movement under some trees indicated that someone was there. Silently, he inched towards it.

He was still some distance away when Morland stepped out of his hiding place to stamp his feet and slap his arms, complaining about the weather and his life in general. As one of the most basic rules of surveillance was silence, and even novices knew not to chatter, Chaloner wondered what the secretary thought he was doing. Morland was answered in monosyllables by a companion whose voice Chaloner recognised as Freer's.

'I should not be engaged in such demeaning work,' Morland grumbled. He was wearing a richly embroidered cloak to ward off the chill. 'I shall complain to the Earl tomorrow.'

'Do that,' said Freer.

'I was assistant to a Secretary of State,' Morland railed on. 'I was privy to great secrets, all of which I passed to His Majesty. I should not be out here like a common watchman. I deserve better.'

'Yes.'

'Is this the way loyalty is repaid? I risked my life by betraying Thurloe, who is as deadly a villain as you could ever hope to meet. Yet here I am, reduced to skulking in the shadows with the likes of you. It is not to be borne!'

'No.'

'You must feel the same way, so why not mention it to the Earl? Then he will dismiss Gery, and appoint me as marshal instead. *I* will not order you to spend all night in the cold, you can be sure of that.'

Freer did not reply, and Chaloner thought Morland's wits must be addled if he expected his companion to agree to such a suggestion. The Earl would probably do nothing other than report the discussion to Gery, at which point Freer would find himself without a job. And Morland? His cunning tongue would doubtless see *him* absolved of mutiny.

But listening to the slippery secretary's litany of complaints was hardly productive, so Chaloner turned his attention to the Post Office. Entering through the front door was obviously out of the question, so he walked to the back instead. Unfortunately, this comprised a tall brick wall that would be impossible to scale without

149

a ladder. Thus the only other possibility was to break into Storey's cottage and enter the General Letter Office via their shared courtyard.

He picked the lock on the curator's door and padded soundlessly through the house to the parlour. There was a faint but unpleasant smell, and he could only suppose that Harriet, Eliza and Sharon still lay beneath their satin covers. He opened the window and scrambled into the yard beyond, frozen weeds crackling beneath his feet.

He stood in the shadows for a moment, watching the building he was about to invade. It was in darkness, and the only sound was a dog barking several streets away. One of its windows had a crooked shutter, so he crept towards it, and had prised it open and climbed through in less than a minute, although speed had its price – he tore his coat on a jagged piece of wood. Once inside, he listened carefully. Timbers creaked as they contracted in the cold, and there was a skittering of small claws. Mice.

He lit a candle and started his search in the Sorting Room, but it was not long before he realised he was wasting his time. The General Letter Office was by definition full of documents, and he could not possibly hope to trawl through them all. He turned to the adjoining offices, but the clutter told him nothing other than that its employees were inundated with business. Discouraged, he made his way up the stairs to the offices occupied by the lesser clerks.

In one, he discovered a pile of letters, all neatly embossed with the date on which they had been posted – a brand known as a 'Bishop-Mark'. O'Neill's predecessor had listened to his customers' complaints about the length of time that letters were in transit, and had

150

devised a system whereby they were stamped when they were received, which meant the Post Office could not lie about how long it had had them. The public had been delighted, although O'Neill had confided at Hannah's soirée that it was a nuisance, as it forced him to be more efficient than was convenient.

Bishop-Marks comprised a circle, with two letters in the top half representing the month and a number below for the day. The handful Chaloner held had been stamped IA 10, indicating they had been posted on the tenth day of January, but a sly squiggle had been added to make them read IA 18, a date yet to come. It was evidence that the Post Office intended to keep them for an additional week, either to give the Spymaster's agents time to read them, or because the Clerk of the Road had too much post already and was unwilling to hire additional horses. It was dishonest, especially as several were marked 'Haste, haste, post haste'.

He ascended to the top floor, and froze when he heard voices. There was a light, too. He doused his candle quickly, and crept towards the sound, peering around a door to see five men. One was slitting seals with a hot knife, three more were making copies of the letters' contents, while the last repaired the damage with sticks of wax. They were Williamson's men, monitoring correspondencc between 'persons of interest'.

Chaloner was about to creep away when disaster struck: his sword scraped against the wall. All five men whipped around to stare at the door. He was going to be caught.

Cursing under his breath, Chaloner ran silently down the stairs and along a corridor, hearing the clerks hot on his heels. Unfortunately, the hallway ended with a locked door – the one that led to the disused wing. He stopped and drew his sword, pressing back into the darkest of the shadows as he waited for the trouble to begin. He tensed as a lamp bobbed closer towards him, hoping he could disable a couple of his pursuers before the fight began in earnest, to even the odds a little. Then the lantern stopped.

'It must have been a mouse,' said one, peering into the gloom. 'O'Neill should set traps before they start eating the post, but he is too mean to buy them.'

It was not many moments before the light receded, and Chaloner was alone again. He released the breath he had been holding, and turned to the door. The lock was robust, and represented a challenge even for his superior skills. He picked it eventually, and stepped through the door. He had just closed it behind him when he heard footsteps. He put his eye to the keyhole and saw a soldier there, holding a lamp in one hand while he adjusted his clothing with the other. It was a guard, and Chaloner had been extremely fortunate that a call of nature had drawn the fellow away at the right time.

Unlike the main building, the south wing was only two storeys high. Chaloner relit his candle, and explored the upper one first. It reeked of damp and mould, and contained nothing but dirty sacks. One had split, spilling letters – all prepaid – across the floor. They were yellow with age. He untied another that looked newer, and discovered missives with Bishop-Marks reading OC 23 and NO 10. It proved that the Post Office regularly accepted correspondence that it never bothered to deliver, and that it had been doing so for some time.

He returned to the ground floor, where he discovered that broken window shutters had been repaired and ashes

152

in one or two hearths told of recent fires. Clearly, the wing was not as abandoned as he had supposed. One chamber contained a desk, covered in papers. He grabbed a handful, and shoved them in his coat to read later. As he did so, something scratched his hand – tiny splinters from the window he had crawled through, which had caught in his ripped sleeve. He brushed them off, and was about to leave when he noticed something wrong with the proportions of the room. It was too narrow, and the ceiling boss was off-centre. He walked to the chamber next door, and saw a similar skewing, but in the opposite direction.

He had been trained to locate hidden rooms, so it did not take him long to discover a concealed handle inside a wooden panel. He grasped it and pulled, wincing when a door sprang open with a rumble that sounded like thunder in the silence of the night. He waited in an agony of tension for the yells that would tell him that it had been heard, but nothing happened, so he stepped inside, raising his candle to look around.

It had been constructed without windows, and its walls had been lined with wads of cloth, presumably to deaden sound. It was longer than it was wide, and crammed with scraps of metal, planks, pots and tools. It stank of oil, and was certainly not what he had been expecting to find. He was about to explore it when he heard footsteps.

Hastily, he pulled the door to, and snuffed out the candle. A lamp flickered in the adjoining room, and through the crack by the hinges he saw three men: Smartfoot, Lamb and the clerk who had intimidated the others. The fellow did not so much walk as prowl, his eyes darting everywhere. He stopped suddenly, and his

153

stillness was so absolute that his companions froze, too. Then he sniffed the air, like a wolf scenting prey.

'What is it, Harper?' whispered Smartfoot.

Harper crouched to touch something on the floor. 'Splinters. Fresh ones. Someone was here.'

Chaloner gaped his astonishment, sure *he* would not have noticed minute fragments of wood in a room lit only by the unsteady gleam of a lantern.

'Then we had better find him,' said Lamb, hauling a cudgel from his belt. 'We cannot afford to have spies wandering around.'

Harper stood, and Chaloner knew he would notice that the door to the hidden chamber was ajar – he was obviously extremely observant – at which point Chaloner would be trapped inside with three armed men blocking the only exit. His only option was to seize the initiative. He burst through it with all the speed he could muster, punching the lantern from Smartfoot's hand and plunging the chamber into darkness.

All that was visible once the lamp had gone out was the merest outline of the door to the corridor. Chaloner raced towards it, but Harper and Lamb anticipated his move, and positioned themselves to stop him, flailing blindly with their weapons as they did so. Meanwhile Smartfoot fumbled to light a candle, simultaneously raising the alarm with a series of yells.

Chaloner did not draw his sword. There was no point – he knew instinctively that the trio would be skilled combatants, and he could not fight them all at the same time. The knife he always carried in his sleeve slipped into his hand, and he lobbed it behind him, towards the window. Lamb immediately blundered towards it, but

Harper did not fall for the ruse, and Chaloner winced when he felt a sword slash close to his face.

He surged forward, crashing into Harper with his shoulder, knocking him off balance. Even so, Harper still managed to aim a blow, and Chaloner felt a slight sting as the blade nicked the tip of his thumb. Then Lamb arrived, and a lucky lunge in the blackness saw him grab Chaloner's arm.

Desperate now, Chaloner resorted to gutter tactics. He kicked at where he thought Lamb's knee would be, and heard a grunt of pain as his foot connected. Lamb's grip loosened just enough to let him slither free. The papers he had stolen fluttered to the floor, but there was no time to worry about them. He shot into the corridor, where the guard had unlocked the door and was coming to investigate. Chaloner felled him with a punch, and raced into the main building.

Unfortunately, Smartfoot's howls had alerted the spies who had been opening the post, too, and three came racing to see what was going on. All were armed, and they blocked the way to the front door, so Chaloner took the only other route available: the stairs. He tore up to the first floor, where he met the other two clerks. He bowled into them before they had gathered their wits, sending both flying. There was a corridor to his left, so he darted along it, but he knew the game was up – his earlier search had told him that all the offices were locked, and he would be caught long before he could pick his way inside one.

'Tom! In here, quickly.'

Chaloner whipped around at the hissed voice, and was startled to see Dorislaus standing there. But it was no time to ask questions, and he was only just inside the

155

room when thundering footsteps indicated that his pursuers had arrived. He closed the door fast.

The Anglo-Dutchman tapped on a panel, which slid open to reveal a hole. Dazed, Chaloner wondered how many more cunningly hidden spaces the General Letter Office contained, and why whoever had built the place should have deemed them necessary. Outside in the hall, he could hear doors being kicked open as Harper and his cronies hunted for him.

'Climb in,' whispered Dorislaus urgently. 'Hurry!'

Chaloner hesitated. Was it a trap? But the alternative was to brave eight armed and angry men – nine including the guard – so he scrambled through the opening, and found there was just enough space to stand upright. His confusion intensified when Dorislaus squeezed in next to him. There was not really room, and it was a tight and very uncomfortable fit.

'You no longer work here,' he said softly, as Dorislaus fiddled to close the panel. He was acutely uncomfortable, his natural distrust of the man filling his mind. 'So why—'

'Hush! Or we will both be caught.'

The panel had only just clicked closed when the door burst open. Through a crack in the wood, Chaloner watched Lamb glance around, see the room was empty and move on. Harper, however, stepped inside, and began sniffing the air. Chaloner held his breath and was aware of Dorislaus doing the same. Surely Harper could not *smell* them?

'He came in here,' the clerk said to Smartfoot, who had come to stand at his side. 'There must be a priest's hole or some such contrivance. Find it.'

Smartfoot obeyed with an alacrity that suggested Chaloner was not the only one who found the man

156

unsettling. He began tapping on the panels, while Harper watched, his face unreadable.

Chaloner's heart was thumping hard, and he wondered whether he would have room to draw his sword when the panel opened, or whether he would be skewered where he stood. He could barely move with Dorislaus pressed against him. Was that what the Anglo-Dutchman intended? To keep him immobile while he was cut down? But why bother with such an elaborate charade? Why not just let Harper catch him?

'How do you know he is here?' asked Smartfoot, when he met with no immediate success.

'Blood,' said Harper softly, and pointed to the floor. 'We injured him.'

Chaloner felt his jaw drop. It was the merest nick, and any drop he might have shed must have been very small. He was good at tracking people himself, but Harper's skills were unnatural. Next to him, Dorislaus began to shake.

Smartfoot had reached the wall behind which they were hiding, and Dorislaus's trembling intensified. Chaloner leaned on him, trying to keep him still. Dorislaus swallowed hard, and the sound it made was so loud that Chaloner was sure Smartfoot would hear. But whatever device operated the panel was too clever for the clerk, and he passed on his way.

Harper was unwilling to concede defeat, though, and ordered him to start again. Time passed, and Lamb and the spies came to help. Later still, more clerks arrived, grimly determined to succeed when informed that an intruder was hiding within. Then there was a flurry of activity in the corridor, and the door flung open to reveal Controller O'Neill. He was bristling with anger.

'Why is no one in the Sorting Room?' he demanded. 'It is well past six o'clock, and you should all be at work. Or do you want the post to be late again?'

'We had an uninvited guest,' explained Harper. 'He came in here, and we are looking for him.'

'In here?' O'Neill eyed him warily. 'Well, obviously it is empty now, so you can—'

'This was once the home of wealthy Catholics.' The softness of Harper's voice was sinister, and Chaloner did not like listening to it. 'There will be a priest's hole.'

'Then ask the fellow who works in this room to point it out to you,' said O'Neill sharply. He had disliked being interrupted. 'Random prodding and poking is unlikely to reveal it. Papists do not design these things to pop open for just anyone, you know.'

'That will be Jeremiah Copping, sir,' supplied the clerk named Rea. 'But he was injured in the explosion, and his sister is looking after him at her tavern on Cheapside.'

'The intruder is not here,' said Lamb, throwing up his hands in defeat. 'He must have escaped.'

'He had better not have done.' O'Neill scowled at Harper. 'I employ you to mind our security, and I have not had cause to regret the appointment so far.'

There was an implied threat in the remark, although Harper did no more than incline his head, and it was O'Neill who looked away first. Then the Controller ordered the bulk of his clerks back to work, leaving Harper with just Lamb and Smartfoot. When they had gone, Harper lit lanterns and handed them to his henchmen, indicating that they should search yet again.

'Did either of you see his face?' asked Smartfoot, rapping on a wall with the hilt of his dagger.

'How could we?' asked Lamb. 'He knocked the lamp

158

from your hand before we knew he was coming. However, he is big and strong, because he all but broke my leg when he kicked me.'

'You can repay him for that when we catch him,' said Harper. 'And we *will* lay hold of him, because we shall not leave this room until we do. No spy eludes me and lives to tell the tale.'

There followed one of the longest, tensest and most uncomfortable days Chaloner ever recalled spending. When his henchmen were unsuccessful, Harper began to search himself, taking an age about it. The air in the hiding place grew hot and stale, and Chaloner's lame leg ached from the enforced stillness, but he dared not move lest he made a sound that gave them away.

Harper came ever closer to their hole, tapping and pushing at every square inch of wall, while Lamb and Smartfoot sat on Copping's desk and watched. Eventually, he reached the panel that concealed the lever, and Chaloner could tell by length of time he spent inspecting it that he had detected something unusual. It was an age before he eventually moved on.

'Perhaps the blood was Copping's,' suggested Lamb, when even Harper was forced to concede defeat. 'He came up here after he was injured in the blast, to collect his coat.'

'Perhaps,' said Harper, although there was doubt in his voice. 'But we have wasted enough time. We should go to the Sorting Room.'

Dorislaus started to move after the trio had departed, but Chaloner stopped him, and it was quite a while before a silent shadow passed the door as Harper finally abandoned his vigil.

'Why did he not find us?' asked Chaloner softly, once he was sure it was safe to speak.

'You need a key,' explained Dorislaus. 'Without it, you can prod all you like, but the panel will never open. However, it did cross my mind that they might take an axe to it.'

'You took a considerable risk by rescuing me.'

'Yes,' agreed Dorislaus shakily. 'And had I known what it was going to entail, I might not have obliged. What did you do to make Harper so desperate to catch you?'

'Nothing,' replied Chaloner, still unwilling to trust Dorislaus, despite what they had just endured together. Perhaps a life of espionage had made him overly cynical, but he was not about to ignore the instincts that had kept him alive for so many years. 'Who is he?'

'He holds the title of Senior Clerk, although his actual remit is to keep the Post Office secure. It is because of him that no one will talk about what is happening. Any number of people have tried to inveigle answers, including Spymaster Williamson, but none have succeeded.'

'You did not reply earlier when I asked what you were doing here. You are no longer a postal clerk, so you should not have been in Copping's office.'

'I will tell you, but not in this place.' Dorislaus reached past him, and tapped something that caused a flap to pop open, accompanied by a rush of cold but musty air. 'I dared not do this sooner. Harper would have heard, and then we would have been doomed for certain.'

'What is it?' Chaloner tried to see, but it was too dark.

'A tunnel that leads to a building on Dowgate Hill. Follow me and no talking. It leads past other rooms, and Harper has ears like a fox. It would be a pity to be caught now.'

Chaloner followed the soft hiss of Dorislaus's breathing along a narrow passage to a flight of stairs. All was pitch black, and he was forced to feel his way, hands braced against the walls. They descended many steps before entering what felt like a tube in the bedrock.

'Now we climb,' whispered Dorislaus eventually. 'Not much farther.'

His mind teeming with questions, Chaloner followed him up a series of ladders. He heard a key turn, and a door opened to reveal a scullery. Dorislaus checked the coast was clear, then walked quickly through it to a room that Chaloner recognised immediately. It was the Antwerp Coffee House. With cool aplomb, Dorislaus sat down and ordered a drink.

Although Chaloner's inclination was to put as much distance between him and the Post Office as possible, he went to perch next to Dorislaus instead. He wanted answers, and the Anglo-Dutchman was going to provide them. He began with the most important question.

'Why do you have keys to secret tunnels in the General Letter Office?'

Dorislaus grinned. 'I have had them since I worked for Thurloe in the Commonwealth.'

Chaloner fell silent when the coffee-house owner came to fill two dishes from a silver pot with a long spout. Dorislaus was obviously a regular customer because the bowl of sugar was left – sugar was expensive, and the courtesy would not have been extended to a stranger.

'His name is Edward Young,' said Dorislaus, apparently reading Chaloner's thoughts. 'He is a sympathiser, and will give us an alibi, should one be needed.'

'A sympathiser with what?' asked Chaloner warily.

'With Parliament, of course,' replied Dorislaus, a little

impatiently. 'The Cavaliers have the Crown, and we have the Antwerp. It has always been that way.'

'And do *they* have tunnels that grant them access to government buildings?'

'Fortunately not,' smiled Dorislaus. 'That particular passage is a closely guarded secret. However, I am surprised Thurloe did not mention it to you, given that you are investigating the place.'

'Thurloe does not know what I am doing,' said Chaloner sharply.

'Oh, come, Tom! He is worried about what might be unfolding there, and you are his favourite spy. Of course he ordered you to look into it. Just as he did me.'

'You are working for Thurloe?' asked Chaloner sceptically.

'Ask him, if you do not believe me. Unfortunately, I have been able to provide him with very little information, which is why I felt compelled to visit the place today – to see what might be learned by snooping. I knew it would be safe for me to use the tunnel, because Copping is still recovering from his wound, and his office is unoccupied.'

'And what did your snooping tell you?'

Dorislaus looked pained. 'Nothing, because the moment I arrived, you caused a commotion. As it seemed you were in danger, I thought I had better help. Thurloe will not want to lose you – it would be a serious setback to his investigation.'

'His investigation into what, exactly?'

'We do not know – Harper thwarts our efforts to find out. However, it must be something dire, or O'Neill would not have hired him. The services of such a man will not come cheap.'

162

'You think O'Neill is at the heart of it?'

'I do. He conspired shamelessly to get Bishop's job, and he is ruthlessly greedy.'

Others had said the same. 'Are all the clerks involved? There must be sixty of them at least.'

'No, it will be a select few, with the others intimidated into looking the other way.'

'Do you think it has anything to do with Thursday's explosion?'

'It seems likely. I do not suppose you got into the disused wing, did you? I have tried twice now, but it is always locked and guarded. It might contain something to help us.'

'Do you have any idea what?' Chaloner wished he had not lost the papers he had grabbed.

'None at all, I am afraid.' Dorislaus was silent for a moment. 'Do you know Mr Bankes?'

'No. Why?'

'Because he has been asking questions about the Post Office, too. But who is he, and why does he offer to pay for information? He is a worrisome mystery.'

Chaloner agreed: Bankes's eagerness to buy intelligence about a state-owned institution was sinister. He changed the subject. 'What do you know about the Post Office clerk who was arrested?'

'Knight? That he was probably innocent of any wrongdoing. He had a reputation for honesty, although I am less sure about his crony Gardner.'

'Then why were the charges brought against him?'

Dorislaus considered for a moment, then beckoned the coffee-house owner over.

'I knew Knight well,' said Young, sitting down and treating himself to a spoonful of sugar. 'He would never

163

have defrauded the Post Office. Those accusations are lies.'

'Did he often come here?' asked Chaloner.

'No – he was a Royalist. I knew him through church. Incidentally, he would never have hanged himself either, no matter how frightened he was. I believe he was murdered, and if I find out who did it, I shall put a noose around *his* neck.'

'I have a feeling Tom intends to do the same,' said Dorislaus. 'What can you tell him to help?'

'That he should speak to Jeremiah Copping, who knows more than most clerks about Post Office affairs. And if he declines to talk, track down a fellow named Bankes, who wrote Knight messages, demanding information. Knight showed them to me: they terrified him.'

'What did these letters say, exactly?' Now Chaloner had two reasons to interview Copping: to ask about the Post Office on Young's recommendation, and the musician on Wiseman's.

'That Bankes would pay handsomely for any intelligence that Knight could provide. They were not threatening exactly, but I would not have liked to receive them. Incidentally, Copping knows Oxenbridge, too. Have you ever seen him? A more sinister fellow does not exist.'

'But he and Copping are friends?'

'Oxenbridge does not have friends,' averred Young. 'No more than the devil does. However, like Satan, evil follows Oxenbridge, and you could do worse than find out what he knows about this shameful conspiracy against Knight.'

* * *

164

Chaloner left the Antwerp feeling he had squandered the best part of a day by hiding from Harper, and a glance at the sky told him it was far too late to beg interviews in Newgate or the Tower. He could, however, call on Copping and enquire after Bankes, Oxenbridge and the musician.

First, though, he had to make an appearance at church. A note was made of parishioners who failed to attend their Sunday devotions, and he did not want to be branded a nonconformist. He took a hackney to St Margaret's, where he exchanged pleasantries with the sexton until he was sure his name had been written in the register, then escaped before evensong began. He disliked his parish church, perhaps because he had been married in it, amid a violent thunderstorm that many guests claimed was a bad omen. He was beginning to wonder whether they might have been right.

Outside, he was about to set off for Cheapside when he saw Roger Palmer. The nobleman's shoulders were slumped, and he looked unhappy.

'White Hall is a pit of ignorance,' he said bitterly. 'We were discussing the King's next soirée, at which guests must dress as Romans, and I asked whether everyone would converse in Latin. Chiffinch and his cronies immediately started calling me a Pope-lover. But Romans *did* speak Latin, and I was only trying to enter the spirit of the thing.'

'Will you go?' Chaloner wondered whether Hannah was right and that the bird-killers would use it as an opportunity to claim another avian victim.

'Certainly not,' replied Palmer indignantly. 'I detest White Hall and spend as little time there as possible. Oh, how I long for Venice, to be among men of culture and learning!'

'Will you return there after our war with the Dutch?'

'No, I have been invited to be the British ambassador in the Vatican, a post that appeals to me greatly. I do not suppose you are free this evening, are you? I should like to assemble a few friends for music, but I find myself sadly short of suitable acquaintances.'

Chaloner knew he should refuse. Hobnobbing with a man shunned by Court was hardly wise, and he had a lot to do. But he had not played his viol in an age, and he liked Palmer. He nodded.

'Come in an hour,' said Palmer, smiling. 'I live by All Hallows the Great on Thames Street.'

As there was not much he could usefully do in an hour, Chaloner abandoned his enquiries about the Post Office, and walked to St James's Park instead. The short winter day was almost over, but Eliot was there, fussing lovingly around his bananas.

'I like it here,' the gardener said. There was a pipe clamped between his teeth, and he was the picture of ease and contentment. 'But I prefer the Inner Temple. Have you seen my hellebores?'

Chaloner shook his head, and was sorry at the man's obvious disappointment.

'You must come when they are in bloom. You will not be sorry, I assure you.'

Chaloner decided to take Hannah. Or would she decline to go? Inspecting flowers was not her idea of a good time. It was not his either, but at least he was prepared to be open-minded about it.

'I suppose you are here for the swan,' Eliot went on. 'I found it this morning. Storey was distraught, of course, and wept so bitterly that I had to take him home.

166

Surgeon Wiseman prescribed a soporific, although it will do scant good – the bird will still be dead tomorrow.'

Chaloner stared at him. 'Damn! I thought there would not be another attack until Tuesday.'

'Tuesday? Why then?'

'Because that is when there will be a noisy soirée.' Chaloner was dismayed. He had been grateful for Hannah's suggestion, but now he saw he was wrong to have trusted it.

'There was a rowdy occasion last night,' said Eliot disapprovingly. 'Lady Castlemaine decided to skate on the Canal by lamplight, and dozens of courtiers came to watch, trampling over the flower beds and jostling the shrubs. They were worse than cattle.'

'So how was the swan killed, if so many people were milling about?'

Eliot pointed. 'The courtiers retired to that pavilion over there for hot wine, and spent several hours cavorting. A herd of elephants could have been poisoned and they would not have noticed.'

He led the way to a potting shed, where it did not take long to ascertain that the bird had been poisoned. Chaloner stared at it unhappily, sorry to see such a magnificent creature limp and motley in death. He borrowed a pair of gloves and prised open its beak to peer down its throat. In it was more blood, along with a mass of what looked to be bread. He walked to the Canal, Eliot trailing at his heels. Near a few white feathers, where the swan had died, were some soggy crusts. He picked them up on the blade of his knife and sniffed them cautiously. He could only smell bread.

'No!' exclaimed Eliot, backing away suddenly as he understood their significance. 'Surely the toxin was forced down their throats? No one would have used bread. It would be despicable – an unforgiveable breach of trust.'

'The culprits *are* despicable,' said Chaloner quietly. 'And using doctored bread would have been a lot safer for them. Storey told me that his swans are not easy to handle.'

Eliot's face was white. 'But this means that I *saw* the crime – with my own eyes. And I let it happen! Last night, after the Lady had finished skating, three fellows lingered here, and I saw one tossing crumbs . . . I thought he was being nice. It is winter, and food is scarce for birds . . .'

'You could not have stopped them,' said Chaloner, to ease his mounting distress. 'And an attempt may have seen you dead, too. Can you describe them?'

'No!' The word came out as an anguished cry. 'They were too far away, and it was dark. They wore gloves, though, because I recall thinking that the greasy bread would stain them. So Storey was right – the culprits *are* courtiers or men of rank. They must be – no one else was here.'

Chaloner was disturbed. Did it mean Storey's list of suspects should be taken seriously after all? That Gery, Morland, O'Neill, Oxenbridge, Wood and Harper should be interviewed? His heart sank. None would be easy to question.

He gathered up the remaining crusts, using his knife to spear them. He was careful to collect the lot, partly so he could provide Wiseman with a decent sample when he asked him to analyse them, but mostly to protect the other birds. Eliot gave him an old plant-pot to carry them in.

'Damn these villains!' the gardener spat angrily. 'Damn them to hell!'

* * *

It was dark when Chaloner arrived at Palmer's house, having stopped en route to deposit the pot and its deadly contents at Wiseman's home. The surgeon had been out, so Chaloner had left a note explaining what he wanted. With luck, the poison would be rare – perhaps even some unusual Italian concoction like Palmer had suggested – and whoever had bought it could be traced. And Chaloner needed some good fortune, given that Leak had proved an effective dead end.

Palmer's home was a modest affair, sandwiched between All Hallows the Great and All Hallows the Less. As both had churchyards, the house had leafy outlooks on both sides, albeit ones that involved a lot of grave-stones. Chaloner knocked on the door and was admitted to a pleasant parlour with a blazing fire and tastefully understated décor. Most of the paintings on the walls were of Venice, all catching that city's unusual light, bustle and colour.

Palmer had been telling the truth when he had claimed to have few 'suitable acquaintances' in London, because there were only two other guests. One was le Notre and the other was Bishop, uglier close up than when Chaloner had seen him across Post House Yard after the explosion. The ex-Postmaster carried his lapdog, and the thing reeked so badly that Chaloner could smell it from the door. Le Notre's eyebrows went up when he saw Chaloner.

'You do appear in some unexpected places! I thought your wife was the Catholic, not you.'

'This is not a religious gathering,' chided Palmer. 'Just one for men who love the viol. Indeed, we shall talk of nothing but music tonight – but in English. Not all my guests speak French.'

169

He gestured towards Bishop, who had been listening blankly to the exchange. Le Notre homed in on him, mischief gleaming in his eyes, and Chaloner saw he had a spiteful sense of humour.

'You must be an aristocrat,' he said in his thickly accented English. 'They always have a dog to hand. Like Prince Rupert, and the yapping article that followed him into battle during the wars.'

'I am nothing,' declared Bishop gloomily. 'Not any more.'

'Oh, fie, Bishop,' said Palmer kindly. 'You have done very well for yourself.'

'But I was Postmaster General until I was accused of corruption. The allegations were entirely false, of course. O'Neill' – Bishop all but spat the name – 'wanted the job for himself. However, it is he who is corrupt. The Post Office is filthy with abuses now.'

Chaloner's recent visit suggested that Bishop was right. 'How do you know?' he asked, wondering whether the man might have heard rumours about what was unfolding there.

'Because O'Neill's profit margins are suspiciously high. He dismissed all the best clerks – men like Dorislaus and Ibson, who knew what they were doing – but their replacements are incompetent, so the place should be losing money, not making it.'

'But you will go down in posterity as having devised the Bishop-Mark,' said Palmer consolingly. 'And the public loves you for it.'

'It has certainly been a thorn in O'Neill's side,' said Bishop with a sudden smile that softened his features and made him seem younger and kinder. 'It forces him to deliver at least some of the letters on time. Of course, I should not be surprised if he changes the dates.'

Chaloner said nothing.

'I cannot imagine that such an invention endeared you to the intelligence services, though,' said le Notre, wide-eyed. 'It will give them less time to sift, opening whatever catches their fancy.'

'Do they still do that?' asked Palmer, surprised. 'I know it was managed with ruthless efficiency during the Commonwealth, but I rather hoped we Royalists were above it.'

'No regime is above it,' replied le Notre, while Chaloner struggled not to gape at the naivety of the remark. 'Not even France. However, you may be right to voice reservations about O'Neill, Monsieur Bishop, because there are rumours of a plot unfolding there.'

'You are very well informed for a foreigner,' said Bishop with a frown. Chaloner was thinking much the same. 'But you are right, as it happens. Unfortunately, none of my old clerks will tell me what is happening, and a fellow named Harper has been hired to prevent gossip. Not even Spymaster Williamson has managed to break through their conspiracy of silence.'

'Would you like to be Postmaster again?' asked le Notre. 'If anything happens to O'Neill?'

Bishop considered the question carefully. 'No,' he said eventually. 'I enjoyed it at the time, but O'Neill has soured it for me now. Besides, nothing will happen to him. He will cling to that job as long as there is breath in his body. He is too greedy to do otherwise.'

Le Notre turned suddenly to Chaloner. 'You have cut your thumb. How did that happen?'

Chaloner struggled to keep the astonishment from his

face. Why should le Notre have noticed such an insignificant scratch? Did he know about the scuffle with
Harper? He forced a smile.

'St Margaret's Church is full of splinters.'

Le Notre's expression was impossible to read. 'I hope
it will not affect your playing tonight.'

It was not long before there were voices in the hall, and
Chaloner was startled when the Major was shown in.
Bishop leapt to his feet and greeted his old friend with
open delight, the dog yapping in his arms. Le Notre
bowed with guarded politeness when he was introduced,
and Chaloner saw a calculating glint in his eyes,
although he could not begin to grasp what it meant.
The Major gave a wan smile when Palmer presented
him to Chaloner.

'We met last Thursday,' he said. His face was the
unhealthy grey-white of the long-term prisoner, and his
eyes were bloodshot. 'You kindly shared your hackney
carriage when I was being taken from the Tower to White
Hall.'

'You have won your freedom?' Chaloner was amazed
that it had happened so fast. In his experience, the wheels
of justice turned rather more slowly.

'No,' replied the Major tiredly. 'Not yet, at least.'

'Then I am astonished that you are permitted to
wander,' said le Notre. 'We do not let inmates of the
Bastille amble where they please. Once they are in, there
they stay.'

'I do not amble where I please,' said the Major bitterly.
'My two Yeomen Wardens are in the hall outside, and I
must be back by ten o'clock. This excursion is just a
reward for my help so far.'

'Your help?' asked le Notre, tilting his head to one side. 'With what?'

'Nothing important.' In a clumsy attempt to change the subject, the Major looked at the table on which refreshments had been laid. 'Is that an eel pie? I have not seen one of those in years.'

Palmer indicated that he was to help himself. 'But the news is good, I hear,' he said amiably. 'You may soon be released.'

'And not before time,' declared Bishop warmly. 'His incarceration is illegal, immoral and all O'Neill's fault – he told terrible lies about the Major, just because he is my friend.'

'It does not matter,' said the Major listlessly. 'But promises have been made, and I hope they will be kept. I have certainly fulfilled my end of the bargain – at great personal risk, I might add. It is dangerous being taken to White Hall when there are rumours of assassins at large.'

'What will you do when you are released?' asked Bishop. 'Produce pamphlets outlining the wicked injustices you have endured?'

The Major smiled thinly again. 'No, I shall go home to Norfolk, and spend my time writing tracts that urge peaceful solutions to our country's problems.'

'I do not blame you for wanting to escape London,' sighed Palmer. 'When this war with the Dutch is over, I shall take up my new appointment in Rome, and I will never return here either.'

'Both my dear friends will leave?' cried Bishop in dismay. 'But what shall I do without you?'

'You will manage,' said Palmer, with an indulgent grin. 'Just as you have done since the Major was thrown in the Tower and I went to Venice. And there are always letters.'

'But that means using the Post Office,' said Bishop, following the Major to the table. The dog, scenting food, began to bark, an irritating yip that hurt the ears. 'And I would sooner die. Incidentally, did you hear about Knight? He was an honest man, and unlikely to have been guilty of corruption. O'Neill is probably behind *those* false charges, too.'

'Speaking of the Post Office, that explosion was a terrible business,' said le Notre. Chaloner was glad the subject had been raised; it would spare him a jaunt to the Tower.

'I imagine O'Neill arranged it,' said Bishop immediately. 'To win sympathy, so that folk will not complain about his ineptitude as Postmaster.'

'It is certainly possible,' said the Major, nodding slowly. 'He is not a very nice man.'

'Do you have any other suspects?' asked Chaloner hopefully.

'I am afraid not,' came the disappointing reply. 'Although I hope we never see its like again. I was with Clarendon in White Hall when it happened. Five dead, poor souls. My family motto is *nil admirari*, but I was amazed by that, and not pleasantly so either.'

'I was so close that I was blown off my feet,' added Palmer. His expression was bleak; the experience continued to haunt him. 'I would have been killed if someone had not yelled a warning.'

Bishop kissed his dog's head. '*She* knew something was amiss, because she started to whine. It encouraged me to leave, and so I was on Dowgate Hill when the cart went up. I returned when the smoke had cleared, though, to inspect the aftermath.'

'I was visiting my friend Storey,' said le Notre. 'He lives next door.'

'Were you?' asked Chaloner innocently. 'He told me he was out.'

'Did I say Storey?' Le Notre gave a careless wave of his hand. 'You must forgive my poor English. I meant to say Wood. He was not in either, but his footman gave me permission to wait in his parlour. I heard the bang, although I did not see the explosion.'

Chaloner nodded, but le Notre's 'poor' English did not explain why he should have used the wrong name. There was something oddly disturbing about the Frenchman, and Chaloner could not help but wonder what was his real purpose in London.

Many people were prepared to put aside personal, political and religious differences for the sake of music. Chaloner was one of them, and although he thought Bishop a buffoon and he was deeply suspicious of le Notre, he forgot their shortcomings when Palmer produced a chest of viols. The instruments had been made in Milan, so the quality of the craftsmanship was exquisite.

They played airs by Rognoni and Ferrabosco, because Palmer had acquired a taste for them while in Venice. He was an excellent violist, while le Notre bowed with a careless panache that matched his character. The Major was technically sound, but his performance was mechanical and devoid of passion; Chaloner suspected he would be a better musician if he was a happier man. Bishop was by far the weakest of the quintet, at least in part because he allowed his dog to distract him. Chaloner was on the verge of running the thing through when

Palmer finally suggested that Bishop might like to listen for a while.

The music immediately improved, and Chaloner soon became lost in it. Thus he was startled when the Major set down his bow, and said he should return to the Tower. It was well past nine, and he was bound by his curfew. Chaloner could not believe the time had passed so quickly.

'When did you say your book will be published?' le Notre asked Palmer as they repacked the instruments in their boxes. 'Rational and sensible though it is sure to be, it will still set London alight, and I must remember to stay in that day.'

'I aim to calm troubled waters, not stir them up,' objected Palmer in alarm.

'Of course you do,' said le Notre. 'However, it will take more than a few pages to soothe London's apprentices. They gather to mutter on every street corner these days. Perhaps that is why the comet is here – to warn us of looming riots and mayhem.'

'Lord!' muttered Bishop, hugging his dog so fiercely that it yelped. 'I hope you are wrong.'

'Will your treatise address the fact that the King should not have the wherewithal to dispense with Lent?' asked le Notre, and suddenly there was no humour in his eyes and his French accent was considerably less marked.

'Lord, is that the time?' blurted Palmer. The King might have made a cuckold of him, but he was still unwilling to indulge in treasonous talk, even with friends. 'We must see you away, Major, or you will be late. I shall summon your yeomen.' He virtually ran from the room.

'How do you know Palmer?' asked Chaloner, after the nobleman had gone. Le Notre he could understand

– they would have met at Court – but Bishop and the Major were unusual acquaintances.

'Through a shared love of fine art,' replied Bishop. 'And good music.'

'And I met him when we conspired to assassinate Cromwell and he provided me with a handgun,' added the Major. 'Unfortunately, Spymaster Thurloe arrested me before I could use it.'

'Is there a political leader you have *not* taken against, Major?' asked le Notre. 'You opposed the old King so fiercely that you are rumoured to be his executioner; you plotted to kill Cromwell; and now you are in the Tower for annoying the current regime. Does no one please you?'

'Not really,' replied the Major with quiet dignity. 'They are all as bad as each other.'

Chaloner was inclined to agree. Then Bishop's dog made a bid for escape, forcing its loving owner to scamper after it, and le Notre went to advise him on how best to catch it. Chaloner used the opportunity to corner the Major alone.

'I was hoping we would meet,' he said in a low voice. 'Clarendon wants to know whether you have any new information about the Post Office.'

The Major regarded him uneasily. 'If I did, I should tell him myself. Besides, Gery is in charge of that investigation, not you, and I took an oath not to discuss the matter with anyone else. Gery terrifies me, and I dare not risk his displeasure by speaking out of turn.'

Chaloner proceeded with his questions anyway. 'Why did the postal clerks in the Foreign Office decide to talk to you, specifically?'

'They do not *talk* to me,' replied the Major, although he was obviously uneasy discussing the matter. 'They write. And they confide because they trust me to handle the information in a way that will not endanger them.'

Chaloner regarded him thoughtfully. 'Your freedom depends on a successful outcome to the Post Office business, but Gery is not up to the task. You may never have what you want, regardless of the risks you are taking with your own life and those of your friends.'

The Major closed his eyes despairingly. 'Do you think I do not know that? Gery and Clarendon decline to listen to all I tell them, and only take note of the parts that catch their interest. I am horribly afraid that they are concentrating on a minor matter when a bigger one may be brewing.'

'What bigger one?'

'I cannot say.' The Major's face was white. 'I told you: they made me promise that any information I gleaned would be shared only with them.'

'I am in the Earl's household,' argued Chaloner. 'I am one of them.'

'You are not! You are regarded with just as much wary hostility as I am – I have heard Gery rail about your Parliamentarian past.' The Major's voice was bitter. 'It is all that stupid Wood's fault. He could have passed my message to anyone, so why did he have to pick Clarendon? I never wanted to be in this vile position.'

'Not even if it means a chance of freedom?'

The Major managed a smile. 'That is the only thing that keeps me sane. But please to do not ask me any more. I dare not give Clarendon a reason to be angry with me, because he will use it as an excuse to renege on our agreement. You see, by setting me free, he is essentially acknowledging that my imprisonment is illegal, and he hates admitting that he is wrong.'

178

Bishop had caught his dog, and Chaloner could hear Palmer returning with the yeomen. There was not much time left. 'You are a patriotic man – you must be, or you would not have brought the matter to the attention of the authorities in the first place – so surely you can see that preventing trouble is more important than some vow you were forced to take? Or even than your freedom?'

The Major looked wretched. 'I know, and I am sorry. But I will die if I do not leave the Tower soon. I do not expect you to understand.'

Chaloner did understand, and sympathised more than the Major would ever know. He started to ask more, but the guards had arrived, and the Major took the opportunity to scurry away. His hand was on the door knob when there was an explosion of smashing glass.

Chapter 6

Chaloner dived to the floor, his first thought that another gunpowder-loaded cart had ignited. But there was no ear-shattering blast, and when a second crash followed the first he realised that the sound came from stones being lobbed through the windows from the street outside.

'What is it?' shrieked Bishop, shielding his dog with his arms. It was barking wildly.

'It must be a mob,' replied le Notre. He had taken refuge behind a cabinet, and did not seem as alarmed as Chaloner thought he should be. 'Or apprentices. But why pick on this house?'

'Because I am Catholic,' explained Palmer. He swallowed hard. 'Or because my wife is . . .'

Chaloner leapt to his feet and darted through the house to the back, where he found a door that led to one of the churchyards. It did not take him many moments to creep around to Thames Street, where he saw that a crowd had indeed gathered to hurl rocks at Palmer's house. It was too dark to see what they were wearing, so he could not tell whether they were apprentices or just louts intent on mischief. He crept forward, past All Hallows the Great, then stopped in surprise.

A man was watching the attack from the safety of the church porch, his unnaturally white face gleaming eerily in the dark. It was Oxenbridge. He started to turn when he sensed someone behind him, so Chaloner leapt forward and grabbed him by the throat, pushing him back against the wall. There was enough light from Palmer's house to illuminate the man's button-black eyes, and Chaloner was reminded yet again of his sister's unsettling doll.

'What are you—' he began, but Oxenbridge shoved him away with surprising strength, and suddenly there was a sword in his hand. Chaloner drew his own, then struggled to fend off the furious attack that followed.

Chaloner was not a fanciful man, but he was unsettled by Oxenbridge's peculiar visage, and his disquiet hindered him in the ensuing struggle. By the time he had forced it to the back of his mind, the sound of clashing steel had alerted the stone-throwers. Oxenbridge's lipless mouth curved into a grin when three blade-wielding men drove Chaloner into a corner, where they kept him pinned down so that Oxenbridge could strike what would certainly be a fatal blow.

'Stop!'

The stentorian cry echoed along Thames Street, and Chaloner saw Palmer running towards them, rapier in hand. The Major, his yeomen, Bishop, the lapdog and large bevy of servants were at his heels, although there was no sign of le Notre. Oxenbridge issued a hiss of frustration when his men melted away into the dark churchyard. He followed, although not before he had fixed Chaloner with a look that made the hair stand up on the back of the spy's neck.

181

Chaloner pulled himself together. Why was he allowing himself to be intimidated? Oxenbridge was just a man. He started to run after him, but someone grabbed his arm. It was Palmer.

'No,' the nobleman said softly. 'You do not want to antagonise him.'

'But he launched an attack on your house. He may do it again if—'

'I shall report the incident to the proper authorities, and they can deal with it,' said Palmer in the same quietly reasonable voice. 'It is the sensible thing to do.'

'There was a note attached to one of the stones,' said the Major unsteadily. He gave a wan smile. 'It seems the assault on your hapless glass was my fault.'

The message, written in bold black letters that could be made out even in the gloom, carried a grim warning. It read, *The Major will die.*

The encounter with Oxenbridge had unnerved Chaloner, and he did not feel like going home to Tothill Street, despite the fact that Hannah's absence meant he could play his viol again. Instead, he walked to his rooms at Long Acre, which were closer – no mean consideration, given the plummeting temperatures.

Long Acre had once been fashionable, home to men such as Oliver Cromwell and John Pym, but it had turned seedy after the Restoration, and was now known for its taverns, brothels and an astonishing number of coach-makers. It was always busy, even at night, which suited Chaloner, as it meant he could blend in with the crowds, although it was often noisy and uninterrupted sleep was never guaranteed.

The house in which he rented rooms was four storeys

high, and he had the attic. The old Parliamentarian named Stokes lodged on the floor below, and Chaloner glanced up at his window as he entered the building. A lamp burned as usual; Stokes had reached the age where sleep was elusive, and he often read well into the night.

Chaloner climbed the stairs, then wished he had gone to Tothill Street when he unlocked the door to find ice on the inside of the windows. He went to bed wrapped in blankets that were stiff with frost, but woke at midnight when a group of apprentices began bawling revolutionary songs in the tavern opposite. They were ones his company had sung during the wars, and the memories they evoked were mixed – camaraderie and pride, but also fear, grief and helplessness.

A rival band attempted to silence them, and a fight ensued. Chaloner went to the window when it spilled out into the road, and saw a pitched battle in progress, knives and sticks flashing in the dim light cast through the tavern door. Then he spotted a man with a faded blue hat and red cloak. It was the musician, lurking in a doorway as he watched the mêlée with unconcealed delight. Clad only in breeches and shirt, and with no weapons whatsoever, Chaloner charged down the stairs.

Unfortunately, the musician detected something amiss when a half-dressed man began to dodge through the mass of cudgels and blades towards him. He whipped around and disappeared down an alley. It took Chaloner several minutes to reach it, by which point his quarry was long gone. He searched for a while, but it was too dark, and he was not equipped for a lengthy chase.

He returned to Long Acre to find the brawl had escalated. He was punched once and kicked twice before he reached his door, only to discover that two drunks had

183

taken refuge there. He shoved past, recognising them as patrons of the Antwerp Coffee House – they had been there the previous day when he had visited it with Dorislaus. He closed the door behind him, but their voices were loud and he could not help but hear what they were saying.

'This would not have happened in Cromwell's day,' one was declaring. 'He knew how to keep order. Not like this licentious King.'

'Mr Bankes will be keen to read an eye-witness account, though,' slurred the other. 'I shall write him one and leave it at the Antwerp. If he likes it, he will send me some money.'

'Why would he be interested in a spat between two packs of hotheads?' asked the other. 'I thought he only wanted information about the Post Office.'

'He appreciates stories about any aspect of London.'

'You should be careful. We none of us know him, and he might transpire to be a Royalist. You do not want to be helping one of them.'

'No, he will be a Roundhead, like us,' predicted the other, 'waiting for the revolution that will oust this corrupt regime. He might even be John Fry himself, come to lead us to victory. He sent me sixpence for my account of that villain Harper, you know.'

'Harper? You do not want to tell tales about him, man! He might find out.'

'I do not care. He is a venomous devil, and I do not want him in my city.'

The fighting eased at that point, and they took the opportunity to stagger away. His mind full of questions, Chaloner climbed the stairs to his attic. Who *was* Bankes, and why was he so intent on gathering information?

184

Could he be John Fry? And was Harper really as dangerous as the two drunks seemed to think?

He turned his thoughts to the musician. The riot was the second violent incident at which he had been present. Was it coincidence, or had *he* played the revolutionary songs that had caused the skirmish? And had he run away because he had something to hide, or because most itinerants were wary of people who looked at them too hard?

Chaloner went back to bed, and woke as dawn revealed a cold, dismal world of frost and clouds. A familiar tapping on the roof told him that the red kites had assembled there, ready to swoop down on any carrion or rotting meat in the street below. These magnificent scavengers were a common sight in London, and he had often thought that they did more to keep the streets clean than the men who were paid to collect rubbish.

When he saw he would have to break through a thick plate of ice to draw water from the barrel in the hall, Chaloner dispensed with washing and shaving. He donned a white shirt that was damply chill against his bare skin, and the black breeches and dark-grey long-coat he had worn the night before. He replaced the dagger he had lobbed in the General Letter Office the previous day, choosing one that was small enough to slip up his sleeve without being obvious, and then was ready to face whatever the day might bring. He met Stokes as he was walking down the stairs.

'Did that fracas keep you awake last night?' the veteran asked. 'It was the printers' apprentices, full of hubris because they threw stones at the Castlemaine coach yesterday. It was empty, so no one was harmed, although I imagine the horses had a fright, poor creatures.'

185

Chaloner wondered whether Oxenbridge had put them up to it, and had arranged for rocks to be hurled at Palmer's windows when the first assault had failed.

'I detest Castlemaine,' Stokes went on. 'He turns a blind eye while his whore-wife makes a cuckold of him, and he will soon publish a tract telling us that we have nothing to fear from Catholics – to lull us into feeling safe before they slit our throats as we sleep.'

'When you read it, you will see that is not the case,' said Chaloner, feeling obliged to defend the man whose hospitality he had enjoyed the night before.

Stokes's eyes widened in surprise. 'I shall not read it, and I recommend you do not either. It will be seditious, and if you are caught with a copy . . . well, suffice to say that such charges are easily made, but not so easily disproved. And I do not want to visit Newgate to hear your viol.'

'I doubt—'

'London has a dangerous feel at the moment,' Stokes interrupted severely. 'And I urge you to stay away from any whiff of treachery – which includes poring over Catholic pamphlets.'

Chaloner was tempted to say he would pore over what he liked, but Stokes was well-intentioned, and he did not want an argument. He gave a noncommittal nod.

'Come with me to Will's Coffee House,' the veteran said, clapping a friendly arm around his shoulders. 'Our fractured night means we could both do with a medicinal draught.'

Will's had been Chaloner's favourite coffee house before he had grown to regard the Rainbow with such affection. However, when he entered its pleasantly smoky interior, which smelled of roasted beans, rather than burned ones, and where the tobacco used by the patrons seemed sweeter and less pungent than that favoured by Farr's clients, he wondered why he had been seduced away.

While Stokes responded to Will's 'What news?' with an account of the brawl, Chaloner picked up a copy of *The Intelligencer*, fresh from the printing presses that morning, and sat down to read it. He was bemused to learn that the government's idea of headline news was that the wind was from the east in Deal. He was about to toss it away in disgust when a notice caught his eye:

Whereas many frauds and abuses have been committed by intercepting letters, and Bills of Exchange; and upon inquiry, one *Knight* (now a prisoner in *Newgate*) is detected to have had a hand therein. And whereas one *Lewis Gardner* lately imployed in the Letter Office, being of known intimacy with the said *Knight*, and since his seizure absenting himself, is more than suspected to have been a principal in the business. Be it known that the said Gardner is of middle stature, bushy hair'd, of a yellowish flaxen, round-faced, well-complexioned, and aged betwixt 20 and 30. Whosoever shall apprehend him shall have 50*l* from Mr Joseph Williamson for his peyns.

Chaloner stared at it in astonishment. Fifty pounds was a colossal sum, so why was the Spymaster willing to pay so much? Or was the prize merely indicative of the seriousness with which the government viewed such charges? Regardless, it was recklessly generous, and

187

Williamson would be inundated with information, most of it bogus, from people determined to have the money. It would take him an age to sort the genuine clues from the false ones.

He glanced up when Stokes approached, a companion in tow. The newcomer was another elderly ex-military man, with baggy grey eyes that looked as though they had seen too much. Like Stokes, he carried himself ramrod straight, and sported a large, old-fashioned moustache.

'This is James Cliffe,' said Stokes. 'A comrade from Naseby.'

'Where we fought bravely,' said Cliffe sourly. 'Only to see our country run by men who have one aim in life: to debauch themselves into oblivion, and to get rich without doing any work.'

That sounded like two aims to Chaloner, but he stopped himself from saying so, suspecting that Cliffe was not the kind of man to appreciate levity when he was griping.

'White Hall is a den of iniquity,' agreed Stokes. 'The Court sleeps all day, and only stirs itself in the afternoons when there are parties to attend.'

'It is Lord Castlemaine's fault,' said Cliffe venomously. 'If he kept his wanton wife in order, she would not be free to bewitch the King and distract him from affairs of state. I did not endure having three toes shot off at Naseby to see my country run by reprobates. It is a vile state of affairs.'

Chaloner stood abruptly. It was hardly sensible to engage in seditious talk in public places.

'Sit down, man,' ordered Stokes irritably. 'You know we speak the truth. And we are not alone in our convictions.

All London is appalled by the way the Court comports itself.'

'Palmer should do the decent thing and take her off to Rome with him,' Cliffe railed on. 'Once her hold over the King is broken, all will be well again. His Majesty will see the sorry state of his realm, and will take steps to remedy the matter.'

Chaloner had started to aim for the door, but Cliffe's remarks made him stop and gape his disbelief. He had heard some naive opinions in his time, but this one outranked the others by a considerable margin.

'He is right.' Stokes nodded earnestly. 'She is ruthlessly greedy, and her gambling debts alone are costing more than the Dutch war. She lost ten thousand pounds in a single night, a bill the King paid with public monies. Palmer should rein her in before she bankrupts the entire country.'

'Oh, damnation!' exclaimed Cliffe, as the door opened and a man strolled in. 'It is that horrible Spymaster again. I am not staying if he is here.'

He left with such haste that Williamson's eyes narrowed. Other patrons glanced up to see what had agitated Cliffe, and when they spotted the Spymaster, there was a general race for the door that had the owner gaping his dismay and Williamson's expression hardening further still.

'The wretched man has taken to coming here of late,' explained Stokes to Chaloner, pulling his hat low over his eyes as he prepared to follow. 'But I wish he would find somewhere else – it is a nuisance having to dash off every time he appears.'

Chaloner sat down with a sigh, feeling that to join the exodus would arouse Williamson's suspicions, and he had enough to worry about without a spymaster thinking he was up to no good.

189

Pulling *The Intelligencer* towards him, he ordered more coffee. One serving was more than sufficient to set his heart racing, but it would have looked peculiar to sit with an empty dish. And vile though coffee was, it was more palatable than tea, which tasted of dead vegetation, while chocolate was just plain nasty with its bitter flavour and oily texture.

He scowled when Williamson came to perch next to him – no one liked to be seen fraternising with a man who was universally hated, feared and distrusted, and he resented the presumption of familiarity. The fact that he was the only customer left, and it was considered poor etiquette to sit alone in coffee houses, was beside the point.

'You are up early,' said Williamson, brushing a few snowflakes from his coat. 'And it is a bitterly cold morning, when most men would prefer to be in bed with their wives. I know I would rather be with mine. Marriage is a wonderful institution.'

He was newly wed to a woman he loved, but Chaloner did not want to discuss matrimonial bliss, acutely aware that his own situation was rather less satisfactory.

'It will never catch on,' he said. The Spymaster regarded him askance, and Chaloner gestured to the mixture in his dish. 'Coffee. We drink it because it is fashionable, not because it is pleasant, and the moment something better comes along, we shall abandon it.'

'I beg to differ. It has become a necessity to most of us, although I am not so sure about coffee *houses*. They are full of seditious chatter, and I would suppress the lot of them if I could. Especially the Antwerp. And its neighbour the Crown, come to that.'

190

'The Crown is a tavern, not a coffee house. Besides, it is popular with Royalists.'

'Yes,' said Williamson grimly. 'But the fanatical kind, who want to kill every man, woman and child who sided with Parliament. What were you discussing just now, by the way? Your companions raced away as though they were on fire when they saw me.'

'You do have that effect on people.'

Williamson regarded him coolly. 'Cliffe and Stokes were officers in Cromwell's army, so they are persons of interest to me. Were they advocating a return to republicanism?'

'Actually, they were bemoaning the fact that Lady Castlemaine is transpiring to be more expensive than war with the Dutch.'

'It is not true,' said Williamson. Then he grimaced. 'But she is doing her best to remedy the matter. She lost another five hundred pounds at cards last night, and her royal bastards are costing a fortune in earldoms and estates. Not to mention her appetite for clothes, jewellery, fine art . . .'

'Speaking of money, was it wise to offer such a large reward for Gardner's arrest?'

Williamson's jaw tightened. 'That was Clarendon's idea. I advised him against it – said we would be swamped with misleading information from unsavoury individuals determined to have the cash – but he is determined to see Gardner in custody. To answer for his crimes.'

'What crimes?' Chaloner was uneasy. Why had the Earl insisted on such a foolish measure?

'Allowing friends and relatives to send letters free of charge.'

Chaloner's disquiet intensified. 'For fifty pounds, I

could send three thousand letters to Dover and two thousand to Bristol. The reward is vastly in excess of the offence.'

Williamson frowned. 'I had not done the arithmetic, but you are right. Does this mean your Earl has learned more about the Post Office than he is telling me?'

Chaloner wished he knew. 'Perhaps he suspects Gardner of setting Thursday's blast. That would explain the huge reward. I did not see him there, but my memory of the whole event is hazy.'

Williamson's expression was bleak. 'I cannot tell you how difficult it is to acquire information about the place. None of O'Neill's clerks will talk to me, and I have used every trick in the book – bribes, blackmail, flattery. My men have even whisked them down dark alleys and put knives to their throats, but they either claim to know nothing or Harper rescues them before they can speak.'

'Surely you have spies among them? You told me you did the other day.'

'Of course I do, but they are worse than useless.' Williamson sounded disgusted and dispirited in equal measure. 'And *I* should be Postmaster anyway. It goes hand in hand with running the intelligence services, and not having control of the mail is a serious hindrance.'

Chaloner imagined it was: Thurloe had been given the Post Office when *he* had been Spymaster, and it was partly why he had been so very good at his job.

'What about Gery? Has he learned anything that might help you?'

Williamson gave a short bark of laughter. 'Him? I doubt it. And even if he did, he would not understand its significance. I admire his persistence, though – he refuses to be discouraged by blank stares and polite refusals, and even declines to be daunted by Harper. He spends a lot of time there.'

Chaloner's thoughts whirled. Was it just tenacity that saw Gery persevering where Williamson had conceded defeat, or did he have another reason for loitering?

'Do you know Clement Oxenbridge?' he asked, changing the subject abruptly.

A pained expression crossed Williamson's face. 'Yes, in that we have exchanged words on several occasions. And no, in that I can tell you nothing about him. I have set my best agents to learn where he lives and how he makes his living, but they have failed. Fatally, in two cases.'

'Can you prove he killed them?'

'No, or I would arrest him – which I would love to do, believe me. There is something unpleasantly eerie about that man, and when he appeared at a soirée that my wife and I were attending the other day, I took her home. I did not want her in the same room as him.'

It was a bad sign when even the Spymaster was intimidated, thought Chaloner.

Most of that day was an exercise in futility. Chaloner arrived at Newgate to learn it was still closed, because the cleaning was taking longer than expected. He was not disappointed to be spared the ordeal of stepping inside, although he knew he was only postponing the inevitable. He went to a tavern for wine to quell his roiling stomach, and asked questions about John Fry and Oxenbridge when several apprentices there claimed to know them. Unfortunately, it took some time to discover that they had never met them, and the brag was a lie intended to impress their fellows.

Next he managed to corner Harper in a Cheapside tavern, but his efforts to engage him in conversation over a pie and ale were repelled, and he was obliged to beat a hasty retreat when Lamb arrived. He went to the Post Office afterwards, to see if *he* could persuade a clerk to talk, and was making headway with Rea – Leak's friend with the taupe eyes – when Gery, Morland and Freer arrived. Gery stopped dead in his tracks when he saw Chaloner, and shook his head in disbelief.

'Do you *want* to be dismissed? And do not say you are sending another letter, because you are too late – the post has gone.' Gery rounded on Rea. 'What were you telling him?'

'Nothing,' bleated Rea. 'But he threatened to break my fingers if I tried to walk away.'

It was untrue, but Chaloner knew there was no point in saying so.

'Arrest him, Gery,' advised Morland, eyes bright with malice. 'His interference may damage our investigation.'

'Please do not,' said Freer wearily. 'Or Clarendon might order us to solve those bird murders, and *I* am not grubbing about by the sides of frozen lakes. Not in this weather.'

'True,' said Gery in distaste. 'I hate ducks.'

'Enough to poison a few?' asked Chaloner coolly.

Gery stared at him. 'What would be the point of that? It would render them unsafe to eat. And now *you* can answer some questions. What were you doing in the Antwerp yesterday?'

It was not surprising that a Parliamentarian stronghold should be monitored, and Chaloner supposed he would have to be careful if he went there again. 'Drinking coffee.'

Gery's expression was triumphant. 'With Isaac Dorislaus, a man dismissed from the Post Office for being a Roundhead.'

Gery had asked Thurloe about Dorislaus, too, thought Chaloner, regarding him with interest. He had overheard part of the conversation at Lincoln's Inn himself. Did the marshal know that Dorislaus had been helping Thurloe with an investigation into the Post Office, and the question to Chaloner aimed to show that Gery had guessed that the ex-Spymaster still dabbled in matters that should not concern him? If so, it was worrying, because Stokes's recent remark was true – accusations of sedition *were* easy to make but difficult to disprove.

'I distrust Dorislaus intensely,' Gery went on when Chaloner did not reply. 'There is a whisper that he is a Dutch spy. However, he is a less immediate problem than you. Morland is right: it would be unwise to leave you free to meddle, so you can spend a few days incarcerated in the—'

'Is that you, Chaloner?' came an amiable voice, just as Chaloner was debating whether to make a run for it or stand his ground. It was O'Neill, Kate at his side. 'Have you come for the post, or is this a social call? I should like to think we are friends now that we have been guests in your home.'

'I came to ask when the post leaves for Spain,' blustered Chaloner. 'Rea was about to tell—'

'Spain?' drawled Morland. 'I do not believe you. But show us the letter you have written, and I shall apologise for doubting your word.'

'No.' O'Neill raised his hand to prevent Chaloner from obliging – not that he could have done. 'We do not inspect the private correspondence of others at the Post Office. How many more times must I say it?'

'I hear Hannah has gone to Epsom,' said Kate, while Chaloner studied O'Neill, trying yet again to decide whether the man was a total fool or a very cunning schemer. 'Will you be holding soirées in her absence? If so, perhaps you would bear us in mind for an invitation. We did so enjoy meeting Monsieur le Notre.'

'Charming man,' nodded O'Neill. 'I might ask him to do something about the courtyard at the back of this building. Bishop allowed it to decay, you see, and now it is very seedy.'

'You should let me see to it,' said Kate. 'However, I shall not plant any tulips. They are Dutch, and it would be unpatriotic. I think we should not exchange post with the United Provinces either. We are virtually at war, and a continued service will only aid their spies.'

'There was only one spy in the Letter Office and I dismissed him,' said O'Neill. 'Isaac Dorislaus, a scoundrel who was almost certainly sending secrets to his Dutch masters. He was one of Thurloe's minions so—'

'No,' said Chaloner sharply, unwilling to see Thurloe maligned in front of the fanatical Gery. 'Thurloe no longer associates with Dorislaus, and has not done for years.'

'I doubt you know either villain,' said O'Neill, patting his shoulder. Chaloner fought the urge to shove him away, disliking both the liberty of contact and the disparaging of Thurloe. 'Hannah would not tolerate it. She is a lady of integrity and good judgement.'

'Not if she married Chaloner,' muttered Morland.

* * *

196

The short winter day was already well advanced, a.
Chaloner had learned nothing of use, despite enduring
encounters with a lot of unpleasant people. Feeling the
need for decent company, he went to Lincoln's Inn, where
he found Thurloe looking harried. He noted with concern
the number of patented medicines that were lined up
on his desk: Rowland Pepin's Cure for Rupture,
Constantine's Strong Coffee Pills, Goddard's Drops,
Sydenham's Laudanum.

'You take too many of those,' he said worriedly. 'What
if one reacts badly with another and—'

'My health is my own concern, Thomas,' said Thurloe
shortly. 'I know what I am doing. Incidentally, the Major
sent me a concoction when he heard I was ailing, one
he says he uses himself when he is low. Do you think I
should try it?'

'No!' Chaloner was appalled. 'You imprisoned him for
trying to kill Cromwell, and he almost certainly bears
you a grudge. Besides, he is hardly the picture of vigour
himself. Where is it?'

Thurloe handed him a phial. 'I would not have taken
it anyway. I am not such a fool as to swallow unsolicited
gifts. I was teasing you.'

It was not Chaloner's idea of a joke. 'Shall I ask
Wiseman to test it? He is already looking at some bread
I found in St James's Park, which was used to kill a swan.'

He perched on the table and gave a concise account
of all he had done and learned since their last meeting.
Unfortunately, it was not very much, and did not take
long. When he had finished, Thurloe leaned back in his
chair and steepled his fingers.

'It is a pity you dropped the papers you took from
that secret room. They might have allowed us to solve

the mystery. And there was certainly no such chamber when I was Postmaster. Still, you did better than Isaac Dorislaus, who has never managed to enter the south wing at all.'

'Yes,' said Chaloner, declining to comment further.

'My sources tell me that Jeremiah Copping is now fit to receive visitors. Go today. And while you are there, see if you can coax his sister, Widow Smith, to talk about Bishop and the Major. One is an ex-Postmaster, while the other supplies the Earl with information. I doubt either is involved in anything untoward, but all intelligence is useful.'

'Does she know them, then?'

'Yes. Her husband plotted to overthrow Cromwell in fifty-eight, but we thwarted him. He was arrested, but died in prison before he could be tried. He blamed Bishop and the Major for betraying him, and she continues to believe it.'

'Did they betray him?'

'No. As most plotters eventually learn to their cost, their fellow conspirators are invariably untrustworthy, despite fervent protestations of loyalty to their cause.'

'Then why did Smith think Bishop and the Major were responsible?'

Thurloe shrugged. 'I really could not say.'

Chaloner stared at him, knowing there was something he was not being told. Then he thought about the date: the year before Cromwell had died, and when the Commonwealth – by then a military dictatorship – had seemed invincible.

'I suppose the culprit was someone who thought his interests would be better served by remaining faithful to Cromwell,' he said, watching Thurloe closely. 'Someone

198

who had a foot in both camps even then, but was driven by self-interest. Morland!'

Thurloe winced. 'You are too astute for your own good sometimes.'

'That snake,' said Chaloner in disgust. 'So he *was* lying when he said he had been a Royalist the whole time he was working for you. As I suspected all along, he changed sides only when the republic was lost.'

'I bear him no malice. He was only trying to salvage something from a terrible situation.'

'By informing on his colleagues and undermining you.' Chaloner could not help but wonder whether the regime might have survived longer, perhaps even permanently, if Morland had not meddled. In his mind, it was a crime that could never be forgiven.

'What is done is done, and there is no point dwelling on it. Please do not tell Widow Smith that Morland is the guilty party. I should not like his death on my conscience.'

'She is the kind of person to kill, then?'

'You will find out when you meet her,' was all Thurloe would say to that question.

The Catherine Wheel was a large, graciously elegant building on Cheapside, although above its door was a vividly painted portrayal of the saint's martyrdom that would have turned even the strongest of stomachs. Two hefty soldiers stood guard outside.

'The tavern is closed,' said one, as Chaloner approached. 'Illness in the family.'

'I came to see Mr Copping,' explained Chaloner. 'I am not here for a drink.'

'You can try knocking,' suggested the soldier, although

his expression said he thought the visitor was wasting his time. 'But do not be surprised when she refuses to let you in.'

Chaloner rapped on a door that was made of best quality oak. 'Is this part of Cheapside especially dangerous?' he asked, wondering how the two men would explain their presence.

'Not really, but Mr Copping was caught in that explosion at Post House Yard, and it frightened him, so Widow Smith hired us to make him feel better. And you cannot be too careful these days, anyway. Did you not hear about the riot in Long Acre last night?'

'There is trouble everywhere,' agreed his companion. 'The Brewers' Guild had a letter from their compatriots in Hull this morning, saying that if they rebel, Hull will stand with them. It has made them mutinously defiant.'

'There have been letters to Londoners from brother guilds in Sussex and Bristol, too,' said the first sagely. 'Not to mention lengthy epistles from John Fry, the famous agitator. All encourage us to revolt. I shall join in when the time comes, of course.'

'To revolt against what?' asked Chaloner. 'Our masters? The government? The King?'

'Oh, not the King,' said the soldier. 'He is a lecherous rascal, but better than his boring father. And probably not the government either, given that we are about to go to war with the Dutch.' He scratched his head. 'In fact, I am not sure what we are against, but it will be something.'

'Definitely something,' agreed the second. 'And it will be important, because John Fry would not concern himself with nonsense. He will appear like a Messiah and lead us to victory.'

At that moment, the door opened. Chaloner had met many formidable matrons in his time, but few compared to Widow Smith. She was a vast mountain of a woman, taller than him by half a head and twice as broad. She wore skirts that accentuated her ample hips, and they swayed purposefully around her ankles. She folded her arms and glowered through eyes that seemed too small for her doughy face, reminding him of an obese and very angry pig.

'What?' she demanded.

'I have come to see Mr Copping.' Chaloner smiled. 'You must be his sister.'

'I am,' she acknowledged. 'Have you heard of me?'

Chaloner was not sure how to reply, because if he answered in the affirmative, she might ask why, and he could hardly repeat what he had been told. 'Just that he was being tended by a loving and careful nurse,' he lied.

Surprisingly, she softened. 'You may enter, then. Follow me.'

Aware of the soldiers' astonished glances that he should have won her good graces so easily, Chaloner stepped across the threshold. She barred the door behind her, and led the way down a corridor with dark panelling and a finely painted ceiling. Then she showed him into an attractive parlour at the back of the house, which was full of elegant furniture and rich curtains that rendered it cosy and light at the same time. Its fine decor would not have looked out of place in a palace.

'Jeremiah was lucky,' she said in a stage whisper. 'He was near the Alibond brothers when the cart exploded, and *they* were killed. I am still picking bits of them out of his hair.'

It was information Chaloner had not needed to hear, and he suspected Copping had not either, because the man who lay on the bed by the window winced and turned his face towards the wall. He was pale, and his neck was swathed in bandages, but he seemed otherwise unscathed.

'It was a terrible thing,' he said hoarsely. He had his sister's princely height but not her girth, lank black hair and a tic in one eye. 'One moment, I was chatting happily with Job and Sam Alibond about the prospect of the government raising postal charges, and the next . . .'

'It was wicked,' agreed Widow Smith. 'Thank God the Alibonds were fat, because that was what prevented Jeremiah from being killed – their bulks shielded him from worst of the blast.'

Copping was staring at Chaloner. 'You are the one who shouted the warning! It saved my life because I managed to take several steps away. But Sam and Job were slower . . .'

'Have you come to demand a reward?' asked Widow Smith, rather dangerously.

'No!' Chaloner was genuinely offended. 'I came to ask whether your brother might know who set the explosion.'

'Why would he?' she demanded aggressively.

'Because someone must, and he seemed as good a person to question as any,' replied Chaloner, meeting her eyes steadily. 'Or perhaps *you* have heard rumours?'

She preened, gratified that her opinion had been solicited. 'I might. But let Jeremiah tell you what he knows first.'

'Not much, I am afraid,' replied Copping unhappily. 'However, I am not surprised it happened. The Post Office has not been the same since Bishop was dismissed.'

'In what way?' asked Chaloner, aware of the angry grimace from Widow Smith at the mention of one of the men she believed had destroyed her husband.

'Bishop was a good Postmaster,' began Copping. He raised his hand when his sister started to object. 'I know you do not like him, but he was very efficient and his mail was nearly always delivered on time. But he was ousted on charges of corruption—'

'He *was* corrupt.' Widow Smith smiled maliciously. 'And I helped prove it. I saw his letter-carriers stop at the tavern across the road and spend two hours sorting through the contents of their sacks before going on their way. I took my tale to O'Neill, and Bishop was discharged.'

'I wish you had spoken to me first,' said Copping wearily. 'There would have been an explanation, because Bishop was not corrupt at all, whereas O'Neill . . .'

'O'Neill what?' asked Chaloner, when the clerk trailed off.

'O'Neill is a dangerous fool,' said Copping tightly. 'The Alibond brothers thought the same. Perhaps that gunpowder was intended for us, for speaking out against him.'

'How did you speak out against him? By approaching him directly? By spreading rumours?'

Copping shook his head vehemently. 'No, that would have been reckless. We asked questions, and started probing certain matters. But I cannot talk about this. It will see me killed!'

'You may be killed if you stay silent,' warned Chaloner. 'It is safer to tell the truth, so that Spymaster Williamson can—'

'Williamson!' spat Copping. 'He cannot stop what has been set in motion, and neither can you. There is wickedness afoot in O'Neill's domain, and the Alibond brothers died for it, even though they were wholly innocent of any wrongdoing. And I do not intend to follow them to the grave.'

'If there is wickedness afoot, you must help me thwart it,' pressed Chaloner. 'It is treason to know of a plot to harm a government institution and do nothing to stop it.'

He had no idea whether it was treason or not, but his remark had the desired effect. The twitch in Copping's eye intensified, and he began to twist the bedcovers with unsteady hands. He was weakening. But then he glanced at his sister and seemed to take courage from her massive presence, because he regained control of himself.

'I know nothing,' he said in a low but firm voice. 'And you cannot prove otherwise, not now Sam and Job are dead.'

'Then tell me about the musician,' said Chaloner, determined to extract something useful from the visit. 'The one who was playing just before the explosion.'

'He was piping "La Mantovana", my favourite song,' replied Copping, his expression distant. 'It is Storey's, too – he lives next to the Post Office – and I recall thinking that it was a pity he was out, because he would have liked to hear it. Then the Alibonds joined me, and we started to chat about business. The next thing I recall is you yelling. . .'

'Do you know Oxenbridge and John Fry? Oxenbridge was in Post House Yard shortly after the blast, and John Fry may be using the General Letter Office to coordinate his—'

'No,' said Copping firmly. 'I know neither of them. But I am tired and do not feel like answering more questions, no matter how much you offer to pay me. I love life more than money.'

It had not occurred to Chaloner to extract the information with cash, but it was obvious from Copping's remark that someone else had. 'Who offered to buy what you know?' he pounced.

'No one,' snapped Copping, clearly furious at himself for the slip. 'It was a figure of speech. Now go away. I can tell you nothing more.'

Widow Smith ushered Chaloner out of the sickroom, where he found himself directed not to the front door, but into another parlour. She shoved him into a chair, and poured two cups of surprisingly decent claret. She smiled rather alarmingly, revealing teeth that were tobacco-stained slabs of brown, and proffered a plate of expensive pastries. He ate one; it was good, so he took another, glancing around as he did so and thinking how peculiar it was that this bristling, threatening, redoubtable woman should live in such delicately elegant surroundings.

'I have things to tell you,' she stated grandly. 'More important things than Jeremiah.'

'I see,' said Chaloner, and resigned himself to hearing a more detailed account of how she had ousted Bishop.

'I have always had an interest in the Post Office,' she began. 'Mostly because my husband was employed there during the reign of the first King Charles. We had always been good Royalists, and I was proud when he tried to overthrow Cromwell.'

'I am sure you were.'

'Well, something untoward is happening there now. And your assumption was correct: my brother *has* been paid to monitor its goings-on. But he has learned nothing of significance.'

'Paid by whom? Bankes? He buys information.'

'By someone whose name I do not care to disclose,' she replied, so haughtily that Chaloner suspected she did not know. 'But *I* have not been paid, although I have more to say. I go there to post letters, you see, and I am observant. For example, I can tell you that if Smartfoot and Lamb are proper clerks, then I am the Queen of Sheba. They are louts, hired for some other purpose.'

'What other purpose?'

'You will have to ask them yourself. Or you could visit Tom Ibson, and put the same question to him. Have you heard of the evil spymaster who oppressed England when the Great Usurper was in power? John Thurloe? Well, Ibson was his jackal.'

'His what?'

'Jackal. It is a predatory animal with a taste for the bones of babies.'

Chaloner regarded her askance. 'What are you saying? That Ibson is a cannibal?'

'I would not put it past him. He is an unsavoury rogue, just like his erstwhile master. However, he knows a thing or two about what is happening in the General Letter Office.'

'Where does he live?'

'I have no idea.' Her eyes narrowed suddenly. 'But you have not told me why you are interested in this affair. Who sent you?'

Chaloner was tempted to say Thurloe, but was not sure he would win the fisticuffs that might follow. 'No one you know.'

'In other words, you will not tell me,' she surmised. 'Well, never mind. Just as long as it is not Thurloe, Williamson, Bankes or the Earl of Clarendon.'

'You have explained why you dislike Thurloe, but what have the others done to annoy you?'

Her expression hardened into something unpleasant. 'Williamson is a fool, Bankes is sinister – not that I have ever met him, of course; I do not associate with scoundrels – and Clarendon has hired a villain named Gery, whom I hate with a passion.'

'I am not enamoured of Gery either.'

Widow Smith scowled. 'He burst in here with half a dozen soldiers and that treacherous little clerk, and he browbeat Jeremiah mercilessly, even though he is injured and knows nothing of any consequence. I would like to repay him for his brutality.'

She had a right to be angry: bullying tactics were hardly appropriate in a sickroom, no matter how annoying the patient. Chaloner murmured something suitably sympathetic, and Widow Smith refilled his cup with claret.

Night had fallen by the time Chaloner finally managed to escape. Widow Smith had told him nothing helpful, so he decided to return to the Post Office, to see whether he could waylay Rea and finish the conversation that Gery had interrupted. The streets were busy, as men left work to go home or visit inns, taverns and 'ordinaries' – places where meals could be bought for set prices. Thames Street and Dowgate Hill boasted a profusion of such establishments, and the many guildhalls that were nearby meant there was no shortage of patrons for them.

Lights burned in the General Letter Office, but its doors were closed, and Chaloner was loath to break in again, suspecting he might not survive being caught a third time. He took up station in the shadows cast by

207

Wood's mansion instead, huddled into his coat against the cold.

Clerks dribbled out in twos and threes, but Rea was not among them. Chaloner was on the verge of giving up and going home when Morland arrived. The secretary glanced around in a manner that could only be described as furtive, and then made for the door. He had a key, but agitation made him clumsy, and it was several minutes before he could get it to work. Chaloner frowned. Why was he behaving so secretively when he had every right to visit the place on account of his work for Gery?

Intrigued, Chaloner forgot his decision not to break in and followed, picking the lock and entering the cavernous Letter Hall, which was as still and silent as a tomb. It was in darkness, and deserted except for Morland, who was just disappearing through the door that led to the offices beyond. Chaloner picked that lock, too, and trailed the secretary to the disused wing, moving with more than his usual caution, because Morland was openly uneasy in the shadowy emptiness of the building, and kept glancing behind him.

The secretary said something to the soldier on duty by the door, and whatever it was made the man hurry back towards the Letter Hall. Swearing under his breath, Chaloner ducked behind a mound of mailbags, and was relieved but not particularly impressed when the soldier passed within touching distance without noticing him. Had Morland sent the man on a genuine errand? Or did he just want him out of the way?

Chaloner had his answer when Morland waited until the guard's footsteps had receded, then took another key and unlocked the door. He did not secure it behind him, suggesting he did not intend to be inside for long.

Chaloner followed, and watched him go straight to the room with the secret chamber. Had he discovered it during his work with Gery, and had come to explore it at a time when the Post Office was devoid of vigilant clerks?

Chaloner was cold, tired and frustrated with his lack of progress that day. His patience snapped. It was time he had answers, and Morland was going to provide them. He strode forward, watching the secretary leap in alarm at his sudden appearance, almost dropping the lantern.

'Christ!' Morland gulped, hand to his chest when he recognised Chaloner. 'You should not be here. There will be hell to pay when Gery finds out.'

'He will only find out if you tell him.'

'Then it will be our little secret.' Morland attempted to hide his disquiet with a sickly smile.

'It is not—' Chaloner whipped around when he heard a sound behind him, and only his instinctive duck saved him from the blow that would have shattered his skull. Morland gave a screech of horror when the cudgel scored a heavy dent in the wall.

'You!' exclaimed Lamb, staggering off balance. He turned accusingly to his companion – Smartfoot. 'I told you he was a spy.'

'This is going to be awkward,' said Chaloner in Dutch. 'I should have stayed outside after all.'

'You speak English,' blurted Morland, bewildered. 'So why gabble in—'

'You see?' cried Lamb, raising his cosh. 'He lied when he pretended to be French.'

Chaloner assessed his situation. It was not good. Lamb and Smartfoot were heavily armed, and could probably summon reinforcements. Moreover, they had him

209

hemmed against the wall, where it would be difficult to use his sword.

'Wait,' cried Morland, as Lamb took aim with his bludgeon. 'The Earl of Clarendon will not want him harmed. Give me a moment to—'

'Piss off!' snapped Smartfoot. 'Unless you want a trouncing, too.'

Morland's eyes went wide with fear, and he turned and scurried away without another word. The moment he had gone, Lamb lashed out with his stick. Chaloner deflected the blow with his arm, but before he could reach for a weapon of his own, Smartfoot had grabbed him by the throat and shoved him against the wall.

'You can tell us what you are doing willingly or we will make you talk,' he said, eyes glittering at the prospect of violence. 'The choice is yours.'

Chapter 7

In the shadowy silence of the Post Office's disused wing, Smartfoot held Chaloner against the wall and nodded for Lamb to advance with his cudgel. Chaloner did not give him the opportunity to use it. He whipped the dagger from his belt, and it was embedded in Smartfoot's arm almost before the man had turned back to him. Smartfoot shrieked and reeled away, blood oozing between his fingers.

Lamb reacted quickly, flailing with his stick and never giving Chaloner the chance to draw his sword. There followed a savage scuffle, during which both demonstrated that they had learned their skills in gutters as well as military camps, and included kicks, punches and even a bite. When Smartfoot recovered enough to join in, Chaloner knew he had to do something fast, or he was going to be killed. He pulled the bottle that the Major had sent Thurloe from his pocket.

'This contains a deadly poison,' he declared, holding it aloft. 'It kills anyone it touches, and if you do not back off, I am going to throw it at you.'

'It does not,' said Lamb disdainfully. 'Such a substance does not exist.'

'It might, though,' said Smartfoot uneasily. 'Leak mentioned a deadly toxin when we were in the Crown once.'

'I do not believe you,' said Lamb to Chaloner, but there was doubt in his eyes now, and neither he nor Smartfoot tried to stop the spy as he backed away. Chaloner locked the door behind him, and had left the Post Office long before anyone heard their outraged yells and came to release them.

The moment he was sure he had not been followed, he flagged down a hackney and asked the driver to take him to Tothill Street. Then he changed his mind and alighted in Fleet Street instead, where he made his way to Wiseman's house.

Wiseman employed a number of servants, all of whom were missing body parts, although Chaloner had never mustered the courage to ask whether their losses were a result of the surgeon's ministrations. The one-legged footman opened the door, and conducted him to the parlour at the back of the house, where Temperance had evidently been at work, because its decor was rather more vulgar than her lover would have selected for himself, and included plush chairs and wallpaper – a frivolous extravagance decried by Puritans, but much in demand by Royalists.

There were also shelves along one wall containing white, yellow and reddish items in glass jars. Chaloner was careful not to look at them, having once been told that Wiseman was not above collecting bits of his family and storing them for their scientific value. There was also a strange smell, which he supposed was the preservatives that kept the specimens from rotting.

Despite its unconventional furnishings, the room was

212

cosy and a fire blazed in the hearth. Temperance was there, already dressed for an evening at the club; she lounged on a bench with the surgeon's ginger cat in her lap. Although she did not make herself available to patrons personally, she still looked the part, with thick face-paints and a low-cut bodice. Meanwhile, Wiseman had donned the peculiar scarlet mantle he wore while relaxing. Neither he nor Temperance smiled when Chaloner walked in.

'I am angry with you,' said the surgeon coldly. 'I know we do not always agree with each other, but that is no reason to put me in danger.'

'I am more than angry,' said Temperance, eyes flashing with a rage Chaloner had not seen before. The cat promptly made itself scarce. 'And if I had a gun, I would shoot you.'

Chaloner looked from one to the other in confusion. 'Why? What have I done?'

'The poison,' said Wiseman stiffly. 'You left a note asking me to test it.'

Chaloner was none the wiser. 'You have done it before. Was there a problem?'

'Yes, there was a problem!' exploded Wiseman. 'It is the deadliest toxin I have ever encountered. The merest crumb killed a rat almost instantly, and I dread to think what would have happened if I had touched it with my hands. You should have warned me.'

'You do not wear gloves when you examine such compounds?' asked Chaloner. It was one of the first things he had learned when he had embarked on a life of espionage.

'Of course I do, but that is not the point. I deserved to be warned.'

213

'I am sorry. But the stuff was used to kill birds. It cannot be as deadly as you say.'

'Obviously, you are involved in something more sinister than you led us to believe,' said Temperance tightly. Her fists were clenched, and he knew she wanted to punch him.

He shook his head. 'It is just a few dead birds. I swear it.'

But then a thought struck him. Smartfoot had backed down very quickly when Chaloner had threatened to lob a phial of poison, and had mentioned discussing such substances with Leak – who would certainly have known what they could do, given that he had used some on the King's birds. Guiltily, he saw Wiseman and Temperance were right to be angry and suspicious.

'Such a potion is unethical,' said Wiseman stiffly. 'And I decline to have any more to do with it. Please do not ask me to help you with anything else.'

'Oh,' said Chaloner, pulling Thurloe's bottle from his pocket. 'Because here is a—'

'Damn you, Thomas!' cried Temperance. 'Go away, and take your nasty bottles with you.'

'Wait,' said Wiseman, as Chaloner turned to leave. The surgeon shrugged at Temperance's immediate outrage. 'He might come to harm if we let him do it himself.'

'Good,' said Temperance sullenly.

'No,' said Wiseman sharply. 'I have not forgotten his kindness last year, when everyone else condemned me and he alone fought to prove my innocence. Put the bottle on the table, Chaloner. I shall examine it tonight and tell you my findings at the charnel house tomorrow.'

'You mean when you examine Mary Wood?' asked

Temperance. 'There are more rumours than ever that say she was murdered, and I am glad you will soon be able to say whether they are true.'

'I doubt they are,' said Wiseman. 'There is a lot of the small-pox around at the moment. The Earl's son was another recent victim.'

'Yes,' said Temperance. 'I was sorry, because he was a promising young man.'

'He was.' Wiseman shot Chaloner a sheepish glance. 'He was strong and healthy, so I confess I wondered why he had succumbed so quickly. To set my mind at rest, I examined him very carefully.'

'You mean you anatomised one of the Earl's sons?' Chaloner was horrified.

'Not anatomised,' averred Wiseman, although his expression was distinctly furtive. 'Just made one or two judicious incisions. But my concerns were groundless. Young Edward died of the small-pox without the shadow of a doubt.'

It was strange to arrive at Tothill Street and find the house empty. The banked fire and a half-packed bag in the kitchen told Chaloner that one or two servants were still around, but whoever it was had gone out. Relishing the solitude, Chaloner took bread, apples and cheese from the pantry, and washed them down with the sweet ale that Joan generally kept for herself. It was the most wholesome meal he had eaten in days, and afterwards, pleasantly replete, he went to the drawing room where he played his viol until weariness drove him to bed.

He slept soundly and awoke refreshed and invigorated just as dawn was breaking, although his happy enthusiasm for the new day faded somewhat when he remembered that he would have to visit Newgate and the Westminster charnel house, neither excursions that appealed.

They were not the only tasks he had, either. Most urgent was cornering Morland, to demand an explanation for his antics the previous night. Chaloner was inclined to do the same with Harper, too, because *he* would certainly have answers. Then he should find Ibson, although if the man had been Thurloe's 'jackal', as Widow Smith claimed, then the chances were that he had already told the ex-Spymaster all he knew. Thus Ibson was low on Chaloner's list, much lower than asking after Bankes and seeing what could be learned about Oxenbridge and John Fry.

As it was Tuesday, he would have to be in St James's Park at dusk, to see if the bird-killers appeared. He was confused about the culprits. Seth Eliot's testimony suggested they were courtiers, and Storey certainly thought so, while all the attacks had occurred during noisy revels, indicating that the perpetrators were privy to the King's social calendar. So why had Leak been involved? Had courtiers hired him, but then been obliged to do their own dirty work when he had died?

But which courtiers? Chaloner thought about Storey's list, which included men who had aroused his interest for other reasons – Gery, Morland, O'Neill, Oxenbridge, Wood and Harper. None were pleasant, and Chaloner could see any of them dispatching birds. He was also inclined to add le Notre, because there was certainly something about the Frenchman that was not quite right.

But lying in bed was not going to bring answers, so he took a deep breath, to brace himself for the chill of an unheated and rather damp room, and flung back the blankets. He hurried down to the kitchen, not surprised to discover that the remaining servants were making the most of Hannah's absence – no one had risen to stoke up the fire or to fetch water to heat over it. He washed and shaved in cold, then raided the pantry for more bread, cheese and apples, which he ate standing up, as it was too icy in the kitchen for sitting. He left the house before anyone else was astir.

He went to White Hall first, supposing he had better report to the Earl. And if Morland was there, then so much the better. It was another bitingly cold morning, with frost hard and white on the rooftops, and coated thickly on the needles of churchyard yews. It was even on the cobwebs above the Great Gate, transforming gossamer strands into hefty strings of white that would not deceive even the most inattentive of prey.

He was just crossing the Pebble Court when he saw two figures gliding through the shadows, and everything about them said they did not wish to be seen. He stepped into a doorway and waited for them to pass. A lamp caught their faces as they came closer, and he was astonished to recognise Oxenbridge's oddly white visage and Gardner's bushy yellow hair. Why were they in each other's company? And more to the point, why were they at White Hall? Were they the 'courtiers' who were killing birds? He decided to find out.

The pair slunk around the edge of the Great Court, and aimed for the jumble of buildings that housed the palace's minor officials. It was a maze, but Chaloner knew it well, and trailing people was his profession. However, they backtracked and zigzagged in a way that told him they knew they were being followed, and eventually he rounded a corner to find them vanished. He whipped around fast, but not fast enough. A blow sent

217

him spinning backwards, and he heard running footsteps. By the time he had regained his wits, Oxenbridge and Gardner had gone.

The Earl's offices were warm, and lamps and a roaring fire cast a welcoming amber glow. Chaloner walked across the thick Turkey carpets and waited until his master deigned to glance up at him.

'Well?' the Earl asked. There were dark smudges under his eyes, and a piece of damp linen on the desk showed he had been crying. Chaloner suddenly felt sorry for him.

'Is there anything I can do for you, sir?' he asked kindly. 'Other than catching the bird-killers?'

The Earl stared at him, and a desperate, yearning hope flared in his eyes. Then it faded. 'No. Just find whoever is dispatching these wretched ducks as soon as you can. Incidentally, Gery tells me that you disobeyed my orders and went to the Post Office again. Is it true?'

'I was mailing a letter to my brother,' lied Chaloner. 'Or would you rather I did not write to my family until Gery exposes whatever is happening there? It might be a while.'

It was a painfully crude way of informing him that the marshal was incapable of solving the case very soon, if ever, but it was the best Chaloner could manage on the spur of the moment.

'No!' exclaimed the Earl, his expression bleak. 'A man's kin are his heart and soul, his very reason for living, so you must communicate with yours as often as you can. Do you ever think of the ones you lost to the plague in Holland?'

The question was so unexpected that Chaloner gave an involuntary start. He opened his mouth to reply, but

218

then was not sure what to say. As it happened, they had been in his mind of late, but it was not something he was inclined to reveal to anyone else. Yet at the same time, he did not want to dishonour their memory by denying them.

'It does not matter,' said the Earl, when the silence became awkward. 'It is just that I find myself thinking about my children a lot these days, especially Edward. My enemies say grief is affecting my judgement, and that I should resign as Lord Chancellor.' He sighed, and gave a wan smile. 'But perhaps they will stop hounding me when I present the King with the villain who is attacking his fowl. So off you go now, Chaloner.'

Chaloner turned to leave, but stopped when he was at the door. 'Do not let them oust you, sir. England cannot afford to lose the only Privy Councillor who does any work.'

The Earl sighed gloomily. 'If only a few more people thought like you.'

Chaloner was walking down the marble staircase when he met someone coming up. It was the Major, with two yeomen in tow. His shoulders were slumped and he moved with the defeated shuffle of a prisoner who was low on hope. He was pale, and he looked as though he had not slept in days. His clothes were rumpled, too, although he had brushed his hair and shaved in an effort to smarten himself up for his audience with the Earl.

'I do not know how much longer I can keep doing this,' he whispered to Chaloner as they passed, speaking softly so his guards would not hear. He need not have worried: Lady Castlemaine's voice was booming in the courtyard below, and they were gazing out of the window at her in transfixed admiration. 'How much longer will Gery's enquiry drag on?'

'Tell me what you have learned,' suggested Chaloner. 'That will expedite matters.'

'How many more times must I say it?' The Major looked pained. 'There is nothing I would like more, but they made me swear to keep silent, and I dare not defy them – I have too much to lose. So do you: several investigators have died exploring this case, and you do not deserve to be one of them. The Earl has excluded you from the matter, so do not rail against it. Be thankful.'

Chaloner nodded, but his resolve to meddle only strengthened. 'Do you have new information to report?' he asked.

The Major nodded. 'But as I have said before, Clarendon and Gery ignore any intelligence they do not understand or that they deem irrelevant. I am deeply concerned . . .'

So was Chaloner. 'If you think the matter is not being properly investigated, you must confide in someone else. You decline to talk to me, but what about a friend? Palmer, perhaps? Or Bishop?'

'I cannot endanger them.' The Major sighed miserably. 'You seem competent, and I wish Clarendon had chosen you over Gery, although not as much as I wish Wood had taken my message to another member of the Privy Council. Buckingham, perhaps; he is a man of action. Or even the King. But what is done is done, and I must make the best of it.'

'Surely you can give me some indication of what is amiss?' Chaloner was reluctant to let him go without learning at least something useful. The Major's misgivings about Clarendon's selective handling of intelligence had alarmed him anew, and he began to wonder whether his master's enemies were right: perhaps grief *was* robbing him of his reason. 'Just a hint?'

The Major's voice was so low as to be almost inaudible. 'Certain abuses will occur in any postal service – clerks "accidentally" losing prepaid letters, letting passengers ride the post horses so there is no room for mailbags, drunken postmen. But there is a question of magnitude . . .'

Chaloner nodded impatiently. 'Of course, but the trouble goes far deeper than mere chicanery. There are tales that the Post Office is behind the unrest that is sweeping across the country, which is a far more serious problem. What do you know about that?'

The Major took a step away. 'Lord! You must have a death wish to speak so boldly.'

'Is O'Neill involved?' pressed Chaloner.

'I hope so,' replied the Major with a rueful smile. 'His lies put me in the Tower, and I would love to see him fall from grace. But the truth is that I do not know. Now please leave me alone. We cannot be seen gossiping. It will endanger both our lives.'

'There are rumours that someone will be assassinated soon, and that you might be the victim,' said Chaloner, desperate enough to use harsh tactics. 'You saw the message on the stone that came through Palmer's window. So, you *are* endangering your life, but because you will *not* talk to me. Gery has been investigating for weeks and has made no headway. It is time to trust someone else.'

A stricken expression crossed the Major's face. 'Do you think I do not know that? Clarendon imagines that bringing me here before dawn will keep me safe, when the reality is that empty streets and darkness only make it easier for killers to strike. And I do not want to die . . .'

'Then talk to me,' urged Chaloner.

The Major stared at him, and Chaloner saw his resolve begin to crumble. He opened his mouth to speak, but at that moment, a door opened, and Gery's voice could be heard echoing beneath them. The Major shot Chaloner an agonised glance and stumbled away.

Chaloner's thoughts whirled as he left the Earl's offices. When he had been sent to arrest Knight and Gardner, he had overheard them discussing a murder. Somewhat unconvincingly, Gardner had denied involvement. Could Knight have been referring to the spies that Thurloe and Williamson had lost, presumably the same men as the 'investigators' to whom the Major had just referred? Chaloner supposed he would have to add finding Gardner to his list of tasks, especially now he knew the clerk kept company with Oxenbridge.

When he reached the Great Gate, someone was waiting for him, shivering and stamping his feet against the cold. It was Vanderhuyden. Chaloner regarded him in surprise.

'Thurloe said you are often here early, so I came in the hope of catching you,' Vanderhuyden explained. His usually jovial face was sombre, and Chaloner's stomach lurched.

'Thurloe? Is he . . .'

'He is well,' Vanderhuyden assured him quickly. Then his expression turned rueful. 'Other than extending affection to men who do not deserve it.'

'Do you mean me?'

'No, of course not. I mean Dorislaus.' Vanderhuyden took a deep breath, and his next words emerged as a gabble. 'I have a terrible fear that he is sending intelligence reports to Holland, and that the Dutch are behind the unrest that grips our country. A rebellion will make England weak and vulnerable, and may tip the balance in the war we shall soon fight.'

'I thought you and Dorislaus were friends,' said Chaloner, not revealing his own suspicions about the man. 'So how can you make such a terrible accusation?'

'We *are* friends.' Vanderhuyden's tormented wail drew the attention of several passing tradesmen. 'And this is not easy, believe me. I have agonised about it for days. Should I turn a blind eye or put the interests of my country first? It is the hardest decision I have ever made.'

'On what grounds do you suspect him?'

'He holds clandestine meetings with peculiar people – O'Neill, le Notre and Gery. Why does he pursue an acquaintance with O'Neill, who sacked him from the Post Office? Meanwhile, le Notre is almost certainly a French spy, while Gery hates old Roundheads, so Dorislaus should have no reason for joining him in shadowy taverns late at night.'

'How do you know all this?'

'Because once my suspicions were roused, I made it my business to monitor him as often as possible. It is difficult, because I have to go to work, but even my occasional surveillance has convinced me that he is a . . .' Vanderhuyden trailed off and looked away miserably.

'Have you told Thurloe?'

'He would not listen; you know how loyal he is to his friends. That is why I decided to come to you – you must have encountered this sort of thing in the past.' Vanderhuyden's voice was thick with misery. 'I thought

I would feel better once I had confided in someone else, but I feel worse. Like the lowest kind of worm.'

Chaloner nodded understandingly. 'But your duty is clear: you must take your tale to Williamson. He will uncover the truth.'

'I was afraid you would say that,' gulped Vanderhuyden. 'And I shall, but not yet.'

'Waiting might allow Dorislaus to do something even more damaging. It may even see you accused of treason yourself, for not stopping him sooner.'

'Then it is a risk I shall have to take, because I refuse to do it without proper proof – written evidence of his perfidy, as opposed to what I have now, which amounts to little more than a series of odd encounters. I shall redouble my efforts. Will you help me?'

'Only if my path happens to cross his. I am too busy to do more.'

'Oh,' said Vanderhuyden, disappointed. 'Then I shall have to ask O'Neill for a few days' leave. I will have to lie, tell him my wife is unwell . . .'

'Speaking of the Post Office, what can you tell me about Harper?'

Vanderhuyden looked surprised, but answered anyway. 'O'Neill hired him to prevent harmful chatter. And it has worked: no one gossips about Post Office business now.'

'No,' agreed Chaloner. 'However, there are tales that the place does a lot more than deliver letters, and keeping quiet about that is dangerous.'

'You mean these claims about our corruption?' Vanderhuyden shrugged. 'The Foreign Office, where I work, is reasonably honest, but the Inland Office is much bigger and some of its clerks probably are abusing the system. But I imagine O'Neill is working to stamp it out.'

'Actually, I was referring to the rumours that say something deadly is in play there.'

Vanderhuyden shook his head impatiently. 'That is a lot of nonsense, as I have told you before. I suspect someone like Bishop is behind those silly stories, to cause trouble for O'Neill.'

Chaloner could only suppose that Vanderhuyden was so intent on Dorislaus's antics that he had failed to see what was unfolding under his nose. He changed the subject, thinking that if the Major would not reveal what his contacts had said, then he would visit them himself.

'The Major has friends in the Foreign Office. Who are they?'

Vanderhuyden stared at him. 'Are you suggesting that the *Major* is behind these silly tales? Because O'Neill was responsible for locking him in the Tower and getting Bishop dismissed? I doubt the poor fellow would have the nerve! He seems singularly lacking in spirit, and I find it very hard to believe that he once gave fiery speeches.'

'Well, he did,' said Chaloner. 'So which clerks were his particular friends?'

'I do not know: I was not employed there when Bishop was in power. But if you help me with Dorislaus, I shall find out. I shall ask about this so-called plot, too. No one in my department will be able to help, but I have one or two acquaintances in the Inland Office.'

'Please do not,' said Chaloner tiredly. Vanderhuyden was not a spy, and did not possess the requisite skills; he would be discovered and killed. 'It is too risky.'

'It is not, because there *is* no plot. Do not worry, I shall be discreet. And asking sly questions of my colleagues cannot be more distasteful than spying on Dorislaus.'

Chaloner watched him leave, unable to shake the conviction that he was letting him walk to his doom. But how was he to stop him? Knock him on the head and lock him up? Bargain with him by saying that he would investigate Dorislaus if Vanderhuyden left the city? But he did not have the time, and Vanderhuyden was no coward, so was unlikely to agree to such terms. He felt the pressure on him mount as he realised there was only one thing he could do to protect his friend: expose the Post Office plot as quickly as possible.

It was still not fully light when Chaloner began to walk up King Street, and as it was too early to go to Newgate, he decided to visit the Rainbow. He did not need a draught of Farr's poisonous brew, because his mind was already sharp with anxiety, but it was better than loitering in the cold, waiting for the gaol to open.

He was almost at Charing Cross when he saw Morland, strutting like a peacock in his splendid clothes. Chaloner strode towards him, grabbed him by the lace that frothed at his throat, and whisked him behind a booth that sold cabbages. The stall shielded them from the road, while above their heads was a large tarpaulin, heavy-bellied with an icy slush of snow and rain. It was somewhere they would not be disturbed.

'You are alive!' A gamut of emotions flashed across Morland's small face, the most obvious of which was astonishment; relief and pleasure were certainly not among them. 'Thank God! I feared they had not listened when I urged clemency, and I am glad I had a hand in saving your life.'

Chaloner released him abruptly. There was something so unpleasantly greasy about Morland that he was disinclined to touch him. 'What were you doing at the Post Office last night?'

'I was on an errand for Gery. We *are* investigating the place, you know.'

'What goes on in that secret chamber?'

Morland scowled. 'I was on the verge of finding out when you appeared. Your antics brought Smartfoot and Lamb running, so I had to leave. You were a nuisance, to be frank.'

Chaloner had no idea whether he was telling the truth, and was not sure how to find out, so opted instead to pursue a subject that might stand a better chance of producing reliable answers.

'What do you know about Clement Oxenbridge?'

Morland's eyes widened fractionally. 'No one knows anything about him. He just appears when he pleases, and then vanishes again. He is a sinister devil, though.'

'What is his connection with White Hall?'

'Well, he is friends with Monsieur le Notre. More than that I have not discovered.'

Le Notre again, thought Chaloner. 'What is—'

He turned quickly when he sensed someone behind him. It was Gery and Freer, both holding handguns. With a squeak of relief, Morland slithered towards them.

'He was quizzing me about the Post Office,' he bleated. 'He asked dozens of questions, but I told him nothing. At least, nothing that is true. However, he represents a serious nuisance, so lock him in a dungeon until this matter is over. It is for the best.'

'Or I could shoot him,' said Gery, the barrel of his gun unwavering.

'In King Street?' asked Chaloner archly. 'At its busiest time of day? Even the Earl will not be able to protect you from the noose if you commit murder in so public a place.'

Gery gestured with his free hand. 'You chose to bully Morland somewhere that is concealed from the road. When witnesses arrive, Freer's dag will be in your hand, and he and Morland will back my claim that you drew first. I shall be feted for saving London from a lunatic.'

Chaloner shrugged. 'Then we must make sure there is some truth in it.'

Slowly and deliberately, he drew his sword. Gery frowned uncertainly, but although his finger tightened on the trigger, he did not pull it. For all his hot words, an innate sense of honour demanded that Chaloner should make at least some hostile move before being gunned down. Morland fled, unwilling to see how the confrontation resolved.

'What are you doing, Chaloner?' cried Freer in alarm. 'Disarm yourself, man! Morland is right: we can lock you in a dungeon for a few days. There is no need for suicide.'

Chaloner held the sword high, knowing that Gery would not fire until he lunged. He stood that way for a moment, then jabbed upwards, at the canvas above his head. There was an immediate cascade of sleety water. Gery jerked the trigger, but nothing happened, and by the time the marshal had dashed the droplets from his eyes, Chaloner was nowhere to be seen.

It was easy to disappear among the teeming masses in King Street, and Chaloner knew that Gery would not catch him. He was disgusted with the encounter, though – he had learned nothing from Morland, and now Gery would hate him more than ever. He entered the familiar, fuggy warmth of the Rainbow, trailing water.

'What news?' called Farr. His jaw dropped. 'Why are you wet? It is not raining.'

'A vindictive apprentice,' mumbled Chaloner.

There was an immediate sigh of sympathy. Farr poured him some hot coffee, Speed the bookseller wrung out his coat, and Stedman gave him a handkerchief to wipe his face.

'Apprentices have been causing far too much trouble of late,' said Farr. 'The tailors fought the soap-makers last night. What has got into them all?'

'The tailors had a letter from Bristol yesterday,' explained Speed, 'in which they were urged to rise up against the wildness of the Court, the Lady's gambling debts, the King's favouring of papists—'

'The King cuckolds one of England's most prominent Catholics,' interrupted Farr, laughing. 'If that is favouring them, then *I* should not like to catch his eye.'

'Speaking of Catholics, Palmer's treatise goes on sale next week,' said Speed happily. 'You have not ordered a copy yet, although I am sure you will all want one.'

'Have you heard the rumours about Mary Wood?' asked Farr, changing the subject in a non sequitur that was typical of discussions at the Rainbow and neatly avoiding being obliged to part with some money at the same time. 'The Queen's dresser. It is said that she did not die of the small-pox, but was murdered.'

'Yes,' nodded Speed. 'Everyone knows it, but no one from Court is investigating.'

'Probably because they are too busy worrying about the Post Office,' said Stedman. 'I heard some of my apprentices talking about it last night.'

'What did they say?' asked Chaloner.

'That something is brewing,' came the unhelpful reply.

'Something has been brewing ever since Bishop was ousted in favour of O'Neill,' said Speed. 'Have you heard that John Fry was seen last night, by the way?'

'What, again?' asked Farr. 'That makes five times in the last three weeks.'

'He has come to lead the revolt,' said Speed darkly. 'He tried to organise one eight years ago, but he was either murdered or died of flux – or perhaps he did not die at all – so he decided to wait for a more opportune time. And that time is now, apparently.'

'I should not like to meet him, dead or alive,' averred Farr. 'He is a fanatic, and I dislike these rumours that he is going to assassinate someone important – the King, Lady Castlemaine, Clarendon, Buckingham, Controller O'Neill, le Notre or the Major.'

Stedman grimaced. 'Why would anyone want to kill the Major? He is in the Tower with no hope of release, and it is said that he is quite broken. It serves him right for executing the old King. We all know that he was the one who struck off the royal head.'

'His imprisonment is illegal, though,' said Speed. 'He has not been charged with anything, and he is continually denied a trial. He will die there, alone, forgotten and crushed in spirit. And talking of crushed spirits, I have Olearius's *Voyages* for you, Chaloner. It makes for grim reading, I can tell you! You should have ordered some of Mr Grey's pills, because you will need them when you peruse these pages.'

Chaloner's heart sank when, leafing through it, the first sentence he saw confidently informed him that Russians were 'brutish, doing all things according to their unbridled passions and appetites.' Farr invited him to read aloud, and when he declined, Stedman obliged, choosing a section about the peasants' love of squalor and the tyranny of their leaders. Chaloner slipped away, suspecting he might have been wiser not to try to prepare himself for the ordeal ahead.

The church bells were ringing for the eight o'clock services when Chaloner reached Newgate. The prison was a formidable structure, and he kept his head down as he approached, knowing that if he looked up at the bleak, soot-stained walls with their tiny barred windows, he would lose courage and walk away. It took considerable willpower to step inside and ask to see Keeper Sligo. His gorge rose at the familiar stench of rotting straw, unwashed bodies, slops and burned gruel.

'You,' said Sligo, when Chaloner was shown into his office. He was a cadaverous man, with a drinking habit. 'When we met last year, you pretended to be someone you were not, and it saw me in serious trouble. I should take the opportunity to lock you in my darkest cell.'

'Do not try it,' advised Chaloner coldly, although the threat sent horror spearing through him. 'I am on Williamson's business today.'

'How do I know you are telling the truth?' asked Sligo suspiciously. 'You lied before.'

And he was lying now. 'Write and ask him. I do not mind waiting.'

Sligo reached for his pen, but then reconsidered, as Chaloner knew he would. 'No, I want you gone as soon as possible, not looming over me while we wait for a reply.' He sighed mournfully. 'Today has brought me nothing but trouble. First there was that letter, and now there is you.'

'What letter?' asked Chaloner politely.

'The one from John Fry, informing me that if I release all the political prisoners in my care, the whole country will call me a hero. Here. Read it for yourself.'

Chaloner did, impressed by the elegant turn of phrase and handsome writing. It had been scribed on expensive paper, and there was a distinctive purple seal that lent it a sense of gravity. It was signed *Your unalterable freinde and servant, Jno. Fry.* He handed it back.

'If you do as he suggests, you are likely to end up incarcerated yourself.'

Sligo sighed again. 'I know, and it is a pity, because I should like to be a hero. So would every gaol-keeper in London – Fry sent the same message to all of us, even the Tower.'

'Do you think anyone might be tempted?' asked Chaloner, suspecting the unrest would gain considerable momentum if all London's rebels and malcontents were freed en masse.

'Some might. It is not easy being a keeper, you know. First, there is the challenge of feeding a lot of people on a very small budget; and second, there is the delicate business of deciding who goes in which cell. One must be careful, or there are mishaps.'

Chaloner did not understand and was not sure he wanted to, but Sligo was warming to his theme, and was already explaining.

'It would not do to put Levellers and Fifth Monarchists in the same room, because they fight. The same goes for Anabaptists and Catholics, while Quakers have to be kept separate from everyone, because they are universally unpopular but are too nice to hit anyone back.'

232

'Knight,' said Chaloner, eager to ask his questions and leave. 'He was brought here last Thursday, but he died.'

'Yes. He claimed he was innocent, but most do when they first arrive.'

'What happened to him?'

'I put him in a cell on his own, but it was a mistake because he hanged himself. I should have put him in with a lunatic, because they can be entertaining and would have kept his spirits up. Would you like to see his corpse? No one has claimed it, but we are obliged to keep it a week before passing it to Chyrurgeons' Hall. Wiseman wants it. It is a nice specimen – well fed.'

'He cannot have Knight,' said Chaloner sharply. 'I will arrange his burial.'

Sligo's pallid face broke into a grin when Chaloner placed several coins on the table. He scooped them up, then led the way through a series of doors, humming under his breath. With each one, Chaloner felt there was less breathable air. He struggled not to cough, afraid he might not be able to stop once he started. Eventually, they reached the dismal little chamber near the kitchens that was used for housing the dead. Chaloner did not know which was worse, the cloying aroma of decay or the stench of the prisoners' dinner.

He knelt and searched Knight's body. There were no valuables of any description, and the clerk was missing his hat, cloak, stockings and shoes. However, the thieving gaolers had left the letter that was tucked inside his shirt. Chaloner was about to read it when he happened to glance at Knight's throat. There were two parallel abrasions. The thicker, higher one had been caused by the rope that was still knotted around his neck; the other was thinner and deeper.

'He was garrotted!' he cried angrily, shoving the letter in his pocket to study later. 'And then strung up as though he had hanged himself. How could you fail to notice such an obvious ploy?'

Shocked, Sligo started to argue, but even he could see the spy was right, and turned abruptly to send for the warden who had discovered the body. It was not many moments before the man arrived, a sullen, unshaven fellow with lice so abundant that they were like snow in his hair. He was startled but defensive when Sligo pointed at the wounds and demanded an explanation.

'We were busy that day with a lot of drunks,' he bleated. 'We never had time to think—'

'What kind of drunks?' interrupted Chaloner. 'Apprentices?'

'Old soldiers, probably. We released them the next morning, when someone paid their fine.'

'Did Knight have any visitors?' demanded Chaloner.

'A vicar. Although none of us had seen him before . . .'

'What did he look like?' Chaloner was struggling to control his rising temper, aware that the warden's careless ineptitude had cost Knight his life.

The man gulped. 'I don't rightly remember. Your size, I think. Brown hair and the kind of broad-brimmed black hat that clerics like. But he was decent – gave us money to drink the King's health. It wouldn't have been him what murdered—'

'Who, then?' snapped Chaloner. 'Another turnkey? You?'

'No!' The warden was growing frightened. 'So I suppose it must have been him. But he seemed so genteel. Polite, like.'

'You should have been suspicious when Knight "committed suicide" with a rope,' said Chaloner to Sligo, disgusted. 'Obviously, he did not bring one with him, and its inexplicable appearance should have raised the alarm.'

Neither Sligo nor the gaoler could answer the charge, and Chaloner left with guilt weighing on him more heavily than ever. He took a hackney to the Westminster charnel house, which allowed him to read the note he had found in Knight's shirt. It informed one Rachel Upton of Scalding Alley that he was innocent of the charges that had been brought against him, and finished with a request for her to post the letters under the bed. Chaloner supposed he would have to locate her – and the bed – as soon as he had finished with Wiseman.

The charnel house did nothing to raise his spirits. It was a dismal building, located between a storage facility for coal and a granary. Caring for the dead was a lucrative business, because its owner, John Kersey, was immaculately attired in a fine woollen suit that Chaloner suspected had been made by a Court tailor. His mortuary was a busy place, and not just with corpses: it attracted interested visitors, and the money he earned from showing off cadavers, along with the small display of artefacts he had gathered over the years, earned him a very respectable living.

'You are late,' he said, as Chaloner entered. 'Wiseman is waiting.'

Wiseman was indeed waiting, and was cross about it. He scowled as Chaloner walked in, but it quickly turned to a frown of concern. 'Are you ill? You are very pale.'

'It has been a difficult day, not made any easier by you laying claim to the body of that Post Office clerk,' replied Chaloner shortly. 'Knight.'

'Why should I not have him?' asked the surgeon indignantly. 'No family has come forward, and his is a nice corpse, much better than the scrawny felons I usually get from Newgate.'

Chaloner glared. 'How can he be a felon? He was not tried in a court of law, so his guilt was never proven. Besides, he said he was innocent.'

'Show me a villain who does not,' challenged Wiseman. Then he relented. 'But I would not have bagged his remains had I known you wanted them. However, I shall be vexed if you sell them to another surgeon. I did see them first.'

'No one will have them,' said Chaloner tiredly. 'I will arrange for them to be buried in St Mary Bothaw. It was their . . . it was *his* parish, I believe.'

'No, leave it to me.' Wiseman bristled at Chaloner's immediate suspicion. 'The rector is my patient, and I have prevailed upon him with this sort of request before. The ceremony will take place late tomorrow afternoon.'

Chaloner did not ask how he knew the minister would be available then – few men were equal to denying the bombastic surgeon and any patient would never dare risk it. He nodded his thanks, and gestured that they should make a start on Mary Wood. Wiseman led the way to a table, on which lay a woman of middling years. Her eyes were closed, and her body was covered in whitish vesicles. Chaloner instinctively stepped back, noting that Wiseman was clad in a thick leather apron and wore gloves.

'The small-pox,' the surgeon explained. 'Not the malignant form, as I was led to believe, but the milder kind, from which most people recover. Mary would have been alive today if someone had not fed her poison. The rumours were right: she *was* murdered.'

He gestured to her face, where four small but distinct contusions lay in a line along her jaw.

'Finger-marks,' said Chaloner. He glanced at the surgeon. 'Does it mean that someone held her head and forced her to swallow a toxin?'

'It appears that way.' Wiseman began to take samples from inside her mouth.

'Why did you not notice the day she died? You said you were summoned to tend her.'

'Yes, but she was dead when I arrived, so I did no more than give her a cursory glance. This is the first time I have examined her properly. I imagine the Earl will ask you to investigate, because she was a courtier, and we cannot have those dispatched with gay abandon. Not even her.'

'You knew her, then?'

'Yes. She had a spiteful tongue and sticky fingers,' replied Wiseman, reiterating what Hannah had said. 'Her husband will have to be told the sorry news, of course. Unfortunately, he went to Chelsey this morning, and will not be home until tomorrow.'

'How do you know?'

'Because I did not want him bursting in on me while I examined his wife, so I made some enquiries about his plans.'

'Perhaps we should ride there and tell him. He has a right to know.'

But Wiseman shook his head. 'She died last Thursday, and it is now Tuesday. Delaying a few hours will make no difference, and I am not eager to shatter his peace of mind.'

'He cannot be that distressed by her death, not if he is gallivanting about the countryside.'

'I imagine you will find out when you visit him. I cannot do it – I am too busy.'

Chaloner was not happy to be allotted such a task, but supposed there might be an advantage in breaking the news. Wood was sufficiently lunatic that he might well be the culprit, and if the Earl did order an investigation, Chaloner would have a head start. He watched Wiseman go to a bench in a corner, and begin to test his samples on some hapless rodent.

'Did you analyse that potion I gave you last night?' he asked.

Wiseman nodded. 'It is Epsom Water – full of natural salts that promote good health. It is expensive, and the phial is crystal, not glass. A handsome gift. Come here. Quickly!'

Chaloner did not move. 'Why?'

Wiseman turned to face him, and Chaloner was alarmed by his sudden pallor. 'It is too late – the rat is dead. I wanted you to see it, because the sample I have just taken from Mary produced exactly the same symptoms as the toxin in the bread you gave me – the stuff that killed the birds.'

Chaloner frowned. 'Is it readily available then?'

'It is not,' said Wiseman with conviction. 'In fact, I have never encountered it before, which means it has either been imported from abroad, or some reckless lunatic has been experimenting.'

'An apothecary?' asked Chaloner.

'I sincerely doubt it. They tend to devise remedies that cure their customers, not kill them. However, think of the repercussions of this vile toxin on your investigation. It means you do not have two separate cases here, Chaloner. You have one.'

Chapter 8

Chaloner accepted the offer of wine in Kersey's sitting room, because he was bemused by the connection Wiseman had made, and wanted to mull it over while the surgeon was available for questions. Wiseman settled his vast red bulk in Kersey's best chair, and began to describe the examinations he had conducted on the victims of the Post Office explosion. Kersey listened with the interest of a fellow professional, while Chaloner thought about Mary and the King's fowl.

Other than the poison, what tied them together? The bird-killers were either courtiers or had access to White Hall, while Mary had been a courtier and so was her husband. Wood was also on Storey's list of suspects. Could Wood have taken against the royal collection for lunatic reasons of his own, and then used the same toxin on his wife? Or was the culprit someone with a grudge against the monarchy, who wanted to deprive the Queen of a dresser and the King of his ducks? Did it mean Gery and Wood could be discounted, because of their Royalist convictions?

'I have not had much previous experience with blast

injuries,' Wiseman was telling Kersey with ghoulish delight. 'So I learned a great deal from the Post House Yard incident.'

'It must have been a huge discharge to mangle the Alibond brothers,' said the charnel-house keeper. 'They were large men. Did you examine those two boys, by the way? Poor little mites.'

'I did, but they were not boys – they were stunted men in their twenties. They should have been agile enough to run, and I do not understand why they lingered.'

'They were going to steal logs.' Chaloner had a vague recollection of a hand reaching out to grab one, and Temperance had seen it, too. 'The cart was full of fire-wood.'

'A tempting target for the poor,' sighed Kersey. 'Especially this weather.'

'But there was money in their pockets,' said Wiseman. 'A lot of it. Why filch logs when they had enough to buy a coppice? You are wrong, Chaloner: they were not interested in wood.'

Chaloner was bemused. 'Then what else would they have been doing?'

'Who knows?' shrugged Wiseman. 'Your warning was perfectly clear, and everyone else ran away. They, on the other hand, moved *towards* the cart. I saw them myself.'

'Maybe it was they who made the thing explode,' suggested Kersey.

'No, there was a fuse,' said Chaloner. 'I saw the smoke, and I smelt it, too. It was burning long before they reached the vehicle.'

'Then perhaps they underestimated the danger, and wanted a ringside seat.' Kersey moved to another subject. 'Is it true that the Company of Barber-Surgeons is dissatisfied with the King, Wiseman? I hear they joined the butchers in a riot last night.'

'Our apprentices have always been unruly,' replied Wiseman stiffly. 'Which is why I never take them on as pupils. I do not mind lecturing or allowing them to watch me conduct anatomies, but I refuse to have them trailing after me while I deal with patients.'

'So is your Company rebelling or not?' asked Kersey impatiently.

Wiseman regarded him coolly. 'Only the students. Their masters have more sense.'

When they left the charnel house, Wiseman invited Chaloner to share a hackney to Fleet Street. As Chaloner intended to visit the Fleet Rookery to find out why the Yeans had died with a fortune in their pockets, he was happy to accept. However, he was not happy when the coach trundled past Wiseman's house and continued down Ludgate Hill.

'We are going to the Crown,' explained Wiseman, reaching forward to stop him from banging on the ceiling to tell the driver to stop. 'Where Temperance will be waiting. No, do not scowl! A decent meal will rebalance your humours, and I do not like the pallor that hangs about you.'

'I doubt Temperance will be pleased. Not if she is expecting a romantic occasion for two.'

'We are never romantic in public; it would not be seemly,' declared the surgeon, leaving Chaloner to wonder exactly what he understood by the word.

Unwilling to jump out of a moving carriage, Chaloner sat back and watched the buildings flash by – Ludgate, St Paul's, Cutlers' Hall – until they arrived at Dowgate Hill. He alighted reluctantly, aware that he was again

241

wearing clothes that were un-Cavalier, and that might see him in trouble somewhere like the Crown.

He felt even more uncomfortable when the first people he saw there were Gery, Morland and Freer. Gery stopped eating to gaze at Chaloner with open hatred, and the spy was sure he would have attacked had they been in a less public place. Freer offered the marshal another slice of pie, which resulted in the dish being dashed from the table with a furious sweep of the arm.

The clatter silenced the rumble of conversation in the tavern, although Wiseman did not seem to notice, intent as he was on meeting his lover. He thrust his way through the crowd, not caring whom he shunted, and Chaloner followed, grateful for the speed with which they were moving away from Gery. However, it was not long before he sensed someone close behind him. He whipped around, anticipating an attack, but it was only Freer.

'Gery sent me to tell you to leave London.' Freer's expression was apologetic. 'You had better do it, Tom – he will not forgive that prank with the icy water. Go while you can.'

'The Earl plans to send me to Russia when the bird-killer is caught,' replied Chaloner, not without rancour. 'So I will not be here for much longer, anyway.'

Freer nodded. 'I will tell him, but be careful. He is a very dangerous man.'

As Chaloner had predicted, Temperance was not pleased to learn that her intimate dinner was to be shared, although she struggled to mask her disappointment when Wiseman shot her an admonishing glance.

'I have ordered woodcock,' she said. 'And gherkins. I

am not sure what gherkins are, but they are expensive, so they must be good. Followed by chicken and quail.'

'Birds,' said Chaloner unhappily.

'Dead ones,' said Wiseman cheerfully, and launched into an account of what had happened to Mary Wood. Temperance listened with rapt attention, while Chaloner supposed he must be growing squeamish, because the grisly monologue deprived him of any appetite he might have had. Wiseman packed some of the food in a cloth, and made him put it in his pocket for later.

At that point, several patrons began a loud-voiced discussion about what they would do to any Roundhead who still approved of Cromwell. They were vicious and uncompromising, and Chaloner was shocked by the depth of their passion. He left as soon as he could do so politely, aiming for the back door to avoid passing them.

He was almost outside when he saw a man sitting alone wearing a thick cloak and a wide-brimmed hat that shielded his face. The disguise did not extend to his hands, though, and Chaloner recognised them immediately: they had played a viol in Palmer's house. Not far away were two yeomen, laughing and chatting with the landlord.

'Oh, it is you,' whispered the Major, as Chaloner slid on to the bench next to him. His face was shiny with sweat, and his frightened eyes were everywhere. 'You startled me.'

'What are you doing?' asked Chaloner. 'Surely not spying? That would be reckless.'

'It is not my idea, I assure you,' said the Major miserably. 'But Gery said I would never be released unless I help him monitor potential rebels.' His hand shook as he shoved a piece of paper across the table. 'So here is my report. Give it to Clarendon.'

'But everyone in here is a Royalist,' Chaloner pointed out. 'The government has nothing to fear from them. They are all like Gery, fanatical in their loyalty.'

'Yes, but they itch to fight Roundheads, so they are a threat to the King's peace,' explained the Major. 'Why do they not understand that violence begets nothing but more violence?'

'If I am to be your messenger-boy, tell me why the Post Office—'

'Chaloner, please!' groaned the Major. 'I *cannot* talk to you, so why do you insist on hounding me? However, if you must meddle, then investigate the threat on my life – this assassination that is the talk of all London. I should hate to be cut down the moment I have won my freedom.'

Chaloner stood. 'You might be safer if you did not spy in places like the Crown. Some folk here will remember that you were in the New Model Army.'

The Major swallowed hard, and Chaloner saw he was on the verge of tears. 'So were you, according to Gery, although you must have been very young. Did we ever meet?'

'Not that I recall,' lied Chaloner. The Major might never trust him if reminded of the arrogantly precocious brat who had barracked him before the Battle of Naseby.

Chaloner hesitated when he was outside, pondering what was more urgent – investigating Oxenbridge, cornering Harper, tracking Gardner, delivering Knight's letter, or asking after the Yeans. He was still weighing up his options when the door opened and the Major stepped out. His yeomen were not with him, and Chaloner wondered whether he was making a bid for escape.

He did not go far. Glancing around with such obvious unease that it attracted amused smirks from passers-by, the Major entered the Antwerp Coffee House. Curious, Chaloner followed, settling in a smoky recess at the back of the room where he pretended to read a newsbook. The Major opted for a seat in a corner, which made it plain that he was there to monitor what was going on. Chaloner cringed when he began to make notes. Did the man *want* to be caught?

Fortunately for the Major, the Antwerp's customers were too interested in bawling their opinions to notice. Their debate was essentially the same as the one in the Crown, the only difference being that it was Cavaliers cast in the role of villain. Landlord Young was busy with his coffee jug, and Chaloner recognised several leading army officers from the wars. His elderly neighbour Stokes was among them, Cliffe at his side, although they took no part in the discussion, and seemed dismayed by the braying antagonism.

The Major did not stay long. Once outside, he cornered an urchin, and paid him a penny to take his report to White Hall. Chaloner caught the lad before he had scampered too far, and offered him sixpence for it. The boy handed it over with a delighted grin.

Chaloner returned to the Crown just in time to hear the Major assure his agitated guards that he had only gone to look for a latrine. His voice shook almost uncontrollably, and one of them took his arm, apparently afraid he might faint. They believed the lie – or were too relieved by his reappearance to argue – and the three of them climbed into a hackney bound for the Tower.

Chaloner hailed a hackney of his own, and read both messages as it conveyed him to the Fleet Rookery. The first was just what had been claimed: a summary of the rabid railings in the Crown with a list of the loudest speakers. The second did the same for the Antwerp, with several patrons named as being particularly bellicose. Chaloner was glad Stokes and Cliffe were not among them.

He stared out of the window, and wondered why Gery was putting the Major through such torments; he could only suppose it was revenge for his Parliamentarian past. It was vindictive, petty and ignoble, and Chaloner saw that Freer had been right to warn him to be wary of the man.

The Fleet Rookery was a jumble of narrow alleys and tiny yards. Its buildings were dilapidated, and people were packed tightly inside them, sometimes as many as thirty to a room. Families often slept in shifts, one group evacuating the beds as another came to rest, and the area was rife with disease, crime and poverty. There were no trees or flowers, and its streets were an unbroken monotony of mud, rotting plaster and decaying timbers.

The forces of law and order rarely set foot there, and any number of dangerous felons had taken refuge inside. Gangs prowled, jealously guarding their territory, and intruders were not tolerated. Chaloner was left alone partly because it was clear he would be no easy victim, and partly because he had a friend there, an old woman who had taken a liking to him. He suspected she was a witch, and that the louts who roamed in undisciplined packs were frightened of her.

He sensed unseen eyes on him as he walked down the

first of the seedy lanes that would take him to her cottage in Turnagain Lane, and the hair on the back of his neck rose in the way it always did when he was in danger. But he did not look around. Eventually, he reached Mother Greene's door, where he knocked politely.

'I thought you must have left the country,' she remarked as she opened it. A waft of warm air drifted out, carrying with it the scent of mint and fresh bread. 'It has been months since you visited.'

'Sweden,' he replied, handing her the parcel Wiseman had packed.

She opened it eagerly. 'Gherkins! How thoughtful. And all the way from Sweden, too!'

She had turned and hobbled back inside the house before he could explain. When he was sitting next to her fire, relishing its warmth and the scent of burning fir cones, she presented him with a cinnamon cake and a cup of milk from the ass that she kept in her yard. The milk was still warm and had a slightly soapy flavour; he drank it only because he did not want to offend her.

'Your wife does not look after you properly,' she said, regarding him critically. 'That is what comes of hiring too many servants: they all think you are someone else's responsibility and you end up being shamefully neglected.'

Chaloner laughed, amused by the notion that any of his staff might be even remotely interested in his welfare, then listened to her talk. It was mostly inconsequential and probably largely untrue; she was merely taking advantage of someone who did not interrupt with stories of his own.

'Why did you come?' she asked eventually. 'I am sure it was not just to bring me gherkins.'

'No,' he admitted. 'Did you know Harold and Henry

Yean? They were killed in the explosion outside the Post Office last week.'

'Yes,' she said, nodding. 'Along with two fat clerks and Sir Henry Wood's servant. I imagine a great deal of fuss has been made about them, but you are the first to enquire after the Yeans.'

Which was hardly surprising, thought Chaloner, given that the Fleet Rookery did not encourage visitors who asked questions. 'What can you tell me about them?'

'They were scamps,' she replied with a fond smile. 'They lived outside the law, and were thieves, of course. But they were good to their mother, and that counts for a lot.'

'I understand they ran errands for the Curator of Birds at St James's Park.'

'Yes. Mr Storey hates foxes, and paid them to bring him dead ones. They hunted the things as far afield as Hampstead and Islington.'

'What else did they do for him?'

'Gathered feathers to take to the Court milliners. They were reliable but dull-witted, and if they had stayed with what they knew, they would still be alive.'

'What do you mean?'

'They became embroiled in something dark, and were out of their depth. They came to me for protective charms, but the evil in which they had enmeshed themselves was too powerful for me.'

Chaloner stared at her. 'What are you saying? That their deaths in the explosion were not a case of being in the wrong place at the wrong time?'

'I doubt it. Unfortunately, they were too frightened to tell me much, although they did mention wicked men – military fellows – who were the root of all their trouble.'

'Did they tell you any names?' She shook her head, so Chaloner made some suggestions. 'Gery, Freer or Morland? Oxenbridge? Harper, Lamb or Smartfoot? Gardner? Le Notre? O'Neill?'

'No. I have never heard of any of them. Except Oxenbridge.'

'What do you know about him?'

'That he is Satan's spawn. He has no home and no roots, and he just appears whenever evil is afoot, as if by magic. You would be wise to leave him alone.'

Chaloner changed the subject, not because of the ridiculous shiver that ran down his spine, but because he knew from the stubborn jut of her chin that she would not elaborate. 'When they died, the Yeans had a large sum of money with them. How did they come by it?'

'I have no idea. But it *was* a large sum, because that nice Surgeon Wiseman sent it to their mothers. However, it was far in excess of what they could have earned from Storey, so it must have come from these dangerous military men. It was a godsend, though. There is fever here, and people are dying for want of food and warmth. Of course, we still need more . . .'

Chaloner gave her all the coins he had, then flinched when she tossed the contents of a small pot over him. She made no explanation, but he suspected he had just been doused with a protective charm. Wryly, he hoped it would be more effective than the one she had given the Yeans.

His next stop was Scalding Alley, to find Rachel Upton. It was where live birds were taken from the Poultry Market to be prepared for the table, and was characterised by hissing boilers, the reek of burned feathers and

an unpleasant sludge underfoot that comprised drop-
pings and bloody mud. Crates holding terrified birds
were stacked along the sides, and the air was full of
piteous clucks.

From the outside, Rachel's house looked as shabby
and disreputable as the rest of the lane, but inside it was
clean, with bunches of sweet-smelling herbs hanging from
the ceiling. A door of exceptional thickness eliminated
most of the racket, and when her landlord – a man
named Morgan – led Chaloner to a set of rooms at the
back of the house, the place was almost eerie in its silence.

He introduced a woman in her thirties with a pleasant
face and clothes that were darned but of good quality.
She was holding a shirt, and Chaloner saw more of them
stacked by the window; she eked a living from mending
and sewing. When she spoke, her diction was refined,
and he supposed she was a gentlewomen fallen on hard
times, no doubt as a result of the wars.

'I have a message for you from Joseph Knight,' he
began. 'He—'

'He killed himself in Newgate Gaol,' she interrupted
harshly, and started to turn away.

'He was innocent,' he said quickly, to stop her from
shutting him out. 'He told me so himself, and I believe
him. Moreover, he did not commit suicide: he was
murdered.'

'Murdered?' she whispered, aghast. 'But that is worse
– sordid and dirty. And to think we were to have been
married next summer!'

'He was going to leave Post House Yard and weave
baskets instead,' explained Morgan.

'We would not have been wealthy, but we would have
been comfortable,' Rachel went on. 'He hated the General

Letter Office, although he was happy there when Bishop was in charge.'

'But things changed after O'Neill took over?' probed Chaloner.

Rachel nodded. 'He said it grew full of vice. He refused to condone it, which was brave, considering that one of the men pressing him to participate was Clement Oxenbridge. Have you ever seen Oxenbridge? He looks like a demon with his white face and black eyes.'

'He does,' agreed Chaloner. 'Did Knight ever mention John Fry?'

'Once, to say that he thought Oxenbridge might be helping him. He wanted to add more, but I stopped him. I did not want to hear anything involving such terrible people.'

Chaloner was sorry, suspecting Knight might have been glad to unburden himself. He handed her the letter, and watched her read it. She frowned, then looked up in bewilderment. 'He says there are letters under my bed, but there are not.'

'Do you mind if I look anyway?'

She stood aside reluctantly, and he entered a room that was clean, neat and that had been made homely with cushions and hand-sewn rugs. It did not take him long to discover that one of the floorboards by the bed was loose. He prised it up to reveal a recess that contained a wad of papers.

'I did not know,' gulped Rachel, watching Chaloner sort through them. She reached out and snatched the one bearing her name. 'You may have the rest. I do not want anything to do with things that result in prison and murder.'

Once out in the lane, Chaloner inspected what he

251

had found. There were twenty or so letters, addressed to such people as Bishop, Wood, Palmer, Clarendon, Morland, Kate O'Neill, and various other courtiers and members of the Privy Council. He was tempted to open them then and there, but common sense prevailed. Nothing would be gained by advertising the fact that they had been read before they were delivered – he needed a hot knife to slit the seals and matching wax to repair them afterwards. Thurloe would have the necessary equipment, so he decided to visit him later, to do it together.

However, he did not mind invading Morland's post, and opened the one addressed to the secretary without hesitation. The message was short and had obviously been written in a hurry:

> *I begg leave to informe you that a Great Evill will soone unfold in our Faire Citie. Look to Clemente Oxenbridge and Jno Fry, who will set it aflame with their tonges and plotts amonge the apprentices. I hear Fry rooms at the Angell Inn in St Gyles Fields. You must silence him before London is aflame and we are at warre again. Your Most Humble Servant, Jos. Knight*

Chaloner shoved the documents in his coat and began to run towards Lincoln's Inn. He would collect Thurloe and they would go at once to corner Fry, returning to open the remaining letters afterwards. Unfortunately, when he reached the Fleet Bridge, breathing hard and with his lame leg burning as it always did after strenuous exercise, he saw the Earl's carriage. Clarendon spotted him at the same time and called him over. Pretending not to hear would have been too risky, so Chaloner had no choice but to go and see what his master wanted. He hoped he would not be delayed too long, impatient now to hear what Fry had to say.

'Where are you going in such a hurry, Chaloner? I assume it is something to do with the dead birds. After all, you have no other enquiry at the moment.'

His cool tone warned Chaloner that it would be unwise to admit that he had disobeyed orders. The spy was even more determined to say nothing when he saw Clarendon was not alone; Morland was in the coach, too, comfortably ensconced in the shadows to one side.

'I am going to St James's Park,' Chaloner lied.

'Good,' said the Earl, and the coach door swung open. 'Climb in. We shall take you as far as Charing Cross.'

'And you can tell us what is so urgent as we go,' added Morland, slyly challenging.

'It will be quicker on foot at this time of day,' hedged Chaloner, backing away. 'And—'

'Nonsense,' interrupted the Earl. 'The traffic is unusually light today. Now get in.'

Chaloner swore under his breath as he did as he was told, struggling to conceal his frustration.

'So, Tom,' said Morland with a nasty smile once they were rattling along. 'I am sure My Lord Clarendon is eager to hear what progress have you made.'

'Quite a bit,' replied Chaloner. He was careful not to look at the entrance to Chancery Lane as they sped past it, lest the secretary noticed and guessed where he had really been going.

'Good,' said the Earl. 'But that is hardly an informative answer. Will you elaborate?'

'Not yet, sir.' To forestall accusations of impertinence, Chaloner trotted out an excuse that Gery had once used.

'I have set traps, and talking out of turn may cause them to misfire.'

He expected some kind of remonstration, and was surprised and a little concerned when the Earl only nodded and turned to stare out of the window. Morland promptly began an ingratiating monologue about the 'significant inroads' he and Gery had made into the Post Office enquiry, carefully attributing all their success to his own efforts. Yet it was hollow chatter, and Chaloner was left with the impression that they knew even less than he did.

'I shall expect a solution to this bird affair tomorrow,' said the Earl, coming out of his reverie as the carriage rolled to a standstill when their destination was reached. 'It would be a pity if someone else exposed the culprits to the King first. Please do not fail me.'

Chaloner alighted from the Earl's coach, and was immediately wary when Morland did likewise. Did the man intend to accompany him to see the birds, to make sure he actually went? Or had he indeed surmised that it had been something else that had set him racing west with such urgency? Chaloner aimed for the park's main gate, feeling he had no choice but to continue the charade.

'I met our friend Thurloe earlier,' said Morland, falling into step beside him.

Chaloner stopped walking. 'I doubt that is how he sees you. Friends do not betray each other.'

'That is water under the bridge and it was for the best.' Morland gave one of his sly smirks. 'We now have our King back, and I am proud of my role in bringing it about. I am sure you are also delighted that we have a monarchy again. Are you not?'

254

Chaloner disliked the secretary trying to entrap him. 'Leave Thurloe alone. Do you hear?'

'I never did him any harm – and I could have done, given the secrets I knew. But he is nothing now, although I did do him a favour today. William Prynne, his fellow bencher, was bitten by a horse, and its owner has threatened to sue. It will make Lincoln's Inn a laughing stock, so I advised Thurloe to intervene. The affair will take him hours to settle, but better that than the alternative.'

So Morland had ensured that Thurloe would be tied up half the night, thought Chaloner irritably – nothing involving the tiresomely loquacious Prynne was ever sorted out in a hurry. When the secretary bobbed his head and moved away, his triumphant grin made Chaloner suspect he had guessed that plans had been scuppered.

Chaloner aimed for the Angel as soon as he was sure Morland had gone, supposing he would have to tackle Fry alone, and was just passing the stump of the medieval monument that gave Charing Cross its name when he heard a flageolet. He stopped abruptly. The player was wearing a faded red cloak and a blue hat.

On a milder day, the musician's merry jigs might have attracted listeners, but dusk had brought a bitter wind, and people were eager to be home. Thus he was standing in splendid isolation, with passers-by giving him a wide berth lest he should ask for money, and Chaloner was spotted long before he could come close. The fellow stopped playing and took to his heels.

Chaloner would have caught him had he been fresh, but his lame leg still ached from his earlier run, and it slowed him down. The musician ducked through a stream of carriages, and was lost to sight. Chaloner spent a few moments hunting for him, but soon realised he was wasting his time. Disgusted, he began to retrace his steps, but then he saw another familiar face. It was the feral Senior Clerk Harper, who was striding purposefully towards the Strand.

Chaloner tugged his hat down, hoping it and the gathering darkness of night would be enough to prevent Harper from recognising him as the man who had waylaid him in the Cheapside tavern the day before.

'Excuse me,' he said, adopting a Buckinghamshire twang to disguise his voice. 'Where can I catch the coach to Dover?'

It was an innocuous question, designed to allow him to strike up a conversation. Thus he was wholly unprepared for the reaction it provoked. Harper whipped around with startling speed, and grabbed him by the front of his coat.

'I do not answer questions,' he snarled in his low, sinister voice. 'Not ever.'

Chaloner tried to push him away, but Harper's fingers were like steel. 'I only want to know about the coach to Dover,' he objected, still playing the bumpkin. 'Is it a secret, then?'

'If you want to live, you will not ask it again,' hissed Harper.

'My mother was right about London,' said Chaloner, finally wrenching himself free. 'It is full of villains and traitors. No wonder the place declared for Cromwell during the wars.'

Harper gave what might have been a laugh, although it was difficult to tell: the square was noisy. 'Then go back to whichever desolate county from which you hail.'

'Buckinghamshire,' supplied Chaloner artlessly. 'Have you ever been?'

Harper scowled. 'That is another question, and you are lucky I do not cut out your tongue.'

Chaloner moved fast, and then it was Harper grabbed by the coat. 'What is the Post—'

He got no further, because Harper was stabbing at his eyes with a knife. He ducked away, and the clerk used the opportunity to land a vicious kick that caught his lame leg. It hurt, and although he tried to limp after Harper, he simply could not move fast enough. Like the musician, Harper disappeared among the traffic.

Disgusted, Chaloner hobbled to the Angel, but his run of bad luck persisted: the landlord informed him that John Fry had indeed been in residence, but he had left that morning for Oxford.

'To return to his mathematics,' he confided. 'I am glad to see him gone, personally. He was a dreadful bore, and drove my other guests to distraction with his angles and cosines.'

'I meant a different John Fry,' said Chaloner. 'The political agitator.'

The landlord scowled. 'That was a nasty lie started by the pot-boys at the Imp next door. Fry the trouble-maker has never set foot in here and never will. This is a Royalist tavern, and his sort is not welcome.'

Chaloner went to the Imp, where the culprits gleefully confessed to what they had done, claiming it was in revenge for the Angel's lads smearing manure on their windows. Chaloner was disheartened. Would Knight's other letters be dead ends, too, and any 'evidence' just more unsubstantiated gossip? He was tempted to rip them open and find out, but then decided against it.

Impatience would serve no purpose, and it would be better to wait for Thurloe and his hot knife.

Meanwhile, he supposed he might as well go to St James's Park. Perhaps the bird-killers would appear, and he would have something to please the Earl in the morning.

Chaloner arrived at the park gate in a sour mood, angry to have lost the leads represented by the musician, Harper and John Fry in such a short space of time. His temper did not improve when he saw Storey and Eliot waiting for him.

'You told Eliot that there might be another attack on my charges tonight,' explained Storey. 'So we are here to stop it.' He grinned wolfishly. 'Those despicable rogues will be in for a shock when they come to do their filthy work.'

'No,' said Chaloner shortly, not liking the idea of amateur assistance. 'Thank you.'

'But there were three of them last time, and you will be outnumbered unless we stay,' argued Eliot. 'Besides, I shall enjoy punching their teeth out.'

'I shall do more than punch,' declared Storey, eyes flashing. 'I shall chop them into pieces and feed them to the foxes. And His Majesty will make me a knight for it.'

'Very possibly,' said Chaloner. 'But I am more efficient when working alone.'

'Then you will just have to adjust,' said Storey, opening the gate with a key, and indicating that Chaloner and Eliot should precede him inside. 'We shall leave this door ajar, to make it easy for them to get in. And then we will pounce.'

'No,' groaned Chaloner. 'It will warn them that something is amiss. *Please* go home and leave them to me.'

'Never,' stated Storey with finality. 'We are coming with you, and that is that.'

'Yes,' said Eliot with equal fervour. 'My bananas are near that Canal, and I would never forgive myself if one was damaged in a skirmish.'

Chaloner tried again. 'The poison they use is unusually strong, and even the merest touch can kill. You will be in great danger if you—'

'You cannot manage poison *and* deranged killers by yourself,' interrupted Storey. 'And our minds are made up, so there is no point arguing.'

'Consider us foot-soldiers,' added Eliot. 'Where would you like us deployed?'

They agreed on positions eventually, farther from the Canal than Eliot and Storey wanted, but too close as far as Chaloner was concerned. He put them together, in the hope that it would be safer, with strict instructions not to talk, even when they became bored.

'We shall remain mum until dawn if necessary,' promised Storey. 'You can rely on us.'

Chaloner suspected they would do nothing of the kind, and that their chattering presence would alert the culprits and drive them off. But there was nothing he could do about it, so he found a thick bush near the water and eased inside, hoping it would not be too long before something happened, because the night was bitterly cold.

Within an hour, the first sounds of fun began to emanate from White Hall, carried on a wind that blew from the north-east. It started gently enough, with flutes trilling what was meant to pass for Roman music, although it was not long before it was shattered by a braying trumpet. The fanfare ended in shrieks of laughter, followed by drums and a series of oddly metallic clashes.

The racket rose in volume and discordance as the night grew steadily colder. Chaloner began to shiver, and his feet and hands were soon so numb that he wondered whether he would be able to do anything if the culprits did arrive. Then he saw three shadows moving towards the Canal.

There was no moon, but starlight allowed him to see that all were swathed in thick coats and large hats, and that one was unsteady on his feet. Chaloner supposed he was drunk. He tensed when they passed the trees where Storey and Eliot were hiding, ready to race to the rescue should curator and gardener be discovered, but the trio did not falter and continued to make for the water.

The birds sensed the presence of hostile intruders, and began to shift and fuss. One of the men cooed softly, and dropped something on the ground, his target the crane with the wooden leg. Hoping the poison would not be eaten before he could destroy it, Chaloner burst from his hiding place, sword in his hand, aiming to have all three in White Hall's prison as quickly as possible.

Storey and Eliot were also racing forward, brandishing hoes and howling like banshees. Chaloner's stomach lurched when the trio did not scatter as most petty criminals would have done, but drew weapons and took up a fighting formation. Clearly, they had done battle together before. He swore under his breath. He had assumed that anyone low enough to hurt birds would be cowardly weaklings, and it had not occurred to him that they might be warriors. It was a foolish mistake, and he sincerely hoped his lapse of judgement would not cost Storey and Eliot their lives.

The tallest stepped forward to meet Chaloner's charge, and they exchanged a series of vicious blows that told him he was dealing with a man of considerable skill. Meanwhile, the drunk jabbed at him from behind, keeping his attention divided, while the third fended off Storey and Eliot with indolent ease. Chaloner saw the fellow was playing with them, biding his time until he grew bored, at which point they would die.

Chaloner intensified his efforts, but so did his opponent, and their swords flashed with such speed and ferocity that any blow finding its mark would have been instantly fatal. Meanwhile, the drunk was an annoying distraction. Chaloner lunged at the tall man, using an unorthodox manoeuvre that had him in retreat for a moment, then jabbed at the drunk with the dagger he held in his other hand. He missed, but the drunk dropped to his knees anyway.

The tall man came at Chaloner again, forcing him to give ground. It drove him beneath a canopy of trees, where it was more difficult to see, and he was hard-pressed to defend himself. His breath came in gasps, and he was sweating, hot for the first time in days. Then his opponent employed a peculiar twisting motion designed to wrench the sword from his hand. It did not succeed, but it jerked his wrist in a way that was unpleasant.

Aware that he was fighting for Eliot and Storey's lives as well as his own, Chaloner used every trick he had ever learned, eventually managing to turn his retreat into an offensive. The tall man met him blow for blow, but Chaloner was winning and was on the verge of delivering a swipe that would decide the outcome permanently when the drunk rallied.

Screaming incoherently, he raced towards Chaloner,

261

barrelling into him with enough force to send him cart-wheeling through the air. Chaloner was vaguely aware of Knight's letters flying from his coat before he landed with a crash that drove the breath from his body. Then there was a lot of yelling, and someone hollered that the palace guards were coming. His senses darkened, and the sounds of panicky confusion faded away.

Chaloner was not sure how long he lay in the frozen grass, but the first thing he did when he was able to move again was scrabble for his sword, feeling naked and vulnerable without it. Once it was in his hand, he struggled to his knees and looked around quickly. The drunk was lying on the ground next to him, being inspected by Eliot and Storey.

'They escaped.' Eliot sounded disgusted. 'Well, two of them escaped. This one will not be going anywhere. Unfortunately, he will not be answering questions either – he is dead.'

'But my birds are safe,' said Storey with grim satisfaction. 'We shall gather up the tainted bread, and when you catch the others, we shall make *them* eat it.'

Chaloner clambered unsteadily to his feet. 'Which way did they go?'

Eliot pointed. 'But you will not catch them. They have too great a start.'

'Where are the palace guards?'

'Oh, I made that up,' said Eliot airily. 'The tall man was preparing to stab you as you lay helpless, so I shouted to our "rescuers" that we were by the Canal. Fortunately, it coincided with a particularly loud bit of the King's soirée, so it did sound like an army was coming.'

'A Roman army,' said Storey drily. 'But it worked. The bastards fled.'

'Did you recognise them?'

'No, it was too dark,' replied Storey. 'These courtiers knew when they decided to fight rather than run that we would never be able to identify them in the gloom.'

'What makes you think they were courtiers?' asked Chaloner, suspecting that the trio had not expected their ambushers to survive, so the darkness had been immaterial. But Storey and Eliot did not need to hear that.

'Because they fought like courtiers,' explained Eliot, as if the answer were obvious. 'All that mincing around with rapiers. You included. And the men I saw feeding poison to the swan last Saturday were courtiers – they had to be, as only courtiers were in the park at the time.'

'How do you know the ones who killed the swan were the men we fought tonight?'

'Because they are,' said Storey impatiently. 'Eliot saw three rogues giving my swan toxic crumbs, and three rogues tried to kill a crane this evening. The first incident happened when there was a courtly rumpus, and so did the second. They are the same people.'

The 'courtly rumpus' was still ongoing, and Chaloner found himself thinking that if His Majesty showed the same dedication to affairs of state as he did to his pleasures, then the country might not be on the verge of war with the Dutch and London would not be in such a turmoil of discontent. Or was that just the old Parliamentarian in him?

'What are you doing?' asked Eliot, as the spy dropped to his hands and knees and started to grope about on the ground.

'Some documents fell out of my coat when I fell. I need them back.'

'I saw the tall man scoop something up before he ran

263

off,' said Storey. 'It was too dark to see clearly, but it was something oblong and pale. Were they very important?'

Chaloner regarded him in dismay, and began to search again, systematically at first, but then with increasing desperation. Storey helped, and Eliot fetched a lamp, but by the time the gardener returned, Chaloner knew it was hopeless: Knight's letters had gone. He was disgusted with himself. It was the second valuable clue he had managed to mislay, counting the papers he had grabbed from the Post Office's secret room.

'That drunk hit you very hard,' said Storey, clearly thinking Chaloner had been knocked out of his wits. 'So we shall escort you home. Are you married? You will need a wife to care for you.'

'Yes,' said Chaloner. Then he recalled that Hannah was away, and he did not want to return to Tothill Street to be sniggered at by any remaining servants. 'No.'

'Yes *and* no,' grinned Eliot. 'Perhaps we had better not ask, Storey. Not every man is as fortunate to have a woman like my Jane.'

By the light of Eliot's lamp, they gathered up the poisoned bread and put it in a pot. Then Chaloner hunted again for the letters, hating the prospect of confessing to Thurloe that he had lost another set of documents that might have provided answers. Afterwards, downcast and full of self-recrimination, he took the lantern and went to inspect the drunk. He turned him over with his foot, then recoiled in surprise.

It was Smartfoot.

Chapter 9

For a moment, Chaloner could only stare at the dead man's face, but then questions surged into his mind. Smartfoot was the second postal clerk to have died in the park, so did that mean the General Letter Office *was* behind the bird killings? That Leak had not just accepted employment from someone else, as his friend Rea had suggested? And if so, was Controller O'Neill behind it all?

But what possible reason could O'Neill have for dispatching the King's fowl? Or for dispatching Mary, for that matter? Was it because she lived in Post House Yard, and she had seen something that necessitated her silence? Storey lived there, too, so was the same true of him, except that he had not been ill in bed, so they had opted to kill his birds instead?

On the three occasions that Chaloner had met Smartfoot, Lamb had been with him. However, Lamb had not been one of the trio that night – he was heavy and brutal, whereas the two swordsmen had been light-footed. Moreover, Lamb's preferred weapon seemed to be a cudgel, not a blade. So who were Smartfoot's companions? Harper seemed a good guess. Or O'Neill. Or Gardner, perhaps. And if Gardner, was Oxenbridge involved, given that the two knew each other well enough to skulk around White Hall in the dark together?

Chaloner pulled away Smartfoot's clothing to assess how he had died, but the only visible wound was a cut on his arm, puffy and inflamed. Chaloner suspected he had inflicted it the previous evening – he certainly recalled Smartfoot reeling away when they had done battle at the Post Office. He sniffed the clerk's mouth, and was surprised when there was no reek of ale.

'Do you know him?' asked Eliot.

'No,' lied Chaloner, thinking the less he and Storey knew, the safer they would be.

'Are my birds safe?' asked Storey, trembling now the excitement was over. 'Have we given these scoundrels such a fright that they will never dare set foot in this park again?'

'Leak's death did not stop them, and Smart— this man's will not either. They have a reason for doing what they do, and until we understand what it is, your birds remain at risk.'

Chaloner, Storey and Eliot carried Smartfoot to the gate, and took him to the Westminster charnel house in a hackney. When the grim business was done, Storey said that he and Eliot were going to return to the park and stand guard there until dawn; Chaloner let them do it only because he was sure the culprits were unlikely to return that night. Once they had been dropped off at the main gate, Chaloner asked the hackney driver to take him to Wiseman's house, wanting the poisoned bread lodged with someone who would appreciate its dangers. He alighted wearily, hoping the surgeon would be in.

He was in luck. Wiseman was not only home, but ensconced in his cosy parlour in front of a roaring fire with his ginger cat on his knees. Chaloner moved towards the blaze gratefully, while Wiseman locked the tainted crumbs in a stout box. When he had finished, the surgeon insisted that they both scrub their hands thoroughly with a foul-smelling abrasive. Only when he was sure they were poison-free did he invite his guest to share a plate of food that Temperance had sent – elegant, expensive delicacies that had been left over from some event at the club.

Afterwards, they sat by the hearth, Chaloner silent and withdrawn as he tried to piece together what he had learned. Wiseman used the opportunity to indulge in a self-serving monologue about a public anatomy he had performed for the King.

'Have you told anyone else that Mary Wood was poisoned?' asked Chaloner, cutting into the tale so abruptly that the surgeon scowled his irritation.

'Just Temperance – in the Crown earlier, when you were with us. But neither of us will talk about it until Wood has been informed. I assume you will visit him tomorrow?'

Chaloner nodded. 'As soon as he is home from Chelsey. Do you know who started the rumours that she died from something other than the small-pox?'

'Well, according to Temperance, they originated with an ex-postal clerk – a plump little fellow with a Dutch name that now eludes me . . .'

'Isaac Dorislaus?'

'The very same! He claims to have seen Mary's body the day she died, and suspected then that something was amiss. He is lying, of course. The servants did not spot

267

anything, so why should he? And what would he have been doing in the Woods' mansion at such a time, anyway? Or do you think *he* fed the toxin to her?'

'If he had, then why draw attention to the murder by starting tales about it? Why not let everyone believe that she died of natural causes?'

'God only knows,' sighed Wiseman. 'The criminal mind is beyond me. However, I should like to rectify the matter, so if you have cause to dispatch him, perhaps you would be kind enough to bring me his head. It would make for an interesting study.'

Chaloner winced at the notion, suddenly assailed with the uncomfortable thought that the surgeon would probably like parts of *him* in his quest for scientific wisdom, too. There were many reasons for not wanting to be dead, but the notion that he might end up on Wiseman's mantelpiece was certainly one of them.

'What would happen if that powerful poison entered someone via a wound?' he asked, changing the subject again, although not to one that was any less comforting.

Wiseman considered. 'It would take longer to work, but death would occur eventually. Why?'

'Because I think that is what happened to Smartfoot. And it was my fault.'

Wiseman regarded him warily. 'Who is Smartfoot?'

'A man I came to blows with in the Post Office last night. I wounded him in the arm with my dagger. He was trying to kill birds in the park this evening, but he was unsteady on his feet, and he fought dismally. Unlike yesterday, when I was lucky to escape.'

'What makes you think you are responsible? It is more likely that he poisoned himself when he was preparing the stuff to feed to the royal fowl.'

'Because I used that particular dagger to pick up the first batch of contaminated bread, and I did not wipe it off. There must have been a residue.'

'Give it to me,' ordered Wiseman. 'Carefully, if you please.'

Chaloner obliged, and while the surgeon busied himself at the table, he stared idly at the fire, recalling how fast Smartfoot had backed away when informed that Thurloe's little phial contained poison. Now he knew why: the clerk had known exactly what contact with it could do.

'There *are* residues on your blade,' said Wiseman, breaking into his morbid reflections. 'And if you plunged it into Smartfoot, then you probably are responsible for his death. It would have taken longer to react, of course, as the toxin seems to be most effect-ive when ingested.'

Chaloner experienced a range of conflicting emotions. He had never liked killing, and poison was a coward's weapon. On the other hand, Smartfoot had tried to dispatch him, and was probably involved in murdering a sick woman and slaughtering the King's birds.

'I have encountered poisons before,' he said, watching the surgeon scrub his hands again. 'But none that are this virulent. You said at the charnel house this morning that no apothecary would have contrived such a substance.'

'Not the ones I know,' said Wiseman drily. 'They aim to furnish their customers with remedies and tonics, not potions that kill. And those who are unscrupulous enough to experiment with deadly compounds will never admit it, so do not waste time trawling their shops.'

'Do you know what is in it?'

'I analysed what we discovered in Mary, and it

contained a number of dangerous ingredients, all of which have been concentrated to an unusual degree – monkshood, henbane, arsenic, some sort of lye. It would not be difficult to manufacture, although one would have to be very careful.'

'You said earlier that it might have been imported.'

'Yes, but it could have been produced here just as easily. You do not need me to tell you that anything can be bought in London, and that includes obscenely potent toxins.'

'And all to kill birds, which seems rather excessive.'

Wiseman's expression was sombre. 'Yet it sends a clear message – that whoever is dispatching these ducks has access to a terrible substance and is not afraid to use it. Perhaps that is why chatter from the Post Office has suddenly dried up – people are afraid of being given a drop of this stuff. Here is your dagger. I have scoured it as well as I can, and it should be safe now.'

Chaloner refused to take it.

Because he was too tired to walk home, Chaloner accepted Wiseman's offer of a bed for the night, and immediately fell into an uneasy sleep that teemed with images of poisoned birds, Russia and Newgate Gaol. It was hardly restful, so when the surgeon's servants began clattering about in the kitchen below, he rose and dressed with relief. It was still dark, but they made no concession to the fact that the other occupants of the house might be asleep.

He walked downstairs, intending to slip out without being seen, but the stairs creaked, and the footman intercepted him. Chaloner knew from past visits that Wiseman's people loved to gossip, and as their master seldom entertained, any guest was seized upon with alacrity. He found himself gripped by the hand and towed into the kitchen, where the other two were eating warm oatmeal.

'Two men died in a fight outside the New Exchange last night,' began the one-eyed groom with salacious glee, handing Chaloner a bowl and ladling some of the glutinous sludge into it. Despite its unappetising appearance, Chaloner ate, not sure how much opportunity there would be for food later. 'The unrest grows worse almost by the hour.'

'It is the same in Yorkshire and Sussex,' put in the cook, who had lost an arm. 'And we are all waiting to see which important person will be assassinated. I think it will be the Major, because he has renounced his principles and become a lily-livered pacifist.'

'No, it will be Controller O'Neill,' predicted the footman. He was missing the lower part of one leg, which lent a grim aptness to his chosen profession. 'Because he is sly and corrupt.'

'It is a bad state of affairs,' sighed the groom. 'And not set to improve when the Court is only interested in enjoying itself and spending money. We should make *them* live in a wooden palace, like the Tsar of Russia. That would teach them to behave.'

'I shall never go to Russia,' declared the cook. 'I have heard that the only drink available is a powerful tonic made from vegetable parings, and a fellow cannot buy ale for love nor money.'

'They do not have money in any case,' said the footman with considerable authority. 'They barter, so if you want to purchase something, you have to pay with gherkins or beetroot.'

'Gherkins,' said the cook with a shudder. 'Surgeon

Wiseman brought one home from the Crown yesterday, and it reminded me of the things he keeps in jars on his shelves.'

'Speaking of unsavoury specimens, Lady Castlemaine's husband was dismayed when he returned from his foreign travels to find his family increased by two babies,' chuckled the groom. 'She told him they were begot by an angel. The whole Court laughed, but all he did was bow and leave. He is a fool to let her treat him with such rank disrespect.'

'She is beginning to lose her looks,' said the footman. 'I saw her in the street the other day, and she looked as old and used as a Southwark whore.'

Chaloner eventually managed to escape, wondering how the King expected to be taken seriously when his private life was so brazenly scandalous. Not for the first time, he felt a wave of sympathy for Palmer, and for Queen Katherine, too. Both deserved better from their spouses.

Fleet Street was strangely deserted as Chaloner began to walk along it, and he wondered why. It was a Wednesday, so should have been busy. Then a bellman's mournful call told him it was four o'clock, and he realised that the servants had woken him ridiculously early.

Yet he did not mind. He had a great deal to do that day – inform Wood that his wife had been murdered; confess to Thurloe about losing the letters; attend Knight's funeral; see what Vanderhuyden had learned about Dorislaus; ask questions about Oxenbridge, Fry, Gardner, Bankes and Harper; corner a clerk and interrogate him about the disused part of the Post Office; waylay Lamb and ask about Smartfoot; and, if there was time, speak to Ibson. Unfortunately, it was too early to

272

do any of it. Except Thurloe. His friend would not mind being woken up.

He climbed over Lincoln's Inn's back wall, and was a silent, almost invisible shadow as he made his way across Dial Court and up the stairs to Chamber XIII. Reluctant to disturb Thurloe's neighbours by knocking, he picked the lock and let himself in. Not surprisingly, the rooms were in darkness and the curtains were drawn around the bed. Chaloner called out softly, then lit a lamp, to give the ex-Spymaster a few moments to gather his wits. When he set his hand to the draperies and a knife slashed at him, he supposed he should have announced himself more clearly.

'Thomas!' exclaimed Thurloe, lowering the weapon. 'Did no one ever tell you that it is impolite to wander about in other people's bedrooms uninvited? You gave me a fright.'

'One you repaid in full,' retorted Chaloner ruefully. 'You almost stabbed me.'

'I thought it was Prynne, and I am angry with him. A horse tried to eat that horrible old hat he always wears, and he was bitten in the battle to get it back. I wasted an entire evening convincing him not to sue the owners, and the owners not to sue him.'

'Was it Morland who came to tell you what had happened?'

'Yes, along with half a dozen others. Their intention was to save Lincoln's Inn from embarrassment; his was to put me in a situation that was demeaning.'

While Thurloe lit a fire, Chaloner told him all he had discovered since their last meeting. The ex-Spymaster regarded him doubtfully when he mentioned Wiseman's contention that it was Dorislaus who had been spreading rumours about Mary's death.

'Isaac would not do that – he and the Woods are friends. He could have spied on them during the Commonwealth, when Wood was a person of interest to me, but he never did. He likes them.'

Chaloner was inclined to see that as evidence that Dorislaus had not been as loyal to Parliament as Thurloe believed. He started to mention Vanderhuyden's suspicions, but changed his mind: Vanderhuyden had tried and had been given short shrift, and he was unlikely to fare any better.

'Isaac has been of incalculable value to me over the past few days,' Thurloe went on. He spoke coolly, as if he had read Chaloner's reservations about the man. 'He managed to prise some excellent intelligence from his former colleagues at the Post Office – before Harper was employed to prevent such gossip.'

'What did he tell you, exactly?'

'Unfortunately, what he learned is confusing and contradictory. Indeed, I am beginning to wonder whether there might be two plots unfolding there, not one.'

'Two?' Chaloner already suspected as much, but it was good to hear it confirmed.

Thurloe nodded. 'One involving dishonest practices, and one rather more dangerous. We shall know soon, because Isaac has befriended a clerk named Smartfoot, who becomes indiscreet when drunk. Isaac plans to take him to a tavern today, and ply him with ale.'

'Oh,' said Chaloner guiltily, and summarised his adventures in St James's Park.

'For heaven's sake, Thomas!' cried Thurloe in exasperation. 'Not only have you eliminated a promising source of information, but that is the second batch of documents you have managed to lose. If you happen

274

across any more, please try a little harder to keep hold of them.'

'I doubt they were important,' said Chaloner defensively. 'The one to Morland said John Fry was at the Angel, but it was untrue – Knight just reported an unsubstantiated rumour. There is no reason to assume the other letters were any different.'

'They were important enough that they were what he wrote about in gaol. And I imagine the one to Morland was the least significant, because Knight could not have been sure of his loyalty to Gery. Indeed, I suspect these reports might have provided the key to this entire affair.'

Chaloner shuffled uncomfortably. 'Why do you think the bird-killers took them?'

'The answer is obvious. They kept their faces concealed but you did not: they almost certainly knew who you were, so of course they were interested in papers dropping from your clothes.'

'The letters were also addressed to Clarendon, Wood, Bishop, Palmer, Kate O'Neill and various members of Court and the Privy Council. Knight had not met the Earl before last Thursday, and I suspect he did not know the others either. Except perhaps Kate. Why choose them?'

'Because they are influential people who would be able to act on the information he provided,' replied Thurloe shortly, making no effort to mask his continuing irritation.

'Do you want me to look for them?'

'I would, if we had any idea where to start. It is a wretched shame they have gone.'

* * *

Chastened, Chaloner left, and it was only when he was out in Chancery Lane that it occurred to him that he should have asked Thurloe about his 'jackal' Ibson. He considered returning, but Thurloe's displeasure was hard to bear, and Ibson was not an important line of enquiry anyway.

It was still too early to begin the other tasks he had set himself, so he walked the short distance to Temperance's club in Hercules' Pillars Alley, aiming to see whether there had been any gossip that might help him. He arrived to find the last of the guests being loaded into hackneys or private coaches, while an army of cleaners moved in to tackle the mess. The weary *filles de joie* climbed the stairs towards beds in which, this time, they would do nothing but sleep.

A few patrons lingered on the steps or in the garden at the front of the house, bidding farewell to Temperance, while her doorman, Preacher Hill, loomed pointedly to remind them that it was time to go home. Hill was a nonconformist fanatic, who earned his keep in the brothel at night, and held forth about the perils of sin during the day. He and Chaloner had never seen eye to eye.

Le Notre was one of the stragglers, thanking Temperance effusively for a delightful evening. The powder on his cheeks was so thick that Chaloner wondered whether he was actually in disguise, and appeared as someone else when he was not parading as a French landscape architect with outrageous tastes in fashion.

After a moment, Oxenbridge appeared. He was also as white as chalk, although not from cosmetics, and there was something distinctly unearthly about the contrasting blackness of his eyes. He was limping slightly. Had he been fighting in the park the previous night or had he strained something in a frolic with the girls? He bowed to Temperance, who shrank away.

It was the perfect opportunity to waylay him, so Chaloner stepped forward. Recognition burned in Oxenbridge's disconcerting eyes – the skirmish outside Palmer's house had apparently not been forgotten – and he gripped the hilt of his sword.

'Good morning,' said Chaloner pleasantly, as the knife from his sleeve slipped into the palm of his hand. 'The Lord Chancellor sent me to ask about your association with the Post Off—'

'I do not answer to him,' snarled Oxenbridge. 'Or to you. Now, if you value your life, get out of my way.'

'If you are busy now, I can come to your house later,' said Chaloner, declining to move.

'Stay away from me,' hissed Oxenbridge. 'I am not a doll, to be pulled this way and that by grand lords and their spies.'

He shoved Chaloner away with considerable force. Normally, Chaloner would have stood firm, or perhaps grabbed him and put the knife to his throat, but he did neither. He told himself that Oxenbridge would not have answered his questions anyway, and pursuing the discussion was a waste of his time, but the truth was that the word 'doll' had flustered him. Logic told him there was nothing sinister about it, and that he was a fool for letting himself be so disconcerted – he should go after Oxenbridge and try again.

He watched as Oxenbridge drew level with le Notre, who linked arms with him, gabbling merrily in French. Chaloner suspected that Oxenbridge did not speak the language, and le Notre was having fun at his expense, although it seemed reckless to make sport of such a fellow. Unless they were friends, of course. But if that were true, then why had Oxenbridge lobbed stones at Palmer's house when le Notre was in it?

He did not want to tackle Oxenbridge with le Notre as a witness, so he trailed them to the lane, where le Notre climbed into a coach that was emblazoned with the Castlemaine coat of arms, leading Chaloner to wonder whether Palmer would have lent it had he known where the borrower intended to travel. It appeared as though he would ride away alone, but Oxenbridge suddenly jumped in with him, and the driver whipped the horses into a brisk trot.

Chaloner ran after it, aiming to flag down a hackney on Fleet Street and follow, but he arrived to find not a one in sight. There was no traffic at that early hour, so the driver gave the horses their head. Chaloner did his best to keep up on foot, but it was hopeless, and it was with a sense of enormous frustration that he staggered to a halt and watched it rattle out of sight.

He returned to the club, which was still disgorging members. Next out was Bishop, lapdog in one hand and some lady's undergarment in the other. He also thanked Temperance for an exquisite occasion, and tottered down the steps into the courtyard, setting his pooch gently on the ground where it immediately squatted and began to water the plants. Chaloner ducked behind a shrub when it snuffled towards him, more so that Bishop would not see him if he needed to boot it away than to conceal himself, although the move did render him invisible.

On Bishop's heels came O'Neill, who seemed taller and more imposing without his wife in tow. His voice was more forceful, too, as he informed Temperance in a penetrating whisper that allowing the likes of Bishop inside the club had lowered its tone.

278

'He is a liar and a cheat,' he stated uncompromisingly. 'And his vile little rat-dog stinks.'

'Yes, it does,' she admitted. 'However, it bit Oxenbridge, which more than compensated for its lack of personal hygiene. And I will hear nothing bad about Bishop. He is a gentle soul, and everyone here loves him for his generosity and thoughtfulness.'

'Ban him,' urged O'Neill, slipping a fat purse into her hand. 'You will not regret it, I promise. And I will let you send free letters for the rest of your life if you poison his dog. I cannot abide the thing. It is worse than birds for its filthy habits.'

Behind the bush, Chaloner frowned. Was this proof that O'Neill *did* engage in nepotistic practices at the Post Office, despite his assurances to the contrary? And was his dislike of animals enough to see him use his clerks to dispatch ducks? When O'Neill aimed for the lane, Chaloner left his hiding place and began to follow, but this time Temperance saw and darted forward to stop him.

'No, Tom,' she said warningly. 'I do not want you harrying my patrons, even the ones I do not like.'

'You do not like O'Neill?'

'Not particularly. He is a—'

She was interrupted by a shout from Hill – O'Neill and Bishop had met in the lane, and were engaged in fisticuffs. Bishop had his dog under one arm and was whirling the other around like a windmill, while O'Neill had taken the traditional pose of a boxer, but did not seem to know what to do next. The dog yapped with irritating intensity.

Bishop lunged, but while his fist missed its target, the manoeuvre brought the dog's sharp little teeth within nipping distance, and they fastened on to his opponent's sleeve. Outraged, O'Neill jerked away, but the dog held on, and both men fell to the ground, where they rolled about, pulling each other's wigs and trading clumsy slaps. Hill tried to separate them, but fell back with a yelp when the dog bit him. Chaloner watched in astonishment.

'Too much to drink,' said Temperance disapprovingly. 'Pull them apart, Tom. We do not allow unseemly behaviour outside the club. What will the neighbours think?'

Chaloner doubted a fight would horrify the neighbours, who were used to very much worse, but obligingly went to lift Bishop off O'Neill. Meanwhile, the dog continued to worry at Hill's ankles, and in desperation, the preacher turned and fled towards Fleet Street. The sight of a pair of heels sent the creature into paroxysms of delight, and it shot after its quarry with a frenzy of excited yips.

'Come back!' cried Bishop in dismay, O'Neill forgotten as he hared after it. 'My darling!'

'I am here on official business,' blustered O'Neill when he recognised Chaloner. His face was scarlet with mortification. 'I did not come for the ladies while my wife is visiting her mother.'

'I shall believe you,' said Chaloner. 'If you answer a few questions about the Post Office.'

O'Neill regarded him in dismay. 'But I never discuss it with outsiders – it would be unethical. Betray me to Kate, then. But if you do, I shall tell Hannah that you were here, too.'

He stalked away, and Chaloner could not help but notice that he was very light on his feet and moved with a compact grace that made a lie of his ridiculous scuffle with Bishop. Had he gone to poison a few birds before enjoying a few hours of leisure at the club?

* * *

280

'That was a dismal attempt at blackmail, Tom,' said Temperance, wryly, when the last of the guests had gone and she and Chaloner turned to enter the club. 'Are you losing your touch?'

'It would seem so,' sighed Chaloner. 'In more ways than one.'

Inside, the mess was appalling. Food was splattered on the walls, and there was more wine on the floor than he consumed in a month. He gazed around in horror, but the cleaners were undaunted, and chatted happily among themselves as they set to work. All would be pristine again by the evening, when the cycle would begin afresh.

'I am exhausted,' said Temperance, leading the way to her private parlour. She flopped into a chair, removed her wig and tossed it on the floor. Hairpieces were both expensive to buy and to maintain, and in that one care-less gesture, she revealed how obscenely rich she had grown.

She reached up to the mantelpiece, and took down her pipe. Once it was lit, she poured two dishes of thick black sludge and passed one to Chaloner. He took it, but had no intention of drinking. It had been made by Maude, her formidable helpmeet, and was coffee so potent that it was rumoured to have killed healthy men. Besides, Chaloner liked having teeth.

'I was surprised to see Oxenbridge here,' he said. 'You told me after the explosion that he was not one of your patrons.'

'Tonight was his first time, and I hope to God it will be his last. I did not see him come in, and neither did Hill. We just looked around, and there he was. It was rather eerie if you want the truth.'

'You could have asked him to leave.'

'I started to, because he was unsettling my other guests, but when he turned those glittering black eyes on me, my nerve failed. I started gabbling silly questions at him instead.'

'I do not suppose you asked him where he lives, did you?'

'I did, as a matter of fact, but do you know what he said? That he lays his head wherever the fancy takes him. What am I supposed to make of that? And when I asked if he had any family, he said they are an encumbrance that he has never deemed necessary.'

'Le Notre seemed to like him.'

Temperance smiled. 'Dear le Notre. He is a lovely man, and likes everyone.'

He had not liked O'Neill, thought Chaloner, recalling how he had warned against furthering a friendship with the Controller and had arranged for him to be blamed for breaking Hannah's clock.

'He had a very nasty experience yesterday,' Temperance went on. 'His carriage was attacked, and he was lucky to escape with his life. Well, it was not his carriage, it was Palmer's. The public mood is against Palmer, but it is his own fault. He should not be planning to publish Pope-loving texts. Were you at Tothill Street last night, by the way? I hear there was a riot.'

'There are riots most nights. Too many taverns.'

'I do not suppose you could secure me a crane, could you?' asked Temperance after a while. 'Lord Rochester has expressed a desire to have one roasted.'

'No,' said Chaloner shortly. 'And do not try to poach one from St James's Park, because they are very well guarded. You will be caught.'

'Anything can be bought in London, if one has enough money. Anything at all.'

'Not a crane,' begged Chaloner. 'Or any other exotic bird. It would break Storey's heart.'

Temperance softened. 'Well, if you put it like that . . . Incidentally, what did Hannah say when you told her you were caught in that explosion?'

'Nothing much. Why?'

'In other words, she did not care. I wish you had not married her, Tom. She is a nice lady, but you are woefully ill-matched.'

'Have you heard any more rumours about the Post Office?' asked Chaloner, changing the subject very abruptly. He was not sure what he disliked more: the fact that Temperance felt free to make such remarks, or the fact that they were true.

Temperance patted his knee in sympathetic understanding, then answered his question. 'There have been plenty more tales, but I do not know if they are accurate. It is said that O'Neill has hired additional clerks, so that every piece of mail can be read before it is sent.'

'I doubt that can be right. The task would be impossible.'

'Then there is a story that abuses are on the increase – mailbags "lost" and business letters sold to rival concerns. And there is a report that something is being built there. It involves Morland.'

'Samuel Morland?'

'I detest him. He slithers about like a snake, and I have no idea whether he is loyal to the King or not. He tried to come here, but I told Hill to toss him out. He was furious, but I was not having the likes of him near my guests when they are too drunk to be sensible.'

Chaloner determined to corner Morland as soon as possible, and this time there would be no rescue from Gery. 'Wiseman wants me to visit Sir Henry Wood this morning, to tell him his wife was murdered. It will not be a pleasant task.'

'No,' agreed Temperance. She was thoughtful. 'Wood says some very peculiar things, but only to those who do not matter. When he is with important people, like the King, he is perfectly sane. Personally, I think he just likes to see folk wrong-footed.'

'Do you think it is possible that he killed Mary?'

Temperance started to say no, but then stopped and was silent for a while, considering. 'I would like to think not,' she said eventually. 'But there is a ruthless streak in him. He slaughtered dozens of Roundheads during the wars, including women and children.'

'Wiseman said you heard it was Dorislaus who started the tales about Mary being poisoned.'

Temperance relit her pipe, while Chaloner studied her shaven head, stained teeth and portly features, and wondered what it was about her that the surgeon found so utterly irresistible.

'Yes,' she nodded. 'Dorislaus is a sly villain, and probably a Dutch spy as well. However, I have no evidence, and only repeat whispers. And there is another rumour about Mary, too, which I heard from the Duke of Buckingham.'

'Yes?'

'His chambermaid was intimate with one of the Woods' servants, a lad named Joyce. Well, according to Joyce, Mary had had a mysterious visitor just before she died – one who was most insistent that he should speak to her.'

'I doubt it is true. Why would he let guests pester his mistress when she was ill in bed?'

'She was on the mend and was bored, apparently – the small-pox is infectious, so no one had been to see her. The caller was well-dressed and told Joyce that he was a friend.'

'Do you know the chambermaid's name?' asked Chaloner, supposing he would have to ask her about the story, given that the hapless Joyce was not in a position to oblige.

'Nancy, but she is a saucy piece, who will whisk you into her bedchamber just as soon as look at you. She wanted to work here, but I considered her too wanton.'

Chaloner left, bemused to learn that someone could be deemed too wanton for a brothel.

Dawn was only just breaking as he walked towards Buckingham's house, but despite the early hour, he saw two men he knew. They were Stokes and Cliffe, marching with backs erect and shoulders back, grey moustaches bristling with military precision.

'We saw Spymaster Williamson join you after we fled Will's Coffee House the other day,' said Stokes in distaste. 'I did not know you were acquainted with that sort of person.'

'I did not invite him to sit with me,' objected Chaloner, unwilling to be considered one of Williamson's toadies. 'He did it because everyone else had disappeared.'

'I always run away when he arrives,' said Cliffe loftily. 'I do not care for such company.'

'Well, it looked suspicious,' said Chaloner. 'As though you had something to hide.'

'We did have something to hide,' averred Cliffe. 'We

285

had just been discussing the licentiousness of Court. There are some who would consider that treason.'

'Although there are many more who agree with us,' said Stokes. 'Especially now Palmer aims to publish books urging us all to love the Pope. Rebellion is bubbling in Yorkshire, Sussex, Nottingham, Bristol and God knows where else. The whole country will be in flames soon.'

'Williamson is next to worthless at quelling trouble,' grumbled Cliffe. 'And he is a fool. Did you know that he is offering fifty pounds for the arrest of that postal clerk? It is a ridiculous sum.'

Stokes's expression was wistful. 'I wish *I* knew where Gardner was. I would love fifty pounds.'

'I am not surprised Gardner is in trouble,' said Cliffe acidly. 'I know him, because he always dealt with my enquiries in the Letter Hall. He looks like a harmless yokel, but I always thought there was something unto-ward about him. Not like poor Knight. I doubt *he* did anything wrong, and the villains who took him to Newgate should be strung up themselves.'

'You are up early,' said Chaloner, immediately uncomfortable. 'It is barely light.'

'We have been to church,' explained Cliffe. 'St Dunstan's does a pre-dawn service.'

'Some of them should try it,' remarked Stokes, nodding to where a coach was rattling past, full of courtiers. They were bawling a tavern song, and one of them hurled an empty decanter out of the window. It smashed against a wall, a sound that elicited drunken cheers.

'Brutes!' declared Cliffe angrily. 'Their behaviour is disgraceful.'

'*She* was in that coach,' said Stokes, lips pursed in furious disapproval. 'Lady Castlemaine. In company with men of dubious character – Sir Alan Brodrick, Will Chiffinch, Lord Rochester. All are dissipated scoundrels who should be locked away.'

'But her husband is nowhere to be seen,' added Cliffe. 'Doubtless he is on his knees in front of the Virgin Mary, muttering in Latin. He should concentrate on bringing his whore-wife to heel, and leave religion until he has time for it.'

Chaloner walked away, thinking that Cliffe could never have been married, or he would know that such advice was easy to dispense, but a lot harder to put into action.

As Temperance had promised, Nancy was indeed a saucy piece, which was doubtless why she had been hired – the Duke liked a romp, and it was clear that Nancy would be a ready and willing partner. She leaned against a bureau in the Duke's best parlour, more than happy to shirk her duties and answer questions put by Hannah's husband.

'Yes, Dick Joyce told me about the stranger who visited Lady Mary before she died,' she purred. 'Perhaps it was as well that Dick was blown to pieces, because if he was alive, he might have been held responsible for the fact that she was poisoned. And she was, you know – all London is talking about it.'

'What did he tell you, exactly?' asked Chaloner.

'That Mary was bored, lying in bed alone, so when this stranger came and said he wanted to speak to her, she told Dick to let him in. An hour later, when Dick went to take her a tonic, the visitor had gone and she was dead.'

'Did he say what this person looked like?'

'He did better than that – he pointed him out to me.'

Nancy adjusted her ample bosom in a way that ensured Chaloner's eyes would be drawn towards it. 'The fellow happened to be passing when we were chatting. It was what prompted Dick to tell me the story in the first place.'

'Where were you when this happened?'

'Outside the Wood mansion in Post House Yard. The villain was on his way to the General Letter Office. To post a package, I suppose.'

'Can you describe him?'

'He was about your height, with bushy yellow hair and a round pink face.'

Gardner, thought Chaloner, whom Knight had asked about a murder, but which had been denied unconvincingly. Was killing Mary the crime Knight had been talking about? Chaloner supposed he would have to find out.

It was still too early to visit Wood, so Chaloner went to the Rainbow Coffee House, hoping a dish of the beverage would sharpen his wits; Farr's charred beans were a lot safer than the toxic sludge Temperance had offered him.

'I would like to invite you all to my shop the day after tomorrow,' Speed was announcing. 'For the first sales of Palmer's book. I promise it will be an interesting event.'

'No, thank you,' said Stedman archly. 'We are not interested in Catholic rubbish.'

'It is not rubbish,' snapped Speed. 'Palmer is erudite and insightful. He is a good Royalist, too, despite what the King has done to his marriage, so there will be nothing seditious either.'

'Speaking of Royalists, how was your visit to the Crown yesterday, Stedman?' asked Farr conversationally. 'It is known to be full of Cavaliers, so you must have felt at home.'

'And so I might,' replied the printer sourly, 'had Clement Oxenbridge not been lounging by the fire. He is so sinister that I could not bring myself to stay.'

'I do not blame you,' said Speed with a shudder. 'There is something disconcertingly spectral about that man, and no one knows anything about him – of his family, his home, his life. It is almost as if he were a ghost. And he spreads trouble like a disease.'

'My apprentices believe he is the devil come to walk among us,' said Stedman in a low voice. He glanced around uneasily, as if he imagined Oxenbridge might suddenly appear and hear him.

'The King held a terribly loud party last night,' said Farr, after a short silence; Stedman's words had unsettled everyone. 'With all his courtiers dressed as Romans. It raised complaints from as far away as Charing Cross, and I have been told that the racket sparked a riot in Tothill Street.'

'Oh, no,' said Stedman. 'The King's soirée had nothing to do with that: a letter from John Fry did. He wrote to the Printers' Guild – on costly paper sealed with fine purple wax – to ask why we pay such a high tax on ink. It set our apprentices alight with indignation.'

'John Fry,' sighed Speed. 'He has become a nuisance with his feisty opinions.'

'I quite agree,' said Stedman. 'But my fellow printers consider him a Messiah, and marched off to tackle the ink factory near Tothill Street. I had nothing to do with it, of course. *I* am no rebel.'

'Complaining about taxes is not rebellion,' said Farr. 'I shall join a demonstration myself later today – one in which coffee-house owners express their disapproval over the increased revenues on sugar. Chaloner is my only customer who does not use it, and it is expensive.'

'Chaloner does not take sugar?' Stedman eyed Chaloner in wary disbelief. 'Why not?'

'He is practising for when he visits Russia,' supplied Farr, patting the copy of Olearius's *Voyages*, which showed signs of having been thoroughly pawed. 'Sugar is not available there.'

A little later that morning, Chaloner knocked on the door to Wood's mansion, and was conducted to a sitting room on the first floor that afforded a fine view of Post House Yard. Bookshelves lined the walls, their tomes about subjects as diverse as cartography, natural history, mathematics and philosophy. However, it was not Wood's choice of reading material that caught Chaloner's eye as much as the fact that he already had visitors: Dorislaus and Vanderhuyden were with him.

'Tom!' exclaimed Dorislaus. He smiled without warmth. 'What a pleasant surprise.'

'Do not loiter there like a cabbage,' snapped Wood. He was standing on a table with a spoon in his hand. 'Come in, where I can see you. Hah! It is Chaloner the regicide. Have you come to conspire with Dorislaus? He is another who worked to see the old King dead.'

Dorislaus stood up and reached for his hat. 'I must be away. I have much to do.'

He bowed and had taken his leave before Chaloner could ask why he had started the rumours that Mary had been poisoned, or why he held clandestine meetings with the likes of Gery, le Notre and O'Neill. Then the spy's attention was taken by Wood, who was scrambling over the furniture with a remarkable agility for a man his age.

'He is chasing a moth,' explained Vanderhuyden, adding in a whisper, 'God knows why.'

Chaloner sat next to him and lowered his voice, taking the opportunity to confer while their host was busy. 'I was hoping to meet you today. Have you found evidence against Dorislaus yet?'

'No, but you saw how quickly he escaped just now. I think he knows I have taken time away from work to monitor him and it has made him uneasy. Should I go after him?'

'Not yet – it will confirm his suspicions. Leave it for a while, then try again. But please be careful. There is little more dangerous than a cornered spy.'

'I am afraid I have not yet asked about the Major's contacts in the Post Office,' said Vanderhuyden apologetically. 'Dorislaus has taken up too much of my time.'

'Good,' said Chaloner, relieved he had not been dabbling in business that might see him killed. He added a lie to keep it that way. 'Dorislaus is much more important. Concentrate on him.'

'Very well, if you are sure. He is—'

'Hah!' exclaimed Wood, breaking into their muttered discussion. He held up his hand, and they saw he had caught the moth. He inspected it carefully, then ate it.

'Christ!' muttered Chaloner. Vanderhuyden winced, but did not seem surprised.

'I have just returned from Chelsey,' declared Wood, coming to sit next to them. 'I went to arrange for Mary to be buried in the churchyard. The vicar agreed, so Dorislaus and Vanderhuyden collected her from the charnel house for me, and we put her in the earth at midnight.'

'Did she hail from Chelsey?' asked Chaloner, wondering how to broach the subject of murder.

291

'She had never been there,' replied Wood airily. 'But it is blissfully free of leeks, and she would not have wanted to spend eternity near those. The vicar was very understanding.'

'Especially once he had been paid twenty pounds,' muttered Vanderhuyden.

'Do you ever drink ass's urine mixed with powder of worms, Chaloner?' Wood asked conversationally. 'Mary used to mix me a draught every morning, and insisted I took it, even though I detested the taste. She said it would strengthen my bowels.'

Chaloner wondered if this had prompted him to dispatch her. 'Speaking of Mary—'

'She was murdered,' interrupted Wood calmly. 'Swallowed poison, poor soul.'

'No, she died of the small-pox,' said Vanderhuyden, kindly patient. 'I cannot imagine who started those nasty rumours, but he deserves to be shot for his malicious tongue.'

'Oh, they are true,' said Wood, and suddenly there was a gleam in his eye that was a long way from lunacy. 'There was blood in her mouth. I inspected her corpse, you see.'

'What?' asked Vanderhuyden in horror.

'I inspected her corpse,' repeated Wood blithely. 'She was my wife, and I wanted to make sure someone had not replaced her body with a parsnip. London is a very peculiar city.'

'Then why did you not tell someone at once?' demanded Vanderhuyden, shocked. 'How will we catch her killer now? She died days ago, and witnesses will have forgotten what they saw.'

'The culprit was clever,' said Wood slyly. 'He waited

until I took everyone away to hunt for carrots in Southwark, and then he struck. It was a pity – Mary was recovering well from her illness.'

'It is more than a pity!' cried Vanderhuyden, leaping to his feet in agitation. 'It is a terrible crime, and I am going to report it. I shall see the bastard caught, Wood, do not worry. I shall demand an audience with the Lord Chancellor himself.'

He left before Wood could respond, and Chaloner saw him emerge in Post House Yard a few moments later, racing towards Dowgate Hill, and yelling for a hackney to take him to White Hall. What would the Earl say when he arrived? Would Vanderhuyden be given short shrift, like Knight, or would Mary's name open the necessary doors?

'Do not look out of the window,' hissed Wood, dragging Chaloner away. His grip was powerful and it, coupled with his nimble acrobatics across the furniture, led Chaloner to wonder whether he might be skilled at wielding swords in dark parks, too. 'The General Letter Office is out there, and you do not want that to spot you. There are onions growing all along its roof, and they are the deadliest vegetables in the world.'

'Who killed your wife?' asked Chaloner, declining to let Wood's eccentricities distract him.

Wood shrugged. 'There are many strange and vicious people in London.'

'Yes,' agreed Chaloner, thinking that Wood was one of them. 'But does anyone in particular come to mind? Vanderhuyden is right: it is a terrible crime, and you must want it solved.'

'Why? It will not bring her back. Besides, vengeance is for celery, which is a vindictive plant.'

'It is not about vengeance, it is about justice. Someone fed your wife a caustic substance while she lay recovering from a serious illness. The culprit cannot be allowed to stay free.'

Wood stared at him. 'But we do not know the culprit. Joyce admitted a stranger, one who did not give his name. And now Joyce is dead, too. We shall never know the killer's identity.'

'Do you not think that Joyce's death so soon after Mary's is a suspicious coincidence?'

Wood raised his eyebrows. 'Why would I? She died of poison, he was blown to pieces.'

Chaloner was becoming exasperated. 'Why did you take virtually your entire household to Southwark when your wife was unwell?'

'Because we cannot have carrots rampaging about, man! Do you not know how much damage they can do? And Mary was almost better anyway. She was happy for us to go.'

Chaloner could not tell if it was the truth. 'Do you know a man named Lewis Gardner?'

'Of course. He is the villain who has been cheating the Post Office, and there is a bounty on his head. Do you knew where he is? If so, I shall fetch my musket and come with you to arrest him.' Wood did a peculiar little dance by tapping his toes on the wooden floor. 'Fifty pounds!'

'Has he ever been to your house?'

'Why would he do that?' asked Wood, although there was a sly cant to his eyes.

'There is reason to believe that he visited Mary the day she died. A witness said—'

'Onions. I told you they were dangerous. *Onions* paid Gardner to come here and murder Mary.'

294

'An interesting concept,' said Chaloner, watching him intently. 'Hiring a killer.'

'Yes,' said Wood, meeting his gaze steadily. 'But I hope you do not suspect me of the crime. I am not an onion. Or a regicide, for that matter. Is that why you are so interested in the onions? You think they might help you to behead another King?'

'No,' said Chaloner, coldly. 'I am not interested in onions. Only in savage, unprincipled brutes who murder sick women in their beds.'

Chapter 10

An interview with the Earl could be postponed no longer, although Chaloner dragged his feet as he walked to White Hall, not liking to imagine his master's displeasure when told that the bird-killers were still at large. He arrived to find the Earl in conference with the King, something that happened so rarely that all appointments had been cancelled for the rest of the day. The Earl had left him a message, though – a stern reminder that if he interfered with the Post Office enquiry in any way, he could expect instant dismissal.

In churlish defiance, Chaloner went to Post House Yard, where he spent several hours asking questions about Oxenbridge, Fry, Harper, Gardner, Lamb and Bankes, although he met with no success. He managed to waylay five different clerks, but none would confide in him – the first four claimed with convincing bemusement that nothing untoward was happening, and the fifth refused to speak at all. Chaloner was about to see whether a knife would loosen his tongue when Harper appeared with two henchman. Chaloner considered demanding answers from them instead, but decided to be sensible when all three drew swords.

He ran, but they followed, and although he was adept at losing pursuers, Harper proved to be unusually dogged. Thus Chaloner was hot, tired and irritable when he finally escaped and made his way to St Mary Bothaw for Knight's funeral.

He had walked past the little church hundreds of times, but had paid it scant attention. It was a simple building, with a low tower and a nave lit by lancet windows. Inside, it was dark and very cold. He heard voices in the chancel, and walked towards them to find Wiseman with Rector Basset, who was a small man with a thin face and long grey hair. They had the coffin lid open, and Chaloner wondered uneasily what they had been doing.

'I thought you might like to be sure we are burying the right person,' said Wiseman, adding archly, 'Given our difference of opinion about what should happen to the corpses of felons.'

'Knight was not a felon,' said Chaloner, guilt flooding through him as he looked down at the man he had arrested.

'No,' agreed Basset. 'I always thought him decent and honest. However, he became oddly withdrawn of late, and his fiancée is probably wise to keep her distance from him today.'

'She is not coming?' asked Chaloner, sorry for it.

'He wrote her a letter explaining his recent actions,' replied Basset. 'But she was hurt and angry to learn that he had squandered their happy future together for the sake of exposing a plot. She thought he should have turned a blind eye, like all the other clerks.'

So Knight had been a brave man, thought Chaloner unhappily, prepared to risk all for his principles. It made the spy even more determined to catch whoever had murdered him.

The service was brief, but even so, the gravedigger had gone to a tavern by the time they emerged, and there was no one to carry Knight to his final resting place. Chaloner grabbed one end of the coffin, and indicated that Wiseman was to take the other. Basset led the way to the grave, which was shielded from the road by yews. They cast deep shadows, and as it was nearing dusk, they rendered the cemetery dark and eerie. Chaloner and Wiseman set the casket on the ropes that had been laid ready, and began to manoeuvre it into the hole.

'Stop!' came a stentorian voice. Chaloner and Wiseman started in alarm, and the coffin jiggled precariously. 'Or we will open fire.'

Chaloner twisted around to see a party of men approaching. All carried muskets. Basset squeaked in alarm, while Wiseman treated Chaloner to a weary look, immediately assuming that he was responsible for whatever was about to happen. The coffin was about halfway down the grave, so was not easy to hold, and Chaloner hoped they would not be expected to keep it there for long.

He assessed the gunmen quickly. There were five of them, all swathed in cloaks and wearing scarves to conceal their faces. However, glittering button-black eyes told him that the speaker was Oxenbridge, and suddenly it seemed bad luck that the cemetery was not visible from the street.

'We are laying someone to rest,' objected Basset unsteadily. 'Will you wait until we finish?'

'No,' snapped Oxenbridge, as Chaloner and Wiseman

started to lower the coffin again. Chaloner felt a musket dig into the small of his back. 'All of you will stand still or I shall kill you.'

'Please,' begged Basset. 'This is not seemly. It will not take a moment to—'

He yelped when Oxenbridge struck him. Chaloner tensed, but there was nothing he could do when his hands were full of rope and there was a musket jabbing at his spine. His arms began to burn with the strain of keeping the casket suspended.

'What do you want?' asked Wiseman. He sounded calm, but Chaloner could see the outrage in his eyes, and hoped he would not do anything rash.

'The letters you took from Knight's woman,' said Oxenbridge to Chaloner.

'What letters?' asked Chaloner, then staggered when the man behind poked him hard with the gun. Several inches of rope skidded through his hands. Wiseman compensated, but the coffin swayed violently regardless. It steadied, but only just.

'The letters you found under her bed,' hissed Oxenbridge. 'She just told us about them, and suggested we come here.'

'I hope you did not harm her,' said Chaloner, meeting Oxenbridge's eyes with a level stare. It was easier to look at him when most of his face was concealed.

Oxenbridge nodded to one of his men, who began to search Chaloner's pockets. Chaloner assessed his chances of survival if he dropped the ropes, whipped out his sword and went on the offensive. They were slim, but they were worse for Wiseman and Basset, who were unarmed. And he fully believed Oxenbridge would do as he had threatened and shoot them.

'Where are they?' demanded Oxenbridge, when the soldier finished and shook his head.

'I posted them,' replied Chaloner. 'As Knight had instructed.'

'Liar! You were too late for yesterday's mail, and there is none today. It is Wednesday.'

Chaloner cursed himself for making such a basic mistake. 'They were all to Londoners,' he blustered. 'The Post Office does not accept letters for the capital, so I hired private carriers to—'

'Pull it up,' interrupted Oxenbridge sharply. 'The coffin. Haul it up.'

'What?' blurted Wiseman, startled. 'Why?'

'So I can see whether you are burying who you claim,' snapped Oxenbridge. 'And then your friend will tell us where he has hidden the letters, or you and the rector will die.'

Chaloner and Wiseman had no choice but to obey. Chaloner pretended the coffin was too heavy for him, and the business took so long that an exasperated Oxenbridge eventually ordered two of his men to take the ropes instead. Chaloner seized the opportunity it provided. The moment their hands were full, he spun around and chopped Oxenbridge as hard as he could in the neck with the side of his hand. Even before Oxenbridge had crumpled, Chaloner had lashed out with his dagger to send the guard behind him reeling away with a slashed face.

Wiseman also reacted with impressive speed. He jerked the ropes savagely, which pulled the two startled soldiers off balance. The casket dropped, and one man tumbled into the grave after it. While his crony gaped in horror, Chaloner clubbed him into the hole, too. He turned to deal with the last soldier only to find himself looking down the barrel of a musket. He thought fast.

'The rector is armed. Shoot me, and he will kill you. Look, if you do not believe me.'

Rashly, the fellow did, which gave Chaloner the split second he needed to snatch the weapon from his hands. Fear flared in the taupe eyes above the scarf that swathed his face. Chaloner recognised their unusual colour immediately.

'Rea,' he said flatly. 'It seems you will answer my questions after all.'

Rea gulped, and glanced to where Oxenbridge was beginning to stir. Meanwhile, the pair in the grave were testing Wiseman by trying to climb out, and the guard with the slashed face had disappeared, probably to summon help. Chaloner did not have much time.

'Give me the letters and leave the city,' whispered Rea. 'Leak is dead, Knight is dead, Smartfoot is dead . . . If you have one jot of sense, you will disappear before you join them.'

'Leak and Smartfoot died killing the King's birds,' said Chaloner. 'And Mary Wood was murdered with the same toxin. What does the Post Office gain from these cowardly acts?'

Rea gaped. 'You should not have made those connections. My masters will not—'

'Who are your masters?' demanded Chaloner, although he was now hopelessly confused. Rea and Oxenbridge could not been involved with dispatching the ducks, or they would not be asking for the letters, given that the bird-killers had taken them. Were there rival factions at work within the Post Office, then? Thurloe had mentioned two separate plots . . .

301

'Men who will kill me if I betray them. So do not think that musket will make me talk.'

'You were ready to speak to me the other day.'

'No – I was ordered to spin you a tale that would send you to a place where you could be quietly dispatched, but Gery interrupted. Who are *you* working for? It is not Clarendon, because Gery is doing his bidding. Is it Bankes? Jeremiah Copping said you were . . .'

'Copping?' pounced Chaloner when Rea faltered, clearly having let something slip that he should not have done. 'What did he—'

But at that moment, Wiseman yelled a warning. Oxenbridge had regained his senses and was climbing to his feet. Chaloner aimed the musket and fired at him, intending to do enough damage to render him harmless but not enough to kill, knowing he himself was not the only one who had questions for Oxenbridge to answer. His deep mistrust of firearms was borne out when the weapon failed to discharge, and nothing more happened than an impotent click.

'You should not have dallied,' said Rea, suddenly gloating. 'Now you will see what—'

Chaloner swiped at him with the musket butt, then leapt towards Oxenbridge, shoving him into the grave on top of the two men already there. There came the sound of splintering coffin and cries of revulsion. Tossing the useless gun away, Chaloner grabbed the terrified rector by the hand and ran, shouting for Wiseman to follow.

'Go home, collect Temperance and leave the city,' he ordered once they were in the street. 'Do not return until I send word to the Stag Inn in Chatham. Take Basset with you.'

'I cannot!' Wiseman was horrified. 'I have duties here – patients. The King.'

'I know.' Chaloner was sorry he had dragged the surgeon into such dark business. 'But Oxenbridge may think you have these damned letters. You will not be safe here.'

'Very well,' said Wiseman reluctantly. 'What will you do?'

'Lead them away so you can escape. Hurry. You do not have much time.'

Moments later, Oxenbridge appeared. He released a bellow of triumph when he saw Chaloner, who then took him and his men on a merry chase, allowing them to come recklessly close to ensure they did not lose interest. Twice they almost outfoxed him by splitting up, and once Oxenbridge even managed to grab his coat. Only when they reached Wapping did Chaloner vanish into the shadows. Then he broke into a steady run, aiming for Scalding Alley.

Rachel's door hung drunkenly on its hinges, and her cosy, neat lodgings were in chaos. There was no sign of her, and a frightened neighbour said she and Landlord Morgan had left London together. Chaloner hoped they would have the sense not to come back.

As Chaloner felt he could not go to Tothill Street or Long Acre that night, he took a room in an anonymous tavern on Cheapside. He was too restless to sleep well, and it was still dark when he left to visit Thurloe, skidding frequently on the ice that lay in slick sheets across the streets. The city was quieter than usual, although an inordinate number of apprentices were out, gathering in sullen gangs. Respectable traders were keeping their

303

premises closed, and many houses had boarded up their windows. London felt much as it had done during the uneasy truces between the civil wars, when no one was sure what was going to happen next.

Chaloner was just walking across Dial Court when he saw a familiar figure. As usual, Prynne's hat was pulled down to conceal his lack of ears, although loose threads indicated that it had not emerged unscathed from its encounter with the horse's teeth.

'You are up early,' said the pamphleteer with keen interest. 'Is trouble afoot? Is Man again hugging his pleasurable sins? Alas, how far are Christians now degenerated from what they were in ancient times; when as that which was their badge and honour heretofore is now become their brand and shame. *Quantus in Christiano populo honor Christi est, ubi religio ignobilem facit?*'

Chaloner regarded him sourly, wondering why the man could not find it within himself to speak plain English. 'I am not sure I want to talk to you, given your recent antics.'

Prynne scowled. 'It was not my fault that wretched horse took a liking to my—'

'I meant what you did last Saturday – taking Gery to Thurloe's rooms.'

'I had no choice,' Prynne pouted resentfully. 'He threatened to chop off my nose unless I obliged. I could see he was in earnest, and I cannot afford to lose any more bits of my face.'

'Have you heard any rumours about the Post Office?' asked Chaloner, supposing he may as well take advantage of the opportunity the encounter provided. Prynne was fond of gossip.

'Oh, yes,' replied the pamphleteer gleefully. 'Half the

clerks are defrauding the government, and the other half are engaged in treachery and treason.'

'How do you know?'

'Because that is why the comet appeared – to warn us about them. And because, as Keeper of Records, I receive the Post Office's quarterly accounts. The corruption and thievery are obvious, and I am surprised that O'Neill puts up with it.'

'What about the "treachery and treason"?'

The vengefully fanatical expression on Prynne's face faded. 'Now there I cannot help you. The Major knows – I sometimes meet him in the Tower when he is allowed out of his cell for air – but he declines to discuss it. He has contacts in the Foreign Office, and spends half his life writing letters begging for information. He is terrified, poor man. Wood did him a great disservice.'

'By taking his story to Clarendon?' Chaloner supposed he should not be surprised that Prynne knew about something that was meant to be secret.

'Yes. He should have used me as a messenger. I would not have gone to Clarendon, because he is blinded by grief for his son. He will not stop what is unfolding, and when the matter explodes, he will lose what little power he has left. And the Major will spend the rest of his life in captivity.'

'Then persuade him to confide in someone else,' urged Chaloner, wondering whether Wood had selected Clarendon precisely because he was distracted – that he wanted him to fail.

'I have tried,' replied Prynne gloomily. 'But Gery has him far too thoroughly intimidated.'

* * *

305

Chaloner was in an unsettled frame of mind when he reached Chamber XIII, and was not pleased to discover that Thurloe already had a visitor. It was Dorislaus.

'I wanted to speak to you yesterday,' Chaloner said, unable to keep the unfriendliness from his voice. 'But you left Wood's house rather abruptly.'

'Yes,' replied Dorislaus, equally cool. 'Thurloe and I have reason to believe that Vanderhuyden is a traitor, and I had kept him company for hours. Then you arrived, and I decided you could take a turn. Spying on one's friends is never pleasant, although I imagine you are used to it.'

Chaloner ignored the jibe and turned questioningly to Thurloe.

'We have been wary of Vanderhuyden for some time, Tom,' explained Thurloe quietly. 'There is evidence that he has been sending national secrets to the Dutch.'

'We have not told Williamson yet,' said Dorislaus, his expression unreadable. 'We must be absolutely certain, given that it will result in Vanderhuyden's execution. Of course, Williamson is so swamped by reported sightings of Gardner that he cannot deal with spies anyway.'

'Why did you start the rumours that Mary Wood was murdered?' asked Chaloner. He was repelled by Dorislaus's perfidy – only very ruthless men sacrificed friends to save themselves. He was aware of Thurloe's disapproval at his curt tone, but he did not care.

'Because she *was* murdered,' replied Dorislaus. 'It would have been unethical to keep silent when I knew something was wrong, so I spoke out. And I am glad I did, because it prompted Surgeon Wiseman to look at her, and my suspicions have been officially confirmed.'

'How did you know?' asked Chaloner, unconvinced by the tale. 'Did you examine her?'

'Yes, although I am not a medical man, so it did scant good. However, I guessed there had been foul play when Joyce told me about her mysterious visitor.'

'Her killer is probably Gardner from the Post Office,' said Chaloner, wondering how Thurloe could be deceived by Dorislaus; the ex-Spymaster was usually an excellent judge of character. 'Do you think he poisoned her on Wood's orders?'

'Of course not,' said Dorislaus impatiently. 'Wood is not sufficiently sane.'

'I suspect he is not as fey-witted as you think,' said Chaloner, recalling the flashes of sly intelligence he had seen in the courtier's eyes. Temperance had also remarked on it.

'Of course he is!' snapped Dorislaus. 'I am fond of him, but even I cannot claim he is rational. Indeed, I am surprised the King keeps him at Court, where he could do more damage with a careless insult to an ambassador than Vanderhuyden could ever do with his betrayals.'

'You have been seen in conversation with dubious people,' said Chaloner, changing the subject abruptly. 'Gery, O'Neill, le Notre—'

Dorislaus flushed a deep red, and Chaloner had the sense that he controlled his temper only with difficulty. 'Surely, you have better things to do than spy on me? However, if you must know, I met those particular men as part of my enquiries for Thurloe.' He turned to the ex-Spymaster. 'If there is nothing else, John, I shall be on my way. I have much to do today.'

He bowed curtly and took his leave. Chaloner trailed him down the stairs to make sure he had really gone, then returned.

'He saved your life at the Post Office last Sunday,' said Thurloe warningly, knowing what was coming. 'He told me. That is not the act of a man who is involved in unsavoury dealings.'

Unless the entire episode had been staged, thought Chaloner, and the 'rescue' had been arranged to convince him that Dorislaus was trustworthy. If so, then it had failed.

'Gery suspects him of something,' he said, disinclined to say that Vanderhuyden did, too. 'At least, he was asking you about him when I came here on Saturday.'

'Gery!' spat Thurloe. 'A fool, whose patriotism does not equal his wits.'

'Will you tell him that Dorislaus was here?'

'I do not betray my friends, Thomas. And I trust Isaac with my life.'

'As you once trusted Morland?'

Thurloe's eyes became twin points of steel. 'That was a low blow.'

It was, but Chaloner had not known how else to make his point, yet he could see there was no point in pursuing the discussion. 'Would you like to know what I have learned since we last met?'

'If you believe it will help us move forward,' replied Thurloe icily.

Chaloner stifled a sigh. He had not intended to alienate the only friend he had left in London, and half wished he had kept his suspicions to himself.

'Mary's murder, the King's ducks and the business at the Post Office are connected, although I do not understand why. Copping knows more than he would tell me, and Knight's letters – the ones I lost – almost cost Wiseman and Basset their lives, because Oxenbridge wants them very badly.'

Thurloe's expression softened slightly. 'It seems you have had an eventful time. Sit by the fire and eat some bread and boiled eggs. Then we shall see if we can make sense of it together.'

In the event, they made sense of nothing, except to underline their certainty that some deadly affair was heading for a dénouement, and they had to work quickly if they were to stop it.

'A witness will arrive in the next few moments,' said Thurloe. 'You should be here when he does. Meanwhile, one of my contacts intercepted this yesterday.'

He handed Chaloner a letter. It was from a man named Jonah McPiperige, and it was addressed to Mr Bankes of the Swan on Cornhill:

You sente a Generuss Summe for Detayles of the Divers Plotts in the Domus of Nuntius. The one is Greede, the other is the Devill's Worke. The Greede you knowe. The Corpse and Kronos's mate are Satan's spawn. I feare to write More. My Affections to your Father.

'Well?' asked Thurloe. 'What do you understand by it?'

'*Domus* is Latin for house, and *nuntius* means letter, so I assume it refers to the Post Office. However, McPiperige is no scholar, or he would have used the genitive—'

'No pompous asides, please, Thomas. We do not have time. Besides, I had reasoned this much for myself. What else?'

'It confirms that two plots are unfolding at the Post Office, as you thought. The first is corruption: "Greede". The second, "the Devill's Worke", is more invidious and has McPiperige frightened. He names Oxenbridge and Rea as perpetrators, calling them "Satan's spawn".'

Thurloe nodded slowly. 'Oxenbridge is the "Corpse", a reference to his appearance . . .'

'And Rhea – Rea – was the consort of Kronos in Greek mythology,' said Chaloner, for once glad of his Classical education. 'Bankes's "Father" must be whoever is paying him to investigate.'

'I have come across Bankes's name on a dozen occasions, always asking for information. But he is clever, and I have never met anyone who has seen him. Who is he?'

'O'Neill, trying to ascertain what is known about his operation?' suggested Chaloner. 'Morland, who is clever enough to gather intelligence without it leading back to him? Wood, who is not as lunatic as Dorislaus believes? Le Notre, who has been a sinister presence from the start?'

At that moment, there was a tap on the door, and Thurloe's expected visitor was ushered in. Chaloner recognised the faded red cloak and blue hat immediately. The musician started in alarm when Chaloner shot to his feet, but Thurloe spoke quickly.

'It is all right, Robin. We only want the answers to a few questions, and then you may go.'

'How did you find him?' asked Chaloner of Thurloe.

'Isaac did,' replied Thurloe pointedly. 'With patience and a lot of footwork.'

Unwilling to pursue that discussion, Chaloner turned to the entertainer. 'You were near the cart when it exploded. What were you doing there?'

'A lot of people had gathered for the noonday post,' replied Robin, although not until Thurloe had nodded to tell him to speak. 'It seemed a good opportunity to earn a few pennies.'

'No one paid you to stay? Or suggested it as a good place to perform?'

'No, I happened on it by chance. I usually work outside the Royal Exchange, but it was windy that day, and I wanted somewhere more sheltered.'

'Was the cart in the yard when you arrived?'

'It was driven in a few minutes later. I remember, because it blocked me off from potential customers, and I was annoyed. Two men were on it. One unhitched the horse and took it away, but he soon came back, and then they both started to fiddle with the firewood.'

'Describe them.'

'Small and scruffy. Like beggar boys.'

'The Yeans.' Chaloner glanced at Thurloe. 'Someone must have paid them to do it – Wiseman found a lot of money with their bodies. But why did they run towards the cart when I warned everyone to move away, especially if they knew what was going to happen?'

Thurloe shrugged, and turned back to the musician. 'Did you notice anyone else loitering?'

'Yes – a lot of people, all listening to me. But there was one fellow . . . He was leaning against a wall some distance away, and I think he was monitoring the Post Office.'

'What did he look like?' asked Chaloner.

Robin considered carefully. 'Drab clothes and a hat with a fake yellow flower. He ran away when you started shouting, as did we all. He did not go far, though, and I saw him after the explosion, watching the General Letter Office again.'

Chaloner nodded his thanks and Robin left. So there had been no attempt to encourage people to stay in a place where they would be harmed, and he had wasted his time by hunting the musician.

'I know a man who wears a hat with an artificial yellow

311

flower,' said Thurloe. 'He was one of my spies in the Post Office, and survived there as a clerk until O'Neill ejected him eighteen months ago. His name is Ibson.'

'Your jackal?' blurted Chaloner.

Thurloe regarded him coolly. 'That was Widow Smith's name for him. It was unkind.'

'She suggested I speak to him days ago, but it looked like an unpromising line of enquiry, so I ignored it. It seems I was wrong.'

'We shall visit him immediately,' determined Thurloe, reaching for his coat. 'He will not talk to you, but he will certainly have time for me.'

Thurloe quickly ascertained that Ibson's current address was a ramshackle tenement in an alley off Holborn. It was a dirty building, which reeked of burned cabbage and poverty. Each room housed a different family, while other folk had paid to inhabit the stairs, so Chaloner and Thurloe had to pick their way across recumbent bodies to reach Ibson's lair on the second floor. His door was closed, although the one opposite was open, home to a small boy who had been given a bone whistle. He blew on it enthusiastically, ignoring his mother's slurred appeals for him to stop. Chaloner wondered how the other residents could bear the incessantly shrill din.

Thurloe knocked on Ibson's door, using a pattern of raps that Chaloner knew could not be random. It swung open, and Thurloe entered. Chaloner followed, but stopped abruptly when he felt the cold touch of a gun against his neck.

'It is all right, Ibson,' said Thurloe quietly, closing the door. 'He is with me.'

'I have been expecting you, Mr Thurloe,' said Ibson.

He had a large, pointed face and a lot of long yellow teeth, so that Chaloner thought Widow Smith's nickname was uncannily apposite – not that he had ever seen a jackal, of course, and his knowledge of them was confined to what he had read in books. He found himself wondering whether there were jackals in Russia.

'We have just learned that you witnessed the explosion outside the Post Office,' Thurloe was saying. 'Will you tell us about it? There is no need for guns, by the way.'

'I beg to differ.' Ibson perched on a table and kept the weapon trained on Chaloner. 'I have not survived these last few weeks by being careless. I trust you, but I do not know him.'

'As you wish. Will you tell us what you know? Quickly, please. Time is of the essence.'

'Two lads from the Fleet Rookery did it. I saw them light the fuse. God only knows why they ran back towards the cart, though. Stupid beggars – victims of their own villainy!'

'Did you see anything else?'

'No, my attention had been on the Post Office. Mr Bankes pays well for good information, and since losing my job as a postal clerk, I am obliged to make ends meet any way I can.'

'Bankes?' asked Thurloe sharply.

Ibson shrugged. 'I have never met him. He sends money here if he likes my reports.'

'And what have your reports told him?'

'That the apprentices are close to exploding into violence. That John Fry has written dozens of letters that encourage Londoners to rebel. That someone will soon be assassinated.'

'What have you learned about the Post Office?'

'Very little, although I suspect O'Neill is at the heart of

313

the evil. He hired Harper to prevent his clerks from gossiping, and he is suspiciously mum himself. I will monitor the place no more, though, not even for you, Mr Thurloe. My contacts there are dead, and I have no wish to follow.'

'The Alibond brothers?' asked Chaloner.

Ibson regarded him sharply. 'Who told you that? Jeremiah Copping? He is an oily devil, and cares for nothing except money. I should have put a knife in his gizzard years ago.'

'You say O'Neill is at the heart of the evil,' said Thurloe. 'But what evil, exactly?'

'First, there is the corruption that everyone knows about, although it is on a massive scale, and will shock the nation when – if – it is exposed. Second, there is something much darker and more wicked. Its perpetrators are using the corruption as a screen.'

'Yes, but a screen for what?' pressed Thurloe, a little impatiently.

'Something that has attracted Oxenbridge like a maggot to rotting meat,' replied Ibson. 'And his helpmeets Rea and Gardner. All are rogues, who want terrible things to happen.'

'Have you ever seen Oxenbridge in the Post Office?' asked Chaloner, thinking that Ibson knew no more about the real plot than anyone else; he was just repeating suspicions and rumours.

Ibson nodded. 'In the disused wing. I got near a window once, and heard him talking to his cronies. Unfortunately, I made a noise and they almost caught me. I was lucky to escape.'

'Storey's parlour overlooks that building,' said Chaloner to Thurloe.

Ibson spat. 'It is no good asking Storey whether he

314

has noticed anything untoward. His only concern is the ducks that are dying in St James's Park.'

'Precisely,' said Chaloner, still to Thurloe. 'Birds poisoned, so he will not care about strange lights and sounds from a part of the Post Office that is supposed to be abandoned.'

'Of course!' Ibson stared at him. 'That makes perfect sense. Why did I not see it?'

'And Mary?' asked Thurloe. 'Is that why she was killed, too?'

Chaloner shook his head. 'The disused wing cannot be seen from her home. However, her death *is* Post-Office related. Gardner poisoned her, and he is a clerk.'

'Gardner did?' Ibson frowned. 'I suppose he might have done. He is a ruthless bastard. He led Knight into turbulent waters, and left him to drown without a backward glance.'

'That implies Knight was involved,' said Thurloe.

Ibson shook his head. 'He was being used. However, he was a clever man, and understood what was happening. He told me the night before he was arrested that he was on the verge of exposing the whole affair, although he had not learned the identities of most of the perpetrators. He had written everything down in a series of letters to important people.'

Chaloner groaned.

'What else?' asked Thurloe urgently. 'Tell us all you know, no matter how trivial it seems.'

'A Dutch spy is using the postal services to correspond with his masters in The Hague – I intercepted one of his reports. I also have papers that prove the corruption of several clerks, and will give them to Williamson when they are arrested.'

315

'Why not before?' asked Chaloner.

Ibson smiled without humour. 'Because I do not want these villains as enemies until they are safely under lock and key.'

'Thank you,' said Thurloe, standing. 'You have been most helpful.'

'There is one other thing, Mr Thurloe. The Major is also desperately trying to learn what is happening. Talk to him.' Ibson glanced at the window. 'He can often be found in the Crown or the Antwerp at this time of a morning, spying on fanatics for Clarendon.'

Chaloner and Thurloe went to the Catherine Wheel on Cheapside first, but were informed by the guards that Copping and his sister had gone shopping, and would not be back until late afternoon. Chaloner wanted to wait – and search the place while he did so – but Thurloe insisted there were more important things to do, such as questioning the Major.

'But he refuses to talk.' Chaloner followed the ex-Spymaster back towards Dowgate. 'He has taken a vow to report only to Clarendon, one he will not break because he is frightened of Gery.'

'Then we must reason with him,' said Thurloe determinedly. 'The Crown first.'

'You cannot enter a tavern full of Cavaliers. They will string you up!'

'Fetch him out, then,' said Thurloe impatiently. 'I will wait here.'

The Crown was busy, and there was an atmosphere of quiet menace that Chaloner had not sensed there before. Patrons wore ludicrously large feathered hats to demonstrate their allegiance to the King, and had donned the kind of ugly, bucket-topped riding boots that had been favoured by Prince Rupert during the wars, despite the fact that most of them had arrived on foot.

'Have you heard that rebels are plotting in Sussex and Hull?' one was asking. 'His Majesty should give me a few cavalrymen. I would go down there and sort them out.'

His foppish appearance and drink-reddened nose made Chaloner suspect he would be incapable of sitting on a horse, let alone fighting from one.

'We should gather the names of all those who fought for the New Model Army and hang them,' declared another. 'They are a danger to our country's stability as long as they live.'

'I am a devoted Royalist,' the taverner muttered, more to himself than to Chaloner as he served the spy with ale. 'But I wish my customers would lower their voices. The Roundheads in the Antwerp might hear, and I do not want my windows smashed.'

The Major was not among the Crown's malcontents, so Chaloner did not stay long. He collected Thurloe, and they entered the Antwerp together, both careful to shield their faces as they did so, lest the place was being watched. The moment they stepped across the threshold, they were surrounded by conversations in which loud-voiced men bemoaned the lost republic. Chaloner saw Stokes and Cliffe there, although the two veterans seemed more alarmed than inspired by the rebellious talk, and left when Landlord Young expressed the hope that it would be the King who would be assassinated by John Fry's brave insurgents.

Thurloe nudged Chaloner, and nodded to where the Major was sitting alone, his face shadowed by a large hat. Chaloner might have missed him, but he was betrayed by his yeomen, who sat near the door reading the latest newsbook. Their uniforms were mostly covered by cloaks, but flashes of red and yellow could be seen around the neck. They tensed when Thurloe sat next to their prisoner, but relaxed when they recognised Chaloner. The Major closed his eyes wearily.

'Not again! I cannot break my oath to Clarendon. How many more times must I tell you? For God's sake go away, so I can complete my business here and leave. I thought I hated the Tower, but it is preferable to what I am charged to do outside it. Why does Gery order me to monitor these places? Why not ask one of his horrible henchmen?'

'That is a good question,' said Thurloe softly.

The Major glanced at him once, and then again. His jaw dropped. 'Thurloe? My God! I did not recognise you. Why are you here? Not to encourage sedition? I thought you had more sense.'

'He is here to thwart trouble, not to cause it,' said Chaloner sharply.

'So am I.' The Major's skin was grey with fatigue, and his hands shook so badly that he had spilled coffee all over the table. 'Although I have a bad feeling that no one will believe me if I am caught. Gery will deny sending me here to spy, and I shall hang. Perhaps that is what he wants, to spare Clarendon the inconvenience of letting me go.'

It was certainly possible, thought Chaloner, given Gery's hatred for one-time Parliamentarians. There was a sudden roar of appreciation from near the hearth, where someone was advocating a second royal beheading. Eager to be gone, Chaloner tried again to make the Major see sense.

'Gery is not making progress with the Post Office

enquiry, no matter what Clarendon tells you. Please tell us what you have learned.'

The Major looked ready to cry. 'I cannot. I gave my word.'

'And that is more important than the security of your country?' asked Thurloe sternly. 'Or your freedom, which you will not win if the Post Office plot succeeds? Indeed, you may even be considered implicit in the affair, and end up being locked away for ever.'

A sickly green flush spread across the Major's face. 'Oh, God! If only Wood had taken my tale to someone else — the matter might have been resolved by now.'

'Then talk to us,' urged Thurloe. 'We shall see this plot thwarted. And afterwards, I shall arrange your release. I may not have the power I once enjoyed, but I still own a certain influence.'

The Major swallowed hard. 'Let me think about it. It is not a decision to be taken lightly.'

'Then do not think too long,' warned Chaloner. 'Or you may be too late.'

'I shall give you my decision tonight. But not here — the place will explode with violence soon, and we do not want to be caught in the middle. Meet me outside the Tower at ten o'clock.'

'You will be allowed out then?' asked Chaloner doubtfully.

'I shall be returning there after yet another foray to meet Clarendon at White Hall. Be prompt, though. I shall have only a few moments before I am shut away for the night.'

'We may need longer,' objected Chaloner.

The Major regarded him soberly. 'No we will not. The business is deadly, but not complicated.'

*　　*　　*

Chaloner and Thurloe went their separate ways after leaving the Antwerp; Thurloe to see what could be learned from his other sources, and Chaloner to visit the Swan on Cornhill to ask about the letter Thurloe's contact had intercepted, and then to check on the birds in the park. It did not take him long to learn what he needed to know from the tavern, after which he turned west, walking through a city where work was beginning to stop for the day and people were already hurrying home, eager to be out of the biting cold.

As he walked along Fleet Street, Chaloner stopped to buy a piece of gingerbread, which transpired to be a heavy slab of stodge that reminded him of army marching rations. He ate half, and was shoving the rest in his pocket for later when he met Maude, the formidable matron who kept Temperance's bawdy house in order. She was pale, and carried a limp bundle.

'I am glad Richard took Temperance away,' she said. 'This would have distressed her.'

'Wiseman's cat,' said Chaloner, pulling the cloth away to reveal ginger fur. He looked at the hapless animal more closely and saw blood in its mouth. 'Poisoned!'

'I am going to take it to Long Acre for the kites, in case Richard boils it up and presents its skeleton to her as a gift. He is not very good at knowing what might win a woman's heart.' Maude handed him a piece of paper. 'This was with it.'

It was a crude drawing of a man and a woman, hanging side by side on a gibbet. Chaloner's only consolation was that the warning had missed its intended target, as his friends were safely away. He offered to dispose of the cat for her and continued towards the park, the sad bundle under his arm. He found Storey and Eliot in one of the sheds, bent over something lying on a bench. Chaloner's heart sank.

'Another swan?'

'Not this time,' replied Storey with triumphant glee. 'A fox. Wood shot it with a musket near Chelsey. He is quite the marksman, although he was disappointed when I told him it was not a brassica. Lord! I hope that is not a bird you have wrapped in that cloth, Chaloner.'

'A poisoned cat. Will you bury it? If the Long Acre kites feed on it, they will die, too.'

Storey nodded. 'Give it to us. We shall ensure it does no harm.'

Chaloner turned to Eliot. 'Do you have room in your house for a guest?'

'Of course,' replied Eliot warmly. 'My Jane loves visitors. How long will you be staying?'

'Not me – Storey. It is no longer safe for him to go home.' Briefly, he explained his reasons, and recommended requisitioning palace guards to protect the birds.

Storey was pale. 'But I *did* see lights burning in the disused bit of the Post Office! Do you think these villains saw me looking out of my window then? It was before poor Eliza was murdered . . .'

'Perhaps it explains why your house was burgled last night, too,' said Eliot.

'I was here guarding my birds,' explained Storey, seeing Chaloner's questioning glance. 'And went home at dawn to find that someone had made off with Eliza, Harriet and Sharon. For their beautiful feathers, I suppose. Milliners will pay handsomely for them.'

But Chaloner suspected that someone was tidying up – removing evidence that might tie dead ducks to a poisoned courtier and whatever else was unfolding in

Post House Yard. And as Rea had been alarmed when he had learned that Chaloner had made the connection, it did not take a genius to guess the identity of the culprits.

'Tell me about the lights you saw,' he ordered.

'Well, ten men or so were meeting there, and I recognised three of them – two clerks named Rea and Gardner, and that eerie Clement Oxenbridge, who looks like a barn owl with his white face and black eyes, although not as handsome.'

'Did you notice anything else?'

'Yes – two others attempting to spy on them. The first was that slippery Morland. He did not stay long, perhaps because it was raining and he did not like getting wet. He left, but it was not many moments before his place was taken by another.'

'Did you know him?'

'Not personally, but I have heard him addressed as Harper. It was amusing to see him press his face against the window as he aimed to hear what was being said, and I laughed uproariously.'

'What happened then?' asked Eliot, while Chaloner thought that Storey would certainly have been fed poison had the clerks known what he had witnessed.

'The meeting ended, and Harper watched them leave. It was then that I saw the expression on his face. It was dark and rather frightening, like a fox about to kill a bird. It made me stop laughing, I can tell you!'

322

Chapter 11

It was nearing dusk by the time Chaloner left the park. The sky was pale blue, fading to a bright orange in the west as the sun set behind the winter-bare trees. The air was still, and smelled of frost and frozen mud. It was going to be another bitter night, although at least a dry one.

It was obvious to Chaloner what had to be done next: arrest Rea, and force him to reveal the whereabouts of Oxenbridge and Gardner. And when all three were in custody, raise the matter of the Post Office, the King's fowl and Mary's murder. But he knew that was not going to happen: the Earl had already promised to dismiss him if he investigated any matter other than the birds, and was unlikely to listen long enough to be told that they were all connected.

He sincerely hoped the Major would come to his senses. Until then, all he could do was return to the Catherine Wheel, and trust that Copping would agree to provide information. Cursing the fact that he had been burdened with such an intractable employer, he started to walk towards Lincoln's Inn to collect Thurloe, but had not gone far before a carriage pulled up beside him. It was a fine one, although plain, and had been provided with thick curtains to keep its occupant warm. One was whisked aside to reveal Williamson.

'It is good to be going home to a loving wife,' said the Spymaster, so smugly that Chaloner wondered whether he perhaps thought that Hannah had gone to Epsom not to prepare the way for the Queen, but to escape from her husband. White Hall was always full of malicious gossip, and Hannah might well have fuelled the rumour mill with some innocently incautious comment.

'I am glad we met,' said Chaloner, electing to ignore the remark. 'You need to arrest Rea.'

Williamson indicated that he was to climb into the coach. It had the luxury of an internal lamp, and its amber glow showed the lines of exhaustion and worry etched into the Spymaster's face.

'I cannot arrest him, Chaloner. Your master will not give me a warrant.'

'Such niceties do not usually stop you.'

'No,' agreed Williamson. 'But half of London is interested in the Post Office at the moment, and I cannot be seen detaining its employees illegally. It would see *me* in the Tower.'

'Rea will probably be able to tell you where Gardner is hiding,' Chaloner pointed out.

'Perhaps, but my hands are tied.' Williamson sighed wearily. 'I must have interviewed a hundred people about Gardner today. We have been hopelessly swamped since Clarendon insisted on offering that reward. It was a stupid idea, and I hope to God it bears fruit. I should not like to think that I have been wasting my time.'

Chaloner strongly suspected that he had.

'If I were Postmaster, I would have had him in custody

by now,' Williamson went on bitterly. 'I could have intercepted letters to and from his acquaintances, and learned where he is hiding. How can the government expect me to succeed with only limited access to the mail? People compare me unfavourably to Thurloe, but they forget that *he* controlled the Post Office.'

'Perhaps the King will give you the position if O'Neill transpires to be corrupt.'

'Perhaps.' Williamson seemed to realise that he was revealing rather more of himself than was professional, and became gruffly businesslike. 'Do you have anything to report?'

Chaloner held out the letter addressed to Bankes, which he had taken from Thurloe, when the germ of an idea had begun to form in his mind. 'No, but I believe this is intended for you.'

Williamson's eyes narrowed, and he did not take it. 'Why would you think so?'

'First, because I have just visited the Swan on Cornhill, and the landlord's description of "Mr Bankes" sounded uncannily like you. Second, because this note is written in terms that an intelligencer might use to his spymaster. And third, because who else but a government official would be able to pay a "generuss summe" for information? Of course it is you.'

Williamson scowled as he snatched it. 'Then let us hope no one else guesses, because Mr Bankes wins considerably more information than poor Mr Williamson.'

Chaloner was not surprised. It was one thing supplying intelligence to an anonymous source, but another altogether to give it to an unpopular spymaster. With the admission, a number of things became clear – and not just about Bankes either.

'It is from Copping,' he said. 'Your mole at the Post Office.'

Williamson regarded him coldly. 'No, it is from Jonah McPiperige, a Wapping tailor.'

'Jonah McPiperige is an anagram of Jeremiah Copping, who inadvertently let slip that he sells information. No wonder he was so terrified when I visited him! He believes he was injured in your service – that the gunpowder was aimed at him.'

'And was it?' Williamson made no further effort to refute Chaloner's conclusions.

'Possibly. The cart was brought by the Yeans, who panicked when they heard me shout. Instead of running away, they tried to douse the fuse, which was why they ran back to it – they were not stealing firewood as we all assumed. I suppose they realised that Copping was going to escape, so decided to postpone the operation. Except that such devices are not easy to put out once they are lit.'

'But you had already seen the fuse burning, so the matter was going to be investigated whether the powder ignited or not,' Williamson pointed out.

Chaloner recalled what Mother Greene had said about them. 'Yes, but they did not have the wits to think it through. Whoever hired them probably wanted Copping's death to be one of many, so you would not realise that your mole was the intended target. But the Yeans left the cart – *sans* horse – in a place that aroused my suspicion. They were well paid, but they were not up to the task.'

Williamson's expression was difficult to read. 'Who is this ruthless villain?'

Chaloner shrugged. 'But you had better tell Copping

to leave London, because the soldiers his sister has hired cannot protect him.'

'Damn,' muttered Williamson. 'He is the only postal clerk I managed to turn, although his injury has kept him from helping me of late. You had better come with me, lest he is inclined to disregard the advice. He does not trust me, despite my best efforts to win his affection.'

'You tried to turn Knight, too,' said Chaloner, rather accusingly. '"Bankes" pestered him relentlessly with demands for information, and when they failed, you applied to Clarendon for an arrest warrant – to frighten him into complying.'

'And Clarendon precipitated me by sending you to implement it,' said Williamson in some disgust. 'Knight would have been perfectly safe in my cells, but he was taken to Newgate instead, where he was murdered. It was a wretched waste.'

'A waste indeed,' said Chaloner coldly. 'Of a decent man.'

Williamson waved a dismissive hand. 'Yes, he was innocent, but Gardner was not. I intended to question them both, then give Knight enough money to live in Limehouse with his woman.'

'The warrant was unnecessary. He was desperate to share what he had—'

'He was only desperate once he was in Newgate. Before that, he was as closed-mouthed as all the other clerks. Why do you think I was obliged to contact him in the guise of Bankes? Because he refused to confide in his Spymaster General.'

'He would have done, had you handled him properly. Your antics with Bankes terrified him – a mysterious man whom no one knows, and who might even be one of the Post Office's criminals.'

Regret flared in Williamson's eyes when he realised he might have miscalculated, but it was quickly masked. He banged on the ceiling and called Copping's address to his driver. Chaloner was about to jump out, preferring to interview the clerk with Thurloe, when it occurred to him that Copping might reveal more to the current Spymaster than a past one. He sat back. He could always take Thurloe to see Copping later, should Williamson's efforts prove to be unfruitful.

Once they were underway, Williamson began to talk about the Post Office, revealing that he knew even less about what was happening than did Chaloner. The only detail the spy did not know was that the Alibond brothers were corrupt. With the revelation, more answers snapped into place.

'Then I suspect Copping is rotten, too,' he said. 'First, because he insists that the Alibonds were innocent when you have proof that they were not. Second, because Rea mentioned his name in a curious way in the churchyard yesterday. And third, because his sister's tavern screams of the kind of wealth that comes with a sudden windfall – a much larger one than you have paid, I am sure.'

Williamson was horrified. 'But that means all the intelligence he passed to me is tainted!'

'Yes,' agreed Chaloner. 'Which explains why the plot has been able to gain such momentum – his disinformation has kept you confused and uncertain. However, if he was the intended victim of the blast, then it suggests that his masters are unimpressed with his efforts. He is probably in considerable danger.'

'Perhaps I should let them have him,' said Williamson bitterly. 'It would serve him right.'

*   *   *

They arrived to find the Catherine Wheel in darkness and no sign of the guards. Filled with foreboding, Chaloner picked the lock. When it snapped open, Williamson followed him along the hall to the parlour in which Copping had been recovering. The gleam of a lamp and murmuring voices indicated that someone was within. Before Chaloner could stop him, Williamson had flung open the door and stalked inside. Copping stood there with his sister, a pair of saddlebags over his shoulder. His neck was still bandaged, although he seemed otherwise recovered.

'You!' he exclaimed angrily when he saw Williamson. His eye twitched convulsively. 'How dare you come here!'

'Please do not leave, Jeremiah,' said Widow Smith plaintively, ignoring the newcomers. 'I can protect you. Me and my guards have kept you safe for a week now.'

'Yes, but you cannot do it indefinitely, and my life has been in danger ever since *he* turned me into a spy.' Copping scowled furiously at the Spymaster. 'I should never have let him seduce me with his traitors' gold. Get out of the way, all of you. I am risking myself no longer.'

'You can go when you tell me who is behind all this mischief,' said Williamson, not moving.

'Go to hell,' snarled Copping, his tic growing more pronounced. 'I am done with you. It is your fault that I am forced to abandon everything I hold dear.'

'You knew the risks,' said Williamson. 'It was your own choice to play the Judas. However, I shall pay a substantial bonus for the name of your master.'

Copping regarded him pityingly. 'You have no idea what you are dealing with, do you! You are as lost and confused as you were two months ago, when all this started.'

329

'Then explain it to me,' said Williamson, manfully swallowing his very considerable pride.

'Why not help him, Jeremiah,' coaxed Widow Smith. 'These villains cannot harm you if they are all arrested. Then you will be free to live here again in safety.'

'He will never best them,' sneered Copping. 'Besides, the answers are obvious. A rebellion is brewing, and they are behind it. John Fry writes letters intended to inflame, and there will be an assassination that will set London alight.'

'Who will be the victim?' asked Chaloner.

'That is obvious, too,' snapped Copping. 'It will be le Notre, to sour relations between England and France – a dangerous thing on the eve of war with the Dutch. Or perhaps it will be the King or Buckingham, whose murders will set the whole country aflame. Or—'

'Give me the names of the perpetrators, Copping,' ordered Williamson. 'If you oblige, I will let you to live here unmolested. Refuse, and you will end your days on the scaffold.'

The threat was barely out of his mouth before fury suffused Copping's face, and he hauled his sword from its scabbard. He hurled himself at the Spymaster with a scream of rage, and Williamson, no warrior, would have been skewered if Chaloner had not leapt forward to protect him. Copping promptly turned his ire on the spy, going after him with a series of swipes that had him retreating backwards faster than was comfortable in a chamber crowded with furniture.

'Stop!' Chaloner yelled. 'You should be thinking of escape, not fighting us. The guards have gone from the front door, and I imagine they have been bribed to leave. You are in serious danger.'

330

But Copping's blood was up, and he was beyond listening to reason. He employed a peculiar twisting motion that almost jerked the sword from Chaloner's hand. The move was familiar, and told the spy that he had done battle with this particular opponent before.

'It was you in St James's Park! *You* went there to kill the royal fowl.'

Copping's only response was to embark on another wild offensive that required all Chaloner's skill to counter. Chaloner's task was not made any easier by Widow Smith, who flailed at him with her meaty fists. Williamson did his best to restrain her, but she was a very large woman.

'Why kill birds?' Chaloner gasped, hoping to distract Copping with questions.

The attack intensified, and the clerk spoke in short sentences between swipes. 'The money is good. I am better than Smartfoot. He only got ducks. And Leak poisoned himself! I bagged a penguin. And a swan. I would have had a crane. If you had not interfered.'

'It was you who took Knight's letters?' Chaloner was tiring, lacking his opponent's enraged strength.

'I sent them to the plotters today. But too late. They are my enemies now.'

When one of Widow Smith's swipes caught Chaloner's sword arm, almost allowing Copping to disembowel him, he knew he needed to do more than defend himself. He lobbed his dagger, and when Copping ducked to avoid it, he surged forward and pinned him against the window, holding him in a grip that prevented him from moving.

Suddenly, there was a crack, and Copping gasped in shock. Then there was another bang, accompanied by the sound of smashing glass. Chaloner dived to the floor, yelling for the others to do the same. Three more shots followed, and Copping slid down the window in silent agony. Then there was silence.

Chaloner scrambled to his feet to see a face peering through the broken glass. He made a grab for it, but hands punched him off. He saw three shadows running away, but could not follow because the glazing bars were too narrow for him to squeeze through. With a sense of enormous frustration, he watched Copping's killers make an almost leisurely escape.

Chaloner declined a lift in Williamson's carriage and went to Lincoln's Inn on foot, using the journey to think about what had happened. His glimpse of Copping's assailants had told him nothing to let him identify them, and Williamson had been too stunned by the incident to provide any intelligent analysis.

Was it Oxenbridge, Gardner and Rea who had killed Copping? Or henchmen sent by some other suspicious character, such as O'Neill, Harper, le Notre or Wood? Chaloner grimaced. His own inability to provide even a vague description meant that Williamson had no grounds to arrest and interrogate any of them, and he hated the fact that murder had been committed right under his nose. What professional spy allowed that to happen?

Widow Smith had been a poor source of information, too. It had quickly become apparent that she had known little about her brother's life, despite the smug assertion she had made when she had first met Chaloner. She had been aware of the arrangement with 'Mr Bankes', but had assumed Copping's sudden influx of wealth had been due to the high quality of his reports, and it had not occurred to her that he might have been playing one side against another.

Chaloner arrived at Chamber XIII, relieved to find the ex-Spymaster alone. The last thing he needed was for Dorislaus, Gery or Prynne to be there.

'Trouble?' asked Thurloe, watching him sink into a fireside chair.

Chaloner described what had happened at the Catherine Wheel.

'Damn it, Thomas!' Thurloe rarely swore, and the expletive revealed the depth of his exasperation. 'How could you have been so careless? He was our best source of information, and his death deals our enquiry a serious blow.'

'There is still the Major,' said Chaloner, painfully aware that he had not comported himself well in this particular investigation. 'We are due to meet him outside the Tower tonight.'

'*I* will meet him,' said Thurloe testily. 'You will not. He is more likely to confide if Gery's loose-cannon of a rival is not looming over my shoulder.'

Chaloner winced at the description. 'But it may be dangerous for you to go alone.'

'I am quite capable of looking after myself. I was Spymaster General, you know. Besides, I am unlikely to come to harm right by the Tower with yeomen to hand.'

'The Major is a target for assassins,' argued Chaloner. 'You may be caught in—'

'So will you, if you are with me. Or do you think you can repel bullets?'

'Killers will not risk discharging firearms outside the Tower.' Chaloner tried to keep the irritation from his own voice, knowing a display of vexation was likely to turn Thurloe even more vehemently against him. 'They

333

will use swords, which I *can* fend off. God knows, I have had enough practice of late.'

'Nothing will happen,' stated Thurloe firmly. He reached for his coat. 'Was there anything else you wanted? I have an important meeting with a contact, and I do not want to be late.'

'Dorislaus?' asked Chaloner uneasily.

'Yes,' said Thurloe with such icy coldness that Chaloner dared not ask more.

He aimed for the stairs, Chaloner following and desperately trying to think of how he might redeem himself. 'I think the best way forward is to tackle Oxenbridge and Gardner. I will corner Rea and force him to—'

'You will not,' snapped Thurloe. 'Even if you find them, which is unlikely – a reward of fifty pounds has not exposed Gardner, while Oxenbridge's lodgings remain a mystery even to my superior detecting skills – you will not crack them. Moreover, if you cause them to panic, they may go to ground. We cannot afford that. Leave well alone, Thomas. You have done enough already.'

Chaloner took his leave subdued, unsettled and unhappy. Reluctantly, he supposed he had better visit the Earl, given that he had been prevented from doing so the previous day. He walked down Chancery Lane, feet crunching on the frost that had settled across the city.

He happened to glance left when he reached Fleet Street, and saw Stokes and Cliffe lurking by the door of St Dunstan-in-the-West. He was puzzled for a moment, but then saw Lord Castlemaine's coach standing nearby. Several burly footmen were lounging near it – Palmer was aware of his unpopularity and had wisely hired guards to protect him.

'*He* is inside,' explained Cliffe, when Chaloner asked what the two veterans thought they were doing. 'Why, when he is not Anglican?'

'A church is a church,' said Chaloner. 'And Palmer is devout. He—'

'But he may do harm in there!' cried Cliffe. 'Or is he surveying it, to see how it might best be blown to pieces, perhaps as part of the revels surrounding the publication of his papist book?'

'I do not suppose you would ask him to come out, would you?' asked Stokes hopefully. 'Even if he is not plotting sabotage, a fellow who cannot keep his wife in the marriage bed has no right to haunt a decent establishment like St Dunstan's.'

Chaloner regarded him coolly. 'Interrupt a man's private communications with God?'

'He will not be communicating with God,' declared Cliffe uncompromisingly. 'He will be communicating with the Pope – through diabolical means. In our church.'

'No,' said Chaloner sharply. 'It is—'

'If you will not stop him, then we must,' said Stokes. His hand dropped to the hilt of his sword, and the guards immediately tensed. 'His henchmen will probably kill us, but at least we shall have died doing what is right.'

'Wait,' ordered Chaloner, unwilling to see anyone skewered in a brawl that could be avoided. 'Stay here. And no caustic remarks when I bring him out. Agreed?'

Both old men nodded, although Cliffe did so grudgingly. Chaloner opened the door and stepped into the scented gloom of the nave, aware that two of the soldiers had detached themselves from their fellows to follow.

He had always liked St Dunstan's, an oasis of peace on one of the busiest thoroughfares in the city. It had a

335

lot of dark wood, but large windows made it airy. He walked towards the chancel, his footsteps echoing on the stone floor. Palmer was standing in one of the aisles holding a lantern, and Chaloner saw that le Notre was with him.

'Chaloner!' exclaimed the Frenchman. 'What a pleasant surprise. If only we had three viols. What beautiful music we should make in this magnificently resonant building.'

Palmer smiled a greeting. 'Its rector said there are some especially fine monuments here, and as le Notre and I share an interest in such things, we decided to inspect them. However, if you have come to pray, we shall leave you in peace.'

'Would you consider returning tomorrow, sir?' asked Chaloner, thinking it an odd thing to do after dark – they would have seen more in daylight. 'With the rector, if possible. He is a liberal man, but his parishioners are not. They are worried about what you might do in here.'

Palmer started to laugh, but then realised that Chaloner was serious. 'Lord! I know some folk are narrow-minded, but I did not realise the extent . . . Well, perhaps my book will correct some of these misunderstandings, and lead both sides to a greater tolerance.'

'Do not hold your breath,' said le Notre sourly. 'Englishmen are not as open to reason as I was led to believe. And now the King has cancelled Lent . . .'

'Come, le Notre,' said Palmer with a pained smile. 'We shall repair to my house and enjoy a little music instead. Will you join us, Chaloner?'

There was nothing Chaloner would have liked more, and it was with considerable reluctance that he declined. He walked outside, where Stokes and Cliffe had taken up station rather indiscreetly behind a cart, watched intently by the guards. To ensure there was no unnecessary unpleasantness, he escorted Palmer and le Notre to the coach.

'I understand you know Clement Oxenbridge, Monsieur le Notre,' he said, recalling how the Frenchman had linked arms with the man outside Temperance's club.

Le Notre looked puzzled. 'The fellow who Palmer tells me smashed the windows in his house the other night? I assure you, I do not.'

'You would remember if you did,' interposed Palmer. 'He is a peculiar-looking specimen – as white as a ghost and with black eyes that look like beads.'

'Oh, him,' said le Notre. A flicker of something unreadable flashed across his powdered face. 'I met him in the club at Hercules' Pillars Alley on Tuesday night. Was *he* the villain who gave us such a fright with that hail of missiles, then? Good God! I would not have chatted to him so merrily had I known. He introduced himself as an expert on French porcelain, a subject close to my heart.'

'Is that what he does for a living, then?' asked Palmer doubtfully. 'Sell crockery? I would not have predicted that.'

Nor would Chaloner, who did not believe it. 'You gave him a lift. Did you take him home?'

'He asked to be dropped at the Smithfield Meat Market,' replied le Notre evenly. 'He said he had business there, but did not elaborate, and I did not ask. I am not very interested in meat.'

'So do you know where he lives?' asked Chaloner, a little impatiently. Le Notre was beginning to annoy him.

'No one knows.' Palmer had answered before le Notre could speak. Was it relief that Chaloner read in the

Frenchman's face? 'He appears and disappears at will. He is quite a mystery.'

'I only met him the once,' said le Notre. 'But I did not take to him, and I shall avoid his company in future, no matter how great his knowledge of Nevers china.'

Chaloner watched their coach leave, wondering yet again about the enigma that was le Notre, and why Palmer should have befriended him.

The temperature had plummeted to well below freezing by the time Chaloner arrived at White Hall, but the Earl's rooms were so hot that he wondered how his master could breathe. Clarendon was sitting at a desk behind a mountain of papers, although it was after seven o'clock and he was almost certainly the only government official still working. Chaloner read one document upside down, and saw it was a letter from his tailor, so the documents did not all pertain to affairs of state.

'Where have you been?' the Earl demanded angrily. 'I told you to report to me yesterday.'

'I tried, sir, but you were with—'

'The King, yes, and he asked me about the villains who are killing his fowl. Well? Are the rogues in custody? Or have I been paying you for nothing all this time?'

'Three of them are dead, sir – Leak, Smartfoot and Copping.' Chaloner took a deep breath and forged on. 'They were all postal clerks. Unfortunately, I do not know why they did it, but if you issue warrants for the arrests of Oxenbridge, Rea and Harper, I shall find out.'

The Earl gaped his disbelief. 'But I told you to stay away from the Post Office.'

'You told me to catch the duck-killers.' Chaloner tried not to sound insolent. 'And that is where the trail led. It

338

also led to Mary Wood, who lives nearby. As does the Curator of Birds.'

The Earl stared at him. 'Wiseman told me that Mary had been murdered, and an agitated clerk named Vanderhuyden came here yesterday, demanding that the matter be investigated.'

'She was forced to swallow the same substance that killed the King's birds,' explained Chaloner. 'Her death and theirs are the same case.'

'I did not know that.' The Earl's face was white. He swallowed hard, and was silent for a moment, but then became businesslike. 'I shall pass the information to Gery, along with your allegations about Oxenbridge, Rea and Harper. He should be along to see me soon.'

'They are not allegations, sir. I have evidence to—'

The Earl flapped his hand, a gesture Chaloner had come to associate with decisions that were reckless or foolish. 'Thank you for bringing this to my attention. You may leave now.'

But Chaloner was not yet ready to concede defeat. 'Oxenbridge is the key to all that is happening. I need to talk to him and—'

'Why must you always argue with me?' cried the Earl. 'I said I want you to leave. And I do not mean White Hall either – I mean London. It is time for you to go to Russia. I have urgent dispatches for the Tsar, and you must take them. At once.'

'What is wrong, sir?' asked Chaloner in a low voice, acutely aware that the Earl's offices were far from secure. 'I may be able to help.'

The Earl hesitated, and for a moment Chaloner thought he might relent and explain what was happening, but then his expression hardened. 'I want you gone. Your wife will not be pleased to lose you so soon, but it cannot be helped. And I doubt she will want to go with you. Not to Russia.'

'May I visit my family in Buckinghamshire first?' asked Chaloner, thinking fast. 'Russia is a long way away, and I should like to tell them . . .' It was his turn to wave his hand, because he was not sure what to say that the Earl would believe.

The Earl regarded him with an expression that was difficult to read, but Chaloner thought he saw sympathy there, mingled rather disconcertingly with guilt. Again, he wondered whether he was being sent to such a desolate part of the world so that Gery might be rid of him permanently.

'Very well. I have chartered a ship, and I suppose we can delay it for a day or two. I shall ask the captain to set sail for Archangel on Sunday night, and I shall expect you to be on it. And do not say that a frozen sea will prevent it from going, because I have already explained that conditions are such that ice will not be a problem this year.'

Chaloner glanced out of the window, where frost lay in a thick white crust on the sill, and where the bowl of water left out for the sparrows had set like iron. 'Are you sure, sir?'

The Earl scowled. 'Yes. Now hire a horse to take you to your family before I change my mind and send you to the Tsar early.'

Three days was hardly enough time to ride to Buckinghamshire and back, but Chaloner had no intention of going anywhere. It was perfectly plain that the Earl needed his help, whether he knew it or not. And Chaloner had just seventy-two hours to give it.

* * *

340

He was glad he had played out the charade of asking for permission to leave London when he opened the door to discover that Morland had been eavesdropping behind it.

'Give my regards to your siblings,' smirked the secretary, smoothing an imaginary crease from his smart coat. 'Russia is a dreadful place, full of endless forests and poverty-stricken villages. It is dangerous, too, so it might be the last time you ever see them.'

'London can also be dangerous,' said Chaloner, gratified to see Morland blanch at the menace his voice. 'Incidentally, there are rumours that something is being built in the Post Office, and as you consider yourself an inventor—'

'I do not *consider* myself an inventor,' interrupted Morland indignantly. 'I *am* one. And nothing is being built in the Post Office, or I would have noticed. However, I am more concerned with you this evening. Have you made a will? You should – you do not want to leave Hannah in the invidious position of not knowing when she might inherit if you fail to return.'

Chaloner took a step towards him, and Morland scuttled behind a desk, although if he thought that would protect him he was badly mistaken.

'Threatening your colleagues, Chaloner?' came a voice that made the spy whip around with his hand on the hilt of his sword. Gery eyed it disdainfully. 'And flaunting weapons in your master's domain? That will not do at all.'

'No, it will not,' agreed Morland sulkily. 'So incarcerate him in White Hall's dungeons until he can be shipped off to the frozen north.'

'There is no need,' said Chaloner, afraid Gery

might do it, and then the Earl would be doomed for certain. 'I am going to Buckinghamshire at first light tomorrow.'

He turned and walked away before the marshal could stop him, running briskly down the staircase and aiming for the door. There was a room at the bottom, which Gery and his soldiers had commandeered to use as a base. It was a disagreeable muddle of dirty clothes, spare weapons and discarded food. As Chaloner passed, he spotted a hat that was broad-brimmed and vaguely clerical, and slowed down to look at it. Freer was there, eating a pie.

'You are working late, Tom,' the soldier said. 'Trouble with the birds?'

'Nothing insurmountable. How is your investigation at Post House Yard?'

Freer tossed the pie on the fire, and walked quickly to the door, looking furtively in both directions before pulling Chaloner inside and closing it behind them.

'Not as well as it should, if you want the truth. Gery only acts on the intelligence that interests him, and I have a bad feeling that he may be ignoring important clues. I fear his negligence may prove dangerous to Clarendon.'

'Then tell the Earl,' said Chaloner.

Freer shot him a weary glance to express what he thought of that suggestion. 'Gery is reputed to be an excellent investigator,' he went on. 'But he is . . . malleable.'

'You think he may have been deliberately misled?'

Freer looked uncomfortable. 'Perhaps. Or he is conducting a shabby investigation deliberately. It is difficult to know when he does not confide in me. Regardless, our failure to expose this plot will almost certainly see Clarendon fall from grace.'

342

'Yes, probably.'

'I cannot say I like the Earl,' Freer went on. 'He is miserly, overbearing and conceited. But I heard the poor old fellow weeping for his son last night, and it broke my heart. I do not like to see a man kicked when he is down, so if you can find a way to help him, I will—'

At that moment, the door flung open to reveal Gery. The marshal's eyes narrowed when he saw Freer and Chaloner engaged in a low-voiced conversation.

'Clarendon has just informed me that you have been meddling where you were ordered not to,' Gery said, anger making his voice unsteady. 'The Post Office is my business, not yours.'

'Does it matter now?' asked Chaloner. 'As I told you, I leave London tomorrow.'

Gery sneered. 'Do not forget to inform your wife, then, although I doubt she will care. I understand the Duke of Buckingham has followed her to Epsom. He will keep her bed warm.'

It was one insult too many. Chaloner surged forward, slamming the marshal against the wall with considerable vigour. Gery started to struggle, but stopped when he felt the prick of steel at his throat. Chaloner was aware of Freer behind him, hovering unhappily and uncertain what to do.

'Will you kill me?' hissed Gery, his eyes dark with a hatred that could not have been normal. 'You will hang if you do.'

Chaloner was about to remark that it might be worth it, when there was a click. He whipped around to see Morland standing in the doorway, holding a gun. Several soldiers were with him, similarly armed. Chaloner reached for his sword, but fingers tightened

343

on triggers, and he knew Gery would love to give the order to fire.

'Assault on the Lord Chancellor's marshal,' said Gery, his face full of vengeful delight. 'That is ample cause to arrest you. Perhaps you will be spared the ordeal of Russia after all, because the Earl will dismiss you for certain now.'

Chaloner fought as hard as he had ever done when Gery's men came to lay hold of him. Once they had finally pinned him down, Gery ordered his hands secured behind his back. The soldiers obliged with alacrity, tying the knots wickedly tight in revenge for the cuts and bruises they had suffered in the scuffle.

When they were satisfied that he no longer posed a threat, they took him to the dismal little cellars that were used as a prison by the palace guards. One contained nothing but a table and two chairs. Morland went to the table, where he began to lay out writing implements. Freer stood with the guards by the door, his face uneasy and strained, while Gery sat on one of the chairs and adopted a relaxed attitude, although Chaloner could tell that his temper was only just under control.

'The Earl told me what you have learned about the birds and the poison,' Gery began softly. 'So it is time we had a little chat.'

Chaloner leaned against the wall, feigning nonchalance. It was not easy when every instinct clamoured at him to make a dash for the door. Common sense told him it would not win him his freedom, but it was still an urge that was difficult to ignore.

'What would you like to know?' he asked pleasantly.

Gery scowled. 'Your insolence tries my patience. Perhaps I should kill you now. The Earl will never find

344

out – he will assume you abandoned him to avoid a voyage to Russia. However, I might be prepared to spare you if you tell me about the birds.'

Chaloner saw no reason not to oblige, given that the Earl had already revealed the essence of it anyway. He described his battle in the park, and outlined what he had reasoned regarding its connection with the Post Office. He did not divulge the role that Storey and Eliot had played in the confrontation, though, wanting them kept out of the matter.

'So you killed Smartfoot,' concluded Gery.

'The poison did. Examine his body if you do not believe me.'

'I tried, but the Westminster charnel-house keeper has released it to Smartfoot's sister. Smartfoot had no sister, of course, and the body has now disappeared. As has Leak's.'

'Eradicating incriminating evidence,' mused Chaloner, impressed by the efficiency of Oxenbridge and his cronies. 'Like stealing the dead ducks from Storey's house. What are you going to do about it?'

'Nothing,' replied Gery. 'Because I do not believe your tale. You invented it, as an excuse to meddle in Post Office business. It is a typical Parliamentarian trick.'

'I have samples of the poison. Surgeon Wiseman put them in—'

'Unfortunately for you, Wiseman's house was burgled last night.'

Chaloner suppressed a groan: loose ends *were* being tied. He glanced at Freer, who was regarding Gery with a troubled expression. Meanwhile, Morland was writing steadily, and suddenly Chaloner knew exactly what he was doing.

'I suppose that is a confession? One you expect me to sign?'

'You will sign it,' stated Gery. 'It will say that you have lied about the poison, and admit to your Roundhead sympathies. Then no one will care what happens to you, not even Hannah.'

'Is this what you did to Knight?' asked Chaloner in distaste. 'He would not sign a false confession either, so you garrotted him? I know it was you who visited him dressed as a cleric.'

Gery's eyes blazed. 'How dare you accuse me of that! You have no evidence.'

'You paid the turnkeys to drink a toast to the King, good Royalist that you are, and I saw the clerical hat you wore to disguise yourself. You should not have left it lying around White Hall.'

Gery's expression was murderous, and Chaloner tensed, wondering how he was going to defend himself with his hands tied behind his back. Freer's mouth hung open in astonishment, while Morland had stopped writing. Both seemed shocked, but would they prevent Gery from dispatching a second prisoner? The marshal came slowly to his feet, fists clenched at his sides.

'It was unfortunate, but necessary,' he said tightly. 'Knight had information, and was prepared to give it to anyone in order to get himself out of gaol.'

'You executed an innocent man,' said Chaloner coldly.

'I stilled a loose tongue that would have damaged my investigation – he threatened to talk to his gaolers unless I let him go. It would have raised the suspicions of those I am trying to catch, so I had no choice but to silence him.'

Morland was concentrating on his writing again, and the soldiers were impassive. Only Freer displayed any emotion, and continued to gaze at the marshal with open revulsion.

'You strangled him while the turnkeys' attention was on an influx of drunks.' Chaloner glanced at the guards. 'These men, no doubt. They were released the next day, when you paid their fine. But what did Knight know that justified his death?'

For a moment, Chaloner thought Gery would refuse to answer, but then the marshal shrugged, obviously of the opinion that sharing information was neither here nor there – which was worrying, because it suggested that he thought Chaloner would never be in a position to use it.

'That abuses are being committed by postal clerks, which are costing the country a fortune. If Knight had bleated, the perpetrators would have gone to ground and I would never catch them.'

Chaloner regarded him in alarm: Freer and the Major had been right to be concerned about Gery's ability to see the bigger picture. 'I am sure some clerks are corrupt, but there is something far more serious that—'

'It is Williamson's fault,' interrupted Gery. 'If he had not applied for those arrest warrants when I was out, Clarendon would not have sent you to expedite them, Knight would not have been taken to Newgate, and I would not have been forced to put an end to him.'

'There are other ways to ensure a man's cooperation besides murder,' said Freer softly. 'It—'

'Gardner is a villain, of course,' Gery went on, ignoring him. 'The fifty-pound reward will see him in custody, where he will reveal the names of his accomplices, and the case will be solved.'

347

Chaloner was appalled by his bullish stupidity. 'The Post Office plot is more deadly than—'

'You are not in a position to give me advice,' snapped Gery. 'And I am tired of talking. Have you finished the confession, Morland?'

The secretary held out a piece of paper still wet with ink. 'Yes, and he does not need to sign it, because I have done it for him.'

'Good,' said Gery, before Chaloner could point out that Morland could not possibly know how he wrote his name. 'Now lock him up before he wastes any more of our time.'

Chaloner was hard-pressed to control his panic when the cell door closed. His dungeon was pitch black, freezing cold, and he could hear from the murmur of conversation outside that his guards were alert and watchful. Moreover, his wrists were still tied. Escape would be impossible.

He sank down on the damp, sticky floor. How long would it be before Gery put a garrotte around his neck and declared him a suicide? Part of him hoped it would be soon: he hated the thought of being incarcerated for days, even weeks, before the decision was made to dispatch him. But he had been trained to stay cool in desperate situations, and despair did not grip him for long. He began to think practically, and decided the first thing he needed to do was free his hands.

Rubbing the rope against a wall until it frayed was more difficult than he had anticipated, because the only suitable stone was high enough to be awkward. He worked until his arms cramped, hearing the palace bell strike nine and then ten. Thurloe would be with the

348

Major, and he hoped they would not need him. Eleven o'clock came and went, and the rope remained as tight as ever.

Just when he was beginning to fear the task was impossible, there was a snap and he was free. He felt better once it was done. Now at least he could punch Gery – at the very least – when the marshal came to commit sly murder.

He explored the cell by groping around in the darkness, discovering that there were no windows, the walls were solid stone and the sole item of 'furniture' was a pallet of straw that reeked of urine and mildew. He paced back and forth, trying to devise a plan. He had been relieved of his sword and knives, and the only thing he had left was the gingerbread he had bought earlier. He pulled it out and weighed it in his hand. It was heavy, but still no kind of weapon, so he ate it instead. The acid churning in his stomach eased, and he realised that he had been very hungry.

The clock was striking midnight when he heard a sound outside the door. He scrabbled about for the rope, and slipped his hands through it – there was no point in exposing the slim advantage he held too soon. He stood against the farthest wall, and watched the door swing open.

'Morland,' he said flatly when he saw who stood there. 'Gery will not kill me himself, then?'

'Hush, Tom. I have sent the guards on a fools' mission to St James's Park – I wrote an anonymous letter saying that another duck was going to be poisoned, and they have gone to save it – but who knows who might be lurking? Now come with me. Hurry!'

'Hurry where?' asked Chaloner, not moving.

349

'Please! I am risking a great deal by doing this.'

'By doing what?' Chaloner was confused and wary.

'Helping you escape,' snapped Morland. 'But if you would rather wait for Gery to garrotte you, then tell me so and I shall leave you to it.'

'Wait,' called Chaloner, as the door started to close. 'Sorry. I was not expecting rescue.'

Morland gave a thin smile. 'Life is full of surprises. Now follow me.'

Chaloner stepped outside the cell, but remained deeply suspicious. 'What happens if someone challenges us? Do you have any weapons?'

'No, but it is midnight, and the only people awake are courtiers who are too drunk to be a problem. However, we shall keep your hands tied, so that I can pretend to be escorting you for further questioning should we encounter any difficulties.'

He was wearing an old uniform coat, and a broad-brimmed hat shadowed his face. The disguise might have worked had he adopted a more military posture, but Morland looked like what he was: a clerk wearing the cast-off garb of a soldier. It would not deceive anyone who was sober and sane. Yet this was White Hall, where Chaloner had witnessed worse inefficiencies. Careful to keep the rope wrapped around his wrists, he followed Morland up the cellar stairs.

'We are going to the river,' the secretary explained, once they were at the top. He took Chaloner's arm and directed him towards the Great Court. 'I have a boat waiting, and I will cut you free when we reach it, so you can row yourself away.'

'Why are you doing this?' Chaloner was still full of mistrust. 'You owe me nothing.'

350

'Knight,' explained Morland tersely. 'I did not know that Gery murdered him, and I was stunned when I heard him confess, as if an innocent man's life was worth nothing.'

Chaloner regarded him sceptically. 'That is the only reason?'

'Well, I would not mind if you repaid me by sharing all you have learned.'

'Nothing you do not already know,' lied Chaloner. He stumbled as he followed the secretary down the short tunnel that led to the Privy Gardens – frost covered the ground, the night was very dark, and it was not easy to balance with his hands behind him. 'The only thing I have kept to myself is that whatever is unfolding will take place in the Crown tavern, not the Post Office.'

Morland nodded his thanks for the information, and led the way around the edge of the garden, where the shadows were thickest. As they passed Prince Rupert's lodgings, Lady Castlemaine's distinctive voice could be heard tinkling within. It was followed by a roar of manly approval.

They exited the palace through a tiny and little-used gate in the narrow lane called Cannon Row. Morland turned towards the Thames, where a flight of wooden steps descended to the shore. The tang of salt filled the air, and Chaloner supposed the tide was out, because he could hear the hiss of wavelets against mud and pebbles.

'What do you know about Mary Wood?' asked Morland, treading carefully as the stairs were slippery with seaweed as well as ice. 'Am I to understand that the poison is the same as the stuff used on the birds, and that Gardner gave it to her?' He must have sensed Chaloner's suspicion, because he turned and shrugged. 'Freer thinks Gery

351

cannot be trusted to see justice done, and I agree. Tell me what you know, and Freer and I will try to act on it.'

'Then arrest Oxenbridge. He will tell you all you need to know, if the right threats are made.'

They reached the shore, which was dimly illuminated by the lanterns that blazed from Prince Rupert's apartments above. The water was velvety black, with pinpricks of light gleaming in the distance from the Lambeth marshes. The hair on the back of Chaloner's neck rose as it always did when he was in imminent danger, and he was suddenly sure they were not alone. He also saw there was no boat. Then there was a flare of light, and Gery appeared with two soldiers. The marshal held a lamp in one hand and a gun in the other.

'Well?' he asked of Morland. 'What did he confide?'

'Nothing of use,' sighed Morland ruefully. 'He thinks Oxenbridge is involved, and believes that any trouble will begin in the Crown tavern.'

Chaloner regarded him in disgust. 'Treachery! I might have known.'

Morland shrugged. 'Spying is a dirty game, Thomas. Surely Thurloe taught you that?' He turned back to Gery. 'He also admitted to lying about the birds. He did it to lead you astray.'

Chaloner was alarmed as well as confused by this particular deception. 'What are—'

Morland whipped around and dealt him a slap that made his ears ring. It was all Chaloner could do not to free his hands and fasten them around the secretary's throat.

'We shall kill him here,' determined Gery, while Morland wrung his smarting fingers. 'Eyebrows will be raised if a second man connected with this case is found hanging in a cell. And if his body is ever found, we shall be able to say, quite truthfully, that Chaloner died trying to escape.'

Chapter 12

Smiling malevolently, Gery aimed the gun at Chaloner, and his finger tightened on the trigger. There was nowhere to run, and Chaloner did not give him the satisfaction of trying; he only stood quietly, waiting for the inevitable. But Gery had reckoned without Morland who, puffed up with a sense of achievement, tried to lay hold of the spy himself. When the secretary stepped between him and the gun, Chaloner flung off the rope, grabbed Morland's coat and butted him hard in the face. Morland screeched in pain and shock as Chaloner hurled him backwards into Gery, causing the marshal to drop both gun and lamp. Then Chaloner turned and ran.

It was much easier to move with free hands, although a rock- and rubbish-strewn ribbon of silt was hardly the place for speed. There was one loud crack, and then another, although neither shot came close. He tried to run faster, but stumbled over a stone. He slowed, knowing it was better to move less quickly than to risk a tumble. He could hear Gery and the guards behind, Morland screaming at them to hurry. Chaloner grimaced. The fact that the secretary was still capable of speech meant he had not done as much damage as he had intended.

He risked a glance behind him. It was too dark to see, but he could hear curses as his pursuers lurched and slithered. Then he reached a part of the foreshore that backed on to the old Palace of Westminster, which was never lit at night. The blackness was absolute.

He stopped running, snatched up a handful of pebbly sludge, and took several steps up the bank, away from the water. Moments later, Gery lumbered past, followed by his two soldiers, with Morland bringing up the rear. When Gery ordered them to stop and listen, Chaloner hurled some of his muck. It dropped some distance ahead, and Chaloner sensed, rather than saw, the quartet surge towards the sound. When they paused a second time, he lobbed more, but harder than he intended, because it plopped into the water.

'He is trying to swim!' yelled Gery. His voice was accusing. 'And I cannot see, because you made me drop the lantern.'

Chaloner threw more mud, this time as far as he could.

'He *is* swimming!' Gery was almost beside himself with rage, and Chaloner heard him shoving his men forward. 'Go after him, or he will tell everyone that we brought him here to be murdered.'

'It will not matter if he does,' said Morland nasally. 'No one will believe him, especially when we report that he murdered Ibson. That will teach him for breaking my nose.'

Chaloner felt matters were spiralling out of control. His mind reeling with questions and solutions in equal number, he left Gery trying to force Morland and the soldiers into the river, and stole back the way he had come. He crept silently through White Hall, and emerged on King Street, every nerve in his body alert for the yell that would tell him that his pursuers had guessed what he had done and had come after him.

He went to Ibson's tenement first, which was full of snuffles and snores as its many inhabitants slept. The door to Ibson's room was unlocked, and he pushed it open to see the former spy lying on his bed, garrotted. As it was the same way that Knight had died, he could only assume that Gery was responsible – that the marshal had gone there with his henchmen, and had overwhelmed Ibson and his single gun.

Chaloner closed the door and stared at the body. Ibson had claimed to possess documentary evidence against the Post Office, and as Chaloner did not believe he would have let such important items out of his sight, they had to be in his home. He lit a candle and began to search, suspecting from scratches and scuffs in the dirt that Gery and his soldiers had been there before him. Fortunately, none possessed his skills, and they had missed the fact that the back of one of the shelves had a slit hollowed out of it.

He prised out the papers, and leaned against the wall to read them. There were accounts proving that money had been bleeding out of the Post Office at an appalling rate, and that Smartfoot and Lamb were involved. There was also evidence that said they were guided by a 'director' of considerable intelligence, although there was no indication as to who it might be. And finally, there were a large number of messages in cipher, which would have to be decoded.

But Chaloner dismissed all these as insignificant when he read what else Ibson had found. There was a letter from John Fry to the Lord Mayor, penned on expensive paper and sealed with purple wax. And there was a series of messages purporting to be from guildsmen in Hull, Sussex and Bristol, urging their fellow tradesmen to rebel. The writing, paper and seals were identical, which meant, Chaloner saw with a shock, that *Fry* was the author of the lot of them.

Was this what Copping had meant by the Devill's Worke? Inciting rebellion? And did it mean that Fry was the mastermind who was using the Post Office's penchant for corruption to screen a more deadly plot?

The last page was in Dutch, and informed the recipient that the British would not be in a position to repel an invasion until summer. This damaging piece of intelligence was signed not with a name but with a crude drawing of a ship, and Chaloner understood its significance instantly: in Dutch, *huiden* could refer to the side of a boat, a play on Vander*huyden*. It meant Vanderhuyden was the traitor, and Dorislaus was innocent – that Thurloe had been right to defend his old friend from Chaloner's accusations.

The letter was dated ten days earlier, and Chaloner knew he had to discover, as a matter of urgency, whether it was a copy or the original – whether the Dutch really did know that a spring invasion would likely see them in London without too much trouble.

Ibson's sword was propped in a corner, so Chaloner buckled it around his waist and grabbed two daggers from the table. Carefully tucking the letters securely inside his shirt, he left the house at a run, aiming straight for Lincoln's Inn. He was not about to lose a third set of documents before passing them to Thurloe.

* * *

He arrived to find Chamber XIII empty, although there was a letter on the table. It was addressed to him, and was in Thurloe's writing. It informed him that the Major had been sent a message saying that he would never see the light of day again if he spoke to anyone else about his discoveries. It had not been difficult to terrorise a man already so near the end of his tether, and Thurloe had been unable to persuade him to break his oath and talk.

The note went on to say that Thurloe was taking Dorislaus to make some enquiries of their own. Its tone was curt, and did not use the cipher he normally employed when he and Chaloner communicated. Chaloner regarded it in consternation. Should he be suspicious of it, because Thurloe was always punctilious of such matters? Or was it merely a sign that the spy was not yet forgiven for his amateurish bungling? He wrote a brief coded message in return, and hid the Post Office documents in a secret compartment inside Thurloe's desk, where he knew the ex-Spymaster would find them. The one from the Dutch spy he took with him.

It was not far to Vanderhuyden's home. A light burned within, but there were no voices: Chaloner's quarry was awake, but alone. He picked the lock, drew his sword and stepped inside. Vanderhuyden was in the process of stuffing clothes into a sack; he paled when he saw Chaloner.

'Did Dorislaus send you? That was sly! He watched my house like a hawk all night, but when he left an hour ago, I really thought he had given up. Obviously, I underestimated his determination to catch me. Where is he? Waiting outside?'

Chaloner held up the letter. 'It is over, Vanderhuyden.'

The Anglo-Dutchman closed his eyes. 'Where did you get that? It should have been sent . . .'

358

'More to the point, where did *you* get the information? No, do not tell me – someone on the Navy Board was rash enough to write it in a letter, and you intercepted it.'

Vanderhuyden took a deep breath, opened his eyes and returned to his packing. 'Dorislaus would see me dead before he let me go, but you will not harm a man whose life you once saved. Put up your sword, Tom. We both know you will not use it.'

'You think I will look the other way while you escape?' asked Chaloner coldly. 'A spy who has damaged my country? You do not know me as well as you think!'

'But I had no choice! I was forced into it – I received horrible letters saying that my wife would die if I disobeyed. Of course I did what they ordered!'

'Show me,' ordered Chaloner.

Vanderhuyden reached into his bag and produced a sheaf of documents. Chaloner glanced through them quickly, recognising the flamboyant writing and purple seal of John Fry, although they were unsigned. They were vicious and uncompromising, and did indeed threaten to execute Vanderhuyden's wife if he did not do exactly as he was told. Chaloner put them in his pocket.

'You should have asked for help. I would have obliged, and so would Thurloe. But by allowing yourself to be coerced, you may have done irreparable harm.'

'And I would do it again,' flashed Vanderhuyden. 'So would you, to save Hannah. There is something nasty about Dorislaus, anyway – we were never friends, no matter what he might have told you – so I do not feel guilty about letting him take the blame for what I did.'

'And what was that, exactly?'

Vanderhuyden shrugged. 'At first, just passing snippets

of Court gossip to The Hague – silly, inconsequential stuff. But in the last few weeks . . .' He nodded at the document in Chaloner's hand. 'I have been instructed to send reports like that.'

'Is this the original or a copy?'

Vanderhuyden inspected it. 'The original. I can tell by the seal. How did you come by it?'

'How many others like it have you sent?'

'A few.' The prickly defiance drained out of Vanderhuyden and he suddenly looked old, tired and defeated. He went to a cupboard and took out a jug of wine.

'So Dorislaus was never a spy,' said Chaloner. 'Did you lie about the Post Office plot, too?'

Vanderhuyden nodded resignedly. 'Yes. There *is* something more serious afoot than petty thievery, but you can see why I was never in a position to admit it. My wife . . .'

'Who are the Major's contacts in the Foreign Office?'

'I never tried to find out – it would have been too dangerous. Christ God, I need a drink!'

Chaloner watched him pour wine with a hand that trembled, but shook his head when Vanderhuyden offered him a cup.

'Wait!' he said suddenly, as Vanderhuyden raised the brimming goblet to his lips. 'Have your rooms been searched today?'

'Yes, but there is nothing here to incriminate me. I am not a total fool.'

He had taken a swig before Chaloner could stop him. He started to add something else, but then clutched his throat and staggered. Chaloner jumped forward to catch him, lowering him to the ground where he lay gasping for breath, his body convulsing violently. There was stark terror in his eyes, but there was nothing Chaloner could do except cradle him while his life ebbed away.

Shocked by the speed with which the poison had killed Vanderhuyden, Chaloner went to the conduit outside and scrubbed his hands until they were raw and aching from the cold. Then he ran to Lincoln's Inn, but Thurloe was still out. He hid the report about the navy and the letters he had taken from Vanderhuyden in the secret compartment, and left. Dorislaus lived on Fleet Street, so he went there next, but his rooms were also deserted.

He knew he needed to tell someone all that he had learned, in case he fell foul of Gery, Morland or someone else who wanted him dead, but who? Williamson was unlikely to be at his office at such an ungodly hour, and Chaloner had no idea where he lived – not surprisingly, the spymaster had never invited him to his home. Meanwhile, Hannah, Temperance and Wiseman were gone, and Chaloner had no other friends in the city. There was only one person left: the Earl's defences had almost crumbled the last time they had talked, and Chaloner believed he now knew the reason for his master's recent peculiar behaviour.

He hurried to Piccadilly, hearing the bellmen call four o'clock. He was surprised that so little time had passed since his escape from the cell. He arrived to find Clarendon House in darkness, so he let himself in through a window with a loose catch and crept past Gery's dozing guards. He aimed for the Earl's bedchamber, sincerely hoping his master had not invited Lady Clarendon to join him that night.

He was in luck: the Earl lay in splendid isolation,

snoring and rather comical in a tasselled nightcap. Chaloner lit a candle from the fire that still smouldered in the hearth, and touched him lightly on the shoulder, but the Earl only mumbled and turned over. Chaloner poked a little harder.

The Earl opened his eyes and blinked stupidly for several seconds. Chaloner said nothing, giving him time to gather his befuddled wits. Then the Earl sat up sharply, hauling the bedcovers around his neck like a virgin about to be ravaged by a particularly ardent suitor.

'Chaloner?' he gulped. 'I thought you had gone to visit your family.'

'Gery arrested me, sir, but I escaped.'

'Then he did not do it with my blessing – I told him to let you go to Buckinghamshire. But why are you here? It is unconventional, to say the least.'

'Yes, but something terrible is about to happen, and if it succeeds, you will bear the blame.'

The Earl frowned in confusion. 'What will happen? And why should I be held responsible?'

Chaloner started to explain, but the Earl held up his hand and climbed out of bed, going to pour himself a goblet of claret. Apparently deciding that unusual circumstances called for unusual measures, he poured one for Chaloner, too, but having so recently watched Vanderhuyden die of contaminated wine, the spy shook his head.

'Who told you your son was poisoned, sir?' he asked softly.

The Earl gaped at him, and the colour drained from his face. 'Edward was . . . But I told no one . . .' He closed his eyes, and his voice became a whisper. 'How did you guess?'

362

'Because it must be expensive to hire Gery, Morland, Freer and their soldiers, and you do not usually squander money. Ergo, someone forced you to take them on. You are not a biddable man, so a particularly vicious method of coercion must have been used. And whenever your son is mentioned, you seem more frightened than grieved.'

The Earl swallowed hard, and when he spoke his voice was thick with misery. 'It was put to me that if I did not employ Gery and allow him to explore the trouble at the Post Office as he saw fit, I might lose another member of my family. I tried to persuade Gery to work with you, but he hates you for your Parliamentarian past, so I had no choice but to order you to stay away.'

'Who made this threat?'

The Earl's face was ashen. 'I received letters.'

Just like the hapless Vanderhuyden, thought Chaloner. 'It is a lie. Your son was not poisoned, sir. He died of the small-pox.'

The Earl gazed at him, hope in his eyes. 'But how did . . . are you *sure*?'

Chaloner nodded. 'Surgeon Wiseman heard the rumours and examined him very carefully, to assure himself that no mistake had been made. And you know you can trust his judgement.'

'Then why did he not tell me?' The Earl's wail was loud, and Chaloner winced, hoping it would not wake the guards. He could not afford to be caught now, when he was so close to winning Clarendon to his side.

'Because he had no reason to know that you feared foul play. If he had, then of course he would have hastened to reassure you.'

A tear rolled down the Earl's cheek. 'But who would do such a dreadful thing?'

363

'Someone who wants whatever is unfolding in the Post Office to succeed, and who does not care that you will be castigated for not stopping it. May I see the letters, sir?'

Wordlessly, the Earl went to the desk by the window. Some of the pile he handed over had been screwed into balls or torn into pieces, as their recipient had experienced fits of impotent rage, but all had been carefully repaired. Chaloner recognised the writing, the paper and the purple seal.

'John Fry,' he said, passing them back. 'Who is determined to see London in flames.'

The Earl flopped into a chair and closed his eyes. Aware that time was short, Chaloner started to add more, but the Earl raised his hand to silence him. In an agony of tension, Chaloner watched the candle flicker, acutely aware that every moment lost was another one for Fry to bring his plans to fruition. It seemed like an eternity before the Earl opened his eyes. He was still pale, but he sat a little straighter.

'Thank you for explaining all this. It eases the pain somewhat. No father likes to believe that he has been responsible for the death of a son, and thinking that poor Edward was murdered on my account has been almost unbearable. You have lifted a great burden from my soul.'

Chaloner nodded a little impatiently. 'No matter what Gery claims, I did not flout your orders, sir. I followed a trail, and it led to the Post Office.'

'Then you had better start at the beginning, and tell me all you know.'

Chaloner perched on the edge of the desk and began, explaining how the King's birds had been killed to distract Storey, and how 'Greede' was being used to screen the

'Devill's Worke', which had resulted in the deaths of Mary Wood, Leak, Smartfoot, Copping, Vanderhuyden and perhaps more. It had also prompted Gery to garrotte Knight and Ibson.

'And John Fry is the ringleader?' asked the Earl when he had finished. His voice was stronger now, and there was colour in his cheeks. He sipped more wine. 'He is behind this diabolical plot?'

'I believe so. But he is not working alone. One of his cronies is Clement Oxenbridge, which is why I wanted to arrest him earlier.'

'Oxenbridge is like mist – you would never have caught him. But I am not surprised he is mixed up in it. There is something distinctly evil about him. Who else is involved?'

'Postal clerks – Rea, Gardner, Harper and Lamb. And there are others who—'

'O'Neill must be aware of what is happening in his domain,' interrupted the Earl. 'And I have recently come to realise that the tales he told to get Bishop dismissed as Postmaster were lies. He fabricated evidence that saw the Major incarcerated, too. Ergo, he is certainly the kind of man to launch sinister plots.'

'How would rebellion profit him?'

'Perhaps he plans to use it as an excuse to raise postal charges. You look sceptical, but we are talking about vast sums of money, and men lose their reason where large fortunes are concerned.'

That was certainly true, thought Chaloner. He continued with his list of suspects. 'Then there is Monsieur le Notre, who seems to have arrived in London just as all this started. And Wood, who has been relieved of an inconvenient wife.'

The Earl was thoughtful. 'So how shall we proceed?'

'We need to arrest Fry, Oxenbridge and the four clerks as quickly as possible. I imagine they will answer questions in exchange for their lives once they are in the Tower.' Chaloner stood. 'If you prepare the warrants and lend me some soldiers, I will set about hunting them down.'

But the Earl shook his head. 'I told you – Oxenbridge is like mist and you will not lay hold of him. Meanwhile, Gardner has evaded Williamson for a week already, and I doubt Fry will prove any easier. Unless you know where he lives?'

'No, but—'

'I think a bold stroke is called for,' the Earl went on. 'One that will smash this nasty plot once and for all. So I suggest we stage an armed raid on the Post Office, and seize every man in it. That will shake loose some secrets.'

Chaloner regarded him askance. 'But some of the clerks are innocent, and such an attack will put them in danger. It is not—'

'I am Lord Chancellor of England,' declared the Earl, a deep, slow anger burning in his eyes. Rage was driving him now, along with determination to repay those who had manipulated him so cruelly. 'And if I say we shall raid the Post Office, then consider it raided.'

'Raided by whom? The palace guards will not be equal to the task, and Gery and his men have their own agenda – which will not include working with us.'

'Williamson will provide troops,' determined the Earl. 'I shall send a guard to appraise him of the situation at once. It is time he did something useful. He has spent the last few days doing nothing but interview witnesses who claim to have seen Gardner.'

366

'Was it your idea to offer such an enormous reward?' asked Chaloner, a little pointedly.

'Gery's.' The Earl was more interested in the task at hand. 'Will Thurloe help us? Ask him immediately, then hurry to the Post Office and monitor it until I bring my army.'

'*Your* army?' The Earl was not a good strategist, and Chaloner was loath to see him head what might be a complex and dangerous operation.

'Yes,' replied the Earl crisply. He surged to his feet and reached for his clothes. 'Now go and carry out my orders. When I arrive, you can provide me with a tactical report of the situation, and we shall attack together, swords in our hands.'

'Oh, Christ!' gulped Chaloner, wishing he had just asked for Williamson's home address.

Stomach churning with apprehension, Chaloner hurried towards Lincoln's Inn. Dawn was breaking, and he wondered what the day would bring. There was certainly something amiss on the streets: the shops of respectable traders were closed, and there were very few carriages or hackneys about. Gangs of youths prowled, many pointing at the comet and murmuring about the omen it represented, and there was an atmosphere of excited anticipation that was rarely felt so early in the day. The scent of trouble was thick in the air.

Chaloner arrived to find Thurloe still out, and the note he had left was unread. He scrawled another sentence on the bottom, describing the Earl's sudden conversion into a man of action. He did not need to add that it was a worrying development: Thurloe would know without being told.

Because he was desperate to find the ex-Spymaster – Chaloner could not stop the Earl from doing anything reckless, but Thurloe might – he went again to Dorislaus's rooms. He felt a surge of hope when he saw a light, but it was dashed when he opened the door to find the Anglo-Dutchman alone. Dorislaus jumped when Chaloner entered uninvited.

'Have you come to see whether I am writing secret messages to The Hague?' he asked coldly. 'I know Vanderhuyden told you that I am the culprit, but any fool should be able to see it is him.'

'Vanderhuyden is dead.' Chaloner leaned tiredly against the wall. 'But he confessed to being a spy first. God only knows what damage has been done.'

'You killed him?' asked Dorislaus uneasily, eyeing the sword at Chaloner's side.

'Someone decided he was no longer useful and left him toxic wine. Have you seen Thurloe?'

'Not since last night. We went to the Tower together, where that cowardly Major decided his personal safety was more important than saving London. Then we visited some of our contacts, but they could not help us, so we separated. He left you a note in Lincoln's Inn.'

Chaloner was beginning to be worried. Was the ex-Spymaster's displeasure with his ineptitude the reason why he had not employed their usual code, or had he been forced to write against his will, so using plain English was a plea for help? And if so, was Dorislaus involved?

'I need to find him,' he said tersely. 'Where is he?'

'He said he was going to see a few old friends. I do not know who – you know how careful he is about such matters – so I have no idea where he might be. Why? What is happening?'

368

Chaloner was not sure what to do. He was desperately tired, his head throbbed with tension, and the bitter weather was making his lame leg ache, so it was difficult to think clearly. He decided to take a chance, although it was one he would have avoided, had there been a choice.

'There will be a raid on the Post Office this morning,' he explained. 'I am supposed to monitor the place until an "army" arrives. I cannot do that and look for Thurloe. Will you—'

'Gery is acting at last?' pounced Dorislaus. 'Good! It is about time he realised that asking questions of liars and cheats will get him nowhere.'

'Hopefully, Gery will not be there. Williamson will.'

'Even better.' Dorislaus started to scribble on a piece of paper, but when Chaloner leaned over his shoulder, he saw it was in cipher. 'No one but Thurloe will be able to translate this. I shall leave it here, so if he visits, he will know where to join us.'

'Us?' asked Chaloner warily.

'Of course. You will need help if you are to present the Earl with an accurate report.'

'One of us should look for Thurloe.'

'How?' asked Dorislaus reasonably. 'We do not know where to start, and he might be anywhere. It is far more sensible for us both to go to Post House Yard.'

Chaloner nodded, but wished he could have read the message. He watched unhappily as Dorislaus propped it against a jug, then went to a cupboard where he withdrew a sword, three knives and a pair of handguns. Chaloner watched with mounting alarm.

'I did not know you were a fighting man.'

Dorislaus shrugged. 'I never used to be, but these are

uncertain times, and I am cognisant of the fate of my father. *I* do not intend to be murdered by men purporting to be my friends.'

Interpreting it as a reminder that Dorislaus was as wary of him as he was of Dorislaus, Chaloner followed him outside. He shivered. It was another bitingly cold morning, and snow was in the air. He glanced up at clouds that were dark, heavy and sullen. He was not usually fanciful, but it seemed they held a message: that the day would bring suffering, danger and despair, and that at the end of it, good men would lie dead.

The Post Office should have been busy, because overseas mail was collected on Fridays, but the door was closed and there was a notice pinned to it. Dorislaus went to read it, while Chaloner lurked in the shadows, watching frustrated customers go away with their letters still in their hands.

'Snowdrifts have closed all the main highways out of London,' reported Dorislaus. 'So no mail is being accepted until further notice.'

'Blocked roads should not stop the clerks from taking post,' said Chaloner, worried. 'Indeed, they should be pleased, as it gives Williamson's spies more time to read it.'

'Yes, but O'Neill controls the General Letter Office, not Williamson,' Dorislaus pointed out. 'I imagine our Spymaster is delighted by what is unfolding here – either endemic corruption *or* a treasonous plot will see O'Neill disgraced. And then who will step into his shoes?'

Chaloner stared at him. Dorislaus was right: Williamson would benefit from trouble at the Post Office. Was that why he had allowed himself to be distracted by the hunt

370

for Gardner? To ensure the plot succeeded? But rebellion was not in his interests either – as Spymaster, he was expected to thwart that kind of thing. Or was he confident that all blame would lie with the Earl for hiring the incompetent Gery to solve the case? Chaloner rubbed his head, trying desperately to think.

'It might take Clarendon some time to raise an army,' Dorislaus went on. 'And we cannot wait here. Someone will notice us, and we should not squander the element of surprise by loitering – it may be the only advantage we hold. We need somewhere to hide until he comes.'

He was right again, and Chaloner cursed his sluggish wits for not seeing it first. He led the way to Storey's house, where he picked the lock on the door. They entered, and Dorislaus whistled at the chaos within: the place had been thoroughly ransacked, presumably by whoever had been detailed to steal the dead ducks. Chaloner hurried to the parlour at the back.

'No wonder they wanted Storey distracted,' breathed Dorislaus, wide-eyed. 'If I had known he had a view like this, I would have moved in with him!'

Lights glowed under the window shutters in the disused wing, and it was so obvious that something was about to happen that every nerve in Chaloner's body thrummed with tension. Dorislaus began to chatter, an annoying buzz that prevented Chaloner from concentrating on the questions that tumbled through his mind.

'Palmer's book will go on sale today, at Speed's shop on Fleet Street,' the Anglo-Dutchman burbled. 'I cannot see that calming turbulent waters, because no one likes Catholics, and London does not want to hear that they are the innocent victims of bigotry.'

'Oh, God!' Chaloner had forgotten that the nobleman's

entry into the world of publishing was scheduled for that day, and Dorislaus was right: it would cause trouble.

'Speed plans to sell the first copies in a couple of hours,' Dorislaus wittered on. 'And Palmer himself will be available to autograph them.'

Chaloner closed his eyes in despair. 'The apprentices are spoiling for a fight, and Palmer might inadvertently provide the spark that ignites a riot. Other factions will join in . . .'

'All fuelled by John Fry's incendiary messages,' agreed Dorislaus.

Chaloner was hopelessly confused. 'But Thurloe says Fry is dead.'

'I know, but a lot of rumours surrounded Fry's "death" eight years ago, and you do not get smoke without a fire. Fry is obviously alive, and poised to lead one of the greatest rebellions that London has ever seen, echoed in Hull, Sussex, Bristol and God knows where else.'

Chaloner knew what would happen then: troops would be called to stamp it out, and the streets would run with blood. Royalists would race to defend the monarchy, Parliamentarians would clamour for a republic, and fanatics of every kind would aggravate the situation with incendiary speeches. London would descend into anarchy, after which the country would be plunged into yet another bout of political turmoil.

'Perhaps we should leave,' said Dorislaus softly, evidently thinking the same thing. 'Leave London, I mean. We are deluding ourselves if we think Clarendon's so-called army can stop what has been set in motion. The rebels will win, and we shall be hanged for trying to thwart them.'

'They will not win,' said Chaloner grimly.

372

'Let us hope you are right.' Dorislaus laughed suddenly. 'What would my father and your uncle think if they could see us now – pondering whether to risk our necks to save the King?'

Chaloner supposed the situation did smack of the ludicrous. But as Thurloe had pointed out days ago, the King was their leader now, and Chaloner was on the Lord Chancellor's staff. He knew where his loyalties lay. So apparently did Dorislaus, because he went to Storey's front door and began to monitor Post House Yard without another word. Chaloner watched the courtyard, but staring at closed shutters was pointless, and it was not long before he joined the Anglo-Dutchman at the front of the house.

'Look,' he whispered after a while, nudging Dorislaus sharply. 'Something is happening.'

Clerks were arriving singly and in pairs. All wore thick cloaks and hats that concealed their faces, but Chaloner identified Lamb by his bulk and Harper by his cat-like prowl.

'Thank God!' breathed Dorislaus, as a slight, almost girlish figure struggled for several minutes before he was able to open the door. 'That is Samuel Morland, which means Gery and your Earl cannot be too far away.'

'How do you know it is Morland?' asked Chaloner warily.

'Because I spent hours watching the Post Office for Thurloe. That latch defeats Morland every time.'

'*Every* time?' Chaloner knew Dorislaus was telling the truth about the door, because he had seen the secretary struggle with it himself. 'How often does he come here?'

'Several times a week, after dark. He comes to spy for Gery, which means he is on our side.'

Chaloner was far from certain about that. 'Did you ever follow him in?'

'Once, when I was sure no one else was there. I trailed him to the disused wing, but he secured the door behind him, and I do not possess your skill with locks.'

Chaloner had all but forgotten the hidden room and its muddle of tools and raw materials. Temperance had told him that something was being built there and that Morland was involved – Morland had denied it, but Chaloner knew better than to believe anything *he* said. But what was being constructed? Some dreadful new artillery piece, which John Fry would use in his rebellion?

'We need to go in,' he said abruptly. 'The key to whatever is happening lies in that wing, and we have to find it before the Earl arrives.'

'But that is why he is coming, surely?' said Dorislaus uncomfortably. 'To expose whatever is in there? Why should we risk ourselves by precipitating him?'

'Because it might be a weapon,' explained Chaloner. 'One that will annihilate Clarendon and his forces, thus ensuring that nothing stands between Fry and his deadly objective.'

'No,' said Dorislaus firmly. 'It is too dangerous. You saw how many clerks went in there. We would be caught and killed in an instant.'

'Not if we use the tunnel under the Antwerp Coffee House. And I am not suggesting we tackle them, anyway. Just assess what is happening.'

'Christ, Chaloner! You must have a death wish! Go, then, if you must. Here are the keys you will need to operate the panels. I will stay here and tell the Earl not to shoot you when he and his soldiers appear.'

* * *

Dorislaus was right to see flaws in the plan, but Chaloner did not know what else to do. Time was passing and it was clear that a crisis was close. As he turned into Dowgate Hill, snowflakes stinging his face, he was aware that the tensions on the streets had heightened – the groups of apprentices were larger, and an aura of dark menace had settled across the city.

Feeling as though he were operating blind and completely alone, he entered the Antwerp. It was packed to the gills, and its mood was sullen and dangerous. He left the door open deliberately, and when everyone's belligerent attention focused on the snow that immediately gusted inside, he used the distraction to duck unseen into the scullery. He located the passage entrance quickly, unlocked it and slipped inside.

He lit a candle, and moved stealthily along the tunnel, soon reaching the entrance to Copping's office. Once there, he listened intently, but heard only silence. Hoping the sound of the panel swinging open would not alert anyone to his presence, he grasped the lever and pulled.

The chamber was empty. Sighing his relief, he padded across it and opened the door. The corridor beyond was also deserted. Dagger in hand, he explored the main building from top to bottom, but none of the offices were occupied. The only person he saw was Morland, who was in O'Neill's room, humming as he rifled through the Controller's private correspondence. Two black eyes and a swollen nose were gratifying reminders of the last time he and Chaloner had met.

The only other place the clerks could be was the disused wing, so Chaloner made his way there, glancing behind him frequently. A guard was at the door, alert and watchful. Pressing back into the shadows, Chaloner scraped his knife against the wall. When the fellow came to investigate, Chaloner struck him smartly on the head and bundled his unconscious body into a cupboard.

He picked the lock on the door, and opened it carefully. The corridor beyond was dark, but there was a light at the end of it. He tiptoed forward, hearing voices in the room that contained the hidden chamber. About twenty clerks had gathered there, and Harper was addressing them.

'We have done well again,' he said in his softly sibilant voice. 'Another huge profit this month, and those investigating us are still chasing their tails.'

There was a low rumble of amusement, although Lamb did not smile.

'We should curb our activities for a while,' he said worriedly. 'I do not like the fact that it was the Alibonds who died in that explosion – they were more talented than any of us at milking profit from our work. Moreover, Clarendon will not overlook Gery's failures much longer. He will appoint someone else to explore what is happening here, and we cannot afford that.'

'You fret needlessly,' replied Harper. 'No one will best us, not if we continue to keep our heads. Besides, it pleases me to thwart Gery – it transpires that he was the one who murdered Knight, and that was unnecessary. Knight knew nothing of relevance.'

'I beg to differ,' countered Lamb. 'Knight was perceptive, and had learned a great deal about our operation. He wrote it all down in a series of letters, apparently.'

'Yes, but he was more concerned with what he called the Devill's Worke,' argued Harper. 'And that has nothing to do with us.'

'No,' acknowledged Lamb. 'But Gery might not

differentiate, and I do not want to be blamed for whatever else is unfolding. It promises to be rather more serious than a few pounds filched—'

'We have filched more than a few pounds,' said Harper with a mocking, hissing laugh.

'You are missing my point,' snapped Lamb. 'It has been easy – too easy – to defraud the Post Office, and I have a bad feeling that someone arranged it so, to disguise this Devill's Worke.'

'I agree,' said another clerk. 'It is suspicious.'

At that moment, footsteps clattered along the hallway, and Chaloner froze in alarm. He was going to be caught between the newcomer and the clerks, and this time there would be no Dorislaus to show him secret passages. The person was humming to himself, and Chaloner instantly recognised the shadow that bobbed along the wall towards him. It was Morland.

Fortunately, Morland was not observant, and although Chaloner felt absurdly visible as he crouched behind a crate, the secretary sailed past with a jaunty step and his head held high.

'You are late,' said Harper sharply. 'We were about to divide up the profits without you.'

'That would have been unwise,' replied Morland. His broken nose made him sound as though he had a heavy cold. 'Gery would have exposed you weeks ago if it had not been for me, and you owe me your lives as well as a share of your earnings. Cross me, and you will regret it.'

'Do not threaten us,' hissed Harper, fingering his sword.

'Then do not threaten *me*,' Morland flashed. 'You know you cannot cope without my help.'

Chaloner was disgusted but not surprised to learn that Morland had managed to profit from the crimes he was supposed to be investigating. The man was nothing if not an opportunist.

'What happened to your face?' asked Lamb in the silence that followed. 'Did Gery hit you?'

Morland lifted a tentative hand to his nose. 'Chaloner did. He is extremely dangerous.'

'We know,' said Harper, his voice dripping acid. 'Which is why you agreed to take care of him for us. However, he is still at large, and poses a serious risk.'

'I did my best – I even enlisted Gery's help. But Chaloner is alone now, and does not know who to trust. He will make a mistake soon, confide in the wrong person. Then we shall have him.'

Chaloner's mind reeled. Could he assume from the discussion that Gery was innocent of any wrongdoing? That he was just an investigator unequal to the task he had been allotted?

'You should have let me deal with Chaloner,' snarled Harper. 'I would not have failed.'

Morland glowered. 'No, but then we would have had Thurloe breathing down our necks. You will not deceive him as you have Gery. Leave Chaloner to me if you value your lives.'

'Thurloe,' said Lamb worriedly. 'I saw him at midnight last night, with Dorislaus. They were walking very fast, and Dorislaus was gripping Thurloe's elbow.'

'What of it?' asked Morland, puzzled.

Lamb's pugilistic face was full of anxiety. 'Well, it made me wonder why they felt the need to tear around at such an hour. Do you think Thurloe has learned something about us?'

'Of course not,' said Harper firmly. 'How could he? We have been more than careful.'

Lamb's tale made Chaloner even more uneasy. Thurloe did not usually walk around arm-in-arm with other men, and if he had been unwell and had needed support, then why had Dorislaus not mentioned it? Or was there a more sinister reason for the gesture, such as that Thurloe had actually been Dorislaus's prisoner? Chaloner decided he would have answers from the Anglo-Dutchman the moment he returned to Storey's house, no matter what he had to do to get them.

He turned his attention back to the gathering, hearing an aggrieved murmur from the clerks as Morland was handed a bulging purse. The secretary was playing a dangerous game, he thought, almost begging to be stabbed and dumped in the river.

'Thank you,' said Morland, struggling to cram it into his pocket. It tugged his expensive coat down on one side, and the answer to another question snapped clear in Chaloner's mind: how Morland could afford to clothe himself so extravagantly. 'And now I have something for you.'

'You have finished it?' asked Lamb with startled eagerness. 'At last?'

Morland nodded, and there was an immediate chorus of delight. One or two clerks even forgot their resentment, and patted him on the back. In the shadows, Chaloner struggled to make sense of what was happening.

Clearly, Harper and his cronies were corrupt, but they were not involved in the Devill's Worke. Therefore, Chaloner should forget about them, and concentrate on the more serious matter of thwarting John Fry. But his fear that Morland had created something deadly kept him rooted to the spot as the clerks followed the secretary into the secret chamber.

He edged forward, glad they had taken the lamps with them, which had left the main room in darkness. But now what? He could not see what Morland was doing, because the secretary was shielded by a wall of men. Then he spotted a streak of light in one of the walls – there was a gap in the panelling. He put his eye to it, and was rewarded with an excellent view of proceedings.

Morland was standing next to a large object draped in a sheet. With a flourish, he whipped off the cover to reveal a complex contraption with levers, presses and a blade. There was an immediate sigh of awe, although Chaloner only stared blankly. It was like no weapon he had ever seen.

'Does it work?' breathed Lamb.

'Of course it does,' replied Morland, offended. 'Give me two letters. I shall open, copy and reseal one. And afterwards, I defy you to tell me which of the pair has been invaded.'

While Chaloner watched with increasing mystification, two missives were procured, and Morland bent over his machine. Wheels turned, gears clanked and there was a lot of shuddering and groaning. Chaloner prepared to dodge away, expecting some of the clerks to wander off while the experiment was in progress, but within moments, Morland was handing the missives back, saying that he had finished.

The clerks craned forward eagerly, and even Harper was obliged to admit that he could not tell which of the two had been tampered with. With a haughty flourish, Morland handed him a piece of paper, and invited him to compare it to the contents of the letter he had opened.

'My God!' exclaimed Harper, looking from one to the other. 'You have it word for word.'

'But how?' asked Lamb, stunned. 'It is not possible.'

'It is all to do with pressing damp paper on to the original, which absorbs some of the ink,' explained Morland. 'But the details are secret. All you need to know is that my invention works.'

Not a weapon, then, thought Chaloner, but something just as deadly in its way. Not only would no one ever know whether his post had been intercepted, but the speed with which the machine had worked meant that hundreds of letters could be copied in the time it had previously taken to duplicate a few. It would revolutionise espionage overnight, and he was not surprised that the disused wing had been provided with guards and sturdy locks.

'Williamson will give his sword-arm for this,' crowed Lamb. 'We shall be richer than ever.'

'We shall not sell it,' said Harper sharply. 'Can you not see its potential? Every business in the country will be at our mercy, and so will every traitor, adulterer and rebel. However, it must remain secret. If people find out what we can do, they will never use the Post Office again.'

'I am glad you are pleased,' said Morland. 'Because I want a higher percentage of your profits from now on. Show me the list of your December earnings, and we shall negotiate a mutually acceptable arrangement.'

The atmosphere went from celebratory to resentful again, and Harper's face was sullen as he tugged a piece of paper from his coat. He handed it to Morland, whose eyebrows went up in astonishment.

'My word! Forging Bishop-Marks is a lucrative business, and so is "losing" prepaid mail. You have done well. Who did you say prepared this document?'

'Our director's identity is something you do not need to know,' replied Harper shortly. He turned to his cronies. 'When you are happy that these figures represent an accurate account of our activities this month, we shall destroy the paper.'

'Of course,' said Lamb irritably. 'We always do. There is no need to remind us every time.'

He snatched it from Morland and the others clustered around him, while the secretary haggled with Harper. Morland was outrageously greedy, but as he claimed that no one except he could operate the machine, Harper had no choice but to yield to his demands.

Seeing their business was done, Chaloner hid in the corridor, sensing it would not be long before they came out. He was right. Morland left within minutes, swaggering along with an expression of great satisfaction. The rest followed, chatting in low voices.

Soon only Lamb and Harper remained. Harper opened the lamp and held out his hand, so the paper could be incinerated, but Lamb indicated that he wanted to study it more closely, to make sure he had not been cheated by the quicker minds of his fellows. Harper rolled his eyes, but left him to it. In the corridor, Chaloner tensed, heart thumping, when Harper stopped and sniffed the air, as if he could smell an intruder. But he walked on after a moment.

Although dishonest officials were the least of Chaloner's worries, the document Lamb held was proof of their crimes, and it was apparently the only copy in existence. He knew he should concentrate on John Fry, but he hated to stand by while an important piece of evidence was destroyed. Lamb's back was to Chaloner, so all he had to do was dart in, knock him senseless and grab it. What could go wrong?

Unfortunately, Lamb had unusually acute hearing, and whipped around at Chaloner's first step. Chaloner managed to snatch the paper, but the blow to render Lamb unconscious was less of a success. The henchman's expression turned from shock to anger when he recognised his assailant.

'You!' he snarled.

Chaloner shoved the page in his pocket and drew his sword just in time to parry the blow from Lamb's cudgel. He knew he had to defeat him quickly, before the noise of the skirmish alerted the others, so he went on a determined offensive. But Lamb had outrage on his side, and he fought like a lion. As Chaloner had feared, the sound brought others running, and he cursed the foolish recklessness that had driven him to tackle the man.

'How did he get in?' demanded one clerk in alarm. 'Harper set guards on all the doors.'

'For God's sake, do not let him escape.' It was Morland, his thin face pale. 'Clarendon was oddly unfriendly when we met at White Hall not long ago, and I have a bad feeling that Chaloner has managed to regain his favour. He cannot be allowed to reveal what he knows.'

Chaloner's blood ran cold. If the Earl was wandering around White Hall, did it mean he had been unable to raise the promised troops, and nothing stood in the way of whatever plot was unfolding? Desperation drove him, and he managed to knock Lamb to his knees before racing towards the door, scattering the officials who blocked his way. He had almost reached it when Harper appeared.

Face lit with a savage grin, Harper launched himself at the spy with a ferocity that was unnatural. Chaloner held his own, but then Lamb recovered and joined in, leaving Chaloner with a choice of being bludgeoned from his left or stabbed from his right. He blocked one blow with his arm, and scored a cut on Harper's neck before retreating behind a table.

'I was right last week,' Harper whispered, dabbing at the blood with his sleeve. Lamb waited for him to finish, so they could attack together. 'There is a secret tunnel into this building.'

'Morland could have told you that,' said Chaloner, aiming to cause trouble. 'He has known about it since the Commonwealth, and has been using it to spy on you, learning your business so he will be better able to inveigle a place in your—'

'Lies!' shouted Morland. 'He is inventing stories, so we will argue, giving him a chance to escape. I know his sly tricks. Now disarm him quickly, before he wastes any more of our time.'

Chaloner had struggled to fight Lamb and Harper at the same time, so when three more clerks joined in, it was not long before he was pinned against the wall, Harper's sword at his throat. He was quickly disarmed, after which Lamb immobilised him with a painful choke-hold.

'Thank God,' said Morland in relief. 'He would have taken over from Gery if you had let him escape, and then he would have had all your secrets.'

'You mean *our* secrets,' said Harper, his eyes cold and hard.

'Yes, of course,' said Morland hastily. 'Our secrets.'

'Kill him,' ordered Harper, and Lamb's arm immediately tightened around Chaloner's throat. Chaloner struggled, but Lamb was a powerful man, and Chaloner felt himself begin to black out.

384

'Wait,' ordered Morland. 'We should consult your director before dispatching anyone.'

'You only suggest it because you want to know his identity,' said Harper accusingly.

Morland raised his hands. 'He may have questions to ask of the man who has been spying on his operation. But if you think he will not mind being deprived of that option, then carry on. However, do not say I did not warn you.'

Harper considered briefly, then gestured to Lamb, and the fierce pressure around Chaloner's neck eased. Another nod sent one of the clerks scurrying away. As he struggled to draw air into his protesting lungs, Chaloner tried to read Morland's face. What game was the secretary playing now?

Suddenly, there was a loud voice in the hall, and every clerk in the room turned in surprise. Murmurs of 'the director' rippled through their ranks.

'Henry!' exclaimed Harper in astonishment, as the newcomer entered. 'I did not expect you in person.'

'I met him in the Letter Hall,' explained the clerk who had been sent to find out what was to be done with Chaloner. 'He says it is safe for him to visit today, because the Post Office is closed.'

The director was Bishop.

Chapter 13

Smelly lapdog under his arm, Bishop listened carefully while Harper gave an account of all that had happened, including Morland's triumph with the letter-opening machine. Morland's eyes were agleam, although whether because he now knew the director's identity, or because Bishop was obviously impressed by the invention was impossible to say.

'Why did no one tell me about this secret tunnel when I was Postmaster?' demanded Bishop, after Harper had explained how he thought Chaloner had broken in.

'Perhaps everyone assumed you knew,' said Morland, when accusing eyes turned on him. He smiled ingratiatingly. 'I certainly did – a man of your knowledge and expertise.'

Bishop regarded him with icy disdain, and Chaloner saw there was more to the ex-Postmaster than an embittered buffoon with a ridiculous pet. The corrupt officials had run a tightly efficient operation under his direction, and any number of people had said that the Post Office had functioned more smoothly with him in charge. Chaloner should not have underestimated him.

'Is O'Neill aware of this device?' Bishop demanded, abruptly turning his attention back to Morland's machine.

'No,' replied Harper. 'He never visits this part of the building. However, Chaloner's presence here suggests our secret is no longer safe. If he knew to break in, so might others.'

Lamb issued a low growl, and Chaloner's air was cut off a second time.

Bishop swung around to look at them. 'I hate to deprive the world of a decent violist, Chaloner, so you will live if you answer me truthfully. Loosen your hold, Lamb. He cannot speak if he is being throttled.' The pressure eased fractionally. 'Who else knows about our business?'

'It is common knowledge.' Chaloner could manage no more than a croak, and Bishop was obliged to lean towards him to hear. 'Your feud with O'Neill is the talk of the city, and everyone knows that you have coerced half his clerks into cheating the Post Office.'

The last part was a lie, because Chaloner was astounded that so many of O'Neill's officials had elected to betray him, and he suspected that most Londoners would not believe it had been possible.

'Coercion was unnecessary,' said Bishop coldly. 'They volunteered. None like working for an incompetent rogue who does not pay them what they are worth. Tom Harper had very little persuading to do.'

'Harper,' rasped Chaloner, noting the easy familiarity between the two men. 'He is the key to the whole operation – those not seduced by promises of wealth could be intimidated into looking the other way. How did you convince O'Neill to hire him?'

'Easily,' replied Bishop, unable to resist a gloat. 'By letting his conceited wife think it was her idea. But I am

387

the one asking questions, not you. What else do you know?'

'Gery did not find the papers that Ibson stole – the ones revealing the extent of the corruption here,' Chaloner went on, desperately trying to think of a way to use Bishop's willingness to listen before Lamb choked off his life. 'I did. They are in White Hall, and will be made public tomorrow. Unless I am there to stop it.'

'Good,' said Bishop fiercely. 'I *want* them published. I know for a fact that one proves dangerous intelligence was passed to the Dutch in a letter. That alone will finish O'Neill, because it is his responsibility to prevent that kind of thing.'

'Several more are copies of accounts that show the extent of your dishonest dealings,' Chaloner managed to gasp. Lamb's grip had constricted again and he was growing light-headed.

'*My* dishonest dealings?' Bishop put his hand to his chest in mock astonishment. 'But O'Neill is Postmaster now, so any hint of thievery is his to bear.'

'You are right,' said Chaloner, struggling to speak loudly enough to be heard by all the clerks. 'Your status probably will allow you to escape prosecution. But your helpmeets will hang.'

'Do not listen to him,' ordered Bishop with haughty authority, cutting across the immediate murmur of consternation. 'None of this can be laid at our door. O'Neill will be blamed, which has been my intention from the start. He conspired to see me ousted, so I vowed to make him pay. Any leaked documents will prove *his* guilt. Not mine and not yours.'

'But you have committed murder,' Chaloner tried again. 'A more serious—'

'We have killed no one,' said Bishop firmly. 'The explosion was not our doing – we lost the Alibond brothers, two of our most dedicated helpers. Smartfoot and Copping were ours, too, but they were involved in other dark business, so their deaths were not our fault either.'

'Wait!' gasped Chaloner, as Bishop, evidently deciding the discussion was over, began to turn away. 'You are in danger. Something deadly will happen here soon, and—'

'That is true, actually,' interrupted Lamb. 'I overheard Rea muttering about it last night. It will be today, and he believes it will shake the entire country to its foundations.'

'Not our concern.' Bishop nodded to Lamb. 'Kill Chaloner and hide his body in O'Neill's garden. Let us see the bastard worm his way out of *that* when I report it to Clarendon.'

'O'Neill is behind the Devill's—' Chaloner managed to gasp before his air was cut off, a desperate plan forming in his mind.

Bishop swung around abruptly. 'What? What did you say?'

With an irritable sigh, Lamb loosened his hold again. Chaloner spoke in a whisper, obliging Bishop to lean towards him as he strained to hear. He could smell the lapdog; it was wearing a diamond-studded collar. He let his voice drop lower still, forcing Bishop to put his head even closer as he tried to catch what was being said.

Morland's eyes widened when he saw what Chaloner intended to do, and he opened his mouth to yell, but Chaloner was already on the move. With all the strength he could muster, the spy butted Bishop hard in the face, moving sharply and violently enough to pull Lamb off balance as he did so. He and Lamb fell to the floor, Bishop staggered backwards and the dog leapt free.

Pandemonium erupted. Bishop bellowed his pain and fury, blood splattering from his shattered nose, while the dog raced yapping through the clerks, creating panic as it nipped at unprotected ankles. Harper stabbed wildly at Chaloner with his sword, oblivious to or uncaring of the fact that he was just as likely to injure Lamb. Screaming for him to stop, Lamb jerked and twisted to avoid the lethal assault, while Chaloner fought just as hard to use him as a shield.

'Stop!'

Assuming the command came from Bishop, Chaloner fought on, grabbing Lamb's hair and thrusting him into the path of one particularly lethal swipe. Lamb shrieked as the blade cut into his shoulder, and Chaloner could see the black rage in Harper's eyes as the sword flashed upwards to try again. The killing blow never came, but Chaloner was too intent on keeping hold of Lamb to consider why. Lamb was struggling violently now, and Chaloner was obliged to use every low tactic he knew to hang on to him.

'Chaloner, please!' came an indignant voice after two bites and a knee to the groin. 'This is the Post Office, not a Fleet Street tavern. Desist immediately!'

With a massive show of strength, Lamb flung Chaloner away from him, but Harper did not strike. Chaloner struggled to his knees, fists at the ready, to see the speaker was Clarendon, resplendent in the robes that marked him as Lord Chancellor. The chamber was full of soldiers led by Gery, and the corrupt officials were lined up against a wall, sullen and frightened. Bishop was among them, a handkerchief pressed to his bloody nose, while O'Neill watched from the doorway.

A hand came to help Chaloner to his feet, but he

390

pushed it away when he saw it was Morland's. The secretary's other hand held a dagger that dripped red.

'I stabbed him just as he was on the verge of dispatching you,' explained Morland. He nodded to where Harper lay dead from a wound in his back. 'Which was extremely noble of me after you broke my nose, so be sure to express your thanks in an appropriate manner.'

Chaloner stared at him, itching to grab the weapon and plunge it into his treacherous heart.

It did not take Gery long to organise his men, ready to march Bishop and his accomplices to gaol. O'Neill smirked gloatingly at his old enemy's stunned dismay, while Morland whispered feverishly in the Earl's ear. Chaloner could not hear what was being said, because Bishop's pooch was loose again, barking in its high-pitched, staccato yip.

'Our raid was a success,' declared the Earl, extricating himself from Morland and waddling to stand with Chaloner and O'Neill. 'Newgate will be twenty villains the richer today, and we have exposed the greatest conspiracy the Post Office has ever known.'

'These men know nothing about the Devill's Worke, sir,' said Chaloner. His throat hurt from being half-strangled, and it was not easy to make himself heard over the dog. 'John Fry is—'

'You cannot arrest us, My Lord,' shouted Bishop, snapping out of the shock that had rendered him mute when the Earl and his troops had stormed in. 'All we have done is gather here to pray. Then your spy arrived and began to—'

'To pray,' repeated the Earl flatly, wincing as the yaps reached a new level of shrillness.

'For the snow to abate,' elaborated Bishop. 'So the mail can resume. We would not want the Post Office to lose money because of inclement weather.'

'Do not lie,' said the Earl coldly. 'We know what you have been doing. We overheard some of what was said, and we can guess the rest. You will not succeed in discrediting O'Neill.'

'No,' agreed O'Neill smugly. 'You will not.'

Chaloner regarded the Controller sharply. Was it just pleasure at seeing an old adversary defeated that gave him his mien of haughty triumph? Or was it delight because Bishop was continuing to provide the perfect foil for the Devill's Worke?

'Discredit O'Neill?' echoed Bishop in mock surprise. 'I assure you, he is quite capable of doing that for himself – with his natural ineptitude.'

Chaloner turned back to the Earl. 'We need to learn what Fry and Oxenbridge are—'

'You arrogant bastard!' spat O'Neill, taking several steps towards Bishop. 'How dare you accuse me of ineptitude when *you* were dismissed because you were corrupt and indolent? At least everyone knows that I am honest.'

'Are you?' Bishop smiled lazily as he addressed Clarendon. 'Check the Post Office accounts, My Lord. You will find wild discrepancies between what is produced in the official record and what is really in the coffers – and between what O'Neill says he earns and what he actually takes home. It was a dreadful mistake to appoint him and—'

'Your hatred has blinded you to reason, Bishop,' interrupted the Earl. 'Has it not occurred to you that your accomplices will tell the truth once they know the alternative is the gibbet?'

392

'They will,' gushed Morland, sidling up to him. 'And I can remember most of the figures on that vital document they burned a short while ago. I shall write them down for you.'

'There is no need.' Chaloner pulled the page from his pocket. Morland shot him a venomous glare, and there were groans from the clerks. 'But this is not important now, sir. We must—'

The Earl snatched it from him, scanning it with the eye of a man who was used to heady figures. Meanwhile, Bishop's dog had decided that Gery was a worthy target for its fangs, and was busying itself around the marshal's legs, barking all the while. The Earl raised a hand to his head.

'Can no one silence that damned beast? I cannot think while it is carrying on.'

'She is not a "damned beast",' objected Bishop, brushing a soldier aside contemptuously as he went to retrieve his pet. 'She is just appalled at the wickedness perpetrated here by O'Neill.'

O'Neill replied in kind and then a spat was under way, raised voices driving the dog into an even greater paroxysm of snaps and yips. Chaloner tried again to reason with the Earl, but could not make himself heard over the hubbub. Then Morland pulled him to one side, an expression on his face that Chaloner did not like at all.

'We both emerged unscathed,' the secretary said silkily. 'Well, you sound like a rusty saw, but that will pass in a day or two. We should thank God for such a successful outcome.'

'You were part of their plot, Morland. Not even your sly tongue will see you slither out of this, because I shall stand witness against you.'

393

'I was working undercover,' objected Morland indignantly. 'Pretending to be part of Bishop's scheme in order to catch him. You must have done similar things during your life of espionage.'

'Not nearly so convincingly.'

Morland bowed. 'I shall take that as a compliment. But you know I am telling the truth, because not once did I urge anyone to kill you – which I would have done, had I really been one of them. I told them to take you prisoner, at which point I would have helped you escape.'

'As you helped me escape from White Hall last night?'

'You survived, did you not? And I have tried constantly to keep you out of danger. How many times did you hear me urge Gery to arrest you? That was to keep you safely locked away.'

'Knight was not very safe when he was locked away.'

'No,' acknowledged Morland. 'And that is a pity. But never mind him. How could you imagine that I would defraud the Post Office? What do you think I am?'

Chaloner would have told him, but the Earl approached at that point and he disliked bad language. 'You accepted bribes,' he said instead.

'Prove it,' challenged Morland.

Chaloner grabbed his coat and shook it, so that the coins jangled in his pocket. Rage flashed briefly across Morland's face, but it was so quickly suppressed that Chaloner wondered if he had imagined it. With cool aplomb, Morland presented the purse to the Earl.

'I almost forgot,' he said with a serene smile. 'Take it, My Lord. It is yours.'

The Earl's eyes gleamed. He liked money and was always claiming that he did not have enough of it. Chaloner's heart sank, suspecting the gesture was enough to 'prove' Morland's loyalty, and might even serve to protect him from awkward questions.

'You treacherous snake, Morland,' shouted Lamb, struggling furiously as Gery's soldiers hustled him away. 'You were always one of us. Indeed, some of the ideas were yours, such as how to forge Bishop-Marks and the machine that opens letters.'

'Will they be hanged, sir?' asked Morland, contemptuously turning his back on him. 'It seems your safest option.'

'No,' replied the Earl. 'I shall ship them to Jamaica. We do not want the general public to lose faith in the Post Office by executing this many felonious officials.'

O'Neill offered to help the soldiers escort Bishop and his clerks to Newgate, and as it was an odd thing for a Controller to do, Chaloner started to follow, but the Earl called him back.

'We have not finished here yet,' he said softly. 'You cannot leave.'

Chaloner watched them go, hoping Gery's men would be equal to keeping hold of their prisoners – and equal to protecting them, too, should O'Neill decide that it might be better for him if they never reached their destination. Then he turned his mind to more important matters. 'The Devill's Worke is—'

'The Devill's Worke!' sneered Morland. 'He does not know what he is talking about, sir. Allow me to explain what is really going on.'

Chaloner chafed with growing agitation as Morland gave a highly subjective, rambling and largely untrue account of what had happened, punctuated by irrelevant asides from Gery, who was eager not to lose too much glory to his self-serving underling. It was a shocking waste of valuable time, but Chaloner could not speak loudly enough to contradict them. Eventually, the Earl silenced Morland with a flap of his hand and turned questioning eyes on his intelligencer.

'Lamb overheard Rea talking yesterday, sir,' croaked Chaloner. 'The Devill's Worke will—'

'He is overwrought,' interrupted Morland, patting Chaloner's arm patronisingly, but desisting hastily when he saw the dark expression on the spy's face. 'Lamb and Harper came close to killing him, and it has affected his judgement. Nothing bad will happen today.'

'It was your own fault that rescue was delayed, Chaloner,' added Gery with a spiteful grin. Chaloner supposed he should not be surprised that the marshal still considered him an enemy, given what had happened on the banks of the Thames. 'I went to the Crown first, because that is where you said this great crisis would be. We lost God knows how many precious minutes before the Earl told us to come here instead.'

'Was Dorislaus waiting to brief you?' Chaloner could only hope that the Earl would remember enough of their earlier conversation to distil truth from all the lies that were being spun.

'Who is Dorislaus?' asked the Earl.

Chaloner's throat hurt too much to explain. 'Where is Williamson?'

'I sent for him, but he never responded,' replied the Earl. 'Perhaps he is away from home. I rounded up as many of his men as I could find, but they were pitifully few, so I was obliged to use Gery's soldiers, too. However, I thought they rose to the occasion ably enough. Where is Thurloe?'

Chaloner shook his head to say he did not know. He was now sure something was wrong, because the ex-Spymaster would have come had he been able.

'You did well, Chaloner,' said the Earl, poring over the paper snatched at such cost.

'We all did, sir,' said Morland smoothly. 'I confess there were times when I thought Bishop might best me, but you arrived to save the day. It is over now, and we can all go home.'

'It is not over and—' Chaloner tried to speak more loudly when Morland interrupted again, but only succeeded in making himself cough.

'Who would have thought that the Post Office would harbour so many villains?' the secretary sighed. 'Thank God we have rooted them all out. We can sleep easy in our beds tonight.'

'No, we cannot,' said the Earl sharply. 'Chaloner is right – this business is far from over. And Freer is fetching someone who may be able to help us decide what to do next. Ah. Here he is now.'

Chaloner turned to see Freer walking through the door. Behind him were the Major and his two yeomen. The Major was ashen-faced and frightened, an expression that intensified tenfold when he saw Harper's body.

'Christ God!' he breathed. 'What is going on? Why have you brought me here?'

'We owe you an apology,' said the Earl briskly. 'Something catastrophic is about to happen, and Gery was wrong to insist that we ignore vital parts of your intelligence.'

Gery opened his mouth to argue, but the Earl glowered so fiercely that he shut it again without speaking. Chaloner sagged with relief that his master was finally standing up to the man.

'Tell us about this Devill's Worke, Major,' the Earl ordered.

'But it is probably too late to do anything about it now,' cried the Major, distressed. 'And why should I believe this sudden change of heart after so many weeks?'

'Because it will be treason to do otherwise,' replied the Earl coolly.

The Major gulped, but remained defiant. 'What will you do? Lock me in the Tower?'

'Oh, I think I can devise something a little more colourful than that,' said the Earl in a softly menacing voice that Chaloner had never heard him use before. 'I have been blind, thinking about my son, but my eyes are open now, and they are looking for felons who harm my country.'

The Major nodded slowly. 'Well, as you seem to be taking me seriously at last, I shall tell you what I suspect, and pray to God that you are in time to act. I have heard whispers about Palmer and the book he is to publish. It is on an unpopular subject by a man London hates – they see him as responsible for his wife's peccadilloes.'

Understanding flashed in Chaloner's mind. 'The assassination? It will be him?'

'I cannot say for certain, but it makes sense,' replied the Major. 'I have been afraid that I might be the target, but on reflection, I do not think I am sufficiently important. Not any more. I might have been eighteen months ago, but I am nothing now.'

'True,' agreed the Earl baldly. 'Chaloner, go and tell Palmer to stay at home until further notice. Take Gery and Freer with you. Palmer is a decent man, and I will not see his blood spilled.'

'He will probably be at Speed's shop on Fleet Street,'

said Chaloner, although he had no idea of the time. 'His book will be sold for the first time today.'

'Well, go there, then,' said the Earl irritably. 'And Morland will walk to Newgate, to ensure that Bishop and his creatures are properly secured.'

'I will go with Morland,' offered Freer quickly, making Chaloner suspect that he was not the only one who distrusted the slippery secretary. 'While Chaloner and Gery save Palmer.'

'You will go where I say,' barked the Earl. 'Well? What are you waiting for?'

'Even an assassination is not the worst you should expect today, sir,' rasped Chaloner, risking a reprimand by not immediately scrambling to obey like the others, Morland smirking gloatingly at Freer as he went. 'There is still John Fry.'

'I know,' said the Earl shortly. 'But unless you have learned something new, we have no idea how to go about apprehending him. However, we *can* save Palmer. And while you do, the Major and I will sit here and review all he has learned. Perhaps we can find answers between us.'

Chaloner was alarmed. 'You cannot stay here! O'Neill may return.'

'He will not. He is enjoying himself too much crowing over Bishop. But why should it matter if he comes back anyway?'

Chaloner did not want to level accusations when he had no solid evidence. Besides, there were more pressing matters to address before he left. 'Thurloe,' he rasped to the Major. 'Last night . . .'

The Major looked away. 'I was a coward, and refused to tell him what he wanted to know. I am sorry, but I was frightened. I still am.'

'Was Dorislaus with him?'

'Yes, although he kept his distance. They left together, but I do not know where they went. Why?'

'Ask this later,' said the Earl warningly. 'You are wasting time and Palmer's life is at stake.'

'Just one more thing,' said the Major, catching Chaloner's arm as he turned to leave. 'I cannot vouch for its truth, but I heard a whisper in the Antwerp that the assassins may be two veterans from the New Model Army. I believe their names are Stokes and Cliffe.'

Chaloner's heart sank. He did not want to challenge soldiers who had fought bravely for their country and were disillusioned with what they had spilled blood to achieve.

'Parliamentarians,' said the Earl with pursed lips. 'I might have known.'

Outside the Post Office, Chaloner glanced towards Storey's house, but there was no sign of Dorislaus. He faltered, his heart clamouring at him to forget Palmer and concentrate on finding Thurloe, but he knew he would be wasting his time – as Dorislaus had pointed out, he did not know where to start.

'I was beginning to think you were not coming,' said Gery, as Chaloner caught up with him and Freer on Dowgate Hill. 'Are you frightened? Stay behind, then. We can manage without you.'

'Ignore him, Tom,' murmured Freer. 'He is just vexed that it was you, not he, who exposed the corrupt clerks after all his efforts. But watch yourself – he is a vengeful enemy.'

Chaloner did not need to be told. He said nothing, concentrating on reaching Fleet Street as quickly as possible. It was snowing, great white flakes settling in a thick carpet that made moving at speed difficult. As before, the roads were devoid of traders and carts, and most of those braving the bitter weather were men who had gathered on street corners or in gangs outside taverns and coffee houses. Many wore items of clothing that marked their affiliation to a particular guild, and the atmosphere was tense and strained.

Chaloner set a cracking pace, partly to reach Speed's shop quickly, but more to prevent Gery or Freer from engaging him in conversation. He was confused, desperately worried about Thurloe, and his throat hurt. Unfortunately, they kept pace. Gery was angry.

'You made me look like a fool,' he snarled. Chaloner was about to retort that Gery had done that all by himself, when he saw the marshal's gaze was fixed not on him, but on Freer. 'You encouraged me to explore the corruption, while all along the real plot was assassination.'

'Do not blame your failings on me,' objected Freer. 'I made suggestions, but you did not have to follow them. It is good that Morland used his initiative, or blood would have been spilled today, and not just Chaloner's.'

'We both know Morland is corrupt,' said Gery. He stopped running, and grabbed the front of Freer's coat. 'And so are you.'

'Me?' Freer struggled to pull himself loose, while Chaloner hesitated, torn between listening to the quarrel and hurrying to help Palmer. 'I have done nothing wrong.'

'You are in someone's pay.' Gery tightened his grip. 'Morland is his own man in that he betrays everyone, but you have a master. Who is it?'

'I do not!' cried Freer. 'You are deranged. Get him off me, Chaloner.'

Chaloner's first instinct was to oblige, to side with the man he liked, but Morland's words about not knowing who he could trust clamoured at him. The secretary was certainly right about that. When he hesitated, Gery flung Freer away and hauled out his rapier.

'Draw,' the marshal said furiously. 'Prove your innocence with your blade.'

'And give you an excuse to kill me?' asked Freer archly. 'I do not think so! We both know you are the better swordsman – you will skewer me in an instant. Now put up your weapon and—'

'You damned traitor,' snarled Gery. Freer ducked behind Chaloner, who was forced to whip out his own weapon to protect them both as Gery flailed wildly in an effort to reach his target.

'Stop him, Tom,' shouted Freer. He drew his sword, but prevented Chaloner from stepping back to let him fight his own battle by taking hold of the spy's coat. 'He has already murdered Knight and Ibson. He would have murdered you, too, if you had not escaped from that cell.'

'Who paid you to betray me, Freer?' demanded Gery, intensifying his attack. He was strong and determined, and Chaloner was hard-pressed to keep him at bay. 'Who is your master?'

'Someone who is twice the man you will ever be,' hissed Freer, a remark that made Chaloner turn to look at him sharply. But not for long – Freer's response goaded the marshal into a series of viciously slashing blows that forced Chaloner to concentrate on him again.

'Enough!' he shouted hoarsely. 'We do not have time for this. Palmer will—'

'Forget Palmer,' snapped Freer. 'He is nothing. Save

me from Gery, and I will tell John Fry what you have done. You will not regret it, I promise. London will burn today, and once it is gone in all its filthy corruption, we shall look to a better, brighter future.'

Chaloner regarded him in horror, and Gery might have used his inattention to stab him had he not been standing in open-mouthed shock himself. Then the marshal shook himself and took a firmer grip on his sword for another assault, but at that moment a huge band of apprentices from the Company of Barber-Surgeons slouched past, identifiable by their scarlet hoods. They were bellowing a Parliamentarian victory song that Chaloner had not heard since his youth. They cast defiant glances at three little gaggles of fishmongers, cutlers and glaziers, but the smaller groups prudently declined to meet their challenge.

'Help!' yelled Freer, pulling off his Cavalier hat and tossing it and his sword away. 'These two villains mean to kill me because I fought for Cromwell. And you can see I am unarmed.'

Rational men would have noticed the discarded weapon and headwear, but the apprentices were spoiling for a fight and Freer's claim provided the perfect pretext. They surged forward eagerly, brandishing sticks and knives.

'We are officers from White Hall,' declared Gery indignantly. Chaloner winced – it was hardly the wisest of claims to make to a mob with Roundhead leanings. 'Back off immediately or I—'

'Two debauched libertines!' shouted one lad. 'About to murder an honest Roundhead. Will we stand by and let this happen?'

There was a resounding howl that they would not.

403

Chaloner was appalled. How much carnage would there be before they realised that sticks and daggers were no match for swords?

'Finish them, lads,' urged Freer. 'Show them what proud Parliamentarians can do.'

'Stop,' ordered Gery angrily. 'We are trying to save the life of a— I said *stop!*'

The youths advanced purposefully, brandishing their staves.

'The world will change today and you two cannot stop it,' yelled Freer over his shoulder as he raced for the safety of an alley. 'Long live the republic and long live John Fry!'

There was an answering cheer from the apprentices. Grimly, Chaloner gripped his sword and waited for the slaughter to begin.

'Wait,' cried the spokesman suddenly, raising his hand just as the skirmish was about to commence. 'This one is a friend of Surgeon Wiseman. I have seen them together several times.'

'Lord!' breathed another. 'We had better let them go then, because we dare not annoy Wiseman. We might end up being the subject of a public anatomy.'

They were gone without another word, linking arms and bawling a rebellious chant as they marched down Dowgate Hill. Chaloner sheathed his sword quickly and indicated that Gery should do the same before someone else saw a drawn weapon as an invitation to attack. Gery did, albeit reluctantly, and hurried to the alley up which Freer had disappeared. It was empty.

'So both were traitors,' he said bitterly. 'Morland and Freer. I supposed you guessed?'

'I have known Morland for a long time,' replied Chaloner carefully, acutely aware that the wrong response might encourage Gery to turn on him, and they did not have time to play out personal animosities.

'And Freer? Did you suspect him of being in John Fry's pay?'

'No. I liked him.'

'I did, too. We have been friends for years. Or so I thought.'

'You are not the only one he used.' Chaloner spoke with difficulty. 'He told me that you were either inefficient or corrupt – he wanted you to bear the blame for the investigation's failure, and me to ensure that Clarendon knew it.'

'But why?' asked Gery, stunned anew.

'Presumably so that when you eventually explained that most of your tactics and decisions were actually Freer's ideas, it would look like sour grapes on your part and no one would believe you.'

'The bastard! I will kill him when this is over and . . . Wait! Where are you going?'

Chaloner wondered whether the marshal had lost what scant wits he seemed to possess. 'To prevent Palmer from being murdered.'

'No! You heard Freer – John Fry plans to destroy London today, and rescuing an unpopular cuckold is hardly the best way to prevent it.'

It was a little late to be worrying about that, thought Chaloner acidly. Fry's plot might not have gained such momentum if Gery had not let Freer convince him to ignore half the Major's intelligence. 'Then return to the Earl and ask him for directions. I am going to Palmer.'

He started running again, thankful when Gery did not

follow. Now he might be able to convince Stokes and Cliffe of the madness of their cause before any damage was done, something that would have been impossible with the marshal breathing fire at his elbow.

His heart sank when he saw the crowd outside Speed's shop, which included unruly apprentices and folk whose austere clothes said that they were the more militant kind of Puritan. All were chanting anti-Catholic slogans. He was relieved to see that none of the Rainbow's patrons had accepted Speed's invitation, although he was more sorry than he could say to spot Stokes and Cliffe among the throng. Bulges in their coats told him that both carried guns.

'No,' he said softly, approaching Stokes and grabbing his arm. 'I know what you intend, and you must stop. It is lunacy and will change nothing.'

'It will make a point,' argued Stokes. He was pale, and Chaloner saw he had no appetite for what he was about to do. 'The Court might be better behaved once it understands that we are weary of its wild licentiousness.'

Chaloner struggled to make himself heard above the belligerent singing. 'You will hang. This "point" is not worth your lives.'

An angry hiss rippled through the crowd as Palmer's coach was spotted in the distance.

'Please, Stokes,' begged Chaloner. 'Stand down before you do something you will regret.'

'Someone must take a stand,' declared Cliffe. 'Or do you suggest we allow *that woman* to destroy our country with her evil ways? Lent would not have been cancelled, were it not for her.'

'But Palmer is a good man,' argued Chaloner, wishing his voice was stronger. 'Who *does* keep Lent.

406

And his book is intended to be a balm to our troubles, not a—'

Cliffe shoved him away, hard enough to make him stagger, and then things happened very fast. There was a collective roar of hostility as the carriage rumbled to a standstill. Stokes reached inside his coat and pulled out a gun; Cliffe did the same. Palmer began to alight. Chaloner tried to shout a warning, but his voice cracked and went unheard in the clamour of insults that was pouring from the onlookers.

He punched the dag from Stokes's hand and stepped in front of Cliffe, blocking him from his target. But Stokes retrieved his weapon quickly, and took aim. Chaloner felt as though he was moving through treacle as he lunged to bat it down again. He touched it just in time, and there was a puff of dust as the bullet struck the ground. The resulting crack turned the crowd's poisonous invective into cries of alarm. Stokes drew a second dag from his belt, even as smoke still curled from the first, so Chaloner crashed into him, knocking him from his feet. There was another bang as that weapon discharged, too.

But Chaloner's move had left Cliffe unguarded, and a third shot rang out. People were running in all directions, howling in fright. Then a whip snapped, and the coach lurched away. Chaloner glanced around to see Palmer's horrified face peering out of the window, but then it was gone, the carriage rattling away with its occupant unscathed.

Chaloner turned back to Stokes and Cliffe. Stokes was gazing after the coach in disgust, but Cliffe was standing in an attitude of defeat, his shoulders slumped and his head bowed. Someone lay on the ground in front of him.

'I changed my mind,' he whispered, white-faced with shock. 'I could not kill in cold blood after all, so I aimed at the Castlemaine coat-of-arms instead. I thought blasting a hole in it might serve the same purpose. But this fellow leapt in front of me. I did not mean to hit him!'

Chaloner knelt next to the stricken man. It was Gery.

Chapter 14

'I saved Palmer,' Gery whispered, and for the first time since Chaloner had met him, he smiled. It softened his dour features and made him look almost handsome. 'The assassin was pulling the trigger, but I took the bullet instead.'

'You did well.' Chaloner was reluctant to tell him that his reckless act of heroism had done no more than save Palmer the cost of having his coach patched up.

'I decided you were right,' Gery went on. His face was an unhealthy grey-white and his breathing shallow. 'He is a good man, a patriot who came home to fight the Dutch, even though it cannot be pleasant for him here. Do you think the King will be pleased?'

Chaloner nodded, although it went through his mind that His Majesty might have been rather glad to be rid of his mistress's husband. He began to unbutton Gery's coat. The hostile crowd had vanished and the prowling mobs paid him no heed. Speed hovered in the door of his shop, but was too frightened to come out, while there was no sign of Stokes or Cliffe.

'Perhaps he will knight me,' whispered Gery. 'It is unfair

that Morland received honours for the dirty business of espionage, while honest warriors like me had nothing. I have always hated spies.'

'Why did you hire him then?' asked Chaloner, still struggling with the buttons.

'He was recommended to me. In fact, everything I have done has been on the advice of . . .'

'Of Freer?' The coat was open at last, but Chaloner had seen enough gunshot wounds to know that this one would be mortal. There was nothing he could do except stay with Gery until he died, although he fretted at the lost time.

'Yes – my so-called friend. It never once occurred to me that he was Fry's mouthpiece. He set me against you from the start – always reminding me of your Roundhead past, saying you would steal the glory if I let you help me.'

'Never mind him.' Chaloner's voice was weaker than Gery's, and he was not sure the dying man would hear it. 'Tell me what the Major said about the Devill's Worke.'

'Freer urged me to keep you busy with nonsense,' Gery whispered. 'I thought the ducks would serve such a purpose, and I was horrified when they led you to Post House Yard.'

'The Major,' prompted Chaloner urgently. 'What did he—'

'Freer suggested the fifty-pound reward for Gardner, too,' Gery went on, either not hearing or disinclined to answer. 'It was a stupid idea – it shackled Williamson by bombarding him with useless information. Of course, now I see that was exactly what they intended.'

Chaloner was nearing the end of his tether, racked with anxiety for what was going to happen, and for

410

Thurloe, so staying calm was not easy. 'Then help me stop them. What did the Major—'

'I was furious with you for arresting Knight.' Gery's eyes were beginning to glaze. 'I thought it would undermine all my work – my hours of patient questioning, my sending Morland to infiltrate those greedy clerks . . .'

And a lot of good that had done, thought Chaloner acidly. '*Please* tell me what—'

'Knight said the Devill's Worke is a distraction, to divert me from the real villains. Ibson claimed the same, so I killed him, too. I did not believe either of them. Ibson also said . . .'

'What?' Chaloner itched to shake the information out of him. He could hear shouting in the distance, and was seized with the fear that the trouble might have started – and that once it gained momentum, it would be impossible to stop.

'That Fry, Oxenbridge and their masters will stage a great revolt today, and that the whole country will reel from it. Freer said it was nonsense, but now I see that Ibson was right.'

'Their masters?' echoed Chaloner. He gripped Gery's shoulder in an effort to make him understand the urgency. 'Who are they? O'Neill? Le Notre?'

'It will start in Post House Yard.' The light was going out of Gery's eyes.

'Wood?' Chaloner swallowed hard as a dreadful thought occurred to him. 'Not Storey, and the business with the birds was a ruse intended to mislead us?'

But Gery was dead.

Shouting for Speed to look after the marshal's body, Chaloner turned and sped back towards the General

Letter Office, his heart pounding with tension as he remembered that the Earl was in it, and perhaps so was Williamson by now. It was even possible that Thurloe had arrived, too. He tried to run harder, but snow was falling thickly, and the ground underfoot was treacherous. He stumbled badly in one pothole, but hands were there to steady him when he started to fall. He struggled away from them when he saw it was Stokes, and that the old soldier still held his gun.

'I do not have time—' began Chaloner.

Stokes cocked the firing mechanism, and Chaloner could tell from his pale face that fear and panic had rendered him unpredictable. When the veteran indicated he was to step into a shadowy alley, Chaloner did not dare refuse, sensing it would take very little to send him over the edge.

'Cliffe does not deserve to hang for killing that man,' said Stokes unsteadily. 'I cannot let you reveal his part in what happened. I am sorry, but he is a comrade-in-arms, and I owe it to him.'

Chaloner did not want to listen to another self-justifying monologue. 'London is on the verge of a crisis and I must—'

'Yes, London is on the verge of a crisis! The gun wobbled alarmingly. 'And it is Palmer's fault. He brought us to this. We should have killed him today, but God was not with us. We came much closer the first time. Indeed, I thought we had succeeded when he was flung back by the blast.'

Understanding dawned in Chaloner's mind. The gunpowder had not been intended for Copping, but for Palmer. And there was Mother Greene's testimony – that the Yeans had been hired by 'military fellows'.

'But it went wrong,' Stokes continued. 'One lad was supposed to engage Palmer in conversation, while the other lit the fuse. Then both would run away, leaving Palmer as the sole victim. But Palmer declined to be waylaid, and when the Yeans saw they would fail, they tried to pinch out the fuse. It was a disaster.'

Chaloner was shocked as well as disgusted. How could Stokes have expected a Yean to keep someone like Palmer entertained? Of course it was a disaster!

'They said they could do it,' objected Stokes defensively when he saw Chaloner's expression. 'And we paid them well. It was not our idea, anyway. John Fry said it would be a vitally important part of a great uprising, which will rid us of corruption and immorality for ever.'

'Were you going to kill him the night he was in St Dunstan's Church?' asked Chaloner.

Stokes nodded. 'But he had bodyguards, and then you arrived . . . We had to invent a tale to explain what we were doing there. Fry was angry with us for failing.'

'You have met him?' The germ of a solution was beginning to unfold at the back of Chaloner's mind, but would he be in a position to act on it?

Stokes pulled a sheaf of letters from his pocket, and shoved them into the spy's hand. All had been sealed with purple wax. 'He wrote. Read what he says yourself. He will lead us to victory today. There will be some bloodshed, but we shall emerge as a gentler, more ethical society.'

Chaloner wondered how to reason with such lunatic beliefs. 'It—'

'But now I find myself uncertain.' Stokes glanced down at the gun. 'Although Cliffe deserves better than to be hunted down like an animal for trying to do what was right.'

413

'I doubt anyone recognised you,' said Chaloner quickly. 'If you leave London today—'

'Turn around.'

Chaloner shook his head, loath to be shot in the back, but Stokes grabbed him roughly and he lacked the strength to resist. He heard Stokes step into position and tensed, but nothing happened. Slowly and carefully, he looked behind him. The old soldier had gone.

Chaloner resumed his journey on unsteady legs, trying to devise a plan should the Earl – and Thurloe and Williamson – be in trouble. Nothing came to mind, and all he could do was hurry to the Post Office and hope that something would occur to him once he had assessed the situation.

People seemed to be reading letters everywhere he looked, huddling in doorways to escape the bitter cold, and conversing in low, urgent voices. Some were laughing, which he found more disturbing than sullen resentment. It suggested a dangerous distancing from reality.

'It is strange that there is post today,' he heard one man say. 'I thought all the roads were closed with snowdrifts.'

'John Fry found a way,' came the proud reply. 'Bad weather will not keep *him* from his noble work.'

Chaloner's legs burned from fatigue when he finally reached Dowgate Hill, and his breath rasped painfully in his damaged throat. He crept cautiously down the lane that led to Post House Yard, only to find the square empty. Footprints in the snow trailed to and from the General Letter Office, and there was evidence that Wood's household had also been active. But nothing stirred now, except two sparrows that hopped along Storey's doorstep in search of crumbs.

Had Gery been wrong to say the mischief would start in Post House Yard? The marshal had not been clever, and may have misunderstood what he had heard or been told. He also could have been fed yet more false information by Freer. Was Fry's plot swinging into action in another part of the city, even as Chaloner loitered uncertainly?

He listened intently. He could hear shouting in the distance. It sounded jubilant, and there was some wild laughter. He did not like to imagine what had precipitated it, and visions of lynching and murder were sharp in his mind.

Because he did not know what else to do, he broke into Storey's house again, every nerve jumping with tension. He aimed for the parlour, where he stared through the window at the disused wing. It seemed deserted, and there were no lights. He climbed out and crept towards it, entering the building through the same shutter that he had forced open the last time. Once inside, he stood still to listen again. The only sound was the thudding of his heart.

With a wave of despair, he saw he had been wrong to go there. Clarendon's raid must have warned Fry that it was an unsuitable place from which to launch an uprising, so he had moved elsewhere. And the Earl? He would have gone home, and ordered the Major returned to the Tower.

A creak made him spin around in alarm, and he found himself facing Dorislaus.

'Good,' whispered the Anglo-Dutchman. 'I was starting to think I might have to do this alone.'

'Do what alone?' Chaloner could manage no more than a croak.

'Rescue Clarendon. Palmer was not the real target today – he is. John Fry sent two fools to shoot Palmer and distract everyone, but Palmer is irrelevant. What is wrong with your voice?'

Chaloner had no idea whether to believe him. 'Where were you when the Earl arrived with his soldiers earlier? You were supposed to intercept him.'

'There was no need,' replied Dorislaus. 'He had more than enough men to catch dishonest clerks, and I was worried about Thurloe, so I left.'

'You have found him?'

'No. I went to Lincoln's Inn, but he was not there. So I came back and—'

'Why were you walking arm-in-arm with him last night?'

Dorislaus raised his eyebrows. 'It was his way of keeping me close so that we could discuss the case without raising our voices. Surely he has done the same with you?'

'No.'

Dorislaus regarded him coolly. 'Then perhaps you are not the trusted confidant you imagine.'

Chaloner did not know what to think, but he had had enough of Dorislaus. He grabbed his arm and dragged him to the secret room in the disused wing, where he shoved him inside and locked the door. The cloth-lined walls muffled the immediate medley of cries and thumps, and would not be audible to anyone in the main building. He put Dorislaus from his mind, and began to prowl.

It did not take him long to locate signs of life. They were in the Letter Hall with its cathedral-like pillars and echoing marble. The window shutters were closed, but although two lamps had been lit, their feeble glow did not penetrate the shadows around the edges. Confident that he would not be seen, Chaloner eased forward, and took up station behind one of the columns.

The Earl was sitting on a chair with his hands bound in front of him. He looked vulnerable and afraid, although he was doing his best to conceal it. Three men guarded him. First, Freer, nervously eyeing the door. Second, Rea, leaning against a wall and affecting nonchalance. And third, Gardner, pacing like a caged lion; his fair, bushy hair was uncovered and his pink face was marred by a savage cut. Chaloner knew exactly how he had come by it: at Knight's burial, when he himself had slashed him with a knife.

He regarded them dispassionately. He could not fight all three at once: Gardner and Rea were experienced brawlers, while Freer, although he had been reluctant to tackle Gery, was still a soldier. Yet it was clear that the Earl was living on borrowed time, so Chaloner would have to act quickly if he wanted to save him. He could expect no help, of course: Williamson would have arrived by now if he was coming, and so would Thurloe, while Gery was dead. He tried to think of something that would give him an edge, half listening to the discussion that was taking place.

'You took a risk coming here, Gardner,' Rea was saying. 'Fifty pounds is a lot of money, and there are those who would sell their children for that kind of reward.'

Gardner scowled at Freer. 'It was a stupid idea, even if it has kept Williamson busy. And if I *am* arrested, I shall expect you two to rescue me. Our leaders will not bother.'

'How much longer will they be?' asked Freer, clearly the most uneasy of the trio.

'You will not get away with this,' warned the Earl, as Chaloner wondered who they were expecting. Oxenbridge and Fry certainly, but who else? 'Chaloner and Gery will come back soon, and they are more than a match for you.'

'They are dead,' said Freer dispassionately. 'Torn to pieces by a mob.'

The Earl looked stricken, although whether at the loss of two retainers or the news that he would not be rescued was difficult to say.

'I do not understand any of this,' he said miserably. 'What will you gain from setting London alight with bitterness and resentment? And why kill poor Mary Wood and the King's birds?'

'Because I was paid to,' replied Gardner shortly.

'Who paid you?' pressed the Earl.

'Why, John Fry, of course.' Gardner's smirk pulled the cut on his face, causing him to wince and raise a tentative hand to touch it. 'He knows what is best for the country.'

'Murdering women in their sickbeds is good for the country?' asked the Earl, struggling for defiance, but managing only to sound fearful.

'She was not as ill as everyone thought,' said Gardner ruefully. 'She put up quite a fight.'

'Did you kill her servant, too?' asked the Earl in a small voice. 'Joyce?'

'Stokes and Cliffe took care of that, albeit unintentionally. You will die soon, too, and so will that meddling Wiseman. I know he has been helping Chaloner and when I dispatched his cat—'

Gardner stopped speaking when shouting was carried on the wind, possibly from Thames Street. The trouble

418

was spreading, and perhaps it was already too late to stop it.

Chaloner took a deep breath and forced himself to think. What he had to do was obvious: attack quickly and free the Earl before Oxenbridge and his cronies arrived. Gardner, Rea and Freer were not expecting him, so he had surprise on his side. He also had speed and shadows. And he could not dally, because once the trio were joined by their masters, Clarendon would die. Moving carefully, he took the daggers from his boot and sleeve, and eased into position.

Without knowing it, the Earl provided the perfect diversion by starting to ask another question, and in an entirely unnecessary burst of violence, Freer slapped him, knocking the wig from his head. Chaloner's first dagger thudded with neat precision into Freer's chest. The soldier gaped at it in disbelief before his knees buckled and he slumped to the floor.

Chaloner's second blade took Rea in the shoulder, and he had drawn his sword and raced towards Gardner almost before it had landed, aiming to incapacitate the clerk before he realised what was happening. But Gardner was no stranger to skirmishing. He met Chaloner's attack confidently, although the force of it sent him staggering backwards.

'Chaloner!' cried the Earl in relief. 'I knew these vile devils would never best you!'

Chaloner found the remark touchingly encouraging, and he went after Gardner with renewed vigour, grati-fied when the clerk was forced to retreat, face white with alarm. He was on the verge of disabling the man permanently when the door opened and Oxenbridge entered.

'Hah!' Oxenbridge's button-black eyes glittered triumphantly in the lamplight as he hauled his rapier from its sheath. 'I am glad you are here. I have a score to settle with you.'

Chaloner sagged, knowing that Oxenbridge's arrival meant the end for him and the Earl. He could not fight him and Gardner together, not even if he had been fresh. Rea was lurching upright, too, and while he would not be joining a skirmish, he was still a threat. Oxenbridge swished his sword through the air, testing its balance, as Gardner advanced on Chaloner from the opposite direction.

'Wait,' said the Earl quickly, struggling to his feet. 'I know you mean to kill us, but will you answer some questions first? You can call it a dying man's last request.'

He glanced at Chaloner, who understood what he was trying to do: give him time to devise a plan – or time to gather strength for a superhuman assault that would see him victorious. Neither was going to happen, of course. Chaloner had no ideas, and his body was numb with exhaustion. He looked at Oxenbridge, and had the peculiar thought that perhaps he had been right to have had nightmares about his sister's doll as a child. It was about to be the agent of his death.

'Answer questions?' Rea regarded the Earl incredulously, hand to his injured shoulder. 'But we are about to—'

'Why not?' interrupted Gardner. Oxenbridge said nothing, his dark eyes fixed unblinkingly on Chaloner; it was unsettling, and the spy wished he would look at someone else. 'It will pass the time, and I doubt Chaloner will keep us entertained for long.'

'Who started all this?' asked the Earl, before the others

420

could demur. 'John Fry is dead. He cannot be your Messiah.'

'You are right: he died eight years ago.' Gardner laughed when he saw Chaloner's surprise. 'But we have reincarnated him as something far more magnificent than he ever was in life – more clever with words, more passionate, more cunning . . .'

'Are you saying that someone has been using his identity?' asked the Earl incredulously. 'Who? Le Notre, because a weakened England suits France? Wood, because he is a lunatic? Isaac Dorislaus, because he is Dutch at heart? O'Neill, because his Post Office lies at the heart of—'

'I can tell you who it is not,' jibed Gardner, smirking at Chaloner. 'Dorislaus.'

'Dorislaus!' spat Oxenbridge. 'Have you killed him for us, Chaloner? We have certainly done our best to make you suspect him of treachery. And it serves him right – I cannot abide incorruptible men.'

Chaloner was heartily glad he had not obliged.

'So you were never friends with Fry,' said the Earl quickly, when Oxenbridge took a step forward. 'And you were not helping him to organise a rebellion. You were helping someone else.'

Oxenbridge inclined his head, but his advance did not falter.

'Copping,' squeaked the Earl frantically. 'Why did you kill him?'

'Because he betrayed us.' Oxenbridge smiled coldly at Chaloner, who could not escape the unnerving sense that it was Death leering at him. 'Thank you for holding him in a position where dispatching him was so easy. Will you do the same for Clarendon? If so, I may let you go.'

'But Copping gave you Knight's letters.' The Earl swallowed hard, as if he imagined Chaloner might be tempted by the offer.

'Yes, thank God,' said Gardner. 'If they had been sent, our plans would have suffered a serious setback. The ones to Palmer, Buckingham and Wood were particularly revealing.'

So Wood was not the mastermind, thought Chaloner numbly.

'There was one to Bishop, too,' said the Earl, as Oxenbridge took another step forward. He spoke flatly now, finally understanding that words could not prevent what was going to happen.

'That was the nastiest stroke of all,' scowled Gardner. 'Bishop would have used it to destroy O'Neill, and we like having him in charge of the Post Office.'

So was that the answer? O'Neill was the arch villain? Or was it just that he was too incompetent to notice what was unfolding under his nose? The Earl seemed to have run out of questions, and Gardner and Oxenbridge advanced on Chaloner in a pincer-like movement. To stall them a little longer, Chaloner asked one of his own.

'Is that why you were helping Knight to escape, Gardner? To lay hold of his letters?'

'What is wrong with your voice?' asked Rea suspiciously.

'Plague,' replied Chaloner promptly. 'So you had better not come near me or—'

'I needed to find out where he had hidden them,' explained Gardner. The lie about plague was contemptuously ignored. 'Then Clarendon kindly issued warrants for our arrests, which was perfect – it threw Knight into my confidence.'

422

'But surely he knew that you were one of the perpetrators,' said the Earl weakly.

'He knew about the plot, but not who was involved,' explained Gardner smugly. 'He would have guessed my role when I took the letters from him, though, after which I would have killed him. Chaloner's arrival was a damned nuisance.'

'What were you and Oxenbridge doing in White Hall last week?' asked Chaloner quickly, as Gardner took a firmer grip on his sword, the memory obviously still rankling. Poor Knight, he thought, doomed no matter how the encounter had ended.

'We went to kill you,' said Oxenbridge, performing a series of fancy manoeuvres with his blade that told Chaloner he was about to be cut to pieces. 'We lured you to a lonely part of the palace, but then it occurred to me that we could not risk Thurloe coming after us, so we let you go. It was a mistake – one we shall rectify today, as he no longer matters.'

Chaloner's blood ran cold. So he had been right to fear that something bad had happened to Thurloe.

'We did not want you racing off to Buckinghamshire either,' added Rea. He flexed his injured shoulder, and Chaloner saw his knife had done less damage than he had intended – Rea would still be a threat in the looming skirmish. 'Where we would not know what you were doing, so Freer encouraged you to stay. You will pay for killing him, by the way. He was a good friend.'

'He was,' agreed Oxenbridge, black eyes bright with loathing. 'So fight me, Chaloner, or I shall kill you where you stand. Gardner, step away. I can take him alone.'

Chaloner only just managed to prevent himself from being run through in the first riposte. He pushed everything from his mind, concentrating entirely on his opponent and ignoring the aching weariness in his limbs. He fought with every ounce of his skill and strength, not the powerful, slashing style he had used against Harper, but the graceful fencing he had been taught as a youth.

Oxenbridge matched him blow for blow, but he had not just learned that his only real friend 'no longer mattered' and so was not fuelled by deeply burning rage. His mouth formed a black circle of surprise when Chaloner scored a cut in his arm. He regarded the blood in astonishment, then fury replaced shock and he attacked in earnest.

Chaloner met the challenge, fighting coldly and scientifically. Oxenbridge yelped when Chaloner's sword nicked first his shoulder and then his wrist. Chaloner continued to advance, driving Oxenbridge backwards, but before he could deliver the final blow, something hit him from behind, knocking him to the floor. Stunned, he was unable to resist as he was divested of his weapons and his hands were tied in front of him.

'There was no need,' cried Oxenbridge indignantly. 'I was winning.'

Gardner did not grace that claim with a reply, and Rea rolled his eyes.

'I still do not understand,' said the Earl. He sounded old, tired and defeated. 'Why do you want to assassinate me?'

'As Lord Chancellor, you are supposed to represent justice,' replied Oxenbridge icily. 'But you imprison innocent men and hold them without trial. Of course you must die.'

And then Chaloner knew exactly who had masterminded the plot – a man who had been unjustly imprisoned himself, and who had not changed from the firebrand he had once been, but who had been acting a role, biding his time. The door opened, and he stood there, portly, triumphant and with the fanatical gleam in his eye that Chaloner remembered so well from Naseby.

The Major strode into the Letter Hall. He oozed confidence, the diffident prisoner vanished, and the arrogance in his step showed that he thought victory was imminent. He was still very pale, though; his fatigue had not been feigned at least.

'You!' breathed the Earl, shocked beyond measure. 'But how . . .'

'I have been planning this ever since you put me in the Tower,' replied the Major coldly. 'And you have been putty in my hands. You and Gery have done everything I – via Freer – suggested.'

'My son,' said the Earl in an agonised voice. 'It was you who wrote . . .'

The Major's eyes flashed. 'Yes, and I am glad it cut you so deeply. You have deprived me of my family these last eighteen months, so you deserve to suffer, too.'

'You said you feared the assassin would kill you,' whispered the Earl, as all became clear. 'But it was a ruse, to deflect suspicion. You were never a target. And if you are purporting to be John Fry, then you do not advocate peaceful political change either. You are a violent lunatic, and I was right to shut you in a place where you could do no harm.'

With weary resignation, Chaloner saw a dribble of purple sealing wax on the Major's sleeve. No wonder he was exhausted – *he* had penned all the missives that had so ignited London! With disgust, Chaloner knew he should have guessed sooner – Prynne had said the Major spent all his time writing in his cell, and it should have been obvious that he had been doing more than begging information from a few Post Office friends.

'I had better make a start,' said Oxenbridge, his pallid face forming what was almost a smile, although not a very nice one. 'We want it done properly.'

'Want what done properly?' squeaked the Earl.

'A fire,' replied the Major. 'You will be incinerated, along with the bodies of my yeomen.'

'Your yeomen?' cried the Earl. 'But they liked you, treated you with kindness.'

'Yes,' sighed the Major. 'But sacrifices must be made in the great fight for freedom.'

He turned abruptly and led the way to the Sorting Room. Gardner and Rea followed, dragging Chaloner between them, while Oxenbridge brought up the rear with the Earl. It was an excellent place for a blaze, given that it was so well supplied with paper.

'You will burn me alive?' gulped the Earl when he saw letters already arranged in a pile.

'I shall offer you a choice,' said the Major stonily. 'Which is more than you gave me. Oxenbridge has a poison that kills quickly. You may drink it, or you may perish in the flames. I recommend the former. It will be far less painful.'

'The substance that killed Mary Wood and the birds?' asked the Earl in a small voice. 'Surgeon Wiseman said it is unusually potent.'

'It is,' said Oxenbridge, pleased. 'I am an apothecary by trade, and I have devised a special process of distillation that concentrates toxins. My potions will be in gifts sent to the King and members of the Privy Council

426

soon – assuming they do not run away to France first, of course.'

The Earl gave a strangled moan, but Oxenbridge ended the discussion by dousing the piled papers in oil. There was a low roar as he applied a flame. Smoke billowed, and he added more documents, along with wood from the hearth. Chaloner coughed.

'You thought I had forgotten you,' spat the Major, rounding on him suddenly. 'The insolent brat who took issue with my speech before Naseby. I knew you would be trouble the moment I heard you were Clarendon's spy. But I bested you with ease, and now I shall have my revenge. I never forget an insult, and you made me look stupid that day.'

Chaloner could think of nothing to say to such a ridiculously exaggerated sense of vengeance. He hacked again as the smoke seared his damaged throat.

'Bishop was your friend,' said the Earl unsteadily, stunned by the depth of the Major's enmity. 'Yet you encouraged him to plot against O'Neill, leading him down a dark—'

'I have *one* friend and that is Oxenbridge,' stated the Major. 'Bishop – and Palmer, too – let me rot in prison without raising a finger to save me. But Bishop is arrested and Palmer will soon be assassinated. My revenge on them is complete.'

'Oxenbridge is no friend to you,' rasped Chaloner. 'It was he who hired the mob to throw stones when you were in Palmer's house.'

The Major regarded him pityingly. 'He acted on my orders, to make everyone think I was a victim of fanatics. And if a missile had injured you, Bishop or Palmer, then so much the better.'

'But you spied for me in the Crown and the Antwerp,'

427

said the Earl, shaking his head in hopeless bewilderment. 'You wrote reports naming the most dangerous villains, yet these will be your foot-soldiers. Why did you betray them?'

'To protect himself.' Chaloner did not bother to conceal his distaste. 'And to ensure it would never cross your mind that he might be the real leader.'

The Major shrugged. 'It worked. And they are unimportant cogs in the wheels I have set in motion. In fact, everything I have done has worked – neither of you guessed that I only pretended to be afraid of Gery. You made it so easy, dragging me to White Hall, giving me leave to write any letters I chose – letters you assumed were for your benefit. Fools!'

'And the information you provided?' asked the Earl in a small voice. 'You mentioned corrupt clerks, but the intelligence about the Devill's Worke was so wild as to be unbelievable.'

'Quite,' gloated the Major. 'I confided my real designs in such outlandish terms that you would naturally disregard them.' He smirked at Chaloner. 'And I told *you* how concerned I was about it, but the reality is that it was exactly what I intended.'

'You aimed to use him,' said the Earl softly, 'by priming him to think that I ignored vital warnings.'

'Which you did,' said the Major. 'I am sorry he followed you here, because it would have been delightful to watch him betray you.'

'You would have been waiting a long time,' muttered Chaloner.

'Being dragged to White Hall suited me in other ways, too,' the Major went on, unable to help himself. 'It generated public sympathy for my plight, and it allowed me

428

to learn when the King planned to hold noisy soirées, so that I would know when to send my poisoners to the park.'

Oxenbridge's blaze was now a bonfire, with flames licking towards the ceiling. He tossed more wood on to it, but some was damp, so it produced a thick white haze. The far side of the Sorting Room was already lost to sight, and it was becoming difficult to breathe. Chaloner's eyes smarted and he tried to move away, but Gardner and Rea were holding him too tightly.

'But why destroy the Post Office?' asked the Earl. He struggled to control the wobble in his voice, unwilling for them to see the extent of his terror. 'It has never harmed you.'

'No, but O'Neill has – his lies saw me incarcerated. However, even if my rebellion fails and he survives Bishop's allegations, he will be blamed for this fire. He will not escape retribution.'

The smoke was growing thicker, and Chaloner coughed again.

'But my uprising *will* succeed today because the regime you support is guided by Satan,' the Major ranted on, his voice growing high-pitched and fervent, just as it had been before Naseby. 'I intend to install a republic – a proper one, not the apology we had under Cromwell.'

'You will not have it,' warned the Earl bravely. 'The best chance was the Commonwealth, and that failed. Now the monarchy is restored, the opportunity is lost for ever.'

'No! The King will flee when London rises against him, and I shall seize White Hall from his debauched followers. Then we shall have a democracy that will be the envy of the world.'

Chaloner coughed harder, then let himself sag, so that

429

Rea and Gardner were obliged either to hold him up or drop him. They struggled for a moment, but then let him go. Everyone's attention was on the Major, so no one noticed when he palmed a metal pen that had fallen on the floor. It was not much of a weapon, but its nib was sharp.

There was a sudden roar, and the fire took on a newer, fiercer intensity. The Major took a step towards the exit as three large sacks began to blaze.

'It seems we must hurry,' he said. 'Poison Clarendon and let us be on our way.'

'Why not just stab him?' asked Rea, fingering a knife. 'Poison is a coward's weapon.'

'We cannot have suspicious holes in his corpse,' snapped the Major. 'It will interfere with my plan to have him accused of helping O'Neill to burn down the Post Office. Now feed him the toxin.'

'Let me,' said Oxenbridge. He withdrew a phial from his pocket, eyes glittering evilly in the dancing firelight. 'I will make him pay for imprisoning you.'

The flames blazed ever more fiercely as Oxenbridge advanced on the Earl and the Earl backed away. They sent sparks flying to the ceiling and filled the Sorting Room with dense, choking smoke. The Major watched the dance between the Earl and Oxenbridge with vengeful glee, while Rea left Chaloner to Gardner, and began to tend the fire, hurling handful after handful of letters on to its greedy tongues.

'I shall kill Chaloner, then,' said Gardner to no one in particular. The Major nodded assent, but did not look away from the Earl and Oxenbridge.

Gardner did not bother with a sword, and drew a

dagger instead. It was his second mistake, the first being to tie Chaloner's hands in front of him rather than behind. The pen shot into his eye, and he reeled away with a howl of startled agony. He stumbled into the fire, where his screams intensified. Rea turned and fled when the burning man tottered towards him, while Oxenbridge and the Major gaped in horror. Chaloner grabbed the knife Gardner had dropped and surged to his feet.

Oxenbridge snapped out of his paralysis. He abandoned the Earl, and there was something approaching madness in his white face as he drew his sword. A dagger was no match for a rapier, so Chaloner put his head down and charged like a bull. Oxenbridge was so taken aback by the unexpected manoeuvre that he was slow to react, and Chaloner slammed into him hard enough to send him flying. Oxenbridge crashed to the floor, where he released an unearthly shriek, while Chaloner's momentum took him stumbling to the far end of the room.

'What?' yelled the Major in agitation. 'What?'

Very slowly, Oxenbridge raised his hand. Blood dripped from a deep gash, pieces of the phial jutting from it. Terror filled his eyes as he realised what was going to happen to him, but then hatred took the place of fear. He stood, eyes bright with the need for reprisal. Meanwhile, the Major lurched from the room, abandoning his only friend without a backward glance.

Oxenbridge picked up his sword. A sheen of sweat coated his face, making it shine eerily in the light cast by the flames, and his eyes were unfathomable pools of blackness. Dispensing with any pretence at finesse, he held the blade like a spear, and began to race towards Chaloner, keening as he did so, a high-pitched wail that made the spy want to put his hands over his ears.

431

As Oxenbridge thundered forward, a vivid memory sprang into Chaloner's mind: it was the same sound that the doll had made when his father had thrown it on the fire so many years before. It rooted him to the spot, and he could only watch as Oxenbridge hurtled towards him.

There was a sharp crack and Oxenbridge's expression turned from fury to incredulity. He continued to advance, but ever more slowly, and when he reached Chaloner, it was only to collapse at his feet. Through the swirling smoke, Dorislaus appeared, holding a gun.

'I discovered a hitherto unrealised talent for picking locks after you shut me in that secret chamber,' he said coolly. 'However, if you do it again, I shall shoot *you*.'

But it was the man standing behind Dorislaus who caught Chaloner's attention. It was Thurloe, gripping a frantically struggling Major. Williamson was with them, and he had brought soldiers. With quiet efficiency, they set about extinguishing the blaze.

'Where have you been?' croaked Chaloner to Thurloe. 'I thought the Major had killed you.'

'Did you?' asked Thurloe in surprise. Chaloner did not have the energy to explain, so Thurloe continued. 'I spent the entire night and much of the day writing letters. It—'

'Letters?' cried Chaloner. 'For God's sake! We are on the verge of a rebellion!'

He shoved past Thurloe and reeled outside. The snow in Post House Yard lay deep and white, but it had stopped falling, and there was a hint of blue in the sky. Screams and howls echoed from Dowgate Hill, and he thought he could hear more in Thames Street. It was too late, he thought despairingly. The Major's plan was already in motion and London would burn after all.

Thurloe had followed him out. He grabbed Chaloner's arm and pulled him across the square and out on to the street. It was full of people, and there was a battle in progress. However, it was not deadly missiles being lobbed, but snowballs.

'My letters,' explained Thurloe. 'They have been delivered throughout the city since dawn. All sent in the name of John Fry, of course.'

'I do not understand.'

Thurloe smiled. 'His great battle is a snowball fight: apprentices versus the rest of London.'

Numbly, Chaloner recalled the laughter he had heard along Thames Street earlier, as people had huddled in doorways with their missives.

'There will be some trouble, of course,' Thurloe went on. 'A core of malcontents will do their best to cause mischief, but Williamson should be able to subdue it.'

'You mean it is over?' rasped Chaloner, slumping in relief.

'Oh, yes,' said Thurloe. 'Do not worry. The Major has lost.'

Epilogue

The following week

Events at the Post Office had been hushed up so efficiently that there was no sign of the fire that had threatened to consume it. Discreet workmen had been hired to repair the damage, while a coffee-seller had opened a booth in the square. Williamson had ensured that he was not a very good one, and the stench of his incinerated beans masked the residual aroma of Oxenbridge's fire.

Chaloner stood outside the General Letter Office with Thurloe, watching the usual bustle as people hurried to catch the noonday post. This time, there were no carts packed with gunpowder, and he found it difficult to believe that the entire episode had started less than two weeks before.

'I am sorry Knight was murdered.' He was still hoarse, and had used it as an excuse not to talk to anyone; Thurloe was the exception. 'Although his letters would not have helped us. He had learned what was being planned, but not who was behind it.'

'Yes, and it is ironic that the mastermind transpired

to be the man who shared the hackney when you took Knight to White Hall to talk to the Earl,' said Thurloe. 'But some justice was served – the Yeans were killed by the very device with which they aimed to murder Palmer.'

'Stokes and Cliffe did not escape, either – they froze to death on the Dover road. I am concerned about the Major, though. I suspect it is only a matter of time before he tries again.'

'He has been transferred to a prison on the Scilly Isles, Tom. Even he cannot cause mischief from there. He was always dangerous and unpredictable, but he surpassed himself this time.'

'He convinced everyone that he was a changed man,' said Chaloner softly. 'But his fanaticism is just as irrational now as it was at Naseby.'

'Do you know what I found most distasteful? The way he preyed on Clarendon's grief. And all the while, he wrote letters, working hard enough to exhaust himself, which convinced us that he was a suffering victim. There was no support from brother apprentices in Hull, Sussex or Bristol – all that came from his poisonous pen.'

Chaloner grinned suddenly. 'We made a nonsense of his family motto, though – *nil admirari*. He was certainly astonished to discover himself thwarted.'

Thurloe smiled back. 'Yes – he thought he was invincible.'

'Can all his crimes be proved?'

'Oh, yes. He and Oxenbridge communicated in code, and Ibson managed to acquire many of their letters – they were in the haul that you retrieved and left in my room. Everything is there: how the birds were killed to distract Storey; how Mary was murdered to frighten off Wood, who had started an enquiry of his own after carrying the message to Clarendon—'

'It did frighten off Wood – he told me several times to stay away from the Post Office. And the Major *did* tell Wood to take his so-called intelligence to the Earl – he lied when he said he wished Wood had picked someone else.'

Thurloe nodded and resumed his list. '—how "Fry's" letters were given credence by sightings of him, all fabricated by his followers; how Vanderhuyden was coerced into spying for the Dutch; how rumours of assassination were started; how Bishop was cajoled into committing fraud to avenge himself on O'Neill; how Gery was manipulated.'

'And all because the Major bears grudges – against Palmer and Bishop for failing to speak out against his imprisonment, against O'Neill for telling the lies that saw him arrested in the first place, and against Clarendon for keeping him in the Tower without a trial.'

Thurloe was sombre. 'He has a right to feel aggrieved. What Clarendon did was illegal.'

Chaloner was silent for a while, his mind playing over the final confrontation in the Sorting Room. 'Did you learn anything about Oxenbridge in the end? Such as where he lived?'

'A rather dull little cottage in Stepney. He had a cat, was kind to his mother and played chess. I was astounded by the banality of the place and the man who had lived there. He was an apothecary, which is why he was able to concoct such a dreadful poison.'

'You make him sound ordinary,' said Chaloner. 'He was not.'

'He was, Tom. We were seduced into thinking him sinister by virtue of his looks and his ability to keep his personal life secret. He played on that.'

Chaloner said nothing, because the sound that

436

Oxenbridge had made before he had been shot continued to haunt him, and there was nothing Thurloe could say that would make him believe he had been a normal man. Absently, he watched people hurry in and out of the Letter Hall. The musician had arrived, and was piping a medley of popular tunes. One included a revolutionary song, but he prudently played something else when he saw Thurloe.

'I misjudged Dorislaus,' Chaloner confessed. 'I thought at one point that he had harmed you.'

Thurloe raised his eyebrows. 'A portly fellow like him? Really, Thomas. Do you have no faith in my ability to look after myself?'

'He armed himself very heavily when he came with me to watch the Post Office – sword, knives, guns. I suspect he is more used to combat than you think.'

'He was just frightened, and wanted the reassurance an arsenal can provide.'

'When you did not write to me in code . . .'

Thurloe shot him an apologetic glance. 'That was an oversight on my part. It did not occur to me that it might worry you. My mind was full of the letters I was going to compose, you see, and I was afraid there would not be time to send them all. Fortunately, Prynne came to the rescue.'

'Prynne?' echoed Chaloner in astonishment. 'That bigoted old—'

'Precisely! He is a pamphleteer with a talent for penning epistles that command attention. He also writes extremely quickly. I suspect that his words were far more effective than mine.'

'Why not ask Dorislaus to help? You trust him.'

'For the same reason I did not ask you – his talents lie in other directions. And if your next question is why did I not confide my plan to either of you, the answer is simple: it would not have worked if you had been captured and forced to talk.'

It was ruthless, but Thurloe had been a Spymaster with the security of a nation in his hands, and he had not earned such a position by being sentimental.

'What about Morland?' asked Chaloner. 'How has he emerged from this affair?'

'He has Williamson's protection, because he claims he is the only one who knows how to operate that letter-opening machine.' Thurloe grimaced. 'He is not, of course. I designed it during the Commonwealth – he stole my plans and built another.'

'Then it is as well he is taking the credit. You cannot be associated with that sort of thing now.'

'True,' acknowledged Thurloe. 'He claimed the fifty-pound reward for catching Gardner, too. He said it was his intelligence that allowed Gardner to be caught and killed.'

'And Williamson believed him?' Chaloner was disgusted.

'No, but Morland petitioned the King, who ordered Williamson to pay. I doubt His Majesty believed it either, but he was enjoying his mistress – Morland chose his time well – and it was quicker to give him what he wanted than to argue. However, Morland has not escaped entirely.'

'No?'

'Someone told Widow Smith that it was he, not the Major and Bishop, who was responsible for betraying her husband during the Commonwealth. And she is vengeful.'

'Good. He can dodge *her* for the rest of his life.'

'Unfortunately your plot misfired, Tom,' said Thurloe

438

mildly. 'She went to confront him, but he employed his cunning tongue. They are now engaged to be married.'

Chaloner gaped at him. 'Is there no predicament he cannot escape? Christ God! He has more lives than a cat and the luck of Lucifer.'

Chaloner did not want to visit Williamson in New Palace Yard, but the Spymaster had demanded a report, and the Earl had ordered him to provide one. He went there the following day, entering the elegant office with considerable reluctance. Williamson was gazing out of his window, looking at the line of traitors' heads that were displayed in a grisly row outside Westminster Hall opposite.

'I have a question for you, Chaloner,' he said, turning and folding his arms. 'Morland's house was burgled last night, and a vast fortune was stolen. I do not suppose you know anything about it?'

Chaloner raised his eyebrows. 'Morland had a vast fortune? How? He cannot earn much working for Clarendon, not even when a fifty-pound reward is taken into account.'

'He declined to say how he came by it. However, every penny has gone, so he will have to rely on the generosity of Widow Smith to keep him in fine clothes now. And she is notoriously mean.'

'Poor Morland.'

'Poor Morland indeed. What do you think happened to the money?'

Chaloner shrugged. 'There is fever and hardship in the Fleet Rookery.'

Williamson regarded him with a complete lack of understanding. 'You could have used it to buy your way out of going to Russia. Or even to purchase employment with me. I am not averse to having my good graces invoked with gold.'

'I shall bear it in mind for the future.'

'Be sure you do. Incidentally, I had a message an hour ago. O'Neill is dead.'

Chaloner stared at him in shock. 'How?'

'Something eroded his guts. Perhaps it was the strain of knowing that, although he lied and plotted to be made Postmaster, he was unequal to running an efficient operation. His wife has been appointed in his stead.'

'Well, she did keep saying she could do a better job.'

'Unfortunately, her husband's death has undermined her confidence, so she has asked me to oblige in her stead. It is a burden, of course, but I have acceded to her request.'

Chaloner's mind raced. Was he to understand that Williamson had dispatched O'Neill to gain control of the Post Office?

'No,' said Williamson indignantly, seeing what he was thinking. 'Of course not.'

'Yet I seriously doubt he died of natural causes. It is too convenient. Would you like me to investigate? It will delay my journey to Russia, but—'

'There is no need. If you must know, Bishop sent him a gift of dried fruits as a peace offering. O'Neill was a fool to have eaten them, but there is nothing we can do about it now, and it is politically disadvantageous to make it known that one Postmaster has murdered another.'

'Bishop is not the culprit,' said Chaloner, thinking Williamson a fool for thinking so. 'How could he send poisoned fruits from gaol? I imagine you have him well guarded.'

Williamson frowned. 'Well, yes, I do. So who is the culprit, then? The Major?'

'Well, he was in the Tower for two days before being sent to the Scilly Isles, which would have given him ample time to organise deadly gifts. He has been a prisoner there long enough to know how to bribe his turnkeys.'

Williamson shook his head slowly. 'God save me from fanatics!'

As it was a fine day, and the snow lay thick and pretty on the ground, the Court repaired to St James's Park for the afternoon. Chaloner rode with the Earl in his private carriage. Foundations were being dug for a new house near the grounds' entrance, and as they passed, the Earl explained that it was for Storey. The curator's experience with the poisoners had taught him that he needed to be nearer his charges, so he intended to leave his cottage in Post House Yard. The area around the new building was already being called Storey's Gate by Londoners.

They arrived at the Canal to find Lady Castlemaine entertaining everyone by designing a line of snowmen in lewd positions. The King stood with his hands on his hips, guffawing heartily, and his courtiers clustered around him to titter. With a prudish glower, the Earl hammered on the ceiling of the carriage to tell his coachman to drive on. Mocking laughter followed.

'She becomes more disgusting every day,' the Earl declared. 'It is a pity the Major did not arrange to assassinate her. I cannot imagine how he convinced Stokes and Cliffe to aim for Palmer, who is more decent and honourable than the rest of Court put together.'

'She is too well guarded,' explained Chaloner. 'But

Palmer was an easy target, because he lives outside White Hall. Besides, there was the excuse of his book.'

'I have read it. A gentle, erudite piece of work, with nothing to inflame. It will do no good, of course. Catholics are unpopular in England, and there is nothing he or anyone else can do about it.'

As they passed the Canal, Chaloner saw the ducks, swans and geese in their usual haunt at the water's edge. The crane with the wooden leg strutted among them, and a flamingo preened nearby. He was glad they were safe from the Major's machinations.

'Le Notre has gone home,' said the Earl conversationally. 'He left magnificent plans for Greenwich, but told the King that nothing can be done for this park. I do not suppose you discovered whether he was a French spy, did you?'

'No, he was just what he appeared: an eccentric landscape architect. Morland tried to confuse me by saying he was Oxenbridge's friend, but it was a lie.'

'Morland,' mused the Earl. 'You may be pleased to know that he is no longer in my service. He had the temerity to inform me that I should reward him for the dangers he had suffered, so I told him he was no longer needed. He will leave for France tomorrow, to join his wife.'

Chaloner frowned. 'He has married Widow Smith already?'

The Earl chortled. 'He cannot do that as long as he is wed to his French lass. I cannot imagine Widow Smith will be pleased when she learns she has been tricked out of her fortune, because I think she fancies herself in love.'

'Christ!' muttered Chaloner, stunned yet again by the secretary's nerve.

'Are you ready to leave for Archangel?' asked the Earl, changing the subject abruptly. 'I received word earlier that the ship I chartered will be ready to sail on tonight's tide. But do not look so glum. I have heard the Russians are very cultured.'

One of the ducks released a raucous laugh, and Chaloner felt no more needed to be said. He had finished reading Olearius's *Voyages*, and was dreading the ordeal that lay ahead of him.

'They have music,' said the Earl encouragingly. 'And I am sure they eat a more varied diet than salted fish and black bread. Besides, my despatches are important. I could not trust them to anyone else.'

'Yes, sir,' said Chaloner flatly.

'It is true.' The Earl lowered his voice. 'They ask for the Tsar's assistance in the event that we lose the war with the Dutch, and may mean the difference between survival and oblivion. Needless to say, no one at Court knows what I am doing. To entertain the possibility of defeat is treason, and these letters will see me executed if they fall into the wrong hands.'

Chaloner was slightly mollified. The Earl was not obliged to appraise him of what the documents contained, and he appreciated being taken into his confidence.

'I am sending a case of valuable jewels, too,' the Earl went on. 'As a bribe. And to be frank, you are the only man I know who will not make off with it. It represents a fortune, and will be a great temptation to anyone who is less than scrupulous.'

Chaloner supposed he would have to develop a dishonest streak in the future, if integrity was to be rewarded with treks to the frozen north.

* * *

The ship bound for Archangel slipped her moorings, and slid soundlessly down the river on the evening tide, her masts and spars stark against the darkening sky. Two men stood side by side and watched her disappear. It was a cloudless evening, so the temperature was already beginning to plummet, and their breath plumed in front of them as they spoke.

'Chaloner will not have a comfortable time of it,' said Morland, his small face pinched with cold and spite. 'The Earl could not have picked a worse month to send him.'

'Was an alliance with Russia Clarendon's idea?' asked Dorislaus. 'Or yours?'

Morland smirked. 'I may have suggested that the Tsar might help in the event of a catastrophe, and that it would be wise to secure his good graces in advance. But it is actually sound advice.'

'I suppose it is,' acknowledged Dorislaus. 'However, I cannot imagine what "good authority" told him that Archangel will be ice-free this winter. Any fool will know it is not.'

'Really?' asked Morland innocently. 'Perhaps I should not have introduced him to a certain sea-captain with a novel theory about tides, sea temperatures and the moon, then. At least, not one who has resided in Bedlam for the last twenty years.'

Dorislaus laughed. 'But your vitriol against Chaloner is misplaced. He did not burgle your house or put you in that invidious position with Widow Smith. He would not have dared.'

'Yes, he would, and he does not like me. However, the Archangel jaunt has nothing to do with them – it is in revenge for him being suspicious of me at the end of the Commonwealth.'

444

'But he was right: you *had* changed sides.'

'Yes, but I did not appreciate him telling Thurloe so. It might have seen me killed.'

'True, and I am glad he did not voice the similar doubts he held about me. I did "lose" his reports, of course, but I would not have wanted Thurloe to know.'

'You were a Dutch agent?' asked Morland in surprise.

'I still am. My father was murdered by Englishmen, and I have never liked this country.'

'Lord!' breathed Morland. 'I am all admiration for your skills. Thurloe has never guessed, and it is not easy to deceive him, as I can attest from personal experience. He thinks of you as a friend.'

Dorislaus nodded. 'But it was harder to convince Chaloner – he even doubted my loyalty when I helped him escape from Harper, spending a horribly uncomfortable day crushed inside a priest's hole with him in order to do so.'

'Why did you not let Harper catch him?'

'At the time, I thought he would be more useful alive.'

'You should not have sacrificed Oxenbridge to save him from being speared, either,' admonished Morland. 'It eliminated the last of his doubts about you, but it was a high price to pay.'

'Oxenbridge was dying anyway, and Thurloe was watching. It would not have been necessary if Gardner, Freer and Rea had been halfway competent – I sent Chaloner to the Letter Hall so they could kill him. Perhaps I should not have encouraged him to investigate the Post Office in the first place.'

'No,' agreed Morland. 'I know you thought his meddling would distract Gery, and they would keep each other in check, but his enquiries almost led to my

445

arrest with Harper and the other corrupt clerks. It was only my clever tongue that saved me – along with a hefty purse and the fact that he was too hoarse to speak.'

Dorislaus gave a short bark of laughter. 'Chaloner, Gery, Clarendon, Williamson, even Thurloe. None are a match for you, and I was never concerned for your safety.'

Morland inclined his head. 'I shall take that as a compliment.'

'Do you know who killed O'Neill, by the way? It was not the Major – his yeomen were too angry about the murder of their two fellows to give him any concessions.'

Morland's face went dark with malice. 'He should not have told Williamson that I tried to sell *him* my letter-opening machine before I hawked it to Bishop. Well, perhaps I did make an offer, but it was ungentlemanly of him to mention it to a Spymaster.'

'How did you do it?'

'Oxenbridge had some of the toxin left over, and I managed to lay hold of it before Thurloe raided his home. I put it in a gift of dried fruits with a message saying it was from the brothel in Hercules' Pillars Alley. Unfortunately, he must have destroyed the note – probably out of fear of his wife – because there have been no reprisals against the place.'

'What has the club done to earn your bile?'

'Temperance would not let me in,' said Morland sulkily. 'She called me slippery.'

'It is a pity the Major failed,' said Dorislaus, changing the subject before he was asked to disagree. 'I had hoped that the letter I wrote him – in cipher, but right under

446

Chaloner's nose – would save the day, but he was arrogant and did not bother to read it. Thus it was the right time to change my allegiance.'

'I suspect you changed it rather sooner than that,' remarked Morland wryly. 'Or you would not have made such a fuss about Mary Wood.'

Dorislaus's expression was grim. 'The Woods were my friends, and there was no need to have killed her. Oxenbridge should not have given Gardner that order. In fact, Gardner should not have been hired at all. He was a fool. Did you know he offered me a substantial bribe to join the Major? Me, the man who gave the Major most of his ideas in the first place!'

'Your indignant refusal made him think you were incorruptible,' said Morland, laughing.

'So the idiot left clues to make Chaloner think that I was part of the plot,' said Dorislaus crossly. 'He thought he was protecting the Major by leaving a "false" trail, but the reality was that I was one of the rebellion's most vital components. It is as well he died in the fire, or I would have to shoot him, too.'

'I should have liked being Secretary of State in the Major's new government,' said Morland with a wistful smile. 'And you would have made a splendid Spymaster – as I am sure the Dutch would agree.'

'We shall try again,' vowed Dorislaus. 'The comet is a sign that we must.'

'Well, we will not need to worry about Chaloner,' said Morland, turning to look at the ship as it disappeared into the dusk. 'He will not survive his journey.'

'Yes – because Archangel will be ice-bound, and the boat will founder and sink.'

'And because he is not carrying the letters that

Clarendon wrote to the Tsar. They are powerful evidence of treason, so I stole them. That will teach him to dismiss me.'

Dorislaus stared at him. 'If you have the originals, then what is Chaloner carrying?'

'Oh, documents asking for much the same thing, but with certain adjustments. The Tsar is a proud, prickly man, and it takes very little to offend him, so Clarendon's letters have been reworded. The Tsar will certainly take umbrage when he reads them, and he executes messengers who bring him insulting communiqués.'

Dorislaus smiled slowly. 'You have been very clever.'

Morland hefted a small sack. 'More than you think. Clarendon enclosed certain jewels with his greetings to the Tsar, but I do not think they should leave the country. I replaced them with coloured glass, and Chaloner does not know enough about such matters to tell the difference.'

'But the Tsar does?'

'Oh, yes,' said Morland. 'He is quite an expert.'

Historical Note

The General Letter Office was a large building, taxed on thirty-three hearths, although its location before 1666 is contentious. One theory is that it stood in a square known as Post House Yard, just off Dowgate Hill. Regardless, it and all its neighbours were lost in the Great Fire, after which the General Letter Office moved to Cornhill.

Secretary of State John Thurloe was Postmaster General during Cromwell's reign, a position that went well with his other occupation as Spymaster. The skill and efficiency with which he used the Post Office to gather intelligence was admired even by Royalists. However, being Postmaster was not only convenient for reading the letters of enemies, it was also extremely lucrative. A series of charters had established it as a monopoly, so the general populace had no choice but to use it.

After the Restoration in 1660, Henry Bishop obtained the office, paying some £21,500 for the privilege. Bishop was not particularly wealthy, and it is possible that the money had come from his friend John Wildman, known to his contemporaries simply as 'the Major'.

The Major was a curious character – an unremarkable lawyer and political thinker who spent almost his entire adult life involved in conspiracies, many of them to dispatch various heads of state. No one seemed to please him, and he happily plotted the murders of Cromwell and Charles II alike. There was even a rumour that he was Charles I's executioner. When not arranging assassinations, he spent his time devising plans for rebellion, and owns the dubious distinction of trying to organise the downfall of five successive regimes.

When Bishop first inherited the Post Office, he kept most of the old staff, on the grounds that they knew what they were doing, and he managed an efficient service. He dismissed Thomas Ibson, though, whom he claimed was Thurloe's 'jackal'. Ibson promptly avenged himself by declaring that several Post Office personnel were traitors to the Crown: these included Bishop himself, the Major, Isaac Dorislaus (the son of an Anglo-Dutchman of the same name who had been murdered by Royalists for his attachment to the Cromwellian regime), and one Mr Vanderhuyden, said to be a spy for Holland. The letter-carrier Smartfoot was also condemned as corrupt.

Bishop vigorously denied the accusations, but his association with the Major was his undoing, especially when coupled with the testimony of one Widow Smith. In 1658, her husband had been involved in a failed Royalist uprising. Bishop and the Major had also taken part, but someone had betrayed them, and Smith was arrested. Smith died shortly afterwards, convinced that the traitors were Bishop and the Major. Bishop was almost certainly innocent, but the Major's role is less clear.

Widow Smith took up her husband's cause with a passion. She owned a tavern named the Catherine Wheel, and when she witnessed two postal clerks illegally opening letters, she seized her chance for revenge. Bishop was dismissed and the Major arrested and taken to the Tower, where the Lord Chancellor, the Earl of Clarendon, quickly saw that here was a very dangerous man. When the Major continued to plot from his cell, Clarendon bundled him off to the Scilly Isles. His incarceration was certainly illegal, which was probably why he was never given a trial.

The Major remained in gaol until 1667, when Clarendon fell from power. Released, he immediately joined forces with the colourful Duke of Buckingham, and was involved in all the major political turmoils that marked the last third of the seventeenth century, merrily plotting against Charles II, James II and William III. He became Postmaster himself in 1689, but was dismissed two years later amid accusations of conspiracy and corruption. By now, he was an extremely wealthy man. He died peacefully in 1693, aged seventy.

During his brief tenure, Bishop is said to have invented the Bishop-Mark, a date-stamp that made it more difficult for the Post Office to delay the mail to suit itself; a similar system is still in use today. After Bishop's dismissal, the position passed to Daniel O'Neill, the King's harbinger and Groom of the Bedchamber. O'Neill did not keep it long. He died in 1664, and it passed to his wife Catherine. She held it until 1667, when it passed to Henry Bennet, Lord Arlington, who was Spymaster Williamson's boss.

Most of the other characters in *Death in St James's Park* were also real people. Andrew Leak, Benjamin Lamb, John Rea, Thomas Harper, and Samuel and Job Alibond were Post Office clerks in the 1660s, as was Jeremiah

451

Copping of the Foreign Office, who was known to pass intelligence to Williamson. 'Mr Bankes' was one of Williamson's aliases at this time.

The outspoken pamphleteer William Prynne was a bencher in Lincoln's Inn, and was made Keeper of Records in the Tower after the Restoration, a clever stroke that turned him into one of the King's most fervent supporters. William Freer was a spy in 1660s London, and Clement Oxenbridge, a sly and villainous character, was a fervent opponent of the Post Office in the 1650s, apparently believing that the state should not have a monopoly on letter carrying, and that it should be open to competition. He would doubtless be delighted by the fate of the Post Office in the twenty-first century.

André le Notre was France's foremost landscape architect, in charge of all royal gardens, and most famously designing the ones at Versailles. He also submitted plans for Greenwich, although it is not known for certain whether they were implemented. Seth Eliot was a gardener at the Inner Temple from the 1640s until the 1680s.

Sir Henry Wood, Clerk of the Green Cloth at White Hall, was a Restoration oddity, with a reputation for saying and doing eccentric things. He was married to Mary, who died in January 1665 of smallpox. She was Dresser to the Queen. Major John Stokes was one of Cromwell's old commanders, who died in 1665, while James Cliffe killed George Gery in a street fight in January 1665.

There was indeed a notice in a January 1665 edition of *The Intelligencer* offering a £50 reward for the arrest of Lewis Gardner for Post Office abuses, along with a physical description; his accomplice Knight was already

452

in custody in Newgate Gaol. There was also an account of the funeral of Clarendon's son Edward, who had died of smallpox, aged nineteen. The January issues of *The Newes* and *The Intelligencer* also carried items that included the King's decision not to enforce the strictures of Lent; advertisements for Goddard's Drops and Mr Thomas Grey's Lozenges (sold by Samuel Speed at the Rainbow); reports about the comet; a list of imports at Portsmouth; and the mass arrest of Quakers in various parts of the country.

There were exotic fowl and other birds in St James's Park, and an entry in John Evelyn's diary for February 1665 mentions a pelican, a crane with a wooden leg, a 'milk-white raven' and a number of swans, ducks and geese. 'Penguins' at this time referred to great auks, now sadly extinct. William Storey was appointed to look after them, and Storey's Gate may be named after the house he occupied.

Roger Palmer married Barbara Villiers in 1659, against the advice of his family. She became the King's mistress a year later, at which point Palmer was made the Earl of Castlemaine. The title came with a stipulation: that it should pass to any children she might bear, as opposed to any he might have. It was a brazen insult, and Palmer left the country shortly afterwards to join the Venetian fleet. He returned to London at the end of 1664 to offer his services in the looming Second Anglo-Dutch War, by which time his wife was the mother of four children, probably none of them his. His first book, *A Catholique Apology*, was published in 1666, and explained why Roman Catholics should not be blamed for the Great Fire.

Perhaps one of the least likeable characters of the

mid-seventeenth century was the ruthlessly self-serving Samuel Morland. He worked for Thurloe, and started to betray his master when the regime began to waver, later claiming he had been a Royalist all along. Thurloe was generally an excellent judge of character, but he was wrong about Morland.

Morland was rewarded with a knighthood at the Restoration, although he was never fully trusted, and limped from post to post, barely making ends meet. He was married five times, and tried to earn a living from his inventions, among which were a speaking trumpet, a fire engine, and fountains for Versailles. He also devised machines for opening, copying and resealing letters. It is unclear how these worked, and they were destroyed in the Great Fire. He resurrected them many years later, and sold them to the Major, then Postmaster General.